DATE DUE

ALSO BY DAVE BARRY AND RIDLEY PEARSON

ALSO BY RIDLEY PEARSON

#3

PETER AND THE SECRET OF RUNDOON

By **DAVE BARRY**

and **RIDLEY PEARSON**

Illustrations by GREG CALL

DISNEP • **HYPERION BOOKS**
New York

Hm 7722
8.99
JF
11/09

For Rob, Sophie, Paige, and Storey: May you always have a little starstuff left.

Copyright © 2007 Dave Barry and Page One, Inc.
Illustrations copyright © 2007 by Greg Call

All rights reserved. Published by Disney • Hyperion Books, an imprint of Disney Book Group. No part of this book may be reproduced or transmitted in any form or by any means, electronic or mechanical, including photocopying, recording, or by any information storage and retrieval system, without written permission from the publisher.

For information address Disney • Hyperion Books, 114 Fifth Avenue, New York, New York 10011-5690.

Printed in the United States of America

First Disney • Hyperion paperback edition, 2009
10 9 8 7 6 5 4 3 2 1

Library of Congress Cataloging-in-Publication Data on file.

ISBN 978-1-4231-2326-2

ACKNOWLEDGMENTS

We thank J. M. Barrie, who imagined one of the most wonderful stories ever, and Paige Pearson, who, upon hearing that story for the first time, asked her father how Peter Pan met Captain Hook in the first place.

Paige's question led us to write *Peter and the Starcatchers*, which led to *Peter and the Shadow Thieves*, which led to the book you're reading now. Our editor for all these books has been Wendy—yes, Wendy—Lefkon. We thank her for her unfailing support of these books, and for her gentle reminders that she cannot publish them until we actually *finish* them.

We thank our amazing illustrator, the quietly brilliant Greg Call, for bringing our words to life.

We thank the people who keep us organized, or at least less disorganized than we'd be without them: Nancy Litzinger and Judi Smith. We thank our copy editors, David and Laurel Walters, and Judi again, for finding and rooting out our many boneheaded errors. Any remaining mistakes in this book are solely the fault of the evil Lord Ombra.

We thank Jennifer Levine for flying us all around the country to talk about a flying boy, and always getting us back home for birthdays.

We thank our smart and beautiful wives, Michelle and Marcelle, for letting us go, and welcoming us back.

Above all, we thank our readers, the young ones and the less-young ones, but especially the ones who came to the bookstores dressed as pirates.

—*Dave Barry and Ridley Pearson*

TABLE OF CONTENTS

CHAPTER 1

THE GATHERING

THE OLD MAN TRUDGED ALONG THE DIRT PATH, pulling his worn coat tighter to ward off the cold wind moaning across the Salisbury Plain. Dusk was near, and the man was glad to see his destination, the village of Amesbury, come into view.

The man glanced toward the cluster of massive dark stones looming in the distance to his left. He had lived near Stonehenge his whole life, and until recently he had considered it an unremarkable feature of the landscape. But in the past few weeks—since the night of the strange lights in the sky—he found that his eyes were drawn to the stones.

The old man turned his head away, disgusted with himself. He was a sensible person; he was not one to believe the stories that had been swirling through the village since that night— stories of evil spirits roaming among the stones, of animals behaving oddly, of people experiencing strange sensations. . . .

"Rubbish," the man muttered to himself as he quickened his pace.

CAW! CAW! CAW!

The bird's cry startled the man. He looked up and saw a large raven swooping across the plain. The man stopped and watched as it passed low in front of him. He was watching the bird, not the ground, so he did not see its shadow pass across his.

But he felt it.

He didn't know it was a shadow; he thought it was a chill. A shudder went through his body, and he drew his coat even tighter. He felt suddenly light-headed and staggered sideways. Catching himself, he started walking again—but not along the path. He veered to the right, toward a clump of trees. He didn't know why he did this; he wasn't thinking clearly.

He reached the trees and saw the strangest sight: animals, a dozen at least—a fox, a rabbit, two dogs, some squirrels, several birds, and a cat. They were lined up in a neat row, perfectly still, ignoring each other, watching the man approach.

The old man stopped about ten feet away; again, he had no idea why. For a moment he stood facing the animals. Then the fox trotted forward, but not directly to the man; it passed by him, such that its shadow crossed his. As it did, two things happened: the man felt another shuddering chill, and the fox looked at him as if suddenly aware of his presence, then ran off.

Next, one of the dogs came forward, and it repeated the fox's actions—crossing shadows with the man, then running away. It was followed by the other dog and, one by one, the other animals.

Each time, the man felt the chill. But now he also felt something else—a new presence . . . a presence growing *inside him*. It was weak, but the man could feel it grow stronger as each animal scampered away, and he understood that whatever it was, it was coming from the animals into him. He understood this, but there was nothing he could do about it except watch, as if in a dream.

When the last animal was gone, the old man returned to the path and, still in his dreamlike state, resumed trudging toward Amesbury. He reached the village as the sun dipped below the hills. But instead of going to his house, where his wife would be cooking his dinner, the man went to the George Hotel, the oldest accommodation in the village.

The old man didn't enter the hotel; he stopped in front of one of the windows. By the lamplight from inside, the man cast a shadow on the road in front of him. He had stood there for less than a minute when a woman walked past. The two knew each other, but neither spoke. The woman crossed in front of the man, her shadow touching his. The man felt the now-familiar chill. The woman let out a soft gasp, stumbled, then recovered and walked quickly away without looking at the man.

In a minute, another woman came by, then a man, then another woman, then a child, each crossing shadows with the man, then departing quickly into the darkness. Now the old man was acutely aware of the presence in him. It was still weak—*wounded*, the man realized—but it was also fiercely determined. And angry. Very, very angry.

In his dream state, the man understood somehow that he was not the target of the anger: whatever the presence was, it was only using him as a means to achieve its ultimate goal. The man did not know what that was. Nor did he want to know.

From down the road came the sound of hooves clopping and wheels creaking. The old man turned his head to see the London-bound coach pulling up to the hotel. The driver, a big, red-faced man in a heavy wool coat, reined in the horses, set the brake, and climbed down from his perch. He nodded to the old man, and getting no response, shrugged, then went into the hotel. He emerged two minutes later with a passenger, whom he helped into the coach. The driver was about to climb back up to his seat when the old man felt himself suddenly step forward and to the side, causing his shadow to cross the driver's.

In that instant, the old man felt the presence rush from

him. He staggered back and almost fell, catching himself against the wall of the hotel. He turned from the driver and stumbled away up the street toward his house. He did not look back. He had already decided that he would not tell his wife what had happened to him. He would never tell anyone.

⟞⬩⟝

Five hours later, the coach reached the London waterfront. The passengers were confused and angry; this was not where the coach was supposed to take them—their stops had all been bypassed. They had been complaining increasingly loudly for some time now, shouting and pounding on the coach roof. The driver had not responded at all. It was as if he didn't hear them.

The coach stopped on a street near St. Katherine's dock. The driver climbed down and walked away, abandoning the coach and its shouting passengers. It was midnight and the docks were quiet, save for the creaking of lines and the slapping of water against the hulls of ships.

The coach driver walked purposefully along the dock to a ship called *Le Fantome*. He walked up the gangway and boarded the ship. A sailor on watch tried to block his path, but the coach driver, a much larger man, shoved him aside easily. The driver strode to a companionway, descended into the ship, and walked toward the stern along a passageway until he reached a door. With a massive fist, he pounded on it five times.

"What?" bellowed an angry voice from inside the cabin. "What is it?"

The door opened, and there stood the captain of *Le Fantome*, a man named Nerezza. There was a hole in the middle of his face where his nose should have been. Usually he wore a wooden nosepiece, but not when he was sleeping.

Nerezza stared at the coach driver, his face a mix of surprise and fury.

"Who the devil are you?" he said, his right hand reaching back for the knife he kept on his bedside table.

The coach driver opened his mouth, but no words came out. Something else did come out, however. It looked like a tendril of smoke—thin and wispy at first, but then thicker, darker.

Nerezza froze, his eyes on the man's mouth. The smoke was billowing out now, forming a thick column, flowing downward toward the floor. Nerezza looked at the coach driver's eyes and saw terror; the man clearly had no idea what was happening.

But Nerezza did. He stepped back into his cabin, away from the dark thing. In a few moments it had fully emerged from the driver's mouth. The big man fell backward, hitting his head against the wall of the passageway. The dark thing was now a swirling black cloud on the floor of Nerezza's cabin. Nerezza stepped carefully around it into the passageway, closing the door behind him. He yelled for his men, and in seconds, several sailors appeared.

Nerezza pointed at the driver.

"Get him off the ship," he said.

The men obeyed, though it took four of them to carry the coach driver up the companionway. They carried him down the gangway and left him lying on the dock, unconscious. He would awaken the next day with no idea how he'd gotten there, remembering nothing but a vivid, hideous nightmare.

Belowdecks, Nerezza stood outside his cabin door. He dreaded going inside, but he had no choice. Taking a deep breath, he opened the door and stepped inside. His cabin was cold now. The dark swirling shape had moved to the corner. It was rising slowly, beginning to take the shape of . . . not a man, exactly, but a cloak with a man inside. Or *something* inside.

Nerezza watched the thing rise, watched it take shape, waited.

Finally the thing spoke. Its voice was weaker than Nerezza remembered, but there was no mistaking it—a low, inhuman moaning sound. Nerezza leaned close to make out the words.

"We sail tonight," the thing said. "For Rundoon."

"Yes, Lord Ombra," said Nerezza. "For Rundoon."

CHAPTER 2

THE SCOUTING PARTY

THREE DUGOUT CANOES, EACH PADDLED by four hard-muscled men, slid through the rolling indigo sea, which was empty from horizon to horizon. The afternoon sun blazed in a radiant blue sky that was equally empty, save for a low white cloud to the east.

The paddlers wore only loincloths. Their skin, sun-baked to a deep bronze, glistened with sweat. Each man's back was almost entirely covered with what appeared to be a large tattoo—a random pattern of dark swirling lines. Closer inspection, however, revealed that the "tattoos" were in fact scar tissue.

The scars had been caused by the tentacles of a particularly nasty type of jellyfish, the poison of which inflicted agonizing pain. Each of the warriors in the canoes had endured an excruciating initiation ritual: as he stood before the tribe, a large, living jellyfish was draped across his shoulders and back, its toxic tentacles searing his flesh like fire. Some men crumpled immediately to the ground, screaming; others passed out. Only those who stood still for a full minute, soundlessly enduring the agony, were allowed to become warriors in this tribe.

Poison played an important role in the tribe's culture. In battle, the warriors sometimes hurled venomous snakes and spiders at the enemy; they also coated the tips of their arrows with a special mixture of toxins that caused horrific, paralyzing pain. It was this practice that gave the tribe its name, the most feared name in this part of the ocean: Scorpions. It was a name that meant misery and death.

The warriors in the canoes made up a scouting party. They had been at sea for three grueling days, searching for an island that, according to their tribal lore, was somewhere in these waters. Their leader, the only man not paddling, sat in the prow of the front canoe. He was a large man, a bit older and thicker than the others, but still very strong. His earlobes stretched nearly to his shoulders, indicating his rank. A braided, black beard hung from his chin like a rat's tail. His dark eyes were fixed on the distant cloud.

He suddenly emitted a series of harsh sounds. Instantly, the warriors began paddling faster, and the canoes shot forward. They rose and fell with the rising and falling of the sea, aiming for the cloud, the men not yet seeing what had excited their leader.

And then, a few minutes later, as an especially large wave lifted them high, they all saw it—a speck on the horizon under the cloud. Now all the warriors were whooping and shouting. The leader raised his arm to quiet them, then spoke. They would wait here an hour, then move to the island as the sun set behind them. Its glare would blind anyone on the island looking in their direction. The warriors nodded, grateful for the rest. They sat in the open water and stared at the distant speck—their prey.

An hour later, with the sun low, the men began paddling again. As they neared the island, the cloud gave them a gift—a small but intense rain squall, which further concealed the canoes from the land. Paddling through the rain, the warriors reached shore just as the squall ended. The showers left behind a damp and steamy island smelling of rotting vegetation.

They climbed out of the canoes, each man carrying a bow and a quiver of arrows. These weapons were to be used only as a last resort: the Scorpions did not intend to be seen. This was a scouting expedition. The attack would come later.

The men dragged the canoes up the narrow beach and hid them in the dense undergrowth. Using palm fronds, they carefully swept the sand clean of their footprints. Then, with the leader in front, they entered the jungle. Beneath the thick tree canopy, a cloak of near-darkness enveloped them, and the sound of songbirds gave way to the hum of insects and the rustle of lizards and snakes.

The men moved as if a single being, one after the other, in complete silence, yet with surprising speed. They dodged monkey-puzzle trees and bushes of ironwood, smelly swamp and patches of fireweed. In time they came to a footpath. The leader bent to inspect it, smiling at the sight of fresh footprints. He rose and signaled the men to follow him, staying in the jungle but now moving alongside the path, which was just to their right. The leader moved more slowly now, pausing every few yards to listen.

He raised his hand, and the line of men stopped. He touched his eyes, then pointed. Just ahead on the path were two boys. They didn't look like islanders; they had light skin and hair. They were talking to each other in a language that sounded strange to the Scorpions.

Chattering away, the boys ambled along the path, oblivious to the men following them. The boys came to a clearing, in the middle of which was a tree stump. As the Scorpions watched with interest, the boys pulled on the stump, tipping it over. Underneath was a hole. The boys climbed into the hole, then pulled the stump back upright and were gone.

The Scorpions' leader left two men to keep an eye on the stump. He led the rest silently forward, still following the footpath but remaining within the cover of the dark jungle.

After a few hundred yards they stopped again. Ahead was a much larger clearing and a high wall of sharpened poles lashed together with vines.

Signaling to his men to stay hidden, the leader crept forward to the wall and put his eye to a crack between two logs. On the other side, he saw a bustling village of thirty or more grass huts, as well as pens holding goats and wild pigs. Dozens of men and women were gathered around cooking fires, eating and talking; children darted about, chasing each other, shouting, laughing.

The Scorpion leader focused on the men, studying the markings on their arms and chests. He tensed with excitement: these were the markings he had hoped to see—the markings that according to legend were used by the Mollusk tribe. The Scorpion leader smiled grimly. The legend was true. They had found Mollusk Island. And soon they would conquer it.

The leader turned and crept back to his men. The expression on his face told them that their scouting mission was a success. Eager now to get back to their canoes, they retraced their steps, traveling alongside the footpath.

By the time they reached the boys' tree stump, night was descending, the sky lit by the last faint rays of the dwindling sun. The Scorpion leader was surprised to find that his two sentries, instead of staying concealed in the jungle, were standing in the middle of the clearing. Furious that they had taken such a risk, the leader ran toward them, only to stop when he saw the fearful expressions on their upturned faces.

Following their gaze, the leader looked up at the sky and saw what had so alarmed them.

A boy.

A *flying* boy.

The boy, his hair fiery red in the sun's dying rays, was swooping among some trees about twenty-five yards away. He shot from tree to tree, knocking coconuts to the ground. Apparently, he had not seen the Scorpions. The Scorpion leader blinked, but there was no question: the boy was not swinging on a vine or jumping. He was *flying*.

For a moment, the leader could only stare, his mouth hanging open. He came to his senses just in time to see one of his men, panicked by the sight of the boy, fitting an arrow to his bow and drawing it back. With a quickness that belied his size, the leader lunged toward the man, reaching him and grabbing the arrow just as the man released it. It burned through his grip, sending splinters into the meat of his hand, but he did not let go.

Angrily, the leader broke the arrow across his knee. He grabbed the man by the neck and lifted him off the ground, holding his face only inches from his own. No words were spoken, but none were needed: this man understood that he had almost ruined everything by giving their presence away.

With his feet back on the ground, the man hung his head shamefully.

Still angry, the leader waved his men back toward the canoes. He went last, constantly glancing backward at the flying boy, who was still darting from tree to tree, growing smaller and smaller until he was finally absorbed by the night. Turning to follow his men, the leader could feel his mind racing as he tried to comprehend what he had seen, and to figure out how much of a problem this boy would be.

These thoughts so occupied him that he forgot altogether about something that, ordinarily, he would have remembered: the broken arrow lying in the mud.

CHAPTER 3

ᴡorrying Questions

Cold rain fell in sheets from the dark London sky. The gusting wind spattered raindrops against the dining-room window of the grand Aster mansion on Kensington Palace Gardens. Inside, at a table large enough for dozens of people, sat just three: young Molly Aster and her parents, Leonard and Louise.

The room was warm and bright, but the mood of its occupants more closely matched the gloomy weather outside. Lord Aster had spent the afternoon in his study, meeting with four men, all of them members of the Starcatchers, a secret group to which the Aster family had belonged for many generations.

Leonard had emerged from the meeting with a somber, troubled look. Both Molly and Louise knew he had something to tell them; they also knew that it would have to wait until they were alone.

Now, with their meal finally served and the household staff back in the kitchen, Molly and her mother looked at Leonard with questioning faces. He glanced at the doorway to make sure he would not be overheard, then spoke quietly.

"I must go to Paris," he said. "There's to be a meeting of the senior Starcatchers."

"Is it about what happened at Stonehenge?" asked Molly. She shuddered, recalling the terrifying night among the massive stones—her father lying on the ground, grievously wounded; her mother a ghastly sleepwalking shell, unable to recognize her husband or her daughter, her life spirit stolen by the hideous shadow creature that called itself Ombra. That night Molly had very nearly lost both of her parents, and the Starcatchers a huge quantity of precious, powerful starstuff, which would have fallen into the hands of humanity's most evil enemies. If Peter hadn't been there . . .

"Yes," said Leonard, his voice low. "It's about what happened at Stonehenge. And some other troubling things, which I was a fool not to recognize earlier."

"What troubling things?" said Molly.

Leonard hesitated before responding, and for a moment Molly thought she had pressed too hard. Until recently, her parents had revealed little to her about the inner workings of the Starcatchers. But since the awful night at Stonehenge, and the courage Molly had displayed there, Leonard had been more willing to answer his daughter's questions.

"Actually," said Leonard, "what's most troubling is something that *didn't* happen. That was a very large batch of starstuff we had—the largest in centuries, at least. Yet we received no warning before it fell in Scotland. That's why the Others got to it first. We were so concerned about getting it to the Return that we didn't stop to ask ourselves why we weren't warned about it in the first place."

"What kind of warning?" asked Molly. "I thought the Starcatchers could sense when starstuff fell."

"Yes, we do feel something when a large amount of starstuff falls," said Leonard. "But the Others feel it, too. The reason we always manage to reach fallen starstuff before they do is that we always receive warnings before it falls."

"Warnings from whom?" said Molly.

"We don't know," said Leonard. "The alerts come anonymously, by various methods. Long ago, it would be an unsigned letter slipped under a Starcatcher's door. More recently—for the last century or so—the warnings have appeared in an Oxford newspaper, the *Observer*."

"Warnings about starstuff . . . in a *newspaper*?" said Molly.

"They were coded," said Leonard. "They took the form of personal notices to a 'Mr. Starr.' Every day for more than a hundred years, a Starcatcher stationed in Oxford has scoured the *Observer* for these notices. Sometimes decades would go by without one appearing. But then, one day, he'd find a notice that said something like 'Mr. Starr: Expect your package Thursday.' We then knew that there would be a starstuff Fall on Thursday. We wouldn't know *where* it would fall, but by knowing *when* we could have teams alerted all over the world, watching the skies for the Fall, ready to go collect the starstuff. That gave us a huge advantage over the Others. We almost always reached it first."

"Until that big lot fell in Scotland," said Molly.

"Yes," said Leonard. "There was no warning for that. Last week we had our man check and recheck the *Observer* for the days leading up to that Fall; he found no notice for Mr. Starr. That's troubling enough. What's more troubling is how quickly the Others got to the starstuff in Scotland. It's as if *they* were warned instead of us."

"When was the last warning, then?" said Molly.

"It was twelve years ago," said Leonard. "In fact, just a few days before you were born. That was the last notice for Mr. Starr that appeared in the *Observer*."

"And you have no idea who's been doing the warning?" asked Molly.

"None," said Leonard. "Whoever they are, they've always kept their identities hidden. And for whatever reason, this time—even with such a dangerous amount of starstuff at stake—they didn't warn us. We were very fortunate to get that starstuff back, thanks to you and Peter."

"And George," said Molly.

"Yes, of course, George, too," said Leonard. "In any

event, we're quite worried that the next time there's a starstuff Fall, we won't be so fortunate. We need to find out why we weren't warned and what we can do about it. That's one reason for the meeting in Paris. The other is this . . . this Ombra creature."

As he said those words, Lord Aster glanced at his wife; her face went pale at the name of the hideous thing that had held her captive.

"Do you think there's a connection?" said Molly. "I mean, between Ombra and the fact that there was no warning?"

"I fear so," said Leonard. "It's difficult to believe it's a coincidence. And whatever this Ombra thing is, or I should say *was*, it's apparently not the only one. Our man Bakari, in Egypt, encountered something quite similar a few weeks ago; we lost five people there. We're very concerned that the Others have allied themselves with some new power—a very dangerous power. That's why the senior Starcatchers are meeting in Paris. We need to find out quickly why this is happening and what we can do about it—*before* the next starstuff Fall."

"How long do you expect to be gone?" said Louise.

"Not more than two weeks, I hope," said Leonard. Seeing the apprehension on their faces, he added: "The house will be guarded. And I promise we'll do a better job than last time."

"It wasn't your fault," said Louise. "You didn't know. . . ."

She faltered, remembering how easily Ombra had taken over the three burly men guarding the Aster mansion when she had been kidnapped.

"It won't happen again," said Leonard. "We know what we're up against now. And whatever that thing was, it was destroyed at Stonehenge."

"Don't worry about us, dear," said Louise, smiling bravely. "We'll be fine. Won't we, Molly?"

"Yes," said Molly. She was also smiling, although she could not help but glance, if only for a moment, at the dining-room window and the darkness beyond. Despite her faith in her father, disturbing questions filled her mind: *How can we be sure that Ombra was destroyed? And do we really know what we're up against?*

CHAPTER 4

"They Will Be Back"

Peter awoke, as he usually did, ahead of the other boys, not having slept well. Since his return to Mollusk Island from England, his slumber had been haunted by a strange and troubling dream.

The dream always began in the same place and at the same moment: that awful night at Stonehenge when—grievously wounded by a gunshot—he had somehow become connected with Ombra, the shadow thing. Their connection had been brief—but a few seconds—yet Peter could not put those seconds out of his mind.

By day, it was possible to turn his thoughts away from that memory. But by night, it came back to him and returned often. In his dream, he felt the coldness creeping into him as Ombra joined him and began to take control, like a snake swallowing him from within. He felt himself fighting to drive the invader out. Most vividly, he recalled the horrible sensation of becoming one with the shadow thing—feeling what *it* felt, thinking what *it* thought.

That was when he always woke up—sweating, disoriented, thrashing around in his hammock, much to the annoyance of Tinker Bell, who slept in his mass of red hair. Sometimes Peter would lie there trying to make sense of the dream, to recapture the thoughts that had seeped into his mind from Ombra's; but the thoughts were always out of reach, drifting away like wisps of smoke.

The nightmare troubled Peter, but something else troubled him more. Since that night at Stonehenge, he had noticed something odd about himself—or, to be specific, about his shadow. Actually, it was Tink who had noticed it first. It had been on a bright, sunny day; Peter, having had a rollicking swim and a splash fight with the mermaids, was standing on the beach that curved around the mermaids' lagoon. Tink had fluttered onto his shoulder and, making her bell sounds, said, *He's watching you.*

"Who is?" asked Peter.

Tink pointed at Peter's shadow. *He is.*

Peter looked down at his shadow. It appeared no different than usual. He studied Tink, thinking that perhaps she was joking, but her expression told him she was quite serious. He glanced again at his shadow, his thoughts flashing back to that encounter with Ombra.

"What should I do?" he asked Tink.

Nothing, Tink answered. *He can't hurt you. He's just watching.*

"Why?"

I don't know.

And that was all she could tell him. Peter tried not to think about it, but it was not the kind of thing you could forget. It never really left his mind. He found himself glancing at his shadow more than usual. He welcomed the sunset, knowing that the coming of night would banish the shadow and bring him some relief from his thoughts of Ombra—that is, until the dream returned.

So Peter was a tired boy when he awoke this particular morning. But as he stuck his head out of the underground hideaway where he and the other boys spent most nights, his spirits were lifted, as always, by the dawn of another fine day on Mollusk Island. After a quick look around the clearing, Peter flew straight up out of the hole and ascended to treetop level, where he turned in a slow circle, eyes scanning the area, just in case there were pirates about. There weren't any pirates, a fact that left Peter feeling relieved but also just the slightest bit disappointed: he loved taunting the pirates.

Peter felt a tickle on his bare legs as a pair of tiny wings fluttered past.

"Morning, Tink," he said as Tinker Bell shinnied up to his eye level.

No, it's not, she answered in melodious tones that Peter, and few others, could understand. *It's the middle of the night.*

Peter laughed. "Tink," he said, "if you want to keep sleeping, be my guest."

Tink crossed her arms and made a noise that could be loosely translated as "hmph." As she and Peter both knew, she did not like to let him out of her sight.

"Morning, Peter," said a voice from below.

Peter looked down and smiled. "Morning, James," he said.

He dropped lightly to the ground as James, always the second to rise, climbed from the hole. The two close friends stood for a moment, enjoying the morning coolness. Peter's enjoyment was tempered by his awareness of how much James had grown recently; he stood a good inch taller than Peter now, maybe two, and he was wider about the shoulders. Peter wondered if James, in addition to being taller, had also become stronger.

Peter's thoughts were interrupted by the emergence from the hole of the two youngest boys, Prentiss and Thomas, who were followed, reluctantly, by Tubby Ted.

"What's to eat?" said Ted, blinking at the dawn.

"There's fresh coconuts," said Peter. "I knocked them down last night."

"Coconuts *again*?" complained Ted.

"It's what grows on the trees," said Peter. "If it was cakes

24

on the trees, I'd knock those down for you. But it's coconuts that's up there."

"Cakes," sighed Tubby Ted. "I'd pay a hundred pounds for a piece of cake."

"The only hundred pounds you have is around your waist," said Prentiss.

Then Thomas complained, "Besides, there's no cake on this stupid island."

Peter glanced at Thomas, whose tone had grown more negative of late. Thomas was also getting taller, as were Prentiss and Tubby Ted; Peter realized that it was just a matter of time before he was the shortest boy in the group.

Tubby Ted sighed again. "Which way to the coconuts?" he said.

"Over there," said Peter, pointing toward a clump of trees.

As Ted trudged off to collect his breakfast, Peter turned to James.

"I thought we might go see the mermaids today," he said.

"Again?" said James.

"You don't want to?" said Peter, surprised by James's lack of enthusiasm.

James looked down. "You go ahead," he said.

"Why don't you want to?" persisted Peter.

"No reason, really," said James. "I just think they like you better, is all. You're more . . . I dunno."

25

"You're more like them," said Thomas, finishing James's thought.

"Magical," said Prentiss.

"I see," said Peter. "Is there something else you want to do?"

"Besides get off this island?" said Thomas.

Peter studied Thomas for a moment, then the others, and in their faces he saw the discontent that he'd been sensing in them more and more since his return from England.

"If you don't like it here," he said to Thomas, "then we can . . ."

"We can *what?*" said Thomas, with a defiance he'd never before shown to Peter.

While Peter was trying to think of an answer, Tubby Ted came huffing out of the jungle.

"Look what I found!" he said, waving something in his hand. As he approached, the others saw that it was an arrow, broken in the middle, the two halves hanging together by a sliver of wood.

"It's an arrow. So what?" said Thomas. "The Mollusks shot at something and missed for a change."

"Let me see that," said Peter, taking the arrow from Ted. As he did, Tink made a warning sound.

"I'll be careful," Peter said. He examined it for a moment, frowning.

"This isn't a Mollusk arrow," he said. "Look at the colors

26

on it. Red as blood. The Mollusks don't do that. And they make the arrowheads from shells. This one is stone."

There was something smeared on the tip of the arrow-head—a dark brown substance. Peter sniffed it, then pulled his head quickly away, surprised by the vile and powerful odor.

"If it's not the Mollusks'," said James, "then whose is it?"

"I dunno," Peter said thoughtfully. "But I think we should take it to Fighting Prawn."

The others nodded, their sleepiness and boredom suddenly gone. Peter rose from the ground, about to zoom skyward and fly to the Mollusk village. But then, seeing the look of disappointment on James's face, he dropped quickly back to the ground and began trotting toward the path.

"Come on," he called over his shoulder—unnecessarily, as the others were already running behind, even the normally slow-moving Tubby Ted.

In a few minutes, they reached the Mollusk village. The Mollusks were gathered around their cooking fires, eating their morning meal; a few waved at the boys, who visited often. Peter hurried to the center of the village, where the largest group was gathered around the largest fire ring. Peter ran straight to Fighting Prawn, the Mollusk chief—a white-haired man with piercing dark eyes, older than the others, but still tall and powerfully built.

Fighting Prawn's face brightened at the sight of the boys.

He was especially fond of Peter, who had once saved his life. But his smile instantly disappeared when he saw the arrow in Peter's hand.

"Where did you find that?" he said, in the impeccable English he had learned in his years as a slave aboard a British ship.

"Tubby Ted found it," said Peter. He handed the broken arrow to Fighting Prawn, who took it, studied it for a moment, and then sniffed the brown substance on the tip.

"Found it where?" said Fighting Prawn. "Washed up on the beach?"

"No," said Ted. "In the jungle, right by our hideout."

The group fell silent. As Fighting Prawn stared at the arrow, an expression flickered across his face that Peter had never seen there before—fear.

"What is it?" asked Peter.

Instead of answering, Fighting Prawn raised his voice and shouted something in the Mollusk language, a mixture of grunts and clicks sounding quite odd to the English-speaker's ear. Immediately, the Mollusk tribe's warriors came running from all corners of the village to gather around their chief.

Fighting Prawn addressed them for several minutes, and although Peter understood none of it, he saw the deep concern on the warriors' faces. When Fighting Prawn finished, the men ran to their huts, quickly emerging with spears, knives, and bows and arrows. They then hurried from the encampment, save for a half dozen who took up guard positions by the gate.

Fighting Prawn turned to the boys. "You will stay here in the village," he said. "You are not to leave without my permission, do you understand?"

"Why?" said Peter. "What's happening?"

"Something I had hoped would never happen," said Fighting Prawn. "Something I have dreaded for a long time."

"What is it?" said Peter.

"This arrow," said Fighting Prawn, holding it up, "belongs to a very dangerous tribe. They are called"—here Fighting Prawn made a hissing sound—"which means Scorpions. This substance on the arrowhead is a deadly poison. The Scorpions are fond of poison."

"Are they here?" asked Prentiss. "On the island?"

"I don't know," said Fighting Prawn. "I have sent men out to search the island; we will know soon enough if they are here. But I suspect they are not. I suspect this arrow was left, carelessly, by a scouting party. If it had been a war party, we would know by now. The Scorpions prefer to strike by surprise with massive force. Now that they've found this island, they will be back, I'm certain of that."

"But now you'll be ready for them," said Peter.

Fighting Prawn hesitated, and again Peter saw the flicker of fear.

"We will post lookouts, yes," Fighting Prawn said. "We

will be as ready as we can be. But the Scorpions attack in great force; their war canoes will bring more attackers than we have defenders. They are vicious, brutal fighters. They have taken many islands, Peter. They rarely fail."

"And what happens to the people on the island?" said Tubby Ted.

Fighting Prawn only shook his head.

"I wish I was back in England," Thomas said softly.

"Maybe I can do something," said Peter. "I could fly over their canoes and drop things. Fire, maybe. Or at least I could fly out to sea and watch for them, and . . ."

"No," said Fighting Prawn. "You will stay here with the others. The Scorpions are expert marksmen. The slightest touch from this"—he held up the arrow again—"and you would fall from the sky like a stone. You must promise me you will not go out there."

Reluctantly, Peter nodded.

"Good," said Fighting Prawn. He put his hand on Peter's shoulder and gave it a fatherly squeeze. "You have great courage, Peter," he said. "I will need your help before this is over."

Then he turned and walked toward the gate, somehow looking much older than he had fifteen minutes before.

Peter looked at the other boys and they at him.

"I wish I was back in England," said Thomas again.

CHAPTER 5

MOLLY'S PLAN

QUIETLY CLOSING HER BEDROOM DOOR, Molly tiptoed down the stairs past her mother's room to the ground floor. Putting on her coat, she walked quietly to the front door—only to hear a familiar voice boom out behind her.

"And where do you think YOU'RE going, young lady?"

Molly turned to face the formidable shape of her governess, Mrs. Bumbrake, who, on hearing Molly's footsteps, had huffed into the hallway.

"Just out for a walk," said Molly.

"A walk to WHERE?"

"I thought I'd visit the Darlings," answered Molly.

The stern expression on Mrs. Bumbrake's face instantly changed to one of approval.

"Going to see young George, then?" she said.

Molly blushed. "Yes," she said. "I'll be back before dark, I promise."

"See that you are," said Mrs. Bumbrake, trying to sound harsh, but unable to hide her pleasure. George Darling was exactly the sort of well-bred young man she thought Molly *should* be seeing. Not like that other boy, Peter, who (in Mrs. Bumbrake's view) had gotten Molly into such trouble aboard that awful ship. . . .

"Bye," said Molly, ducking out the door before Mrs. Bumbrake could say any more. Pulling her coat front tight, she crossed the broad, mansion-lined street in front of her house and entered Kensington Gardens, the massive form of Kensington Palace looming through the fog. She took the path through Hyde Park, then crossed Kensington Road into a street lined with fine homes. Reaching the Darlings', she climbed the steps, rang the doorbell, and told the servant who answered that she was there to see George.

In thirty seconds he was bounding down the stairs, gangling and awkward, but showing more and more indications of the handsome young man he was becoming.

"Hello, Molly," he said.

"Hello, George."

There was an awkward pause, which was not unusual; Molly and George spent a good deal of their time together pausing awkwardly. Finally Molly broke the silence.

"I wondered if we could talk," she said.

"Of course!" said George. "What about?"

"I meant talk, uh, quietly," said Molly, glancing toward a servant dusting the mantel in the next room.

"Ah!" said George, feeling idiotic, which made him turn even redder than usual. "Of course. Father's study is empty. He and Mother are traveling." He rolled his eyes. "Again."

They went into the study, and George closed the door.

"Is something wrong?" he said.

"Yes," said Molly. "At least, I think so."

"The Starcatchers," said George.

A few months ago, Molly would never have discussed the Starcatchers with George, or even acknowledged their existence. But George had been with her and Peter that night at Stonehenge; in fact, without him, none of them would have gotten there at all. He had been very brave that night, and though he was not a Starcatcher, Molly trusted him absolutely.

"Yes," said Molly. "The Starcatchers."

Quickly she summarized what her father had said about the meeting in Paris and the Starcatchers' concerns.

When she had finished, George said, "I don't blame them for being worried—that Ombra thing was quite alarming. But it sounds to me as though, now that they're aware of the situation, they're taking steps to deal with it."

"I don't know," said Molly. "Father seemed so *worried*— more so than I've ever seen him. I wish there was something I could do to help."

"Such as what?"

"I've been thinking," Molly said. "About the starstuff warnings."

"The ones they're not getting anymore."

"Yes," said Molly. "Father said they appeared as personal notices in the Oxford *Observer*. For more than a hundred years, he said. That's a long time, George."

"It is a long time," said George, not sure what she was getting at.

"So," said Molly, "I was thinking that perhaps somebody in Oxford—somebody at the newspaper—might know who placed those notices."

"Perhaps," said George.

"So," said Molly, "I was thinking that perhaps somebody could go up to Oxford and look into that."

"Somebody?" said George.

"Me, actually," said Molly.

"Do your parents know about this plan?"

"No," confessed Molly. "They'd never allow me to go. But they needn't know, George. It's only an hour or so by train to Oxford. We could go there and be back in a day."

"We?" said George.

Molly blushed. "I was hoping that . . . I mean, you're the only person outside my family who understands the situation, and I know it's a huge imposition after all you've done, but I . . ."

George put his hand on Molly's, stopping her and send-ing a current through them both.

"Of course I'll go to Oxford with you," he said.

"Thank you," she said.

They self-consciously separated hands.

"I can get away easily, with my parents gone," George said. "But how will you escape the clutches of the formidable Mrs. Bumbrake?"

Molly smiled. "I shall use you as an excuse. I shall tell her you're taking me to the National Gallery tomorrow, and that we plan to spend the day there, as there are so many fine paintings to admire."

"Indeed there are," said George. "But will the formidable Mrs. B. entrust you to me?"

"She will," said Molly. "The formidable Mrs. B. is quite fond of you."

Molly was on the verge of saying something more, but settled instead for another awkward, blushing silence, this one broken by George.

"All right, then," he said. "Shall I come 'round tomorrow at nine? For our visit to the National Gallery?"

"Nine it is," said Molly. "Thank you, George."

"It's my pleasure," he said.

He saw her to the door and they said good-bye. As Molly retraced her steps back to her house, she thought warm thoughts about George's loyalty and his willingness to help.

Then a different thought began to intrude: *The last time George helped me, he wound up in great danger. Am I putting him in danger again?*

Molly pondered that, and decided she was being silly. *What harm can possibly come from a trip to Oxford?*

Comforted somewhat by that thought, Molly hurried forward into the swiftly falling night.

CHAPTER 6

RUMOR SPREADS

LE FANTOME CHARGED THROUGH the roiling seas faster than she'd ever sailed before. Captain Nerezza pushed the vessel to her limits, putting up more sails even when it seemed the added cloth might tear the ship apart. Night and day, she surged forward, leaving a wake of bubbling white on the dark, open ocean.

The sailors were as eager as their captain to reach their destination and discharge their unwelcome passenger. Rumor had spread quickly through the crew that he was back—the hooded, shadowy shape living in the darkened cabin. At first, some dismissed the rumor, insisting that Ombra had died at Stonehenge—why, people had seen it.

But the rumor persisted. For one thing, there was the cold: the nearer one got to that dark, forbidden cabin, the colder the air grew, to where a man could see his breath.

Then there was the sound—a raspy, wheezing sound, like

some kind of beast in pain. Sometimes late at night it could be heard on deck, moving from one end of the ship to the other, though the men on watch, when they dared to look, saw nothing but shadows.

With each new report of strange occurrences, the ship's mood grew gloomier. What might have been a cheerful crew—for sailors loved a fast ship—became an ever less happy one. Captain Nerezza's mood remained foul, with an almost frantic edge, as he stood for hours on deck brooding, always trying to eke another half knot out of a ship already shuddering under the stress of too much sail. The helmsman fought to hold the great wheel, never a song on his lips or a smile on his face. The cook produced uninspired gruel. There was no music to be heard, not a single laugh.

They all felt it—the thing in the dark cabin. Every man felt it. And then one night, as sailors lay in their hammocks trying to find sleep that wouldn't come, a young boy spoke three words that carried through the lower decks like a bone-chilling wind. He spoke them just after prayers, when the only sounds were the swishing of water against the hull and the groan of the ship as it buckled and bent under the captain's demands. Those three words rippled through the hearts of all those aboard, for everyone had been thinking the same thing: "It's growing stronger."

CHAPTER 7

THE SECRET

THE SUN BLAZED HOT IN THE BRILLIANT BLUE SKY; the still, humid air hung heavy on Mollusk Island.

Peter and his mates sat in a bored clump in the middle of the Mollusk village. Normally, this was a lively place, where children's laughter mingled with tribal gossip. But today there was almost no sound other than the muffled roar of waves crashing onto the beach several hundred yards away. Nobody felt like talking; everyone except the youngest children was waiting.

They were waiting for a sound nobody wanted to hear but everyone expected—the sound of a conch-shell horn, blown by one of the sharp-eyed Mollusk warriors posted high on the mountainside. The conch horn would mean that a lookout had sighted war canoes on the horizon.

It would mean the Scorpions were coming.

But for now, there was nothing to do but wait.

And waiting was something Peter did very poorly. He glanced at his shadow; it was just the slightest bit longer than the last time he had looked at it. Would this day never end?

Peter looked at the others. Tubby Ted was sleeping, his chin sticky with juice from the coconut he'd been eating before he dozed off. Prentiss and Thomas were playing perhaps their hundredth game of tic-tac-toe, drawing the grid in the dirt with sticks. James sat nearby, trying to catch a bright green jungle fly as it darted around his head.

Peter shifted closer to James, moving carefully so as not to wake Tinker Bell, who was dozing in the bushy red mass of his hair. Keeping his voice low, he said, "The moon is full tonight, isn't it?"

"I believe so," said James, swatting unsuccessfully at the fly. "Why?"

"I'll have a good view of the ocean, that's why," said Peter, grinning.

James, abandoning the fly, turned to Peter. "You wouldn't," he said.

"Yes, I would," said Peter. "I'm tired of staying in the village."

"We all are," said James. "But you promised Fighting Prawn that . . ."

"I *nodded*," interrupted Peter. "A nod isn't a promise. Fighting Prawn doesn't have to know I went out there—that is, unless I find the Scorpions. And then he'll be *glad* I went out."

"But what about the poison arrows?" said James. "Fighting Prawn said . . ."

"They can't hit me if they can't see me," said Peter.

"When do you plan to go?" said James.

"Tonight," said Peter. "Keep it a secret, all right?"

"All right," said James reluctantly. "But I don't think it's a good idea."

"I'll be careful," said Peter, grinning. "Aren't I always careful?"

"No," said James.

CHAPTER 8

THE FIRE GOES OUT

A QUARTER MILE INLAND FROM the western shore of Mollusk Island rose a ramshackle wall of palm-tree trunks, sharpened to knife points at the top and lashed together to form a respectable fort. At one corner, a live palm towered over the fort with a platform built atop it, creating a lookout. Upon that platform sat a deeply tanned man clothed in what would barely pass for rags, with few teeth in his mouth and hair down to his shoulders. Eagle Eye Potts—so called because he could spot a lizard scratching itself three-quarters of a mile away—spent a good deal of time in the lookout tree, watching for signs of trouble.

But right now he was troubled by something he *didn't* see. He'd been thinking hard for the better part of a half hour, trying to figure out what it was. Suddenly it came to him.

"No smoke," Eagle Eye muttered. Then he shouted it: "Smee! There's no smoke!"

Below, in the shade of the fort wall, a very round man with a very round, red face jerked awake from his catnap and wiped some drool from his stubbly chin. This was Smee, the captain's first mate at sea and his lackey on land.

"What?" he shouted up to Eagle Eye.

"There's no smoke!" repeated Eagle Eye.

"Smoke?" shouted Smee. "Where?"

"No! There's NO smoke," shouted Eagle Eye.

"Where is there no smoke?" shouted Smee, confused.

"Anywhere!" said Eagle Eye.

Smee thought about that for a moment, then suddenly understood. He rose and scurried to the captain's hut, a makeshift affair of stick walls and a palm-frond roof.

"Cap'n!" he said, tapping tentatively on what passed for the door.

"Get in here, Smee!" answered a gruff voice.

Smee stepped into the hut, which was occupied by a tall, gaunt man with long, tangled, black hair and a sharp steel hook where his left hand had once been. He was called Captain Hook by his men, though he had once been known as Black Stache, the most feared pirate on the seven seas. A prodigious display of facial hair sprouted beneath his nose, greased and curved on the ends and stretching nearly ten inches in length when fully extended. His focus at the moment was his long feet, and in particular his thick, yellow toenails, which curved around his toes like claws. He was

43

rubbing the nail on his big toe with a piece of lava rock, attempting to grind it down.

"Cap'n, sir," Smee said. "Eagle Eye . . ."

"It ain't no good, Smee," interrupted Hook, not looking up. "Either the nail is too hard or the rock too soft, but it don't answer. Get down on your knees there, and give us a bite."

"A bite?"

"My toenail, you idjit."

"But, Cap'n . . ."

"Now!"

Smee shuddered, edged forward, and went down on one knee. He stared at the grotesque yellowed fang that protruded from the captain's dirty big toe.

"But, Cap'n . . ."

"Just give it a nip there on the side. I can tear it off after that."

Smee closed his eyes, held his breath, and did as he was told. He had five teeth and only two that met. He pressed these together, bit down hard, and heard a click. His mouth tasted like . . . he couldn't think about it.

"Splendid!" said Hook, examining and then peeling the excess nail away from his toe. "Fine job, Smee."

Smee spat onto the sand floor and said, "Cap'n, Eagle Eye says there's no smoke comin' from the native side."

"What?" said Hook, looking up from his toenail.

"The natives has put out their fires."

"But they never put out their fires," said Hook.

"That's the point, I believe, sir."

"Shut up, Smee!" snarled Hook. "I *know* that's the point." He pondered for a moment, then said, "Send out a scouting party. I want six men who can work the jungle quiet as snakes. They're to cross the mountain to the other side—"

"But—"

"Don't 'but' me, Smee. To the other side. Get as close as they can and find out what them savages is up to. No good, is what I'm guessing. Planning some kind of trap, some raid on yours truly."

"But—"

"Shut up, idjit."

"Aye, Cap'n," said Smee, turning to leave.

"And before you go, Smee . . ."

Smee turned around to see the captain wiggling his toe talons in the air.

"Nine to go," said Hook.

CHAPTER 9

A Mysterious Gentleman

Enveloped in the *bumpity-bump* and *clickity-clack* of the train car they'd boarded in Paddington Station, Molly and George made the hour's journey to Oxford, looking at the scenery and sipping tea. It was a beautiful, sunlit day with only the occasional puff of cloud dotting the rich blue sky.

They passed thatch-roofed farmhouses, green fields surrounded by stone walls, horses and cows, dogs and ducks. Occasionally one of them would attempt conversation, but it was awkward; both were nervous about being away from home on their own, and all too aware of being together, boy and girl.

As they neared Oxford, George, after a long gaze out the window, turned to Molly and said, "I don't want to be negative, but I don't see how we'll ever find out who placed these personal notices. There are far too many for anyone to remember a particular one, especially given that the last one your father mentioned ran in the paper more than twelve years ago."

"There was a name in the ad: a Mr. Starr."

"But even so . . ." George complained.

Molly lowered her voice. "And we have a date. Father said the last notice for Mr. Starr was placed twelve years ago, just before I was born. So we can start looking at the newspapers right around then."

George nodded. "I suppose that's a start," he said.

"Yes," said Molly. "It's better than nothing." She hesitated, blushed, then added, "I'm ever so grateful you've come along."

It was George's turn to blush. "I wouldn't miss it," he said.

After that they spoke little until they arrived in Oxford, where they took a cab to the Oxford *Observer*, which occupied a massive stone building on High Street. The lobby, smelling of ink and glue, was busy with people bustling this way and that.

A receptionist directed Molly and George to the Archives Department, on the third floor. They climbed the stairs and found themselves in a large, musty room that looked like a sort of library, with bank after bank of racks filled with newspapers hanging from wooden rods. Molly filled out a request slip and gave it to a clerk, who disappeared among the racks and returned ten minutes later with several weeks' worth of newspapers. The clerk passed these across the counter to Molly and George, who took them to one of the long wooden tables where several other people sat poring over old editions of the *Observer*.

Molly and George began paging through the twelve-year-old newspapers, starting with the one published on Molly's birthday, then working back. It was slow going—scanning page after page, reading dozens upon dozens of notices printed in small, cramped type. At the end of an hour they had gone through three issues and found nothing, and Molly was beginning to worry that their trip had been a waste of time.

And then, on the thirteenth page of the issue printed four days before her birthday, she saw it.

"There!" she whispered, gripping George's arm with one hand and pointing with the other at a two-line notice on the bottom of the page:

Mr. Starr: Expect your package Friday the 18th.
(DS5G3—10/2)

"Capital!" exclaimed George. "But what are those letters and numbers?"

They put this question to the Archives Department clerk, who explained that the letters and numbers were a billing reference used by the Accounts Department. The date that followed represented the first day the notice had been posted; it had run for over two weeks before the current issue. Molly wrote down the billing reference and the date of the notice, and, following the clerk's directions, she and George went down to the Accounts Department, which was on the floor below ground level.

They found themselves in a dimly lit hallway, which they followed to a door marked ACCOUNTS. George knocked, and they were called inside by an ancient-looking man wearing thick glasses and seated behind a cluttered desk piled high with ledger books. A plaque on the desk read: MR. RINGWOOD.

"May I help you?" His voice sounded dry and fragile, like the paper in his old ledger books.

"Yes," said George. "We're interested in . . . that is to say, we're trying to find out . . . That is, we'd like to know . . ."

Molly, rolling her eyes, interrupted. "Someone placed a personal notice some years ago in your newspaper. It mentioned a package and a man's name—Mr. Starr. That's my, ah, father, and . . . well . . ."

Molly ran out of steam. Ringwood sat patiently, waiting.

"Her father has taken ill, I'm sorry to say," said George. "This person who placed the ad, he . . . he . . ."

George looked at Molly for help.

"I believe he may be my father's brother," she said. "A long-lost brother, that is. My uncle. I'm hoping you might have his address, as it's quite important we locate him. Our business with him involves my family's estate."

Ringwood sighed, then carefully placed his pen in its holder and slipped a wooden disk over his inkwell. He gestured at the shelves behind him, which were filled with hundreds of fat ledger books like the ones on his desk.

"Young lady," he said, speaking slowly and carefully, as though afraid his words would break. "The *Observer* has printed a great many personal notices. Could you be a bit more specific as to when your uncle . . ."

"Yes, of course," said Molly, hastily pulling out a piece of paper. "I have the date of the notice and the billing reference."

"Well," said Ringwood. "That's another thing altogether." He took the piece of paper in shaking hands and peered at it through his thick lenses. Then he slowly stood and turned to consult his ledger-lined shelves. He dragged a ladder that moved on rollers to a certain spot, and with some difficulty, climbed up several steps. He withdrew a leather binder, climbed down, and returned to his desk. There he began to turn the pages far too slowly for the impatient Molly, who was intensely aware of the need to get back to London before nightfall.

Finally, Ringwood found the page he wanted. He ran a bony finger down a column of writing.

"Ah, yes," he said. "Here it is."

George and Molly waited. Ringwood read the ledger entry, then looked up at Molly and frowned.

"Interesting," he said.

"What?" said Molly. "Do you know him?"

"As it happens, I did," said Ringwood. "I wasn't a personal friend of the gentleman, but he was a customer here for a number of years. Put in a notice only every few years, but it always ran several weeks. And he had a . . . memorable way about him."

"You speak of him in the past tense," Molly said softly.

"Yes, miss. Sadly, I do."

"What happened?" said George.

"Bit of a mystery, actually," said Ringwood, eyeing Molly. "The gentleman and his wife went missing under . . . odd circumstances. They simply disappeared. Vanished. The police searched for weeks on end, but they were never seen again, at least not here in Oxfordshire. It was on the front page of this very newspaper for days. Weeks."

"What kind of odd circumstances?" George asked.

"You can read the articles," Ringwood told him. "We'll have copies upstairs in Archives. But as I recall there was a child—a son, just a baby, left behind. Terrible thing."

"A boy," said Molly, suddenly feeling a strange chill. "Do you know what happened to him?"

"As I recall," said Ringwood, "he was not claimed by family, so he was placed in an orphanage."

Molly felt light-headed. "What orphanage?" she said.

Ringwood frowned and rubbed his chin. "Saint Somebody's, I believe. St. Nigel's? No, that's not it . . ."

"St. Norbert's?" Molly whispered.

"St. Norbert's! That's the one," proclaimed Ringwood.

Molly, her face pale, grabbed Ringwood's desk for support.

"Are you all right?" said Ringwood.

"Yes," said Molly, though she was obviously shaken.

"Well, in any event," said Ringwood, "this man could not have been your father's brother."

"Why not?" said Molly, looking up.

"You said your father's name is Starr," said Ringwood.

"I . . . uh, yes. Starr," said Molly.

"This man's name was not Starr," said Ringwood. He looked down at the ledger. "Quite a mysterious gentleman," he muttered.

"What was his name?" said Molly.

Ringwood looked up; his eyes met Molly's.

"The gentleman's name," he said, "was Mr. Pan."

CHAPTER 10

THE JACKAL

LE FANTOME TACKED TO STARBOARD under a cloudless, moonlit sky. The coast of Africa now loomed close ahead; Spain was somewhere astern.

It was just past two in the morning when the ship slid past the ancient stone jetty outside the harbor of Maknar, the primary port city of the kingdom of Rundoon. Helped by an onshore breeze, the ship made straight for the main wharf, where a carriage hitched to two horses awaited. Standing next to the carriage were four guards wearing the loose-fitting pantaloons and red tunics of the Rundoon Royal Guard. Each man had a large, curved sword at his belt.

Le Fantome was quickly tied up, and her gangway lowered. Nerezza thumped three times on the deck with the heel of his boot. A moment later, the dark shape emerged from the aft companionway. It flowed across the deck and down the gangway. Some of the crewmen turned away; others stared in open horror at the hideous thing that they had been traveling with.

Nerezza watched also; his expression was blank, but he hoped this was the last he would see of Lord Ombra. The instant the thought formed in his mind, the shadowy shape stopped on the gangway and turned slowly, until his face—or, more accurately, the opening in his cloaklike shape where a face should have been—pointed directly at Nerezza. For several very long seconds Ombra faced him, and in the darkness Nerezza thought he could just make out two red orbs, like glowing coals. Then the shape turned away and resumed descending the gangplank, and Nerezza could breathe again.

Ombra glided onto the wharf and slithered—*floated*—up into the carriage. The horses skittered nervously, unsettled by the dark creature. The guards, hiding their own nervousness, closed the carriage door and took positions on the exterior footholds. The driver flicked the reins, and the carriage rolled off the wharf, into the night.

It climbed the deserted road toward the center of Maknar. The air was dry and warm even at this hour. The road itself was made of sand and dirt packed hard as stone. Rising directly ahead was the royal palace of Rundoon's supreme ruler, King Zarboff the Third. It was an enormous, sprawling castle made of gold-hued stone, with a series of sharply pointed spires rising high into the night sky. But the carriage did not go to the palace; instead, it veered to the right, onto another road that carried it through a market-place, deserted at this hour, and then down a hill. The road snaked through a series of progressively more crowded neighborhoods consisting of ramshackle mud huts built close together. A long snake slithered across the road as the carriage left Maknar altogether and entered the open desert.

The road here was no more than ruts in the moonlit sand; the horses strained to maintain the momentum of the carriage, a vehicle ill-suited to desert travel. A mile, two miles, three—and then a foreboding shape loomed on the horizon. As the carriage drew closer, the shape grew more distinct, and its great size became increasingly apparent.

It was the head of a jackal, a wild predator related to the dog. The symbol of death.

The Jackal was made from enormous carved blocks of stone: two sharply pointed ears—each sixty feet high—rose on either side of a massive head with cavernous, staring eye holes above a huge, cavelike mouth lined with rows of jagged teeth.

The Jackal had been built a thousand years earlier by a conquering tribe from the east, brutal warlords who had enslaved Rundoon for centuries. They had used the Jackal as a temple, a place where they conducted their rituals, many of which involved human sacrifice. Since their departure long ago, the Jackal had stood unused, abandoned—and feared.

The people of Rundoon believed the Jackal to be

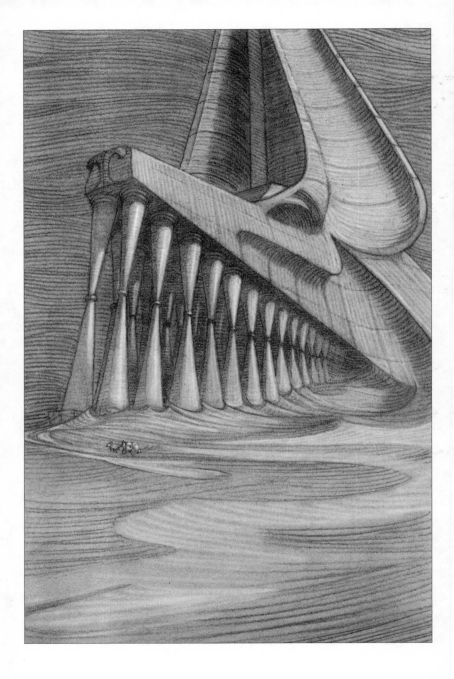

possessed by evil. Indeed, many travelers, having made the mistake of passing too close, claimed to have heard strange sounds or seen dark shapes moving about. The carriage guards had been handpicked for their bravery, but to a man, they were intensely uneasy as they drew closer to the huge jagged-toothed maw opening above them in the moonlit desert. The horses also grew skittish; finally they stopped, ignoring the driver's whip, refusing to go any closer. The mouth of the Jackal was still fifty yards away.

In the sudden stillness, the driver and the guards exchanged nervous glances. Nobody knew what to do; nobody wanted to approach the coach door.

There was no need. With a creak, the door swung open. The dark shape oozed out of the carriage onto the sand. It turned toward the driver and, with a groaning voice no human throat could have uttered, said a word that in the language of Rundoon meant "Wait." The driver nodded, unable to speak.

Ombra turned and glided toward the Jackal's mouth. The moonlight seemed to press down on him, flattening his shape. He left no footprints in the sand.

Ombra reached the mouth of the Jackal and glided inside. As he went from moonlight to darkness, he rose to full height. Passing between the rows of huge stone teeth, he moved deeper and deeper into the giant mouth until he came to a low stone archway where the Jackal's throat would be.

Without hesitating, Ombra glided through the archway into the pitch blackness beyond. He descended a steep, narrow stone stairway, the air growing cooler the deeper he went into the earth. Down and down he went, the stairway switching back, then switching again, then again and still again. Finally it opened into a large underground chamber, utterly dark to human eyes, though there were no humans there. The beings there did not need light, nor did they want it.

Ombra glided to the center of the room and stopped. What followed was a conversation of sorts between Ombra and the other beings in the chamber. It was not held in spoken words; it was essentially a mingling of thoughts. Loosely translated, it went as follows:

I failed, said Ombra. *The starstuff is gone. The Starcatchers returned it.*

How did this happen? said the beings.

I met unexpected resistance, said Ombra.

From whom?

A boy.

A human boy?

Yes. But not an ordinary human.

A Starcatcher?

He is allied with the Starcatchers. But he has powers beyond theirs.

What powers?

Flight. And more. I touched his shadow, but I could not take it. He resisted me with great strength.

Is he a Watcher?

It is possible. But if he is a Watcher, he does not know it. He only recently learned about the Starcatchers. He was on the ship that was to carry the starstuff to Rundoon; he came into contact with it on the island. It should have killed him, but it did not. That is when he began to acquire these powers.

How do you know this?

When we struggled, I felt his thoughts. What is troubling is that, at the same time, he felt my thoughts.

What did he learn?

I do not know.

Could he have learned about the Reversal?

It is possible.

That is very troubling.

Yes. I came as quickly as I could to report this. I was damaged.

Where is the boy now?

I do not know. But I believe he has returned to the island. When we struggled, I sensed that he felt strong loyalty to his friends there and would return as soon as possible.

You must find him and bring him here. We must determine what he knows and what he has told the Starcatchers.

Yes. And the Reversal?

We will continue with our plan. But we cannot create the

Reversal without more starstuff; we must arrange for another Fall. The boy may be able to help us with that as well, if he is a Watcher.

I will find him.

How far to the island?

By ship, a week.

That is too long. The time for the Reversal is close. You will travel in the pod.

Yes.

Bring the boy. Do not fail again.

I will not fail again. I will bring the boy.

CHAPTER 11

THE UNSEEN ENEMY

WE SHOULD GO BACK, said Tinker Bell, for at least the two-dozenth time. *There's nobody out here.*

"One more time around," said Peter.

That's what you said last time.

"This time I promise."

Hmph.

"You can go back if you want," said Peter, angling his body into a gentle turn, knowing that Tink would be right behind him. They were flying about five hundred feet above the sea in a sky unmarked by a single cloud. To Peter's right the moon shone brightly, twice—once in the sky and once reflected below in the warm and placid water.

Peter and Tink had been out for more than two hours, patrolling in widening circles, gradually increasing their distance from Mollusk Island, which rose sharply from the sea about twenty-five miles off to Peter's left. They had seen nothing, and Peter knew he would have to return to the island soon, before dawn revealed his absence from the Mollusk village. He would be glad to reach land again; his neck was aching from keeping his head up while scouring the horizon for . . .

Boats!

Tink's warning chime startled Peter, causing him to swerve and almost tumble head over heels in the sky.

"Where?" he asked, regaining his balance.

That way.

Peter looked in the direction indicated by Tink's tiny pointing finger—almost straight ahead but slightly to the right. He saw nothing, but that didn't surprise him; Tink could see like a hawk. He altered his course slightly and increased his speed.

Why are you going toward them? Shouldn't we go back and tell the Mollusks?

"We need to find out how many there are."

Many, said Tink.

Peter, wanting a more accurate count, kept flying toward the horizon. In a few minutes he could make out a few dark shapes on the water, then more, then more . . .

And then Peter felt a hollowness in his stomach as, suddenly, the whole sea ahead seemed to be covered with long, low war canoes. They were manned by teams of paddlers who sent the sleek craft surging through the water, each hull creating a ghostly moonlit wake of dozens and dozens—perhaps hundreds—of white smudge lines on the dark sea.

Now can we leave?

"In a minute," said Peter, determined to bring back a good estimate of the size of the Scorpion war party. "Just a little closer." He dropped lower, thinking that if he stayed close to the sea he would avoid detection. What he did not realize was that by reducing his altitude he was not only getting closer to the canoes, but he was also silhouetting himself against the brilliant moon.

Closer he flew, closer . . .

Look out!

Peter heard the warning an instant before he heard the sound, a hiss of air as something shot past him no more than five feet away.

An arrow.

Look out!

This time there were three hisses, one of them so close, Peter felt the air move as it went past. He banked hard to his right and flew straight up in an evasive corkscrew pattern, praying that he was not flying into the path of one of the arrows—there were many now—hissing into the sky, hunting him like invisible airborne snakes.

Altitude was the key, he knew; if he could get high enough, they couldn't—

LOOK OUT!

Peter felt it on the outside of his right thigh just above the knee, a sharp pain like a bee sting. He looked down, fearing he would see an arrow in his flesh. His fear turned to relief when he saw that the arrow had merely grazed him. He was bleeding, but it wasn't a serious wound, just a scrape . . .

"Uhh!"

Peter grunted as the muscles in his right leg suddenly contracted in violent cramps, which almost immediately spread to the rest of his body. He doubled over in excruciating pain, and, unable to control his flight, began to tumble from the sky.

Peter! Peter!

He could hear Tink shouting as she flitted around him, but he couldn't answer her, couldn't do anything except moan in agony as he tumbled through the air while waves of cramps racked his body. It was the poison, he knew. The arrow had barely scraped him, but still the pain was almost unendurable. Fighting Prawn had warned him. He had not heeded. And now . . .

Peter!

With great effort, Peter fought to straighten his body; he could see the water now, no more than fifty feet below him and getting closer. Somehow he managed to stop tumbling and slow his descent. With the sea just a few feet away, he began to fly forward, wobbling badly but at least no longer losing altitude.

You're going toward the boats!

Peter veered left, then left again, reversing course in an ugly erratic turn, his legs brushing the water.

"Which way?" he gasped, struggling to regain a few feet of altitude.

This way.

Tink flitted ahead, flashing brightly so Peter could follow.

Can you go higher?

"No."

Grimly, Peter focused on following the tiny streaking light ahead, trying to ignore the agonizing pain in his muscles and the water just below him. He tried not to think about how far they were from the island. Too far, he knew, as his toes brushed the sea. He would not be able to stay aloft for all those miles.

"Tink," he gasped, "I can't keep flying."

Yes you can. You must.

"I can't."

Can you see the island?

With painful effort, Peter raised his head and saw the steep volcanic cone of Mollusk Island. It was directly in front of him—but still much too far away. He would not make it.

"I see it, but—"

Keep flying toward it. Don't stop flying!

"I don't think—"

But he was talking to no one. Tink was gone, a tiny darting light now far ahead, leaving him alone just a few feet over the dark water.

Peter gritted his teeth and forced himself to keep going, trying to ignore the throbbing that convulsed his entire body. He flew for five minutes, ten, fifteen, raising his head every minute or so to check his course. He was getting closer, but he knew he would not make it to the island in his pain-weakened state.

Time and again his feet, then his shins, touched the water. Finally, he could fly no more. As he settled into the sea, he felt the warm water cover the length of his body, swallowing him; as it reached his neck, he made a few feeble attempts to swim, but his pain and fatigue were too great. He slipped beneath the surface and started to sink, staring up at the water turned golden green by the bright moon, which wobbled above him, growing dimmer as he descended into the depths, almost grateful that the pain would soon be gone.

But it did not go. In fact, it got worse, and Peter, barely conscious now, sensed that this was because he was moving . . . *upward.* He felt himself burst through the surface, coughing water and gulping sweet salt air into his burning lungs. Tink was zipping about his head, asking over and over if he was all right, but he could not speak, only cough and gasp, cough and gasp . . . and wonder *what had brought him up?*

Then he felt the tightness around his chest and looked

down to see a pair of strong, pale arms around him, hands interlocked in front. Then he heard a familiar voice—not with his ears but in his mind—say his name, and he knew who his rescuer was.

Teacher, he said, not aloud but with his mind.

Yes, answered the mermaid.

Thank you, he said.

Don't thank me, said Teacher. *Thank Tink.*

That's right, said Tink, who had never been happy about the mermaid's obvious fondness for Peter.

"Thanks, Tink," Peter gasped.

Propelled by graceful thrusts of Teacher's powerful tail, Peter shot through the water. Within a half hour he was stumbling ashore on Mollusk Island. He collapsed on hands and knees in the sand, catching his breath. Then, despite the pain that still racked his body, he stood up, intending to get to the Mollusk village as quickly as he could. Head down, he stumbled forward a few feet, and then with a moan, fell . . . into the strong arms of Fighting Prawn. The Mollusk chief had just trotted out of the jungle, followed by two warriors.

"Lie down," said Fighting Prawn, setting Peter gently onto the soft sand.

"How did you know—" Peter began.

"Your bright little friend," said Fighting Prawn, pointing to Tink, who glowed radiantly. "She sent the mermaids around to fetch us."

"Out there," Peter said, pointing toward the sea. "Canoes. They shot me with an arrow. There were—"

"In a moment," said Fighting Prawn. "First let me see your wound."

By the bright moonlight, Fighting Prawn examined Peter's thigh. There was a thin, straight red line in the skin, apparently caused by the side of the passing arrowhead; the flesh around it was swollen and purple.

Fighting Prawn frowned, then grunted something to the warriors, one of whom turned and sprinted into the jungle.

"He will bring the medicine woman," Fighting Prawn said to Peter. "You will do what she says and swallow what she tells you to swallow, no matter how bad it tastes."

"Yes," said Peter.

"You are very fortunate, Peter. Had the arrow pierced you directly, you would be dead now. To be honest, you should be anyway; very few people survive *any* dose of Scorpion poison."

Peter hung his head.

"I shouldn't have gone out there," he said.

"No, you shouldn't have," agreed Fighting Prawn. "But since you did, tell me what you saw."

"Canoes," Peter said. "More than a hundred of them."

"Which direction, and how far out?"

"That way," said Peter, pointing. "They're probably about twenty miles away by now."

"They will be here at dawn," said Fighting Prawn. He stood and looked out to sea. "You did well, disobeying me," he said. "I expected them to come from the west, but they circled around, intending to surprise us. They won't surprise us now. Though in the end I don't know how much difference it will make."

Peter looked up, surprised; he had never heard Fighting Prawn sound so uncertain.

The Mollusk chief turned to the remaining warrior and, with the tone of confident command back in his voice, grunt-clicked an order. Then he turned back to Peter.

"He will stay with you until the medicine woman gets here," he said. "I must go and redeploy the warriors. We must prepare to defend our island."

He turned and ran back into the jungle, leaving Peter and Tink with the warrior on the beach, all three of them looking out to sea toward the unseen enemy coming toward them.

CHAPTER 12

St. Norbert's

THE CAB, PULLED BY A LOWLY OLD NAG with a swayback and heavy hooves, moved down a rutted muddy lane lined with trees, their gnarled black branches reaching like skeleton arms into the rainy sky, which had turned from sunny to dark in an instant.

"Do you think we'll learn anything?" Molly said, peering doubtfully out the cab window. "All we have is the date from the newspaper articles. I'm worried that we'll need more than that."

"We have money," George said, patting his pocket. "My father says money can loosen tongues faster than all the chocolate in the world. You remember the cabdriver in Salisbury? A few quid went a long way with that one."

"Yes, it did. Still, I hate to have you spend your own money on this."

"Don't be silly," said George. "It's actually Father's money, and I rather enjoy spending it."

Molly smiled—her first smile of the day. But it faded quickly as the carriage pulled to a stop in front of a rusted iron gate, each of its two sagging halves bearing the letter *S* wrapped snakelike around the letter *N*—the insignia of St. Norbert's Home for Wayward Boys. Beyond the gate, past a gravel drive that was more mud than gravel, loomed a massive gray stone structure with a slate roof in such poor repair that it appeared ready to slide off.

As Molly and George got out of the cab, the drizzle turned to a downpour. Molly lifted the hood of her cloak, and George tugged up the collar to his overcoat.

George, handing the fare to the driver, said, "Two hours."

"Aye, Guv'nor," said the driver. "But I can't imagine why two fine young people like you would want to spend two hours in that place." He nodded toward the building. "Ain't nothing in there but sorrow, you mark my words."

"You wait for us!" George repeated.

The cabbie nodded again, his bowler spraying water from the rim, and gently flicked the reins, sending the old sway-back horse back down the skeleton-lined lane.

Picking their way among the many mud puddles, Molly and George walked up the driveway to the massive oak door of St. Norbert's. There was an iron door knocker, but it was broken; so George pounded the door with his fist. After a wait of a minute or so, they heard the sound of a bolt sliding, and the door swung open to reveal a bent-over man with a two-day growth of gray beard.

"What do you want?" he complained. His eyes were bloodshot and constantly moving.

"My name is Molly McBride," said Molly. "This is George, um . . ."

George, seeing Molly's hesitation, stepped in. "George . . . Chester . . . Maybeck . . . Dooling," he said, causing both Molly and the man to raise their eyebrows. He held out his hand. "And you, sir, are . . ."

"My name's Grempkin," said the man, ignoring George's hand. "I'll ask again: what do you want?"

"We'd like to meet with the director," said Molly.

"Would you, now," said Grempkin.

"We've come all the way from London," said George, following the plan he and Molly had worked out. "There's been a tragedy in Miss McBride's family—her parents, you see—and some information has come to light that suggests, strange as it seems, that a relative of hers may be here. At St. Norbert's."

Grempkin's eyebrow arched high into his hairline. "A relative, is it?"

"Possibly," said Molly.

Grempkin took a closer look at Molly and George, both dressed in the manner of people who come from families with money. He tried to smile, but since he was not used to smiling, what he produced was more of a grimace. When he spoke again his tone was considerably more welcoming.

"Well, now," he said. "Why don't you come in from the rain, and I'll take you to the headmaster."

The foyer smelled musty, as though no door or window had been opened in years, as if the sun had never shone into this place. From somewhere up the enormous wooden staircase came the cry of a boy, and then a long groan. From somewhere else came the sound of vicious barking.

Grempkin led Molly and George down a long corridor lit by hissing gas lamps. He stopped at an office door with faded lettering that announced that its occupant was MR. CHALMERS GREYSTOKE, HEADMASTER. Grempkin knocked and was summoned inside.

Greystoke, a thin-lipped man with a pinched, pale face, sat behind an ancient desk covered with a formidable layer of dust. He did not appear busy, but he also did not appear to be pleased by the interruption.

"Master Greystoke," said Grempkin, "this young lady has reason to believe she has a relative here at St. Norbert's. And since these young people seem to be from *fine families*"—here Grempkin arched his eyebrows to make sure Greystoke got the point—"I thought you'd want to talk to them."

"Of course," said Greystoke, his nostrils flaring at the

aroma of money. Molly and George introduced themselves—again using the false names, although George got his in a different order—and Grempkin, after excusing himself, left the room.

"So you believe your relative is at St. Norbert's," said Greystoke, looking at Molly.

"Possibly," said Molly. "His father and mother—my mother's cousin—went missing twelve years ago, and we believe their infant son was brought here."

"And the name?" said Greystoke.

"I don't know the infant's name," said Molly. "It wasn't in the newspaper articles. But the father's surname was Pan."

At the mention of the name, Greystoke's eyes widened just a bit. He hesitated, his eyes darting from Molly to George.

"Unfortunately," he said, "I cannot . . . that is, our *policy* is not to divulge specific information of that nature about our charges unless certain, ah, *procedures* are followed."

George nodded, stood, reached into his pocket and pulled out a wad of currency. "I was charged by Miss McBride's solicitor to defray any legal expenses necessitated by this inquiry," he said. "Would this be sufficient?"

George set the stack of bills on the desk and sat down. Greystoke quickly swept the money into his top drawer, along with a puff of dust.

"Mrs. Wilson!" he called, so loudly that both Molly and

George jumped in their seats. An elderly woman appeared from a side room.

"The Pan boy," Greystoke said. "Twelve years back. Parents went missing. Terrible thing."

"Yes, sir. I remember it well."

"Get me his file," he said, giving Mrs. Wilson what Molly thought was an odd look.

She returned with a file so quickly that Molly wondered if it was actually the right file Greystoke was now consulting—or if they showed the same file to every inquisitive visitor. Greystoke muttered to himself, then shut the folder. He laid it on his desk, sending up a small dust cloud.

"A fine boy," he said. "I'm sure he's a fine ambassador for St. Norbert's."

"Ambassador?" said George. "To where?"

Greystoke cleared his throat, sounding as if he were gargling glue.

"Many years ago," he said, "the Board of Trustees saw fit to establish a program abroad for our more excellent boys. To broaden their perspective. To widen their horizons, quite literally. I'm happy to say that your cousin—or is it cousin once removed?—qualified for this most generous program."

"You sent him away," George said, his voice carrying a hint of challenge.

"We afforded him an *opportunity*. It is our role as legal guardians to offer our lads the best that life can offer."

I can see that, thought Molly, recalling the cries she'd heard in the foyer. Aloud, she said, "And when exactly did you send my cousin away? And to where?"

Greystoke consulted the folder again, turning a few pages without appearing to actually look at them.

"It would seem that our records are incomplete," he said finally. "I don't seem to see either a date of departure or a destination. Though I'm sure your . . . *relative* is in the best of hands."

"But you took my money!" said George.

"Yes," said Greystoke. "And then I performed the service of checking the records. Which, as I say, are unfortunately incomplete."

"You sent him away, and you don't know *where?*" said Molly, her voice rising. "Can you at least tell me *when?*"

"I'm sorry," said Greystoke, sounding not at all sorrowful. "I can't help you there. Although perhaps Mr. Grempkin can. He handles the arrangements for the boys who are sent to Run . . . abroad."

Molly and George both caught the name Greystoke had half uttered, but neither reacted.

"Well," said Molly, "can you tell me *anything* about him? Can you at least tell me his *name?*"

Again Greystoke leafed through the folder, which Molly was now certain was just a prop. He looked up, shrugged, and said, "I'm afraid we don't—"

"You said he was a fine boy," interrupted George. "But you don't even know his name."

"We have so many boys here—" Greystoke began.

"I want my money back," said George, standing up.

"Hold on, there," said Greystoke. "Mrs. Wilson!" Immediately the old lady appeared.

"Yes, sir?"

"The Pan boy," Greystoke said.

"Yes, sir."

"I've put these young people on to Grempkin for the details of the program abroad. But what was the boy's given name—do you recall? It's lost among the cobwebs, I'm afraid." He tapped his head and tried on a smile that didn't fit.

"Oh, yes, sir. I remember him well. Peter, he was. Peter Pan."

Molly suppressed a gasp. This was the name she'd been expecting. But hearing it was altogether different. "Peter," she said.

"A lively boy he was," said Mrs. Wilson. "A shame that—"

"Thank you, Mrs. Wilson," interrupted Greystoke. "That will be fine. Now I must ask you two young people to leave. I've a great deal of work to do."

"Yes, I'm sure you do," said George, looking pointedly at Greystoke's empty desk.

Greystoke glared at George, then turned to Molly. "I

wish you luck in finding your relative," he said. "I wish I could have been more helpful."

"Do you?" said Molly, staring at Greystoke until he turned away.

Leaving Greystoke's office, Molly and George retraced their steps down the corridor. They found Grempkin waiting in the foyer; he took five pounds from George but revealed little in exchange. He said he had taken the boy Peter, along with four others, to London, and put them on a ship headed abroad, but he claimed to have no recollection of the name of the ship or its destination. By this point Molly and George knew they would get little more from St. Norbert's, so they went outside, where the cab was waiting. They spoke quietly on the ride back to the train station.

"I can see why they don't want to tell us anything," said George. "They're obviously selling the boys as slaves to Rundoon."

"Yes," said Molly. "And one of those boys was Peter. That's quite an amazing coincidence, don't you think?"

"What do you mean?"

"Well," said Molly, "first we find out that the person who had been warning the Starcatchers when starstuff was about to fall was this Mr. Pan. Then we learn that he disappeared under mysterious circumstances and that he had a son. Now we learn that the son was our own Peter."

George flinched; he did not like the possessive tone

Molly used when she talked about Peter. George sometimes wished there *was* no Peter.

"But it gets even odder," continued Molly. "Peter, after years at St. Norbert's, was sent to Rundoon, and it just so happens that the ship he was placed on was the same ship that *I* was traveling on. And, more important, it was the ship secretly carrying the largest starstuff Fall in many years. Now do you think that could possibly be a coincidence?"

"No," said George.

"I don't either," said Molly.

"So what do you think it means?" said George.

"I think Peter was meant to be on that ship," said Molly. "I don't know *who* meant him to be there. I suspect the gentlemen at St. Norbert's do, but clearly they don't intend to tell us. But he was meant to be there, I'm sure of it, and it seems likely the reason has something to do with his father, the mysterious Mr. Pan. And I wonder if . . ." Molly trailed off, looking out the cab window.

"If what?" prompted George.

"If perhaps this explains Peter's unusual powers."

"I thought that was the starstuff," said George. "When he was exposed to it, he suddenly could fly and so on."

"Yes," said Molly. "But that exposure should have killed him. Instead, it changed him. Father said that was very, very unusual. I think the reason it happened has something to do with his father."

"But what?"

"I don't know," said Molly. "But I believe there's a connection between Peter's father going missing and Peter's powers and the fact that the Starcatchers are no longer being warned about the starstuff Falls. And I strongly suspect that the Others have something to do with all of this. I need to tell my father about this immediately."

"But your father is in Paris."

"Then we must go to Paris."

"All right," said George. "We'll go to Paris."

"Thank you, George," said Molly, resting her hand on his for just a moment. In that moment, George felt two strong and conflicting emotions: the thrill of setting off on another adventure with Molly and resentment over the fact that, once again, the adventure revolved around Peter.

CHAPTER 13

THE POD

THE POD SLID SWIFTLY THROUGH THE SEA, deep enough to leave no sign, not even a ripple, on the surface above.

The pod was made of metal, but not an earthly metal; it was blacker than coal, harder than diamond, stronger than steel. It was a sleek cylinder, seventy-five feet in length and tapered to a sharp point at each end.

The interior was divided into compartments. At the moment the one at the forward end, a small, totally dark enclosed chamber, held only Ombra. At the aft end of the pod were four large cages. Between these and Ombra's chamber was an open main cabin, lit by a lone swaying lantern overhead and occupied by eight members of the Rundoon Royal Guard.

They were hand-picked men—strong, skilled, well-armed fighters. Each one was brave, battle-tested, and—at the moment—quite terrified. They did not show their fear; they were too disciplined for that. But they were afraid nonetheless—of the thing in the forward compartment but also of the bizarre vessel in which they were traveling.

When they had been ordered to report to the harbor in Maknar, they had expected to be boarding a sailing ship. Instead, on arriving at the appointed dock, they had been surprised to find . . . nothing. Where a ship should have been, there was only a patch of murky water. The guardsmen waited a few minutes, not knowing what to do.

Then the murky water began to bubble and swell. As the men stared, a long black shape broke through the surface and rose, settling itself against the dock. A section of the hull slid open smoothly, creating an opening about six feet wide, with stairs leading to the dim interior of the hull. The guardsmen looked at it uncertainly, none of them moving.

Then a voice came from inside the hull, an inhuman groan.

"Enter," it said.

The guardsmen did not want to enter, but they were disciplined soldiers, and they knew the horrible price they would pay if they disobeyed an order. And so, one by one, they descended the stairway into the main cabin. The instant the last man was inside, the opening slid silently shut. They were now trapped inside this strange vessel.

"You will remain in this cabin," said the groaning voice.

The men looked forward and saw its source: the dark shape of Ombra, nearly invisible in the gloom.

"We will travel for one day," he said. "I will give you further orders when we arrive at our destination."

Ombra turned and glided through the opening into his forward chamber. The door closed silently. The guardsmen looked at one another. Each had many questions; none had any answers.

They felt the vessel descend. They heard the water sloshing against the sides and then overhead. They were underwater.

And then they were moving—slowly as they left the harbor, then faster and faster, until the swooshing sound of water slipping past the hull made conversation difficult. The guardsmen could see nothing, as the vessel had no portholes, but it felt to them as though they were moving far faster than any normal sailing ship. And, in fact, they were.

The men heard no engine sound; they did not know how the vessel was moving. It was just as well that they didn't. Their fear would have grown tenfold had they been able to peer into the gloomy water ahead to see what moved the pod so swiftly through the water.

It was pulled by four gigantic squid.

The creatures, each well over a hundred feet from the tip of its huge, dome-shaped, broad-finned mantle to the ends of its longest tentacle pair, were wearing special harnesses

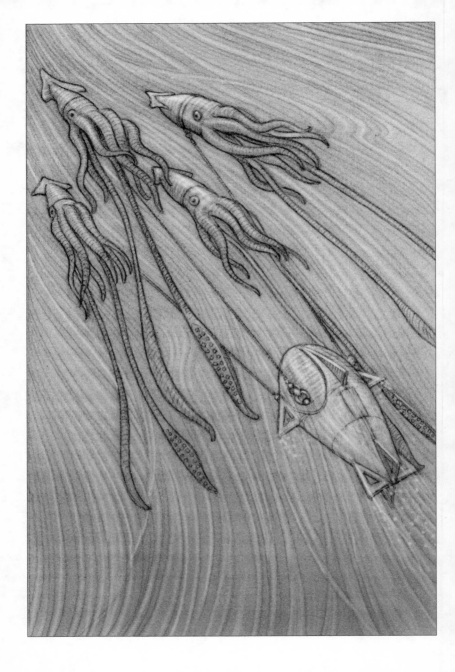

attached by steel cables to four rings on the front of the pod. The monstrous creatures worked rhythmically, sucking huge quantities of water into their mantles, then contracting to eject the water out the back with immense force, causing themselves and the pod to surge forward. They responded to unspoken thought commands from Ombra, whose presence they felt intimately, and who could sense, through them, everything in the sea near the pod.

At the moment there was little to sense; save for a few small fish and the strange vessel passing through, the sea here was open water. But soon enough that would change.

Soon enough, because on its present course, the pod would arrive at Mollusk Island.

CHAPTER 14

THE OTHER TRAIN

MOLLY GLANCED LEFT, THEN RIGHT; *no one was looking. She eyed the ship, mentally measuring the distance. She took George's hand and counted softly.*

"One . . . two . . ."

When Molly and George returned to London, Louise Aster was furious at them, especially Molly, for having left London without permission. But her anger evaporated when the children told her what they had learned in Oxford. Louise immediately sent a telegram to her husband in Paris to let him know that she and the two children would be joining him there on urgent business. George's parents were, as usual, traveling, but his governess readily gave permission for George to travel with the Asters.

Leonard Aster met Louise and the children at the train

station in Paris and took them to his hotel suite. There he listened intently as Molly and George recounted what they had learned in Oxford: that the cryptic personal notices in the *Observer* had been placed by a Mr. Pan; that Pan and his wife had disappeared under suspicious circumstances; that their son had been sent to St. Norbert's; and that the boy's name was Peter. The last piece of news drew a gasp of surprise from Leonard.

When Molly and George were finished, Leonard quizzed them until he was satisfied that he had extracted every last bit of information from them. He then gave them a lecture about having gone to Oxford without permission. But he was so obviously impressed by their detective work that Molly could barely suppress a smile of pride.

It was nearly midnight when Leonard sent the children to bed. He then left the hotel to share their findings with the other senior Starcatchers meeting with him in Paris.

The next morning, Leonard, Louise, Molly, and George ate breakfast around a table in the hotel suite next to a window with a grand view of the Seine. Molly noticed that her father's trunk had been packed and placed by the door, but, following her father's lead, she said nothing until the waiter had left the suite.

The door clicked shut. Leonard said, "I sail today for Mollusk Island." Molly started to speak, but her father held up his hand to stop her. "I believe Peter is in grave danger," he said. "I never should have let him go back to the island. I had a nagging feeling that it was a mistake, but he was so eager to get back to his mates, and he'd done so much for us, I just couldn't bring myself to stop him. Now I wish I had."

"I don't understand," said Molly. "Why is he in danger?"

"The Others," said Leonard. "I fear they'll come back for him."

"But why?" asked George. "They were after the starstuff, and that was returned at Stonehenge. The Others know that. What good is Peter to them now?"

Leonard paused, as if deciding how much to reveal. "Peter may have certain abilities that could be very useful to them," he said.

"You mean flying?" said George. It bothered George that Peter could fly.

"No," said Molly, looking at her father. "It's not flying. It's the falling starstuff, isn't it? You think Peter can do what his father did."

Leonard smiled at his daughter's insight. "Yes," he said. "This Mr. Pan apparently had the ability to predict starstuff Falls. And if Peter is, in fact, Mr. Pan's son . . ."

"Then he might have the same ability," said Molly.

"He might," said Leonard. "He certainly has other unusual abilities. And if he can, in fact, predict starstuff Falls, he would be very valuable to the Others."

"But Peter would never help the Others!" said Molly.

"Not willingly, no," Leonard said softly. "But I doubt they would give him a choice."

Molly was silent for a moment. "So," she said, "it *wasn't* coincidence that Peter was put aboard the *Never Land*." She thought back to the day she had met Peter, both of them passengers aboard an old, ill-fated ship carrying a mysterious trunk.

"I now believe it was not," said Leonard. "I believe Peter was being sent to Rundoon to be used by the Others. I think the same thing may have happened to his father."

"You think Mr. Pan was taken to Rundoon?" said George.

"Possibly," said Leonard. "That would explain why he disappeared a dozen years ago, and why we received no warnings from him after that—*and* why the Others knew about that last starstuff Fall in Scotland."

"But if the Others have Peter's father," said Molly, "why would they need Peter?"

"I don't know," said Leonard. "Perhaps to keep him away from us. Or perhaps something happened to his father, and they want Peter as a replacement. If that's the case, they'll want him even more now. We managed to get that last batch of starstuff away from them. It was obvious they wanted it very badly—sending that Ombra creature after it. They'll be looking to get more."

"And they'll try to use Peter to get it," said Molly.

"I think they might," said Leonard. "We can't take any

chances. I've arranged for a ship to leave Le Havre tonight. Whether Peter wants it or not, I'm going to bring him back to London, for his protection as well as ours."

"When do we leave?" said Molly.

"*We?*" The exclamation came simultaneously from both of Molly's parents.

"Oh please, can't George and I go?" said Molly.

"Absolutely not," said Louise.

"It's far too dangerous," said Leonard. "You, your mother, and George will return to London, where you'll remain under protection." Seeing Molly's disappointment, he softened his voice. "I'm sorry, Molly. I—all of us—very much appreciate all the good work you and George have done."

"If you appreciated it," said Molly, "you'd let us go with you and stop treating us like children. Without us, the Others would have the starstuff and you'd be—"

"That's quite enough, young lady," said Louise, in a tone that did not allow for a reply.

Molly said no more, but she seethed with disappointment and anger. She felt betrayed. To be treated like this after all she had done . . . and after Peter had risked *his* life to come to her rescue in London. Now, when he was in trouble, she was being denied the chance to help him. It wasn't fair!

For his part, George didn't look too unhappy about not being included in the voyage to find Peter. He and Peter were not exactly best friends. "Your father's right, you know," he said to Molly. "Perhaps there's more to be done in the libraries and public records to—"

Molly shut George up with a glare that told him she was not interested in libraries or public records. She wanted one thing and one thing only: to be on the ship bound for Mollusk Island.

Three hours later, Molly, George, and Louise Aster boarded a train for Calais, where they would board a ship to England. But Molly's mind was on another train in the same station: the train her father had just boarded for Le Havre. The two trains were scheduled to leave only minutes apart.

As her mother was supervising the storage of their luggage, Molly pulled George into their train compartment and whispered, "You can do what you want, but I'm going with Father."

"What?" George said. "Are you *insane*? How . . ."

"*Shh!*" Molly said as her mother entered the compartment. "Mother," she said, "George and I are going to explore the train. Can I bring you anything from the dining car?" She knew her mother was never far from a cup of tea.

"Some tea would be lovely," her mother said. She dug into her purse and, after searching a bit, frowned and said, "All I have is a twenty-franc note." Handing it to Molly, she said, "Make sure you get change."

"Oh, I will," said Molly. She saw the worry in George's eyes, and for a moment she feared he might reveal her plan. Louise also noticed George's expression.

"George, are you all right?" she said.

"Yes, Mrs. Aster," George answered. He forced a smile. "One tea, coming up!" He turned and followed Molly into the train corridor.

"Molly," he whispered. "You can't be serious. Your parents will . . ."

"I am completely serious," interrupted Molly. "If you wish to stay, fine. But don't you dare give me away until the train is under way. Do you hear me, George Darling? If you muddle this up, I will never speak to you again, *ever*."

"I'm not going to muddle anything," George said quietly. "I'm going with you."

Molly stopped and turned to look at him.

"Are you sure?" she said. "It may be dangerous."

"I'm sure."

"Thank you, George," she said, and both of them blushed.

They moved into the next car. Molly bent and peered out a window until she caught a glimpse of the train to Le Havre, three platforms away.

"What time is it?" she said.

George consulted his pocket watch. "Three minutes before the hour."

"There's no time to lose," Molly said. As she spoke, the train car lurched and began to move. "Hurry!" said Molly. With George right behind, she ran to the end of the corridor, opened the coach door, and descended the steps. The train was moving quite quickly now; the end of the platform was near. Molly looked at the platform and prepared to jump.

"It's too late!" said George. You can't possibly . . ."

But Molly had already jumped. The train's momentum sent her stumbling alongside the train, almost falling. She caught her balance and turned to see that George had been unable to catch his; he was sprawled on the platform, wincing in pain.

"George, are you all right?" she said, reaching to help him up.

"I'm *fine*," he snapped, ignoring her offer of help as he scrambled to his feet, his face beet red with embarrassment.

The train rumbled out of the station carrying Molly's mother, not to mention Molly's luggage and any hope Molly might have had to avoid infuriating her parents. All she had now were the clothes she wore and the twenty-franc note she clutched in her hand. And, of course, George.

"Hurry," she shouted, running toward the platform stairs. "Father's train is about to leave!"

＊

The train station in the port city of Le Havre smelled of coal smoke, with hints of salt water and fish. Molly and George emerged cautiously from the third-class coach they had ridden in to avoid being seen by Molly's father. The night sky was cloud-covered and dark. Molly and George hid behind a column on the bustling station platform and watched as Leonard Aster descended from the first-class coach. He was met by two men and a porter to carry his trunk.

Hanging back in the crowd, Molly and George followed Leonard and the other men downstairs to a waiting horse-drawn carriage. A few minutes later, the children were in a taxi following the carriage along bumpy cobblestone streets lit by flickering gaslights.

They soon arrived at a busy wharf lined with tall sailing ships in various stages of being loaded and unloaded, with sweating dockworkers moving heavy barrels and crates this way and that. Keeping well back, Molly and George followed Leonard Aster and the other men to a large, handsome ship that bore the name *Michelle* in gold lettering on her bow. The men walked up a gangway onto the deck, followed by a dock man with Leonard's trunk.

Molly and George got as close to the ship as they dared, concealing themselves behind a stack of wooden crates.

"We can't just walk up that ramp," George whispered.

"No, we can't," agreed Molly, looking desperately for some other way to board. She touched the locket she wore around her neck. It held a small amount of starstuff, enough to enable her and George to fly onto the ship. But it had been given to her by her father to be used only in the gravest of emergencies. She wondered if this qualified.

Molly studied the *Michelle*, whose crew was preparing the ship for departure. All of the activity, she noted, was taking place toward the stern. At the moment, there were no crewmen at the bow, which was attached to the dock by a thick line.

"Can you climb a rope, George?" she whispered.

"Of course I can," George said, his gaze following Molly's. "But you can't seriously be thinking about . . . *are* you?"

Molly's look answered his question.

"We run across to that pile of nets," she said. "From there, it's straight to the bow line. And up. Quickly, George. It's our only chance. All set?"

George was about to say that no, he was not all set, but Molly wasn't interested in his views.

"On three," she said. She took a deep breath, looked both ways, and took George's hand.

"One . . . two . . ."

CHAPTER 15

Hook's Plan

THE EASTERN HORIZON HAD barely begun to lighten with the first pink hint of dawn when the mournful sound of the conch horn came echoing down the mountain.

The Mollusks had been expecting it; most had been up all night waiting for it. Yet it still came as a shock, confirming the brutal reality: the attack was coming.

Fighting Prawn, followed by a half dozen of his senior warriors, stood at the edge of a rock outcropping on a steep cliff overlooking the eastern side of the island. He stared out at a place where the indigo water met the lightening sky. His eyesight was still superb, but it was a minute before he could see the black shapes of the lead canoes. He stood motionless, watching as more canoes came into view, then more, then still more, until they seemed to cover the horizon. Each canoe, he saw, carried ten men at least, perhaps more. Fighting Prawn did not allow his face to betray the despair he felt upon seeing the size of the attacking force. But he saw the worry in the eyes of his men as he turned to face them.

In a calm voice, he grunted a brief command. There was little to say: his men knew what to do. They trotted off, heading for the various stations from which they would try to defend their island.

Fighting Prawn, alone now, turned back to the sea and watched the flotilla of black canoes coming relentlessly closer, bringing terror and death to his peaceful island.

High above the outcropping where Fighting Prawn stood, a pirate by the name of Boggs was hidden in the foliage near the top of the island's mountain ridge. He was also looking at the oncoming canoes and trying to count them, but he gave up after reaching thirty-nine, which was the highest number he knew. Then he turned and began running toward the pirates' side of the island.

It took him nearly an hour to reach the pirate camp. Out of breath, he ran straight to Hook's hut and gasped out the news.

"Canoes, Cap'n. Coming from the east. Big ones. Lots of 'em. A war party is what it looks like."

Hook was on his feet in an instant, his close-set black eyes glittering.

"How many canoes?" he rasped.

"More'n thirty-nine," said Boggs. "A LOT more."

"Big ones, you say?"

"Aye, Cap'n. Each carrying ten men."

"SMEE!" bellowed Hook, stepping out from his hut.

"Coming, Cap'n!" said Smee, approaching the hut at a rapid waddle, mango juice dribbling from his chin.

"Round up a small party of the best men," said Hook. "Tell them to bring their weapons and as much food and water as they can carry. We're getting off this cursed island."

"We are?" said Smee. "How?"

"Boggs here has spied a war party of savages approaching in canoes," said Hook. "We're going to borrow some of their canoes and take our leave of this wretched place."

"But, Cap'n," said Smee, frowning. "Do you think the savages will let us borrow their canoes?"

Hook stared at Smee for three long seconds.

"Smee," he said finally.

"Aye, Cap'n?"

"You have the brain of a sea urchin."

"Aye, Cap'n."

"We ain't going to *ask* the savages to borrow their canoes, you idjit. We wait until they's fighting the local savages. While they ain't looking, we slip off in their canoes."

"Ah!" said Smee, brightening. "It's a fine plan, Cap'n."

"Of course it is," said Hook. "Now assemble the men."

As Smee waddled off, Hook allowed himself a moment

to reflect upon his genius and savor the knowledge that, within a few hours, he would be leaving this hideous island behind forever. His only regret was that he would not have a chance to get his revenge on that cursed flying boy.

CHAPTER 16

A LIABILITY

GEORGE AND MOLLY QUICKLY found a good place to hide. Near the bow of the ship there was a dory turned upside down and lashed to the deck. George loosened one of the lines and lifted the edge; the two slipped underneath and retied the line. It was cramped and dark under the dory, but safe.

Trying to ignore their hunger, they fell asleep beneath the little upside-down boat, out of the wind, the salt spray, and the view of crewmen. In the morning, with the pink light of dawn showing through the gap where the boat met the deck, George was awakened by Molly's hair tickling his nose. Forgetting where he was, he tried to sit, and bumped his forehead on the dory's bench.

"Ow!"

The sound woke Molly, who blinked a few times, remembering where they were and how they'd gotten there.

"I'm starving," whispered George, rubbing his head. "How long do we have to stay out of sight?"

"Long enough so they won't turn the ship around and take us back. Two days at least."

"Two *days?*"

"No one made you come along," Molly reminded him.

"We'll starve!"

"No, we won't," said Molly, though she was quite hungry herself. "We'll find some food tonight."

"*Tonight?* Are you saying we're to go without food the entire day?"

"Apparently, I am."

George groaned and lay back down. They spent an unhappy morning under the dory, saying little, listening to the sounds of the ship and the grumble of their stomachs. Molly grew quite thirsty and knew that George must be thirsty, too. She was grateful he didn't complain.

The first suggestion of the storm was the dimming of light where the dory met the deck. The next sign was the rise and fall of the ship, which went from gentle rocking to a much more violent motion, the bow lifting high and then crashing loudly down into the sea. The dory rattled and shook, and Molly began to feel sick to her stomach. Things were not going as she'd planned.

She looked at George. By the dim light filtering under the dory, she saw that his face was as gray as driftwood.

"I need some air," he whispered.

"Please don't be sick," she said.

"I need air *now*," he said.

But it wasn't air George got: it was water. There was a sudden, loud drumming sound on the dory hull, then rivulets of cold rainwater surged across the deck and under the dory, soaking Molly and George. With the rain came an even more violent motion of the ship's deck, now rolling right and left as well as rocking up and down.

George made an ominous sound and clapped his hand over his mouth.

"George . . ." Molly warned.

"Sorry, I . . ." George turned away from Molly just as his unhappy stomach rebelled. Instantly an awful stench filled the upturned dory; Molly, now retching herself, frantically untied the line holding the dory down and lifted the boat off with her back. At once, she and George were blasted by torrents of wind-driven rain; they scrabbled along the heaving deck, looking for something to hold on to. George was still retching pitifully.

"Hey!" a deep voice boomed over the roar of the wind. "You there!"

Molly turned to see a burly seaman fighting his way forward. He grabbed the sliding dory and quickly secured it to the deck, then turned to the children.

"What's this, now?" he boomed. "Stowaways, is it?"

"I'm the daughter of Lord Aster," Molly shouted. "If you please, sir, I wish to be taken to him at once."

"His lordship's daughter, hiding under a dory?" said the seaman, smiling skeptically. "And who might this be?" he asked, pointing at the retching George. "A duke, perhaps?"

"He's my friend," said Molly. "Please, just take us to my father."

"All right, then," said the seaman, eyeing George's clothes, which were covered with what had once been the contents of his stomach. "But first we need to make the duke more presentable." He turned and walked astern, returning moments later with a bucket.

"Here, your lordship," he said. As George, still on hands and knees, looked up, the seaman splashed him with a full bucket of cold seawater.

"That's much better," said the seaman, laughing as he reached out a hand to help the sputtering George to his feet. "Welcome aboard the *Michelle*, my lord and lady."

———◆———

Leonard Aster paced the captain's quarters, walking back and forth in front of two chairs. In one sat Molly; in the other, George; both were wrapped in rough wool blankets.

Leonard's face was grim and pale save for two red spots,

one on each cheek. Those spots, Molly knew, meant her father was furious.

For more than a minute, Leonard strode back and forth, too angry even to speak. When he finally did, his voice quivered with rage.

"I cannot believe you would do this, Molly," he said.

"But, Father . . . it's Peter."

"*Silence.*"

Molly's mouth snapped shut.

"I am extremely disappointed in you, Molly. And George, you . . ."

"I talked him into it," Molly said.

"No, she didn't, sir," said George, "I . . ."

"*Silence,* both of you."

Molly and George sat still as stones as Leonard paced for a full minute more.

"You've created a very bad situation, Molly. If I take you to the island, I expose you and George to danger, not to mention the fact that your mother and George's parents will be frantic with worry, not knowing your whereabouts. But if I order the ship turned around to return you to France, we lose precious time getting to the island. Precious to the Starcatchers. Precious to Peter."

Molly started to speak, but her father's look quelled that idea.

Leonard paced some more.

"Here is what I have decided," he said finally. "We will proceed to the island. Peter's well-being is paramount. We will try to get word to your mother through the porpoises; she can contact George's parents. For the remainder of this voyage, you and George will remain on this ship, under close supervision. You will not go onto the island; you are a liability on this expedition. So you *will* remain on the ship, and when we return to England"—here Leonard stopped pacing and looked into Molly's eyes—"there will be consequences. Do you both understand?"

"Yes, Father," said Molly.

"Yes, Lord Aster," said George.

"The crew are making up cabins for you both," said Leonard. "You will go to them now and clean up as best you can. I will see you at dinner." He turned his back, dismissing them.

The two children left. Although they hadn't eaten for a day, neither was looking forward to dinner: George was still quite seasick, and Molly was not at all eager to face her father again. She'd been so sure that stowing away was a good idea—that her presence would, somehow, help Peter. Now it seemed that all she had done was muddle the rescue effort.

A *liability*, that's what her father had called her.

Neither Molly nor George spoke as a crewman led them to their cabins. When she reached hers, Molly closed the door and looked around the tiny space, which had barely enough room for a chest and a bunk bed.

Molly sat on the bed, put her face in her hands, and wept.

CHAPTER 17

THE ATTACK

FIGHTING PRAWN STOOD ALONE on the beach, watching the war canoes surging ever closer. Behind him, his Mollusk warriors lay in wait, hiding in the jungle.

He'd done all that he could: thanks to Peter's warning, he knew where the Scorpions would land; he'd set his defenses accordingly. His best archers were perched high in the palm trees lining the beach, ready to rain arrows down on any attackers. The trails leading inland from the beach were bristling with traps—concealed pits, trip vines, and other surprises. More Mollusk warriors, armed with bows, spears, and knives, waited to ambush. Well beyond them, the gates—both front and rear—to the Mollusk village were secured shut, and still more warriors had been posted as defense along the top of the compound's towering log wall. On the mountainside rising above the village, Fighting Prawn had prepared other unpleasant surprises for the attackers.

He was as ready as he could be. But . . .

It looked as if there were at least a hundred Scorpion canoes coming straight at him, possibly more. And with ten warriors in each canoe . . . it made a thousand warriors attacking Mollusk Island. Fighting Prawn had fewer than two hundred Mollusk men with whom to defend it. They were fearless fighters and skilled in the use of their weapons. They would do anything their chief asked of them, as would the women and children back in the village. They would fight to the death—all of them—if asked.

If *he* asked. The decision to fight, and how long to fight, weighed on his shoulders like a stone.

The Scorpions' lead canoes pulled close enough now that Fighting Prawn could see the men doing the paddling. Their faces and chests were covered with blood-red war paint. A Scorpion warrior stood in the lead canoe, his teeth showing bright white against his red-painted face. He raised a bow and fitted an arrow to the string. Fighting Prawn turned his back to the man and began to walk up the beach toward the jungle. His pace was unhurried. He would not let his men, or the Scorpions, see him run. As he reached the line of palms he heard one of his men shout, but he did not react. He kept walking calmly forward.

THUNK!

The arrow drilled deep into a tree trunk a foot to the right of Fighting Prawn's head. He did not flinch. He continued walking into the shade of the trees, where he grunted an order to a man holding a conch shell.

"Sound the battle call."

<hr />

Peter, awakened by the low moan of the battle conch, tried to sit up. He was lying on some palm fronds on the floor of the hut. Normally the boys slept in their underground hideout, but with the Scorpions approaching, Fighting Prawn had insisted that the boys move to their driftwood hut, which was closer to the protection of the Mollusk village.

As Peter struggled to raise his head, Tink flew in front of his face and emitted a deafening burst of chimes.

"All right! All right!" said Peter, weakly trying to brush Tink away.

"What did she say?" said James, who'd been sleeping next to Peter on the mat.

"She wants me to drink my medicine."

"What was that horn?" asked Tubby Ted. "Is it breakfast?"

"It's the battle," said James. "It's starting."

"I have to help them," Peter said, again struggling to rise.

Another furious flurry of chimes. Tinker Bell landed on Peter's nose, forcing him to look at her cross-eyed.

"I think she wants you to rest," said James.

I want him to grow a brain, said Tink.

"But I can help," said Peter. "I can fly out and . . ."

You can't even sit up, said Tink.

"You can barely sit up," said James.

That's what I said, said Tink.

"What'd she say?" asked James.

"She agrees with you."

No, he agreed with me.

"Tink," said Peter, "please get off my nose."

"She's right," said James. "You can't fly, and even if you could you'd get shot again. You need your medicine, and you need more rest."

"I need breakfast," said Tubby Ted.

James picked up a cup made from a hollow coconut. It contained a thick, greenish-brown liquid—made by the Mollusk medicine woman—that smelled like a combination of trail mud and rotting seaweed. Peter turned his head. Tink flew in front of his face.

Drink it, she chimed.

"It's foul," Peter complained.

Drink it, or I'll pour it in your ear.

"But it's disgusting!" said Peter, pushing the cup away.

Tink's chimes softened. *If you drink it, I'll fly out over the beach and tell you what's going on.*

Peter eyed the cup. "All right," he said. "But as soon as I feel a bit stronger, I'm going to fly out there myself."

He took the cup in one hand, held his nose with the

110

other, shut his eyes, and choked down the malodorous brew in two hasty gulps. He then rolled sideways on the mat, gagging.

"Are you all right?" said James.

"No, I'm *not* all right," said Peter. "I think this medicine is worse than the poison." He turned to Tink. "I held up my end of the bargain. Now go find out what's happening."

With a burst of bells that Peter would not have wanted to translate, Tink soared skyward in a brilliant blur and shot over the village wall. Peter resumed gagging.

"When's breakfast?" asked Tubby Ted.

———◆———

The Scorpion war canoes charged straight at the beach, the warriors paddling furiously to catch the breaking waves and surge high onto the sand. The Mollusk marksmen, following Fighting Prawn's orders, waited patiently until the canoes came to rest, then let loose a fearsome volley of well-aimed arrows from the treetops. The Scorpions, clearly expecting the arrows, quickly raised shields made from the shells of sea turtles. A few of the Mollusk arrows found their targets, but most clattered harmlessly off the shells and onto the sand.

As the Mollusks reloaded their bows, the Scorpions leapt from their canoes, pulled them high up onto the beach, and raced forward toward the trees, shrieking a high-pitched, hideous-sounding war cry. The Mollusks fired another

volley; again the raised shells blocked most of them. From behind the wall of shields, Scorpion marksmen returned fire, sending dozens of poison-tipped arrows hissing toward the tops of the palm trees. A scream, then another, then still more—and Mollusk warriors began to fall from their perches.

Fighting Prawn immediately ordered another volley of arrows, this time fired by his men on the ground. Then, as the attackers crouched defensively under their shells, he ordered his men out of the trees. As they slid swiftly down the palm trunks, Fighting Prawn turned to the man with the conch shell.

"Sound regroup!" he grunted.

The conch sounded; the Mollusk warriors moved back into the jungle, some carrying wounded comrades who moaned in agony from the sharp arrows and the poison.

Fighting Prawn, the last to leave, looked back to see the red-painted Scorpions moving steadily up the beach—*his beach*—shrieking in triumph. They had good reason to sound triumphant: they had easily routed the initial Mollusk defenders and were now established on the island in force. The Mollusks knew the island better, of course, and they had laid some clever traps that were yet to be revealed. But they faced far superior numbers.

Worry gnawed at Fighting Prawn as he trotted into the jungle, where his men were taking up defensive positions.

How long could they hold out?

"One man's misfortune is another man's opportunity," said Hook, peering through his spyglass with a smile that revealed two jagged rows of brown tooth stumps.

Hook and seven of his men had observed the battle from a hidden perch on the jungle-covered mountainside. They witnessed the landing of the huge flotilla of war canoes; they watched with a mixture of awe and fear as the howling horde of red-painted invaders easily routed the Mollusk beach defenders.

Now, as the attackers charged into the jungle below, the pirates looked nervously to Hook.

"What's the plan, Cap'n?" asked Smee.

With the sharpened point of the curved blade attached to his left arm, Hook scratched the thick black bristles of his foot-wide moustache. "The plan?" he said. "We steal one of them nice big savage canoes and we get ourselves off this blasted island. That's the plan."

One of the men frowned, then said, "But, Cap'n, what about the men back at the fort?"

With lightning speed, Hook shot out his left arm and placed the point of his razor-sharp hook into the man's right nostril.

"I don't recall asking for your opinion," he said. "Do *you* recall me asking for your opinion?"

With his crossed eyes on the hook, the pirate shook

his head, barely moving it so as to avoid cutting himself.

"Then let's leave the captaining to me, shall we?" said Hook, who was not certain that "captaining" was a word, but *was* certain that nobody would question him on this point.

"Now, listen, men," he said. "We ain't got time to go back to the fort. By the time we get all the way there and back, these attacking savages will control the whole island. We'd never make it to the canoes. We need to strike now, while the savages is busy killing each other. Savvy?"

Some of the men were frowning.

"So what we do," said Hook, addressing the frowners, "is we snatch ourselves a canoe and put to sea, then we go 'round the other side of the island and get the men at the fort, time permitting. How's that sound, men?"

The men nodded slowly, though they had their doubts about "time permitting" them to rescue the others.

"All right, then," said Hook. He pointed off to the right. "Looks like them red-painted savages is heading to the local savage village; so that's where the big battle will be. Massacre is more likely, but that's not our concern. While that's under way, we'll sneak down to the beach, careful as cats. We'll stay to the left there, away from the fuss. Are you with me, men?"

The men nodded again. Hook smiled, for two reasons: one was that he was, at last, about to get off this cursed island; the other was that the path to the beach went right past the hut where the cursed flying boy was sometimes found. Ordinarily, the pirates didn't cross to this side of the island, didn't go near that hut—not with the village so close. But now the savages were fighting for their lives, which meant that Hook might—just *might*—be able to manage one last encounter with the boy who'd cost him his treasure, his ship, and his hand.

If the boy was in that hut, he intended to take his revenge.

———◆———

The Scorpion warriors swarmed along the jungle paths like fire ants. Some succumbed to the traps set by the Mollusks—tumbling into hidden pits lined with sharp stakes, tripping on vines, becoming ensnared in falling nets. Some were felled by defenders waiting in ambush.

But not nearly enough of them. For every Scorpion who fell, ten red-painted attackers came shrieking right behind. Fighting Prawn, who could still move more swiftly through the thick jungle than anyone in his tribe, raced from place to place, constantly repositioning his warriors, placing them where they would be most effective.

His men fought with great courage, but the numbers were overwhelmingly against them. Relentlessly, brutally, the Scorpions pushed the Mollusks back through the jungle, closer and closer to the high-walled Mollusk compound.

Finally, Fighting Prawn had no choice but to order his men into position for a last-ditch defense of the village. His marksmen mounted towers around the log wall, aiming across the clearing into the jungle. As the Scorpions started across the clearing, the front line was felled instantly. The remaining warriors retreated quickly into the jungle, but Fighting Prawn knew they would regroup and return soon with their shields protecting them.

He had one last hope to save the village.

"Now," he grunted to the warrior with the conch shell.

Immediately, the conch sounded four short bursts. Fighting Prawn turned his gaze to the mountainside rising behind the village. He saw a group of his warriors using logs as levers to maneuver massive lava boulders into earthen chutes that he had ordered dug years ago, hoping that he would never have to use them. At the same time, men with burning torches raced across the clearing to a long, shallow ditch filled with dried grass and fish oil. Seconds later, a curtain of dark smoke rose.

Fighting Prawn squinted through the smoke and saw that the Scorpions were again coming out of the jungle, this time behind shields. He nodded to the conch man, who blew another four blasts. The men on the hillside yanked on their logs, and a dozen boulders came rumbling down the earthen chutes, which were angled so that the boulders shot across the field and over the shallow ditch, bursting through the smokescreen and into the oncoming mass of attackers. Perhaps twenty-five Scorpions went down, maybe a few more. But as a gust of wind cleared the smoke for a moment, Fighting Prawn saw it was not enough. Not nearly enough.

The Scorpions had only been slowed, not stopped. They continued forward relentlessly as Mollusk arrows glanced harmlessly off their upright shields. In a moment they would reach the compound wall. Their numbers were far too great. They would soon destroy the village, killing every man, woman, and child. They would exterminate the Mollusk tribe.

Unless . . .

Fighting Prawn's shoulders sagged. He turned to the conch signalman and gave an order that had never been given, in untold generations, by a Mollusk chief.

"Sound the surrender."

The signalman stared at Fighting Prawn, stunned.

"Sound it!"

The man blew seven long, slow, mournful blasts. The Mollusk archers stopped shooting. The Scorpions stopped advancing and peered warily out from behind their shields. The clearing fell eerily silent.

Fighting Prawn, carrying his spear, walked forward alone. He stepped through the smoke and stopped, facing the Scorpions. Slowly, he raised the spear over his head, then brought it down over his knee, breaking it into two pieces with a loud snap. He dropped the pieces onto the ground.

The Scorpions, with howls of glee, surged forward to claim their prize.

⸻

Peter lay on his mat, too weak to sit up, listening to the sound of shrieks and screams muffled by the jungle. A terrible battle was raging, that much was obvious; but who was winning? Tink, as promised, had gone to see, but she had yet to return with a report.

James, Prentiss, Thomas, and Tubby Ted huddled in the driftwood hut with Peter, listening to the horrible sounds.

"Peter," said Prentiss, "I'm scared."

"It'll be all right," whispered Peter.

"You don't know that," said Thomas.

"Be quiet," said James.

"Is there any more food?" said Tubby Ted.

"But he can't even fly," said Thomas. "How can he know it's all right?"

"Peter is our leader," said James firmly.

"I'm going to go look for coconuts," said Tubby Ted, opening the ship's hatch that served as the door of the hut.

"Ted," said Peter, "don't . . ."

But Ted was already pulling the door open.

And then he was screaming.

"Well, well," said Captain Hook, shoving Ted backward and stepping into the hut. "What have we here?"

Thomas made a move to dart around Hook, but stopped when he saw that the doorway was blocked by more pirates. The boys froze as Hook sauntered over and crouched next to Peter's pale form.

"Feeling poorly, Peter?" he said. "You seem hot to me." He touched his steel hook to Peter's forehead, then roared with laughter at his own joke.

Peter fought to keep from sounding as weak as he felt. "Let the others go," he said. "I'm the one you want. You don't need them."

"You are, indeed, the one I want," said Hook agreeably. "But I don't have time to deal with you properly right now, so I'm going to take you with me." He turned to his men. "Grab the flying boy. I want two men holding him. Grip him tight and slit his throat if he tries to fly." He looked around at the four other boys. "Take these, too," he said.

"But, Cap'n," said Smee. "Won't they . . ."

"Avast gibbering, ya gibbering idjit," barked Hook.

"Aye, Cap'n."

"We've a long way to travel in them canoes," said Hook. "We could use some extra paddlers, and these boys'll do nicely. If they get too tired, or this flying boy gives us trouble, why, we'll toss 'em to the sharks." Hook smiled as these words had their intended effect on the terrified boys. "Let's go then!" he said. "Sounds like the savages is finishing the fight, so we'd best grab a canoe while we can."

Two of the sailors grabbed Peter and hoisted him roughly onto their shoulders. The others herded James, Prentiss, Thomas, and Tubby Ted out the door. Carrying Peter and shoving the other boys along, the pirates, led by Hook, ran down the path to the beach, which was lined in both directions with war canoes pulled high up on the sand, out of the reach of the waves. Hook quickly selected one of the larger ones, noting with pleasure that it was well equipped for a long journey, with water gourds, fishing line, and even an auxiliary sail. He ordered the men to drag it down to the surf. He then directed the boys into the canoe; Peter was placed on the floor, near the bow. Hook then climbed in himself, taking a seat right next to Peter so he could make sure the boy made no attempt to flee. When Hook was comfortable, he shouted, "Shove off!"

The men pushed the canoe into the surf and clambered aboard; the last to make it was Smee, who avoided being left behind thanks to a desperate heave of his round body.

"Grab them paddles, men!" bellowed Hook, who did not grab one himself.

The pirates, happy to get away from the island, responded eagerly, and the canoe shot briskly through the waves. Within minutes, they were in the open sea, Mollusk Island growing smaller behind them.

Hook was nearly delirious with joy. His fondest hopes

had been realized: he had gotten off the cursed island *and* he had the cursed boy! What's more, the savages' canoe was superbly crafted—fast and stable. It would take Hook to civilization, he was sure of that. The boys would not make it—certainly the flying boy would not—and some of the men might have to be sacrificed as well. But he, Captain Hook, would make it. Of that he was certain.

Prentiss, Thomas, and Tubby Ted huddled glumly at the stern of the canoe. Peter lay on the floor near Hook's black boots. James sat next to Peter, looking worriedly at his friend, who lay with his eyes closed, his face pale as paper.

"Peter, are you all right?" James whispered.

"Yes," Peter mumbled, barely mustering the strength to speak. "I'm fine."

In fact, Peter was far from fine. His body still throbbed with pain from the Scorpion poison, and he was weak from hunger, having been able to swallow nothing other than the horrid Mollusk medicine. Almost worse than the physical pain was his feeling of helplessness. He, who had always looked after his mates, was now unable to lift a finger, let alone fly, as Hook carried them off to sea, to an unknown—and almost certainly unpleasant—fate. He had no idea where Tinker Bell was, and he knew that would worry her even more than it did him. And beneath all these woes and worries, Peter felt something else—a sense of dread, of something evil nearby, and getting nearer. . . .

"Cap'n!" shouted one of the men. "Something ahead!"

"What? Where?" said Hook, scanning the horizon.

"The water, Cap'n! Dead ahead!"

Hook looked down at the waves and saw it: a strange patch of sea, boiling and roiling, with huge bubbles breaking the surface.

"What is it, Cap'n?" said Smee, his voice trembling with a fear that all of the men felt.

"It ain't nothin' but a little sea gas," said Hook. "You idjits never heard of sea gas?" Hook himself had never heard of sea gas, but he didn't mention this. "Steer clear," he ordered the paddlers. "Leave it to starboard."

The men complied, turning the canoe to the left so the odd patch of sea would be off to the right side. But they turned too late. The patch moved toward them and grew in size, putting the canoe right in the middle of the turbulence, which was fast becoming more violent.

"What's happening?" screamed Prentiss. "Are we going to sink?"

"Shut your hatch, boy, or I throw you over now!" bellowed Hook. "We ain't sinking! This here is just a . . ."

Hook never finished the sentence, as the canoe suddenly rose straight up, and then, as if grasped by some force from below, tilted sideways, sending men and boys flying into the boiling, roiling sea. They struggled, gasping, to the surface, flailing their arms, looking for something to hold on to.

James, a decent swimmer, whipped his head desperately around, looking for the other boys, especially Peter, who was far too weak to swim. He saw Thomas, who began swimming toward James but then froze, his face twisted in terror.

"My leg!" he screamed. "My . . ."

Before he could say another word, he was gone, pulled straight down into the bubbling sea. James swam to the spot where Thomas had been and was about to dive when he felt something wrap around his right leg. He kicked at it with his left, but the grip tightened painfully. He reached down and felt something thick and slippery. . . .

And then he, too, was gone.

For another minute, the sea continued to bubble and boil, as one by one, other desperate swimmers were suddenly sucked below. Then, at once, the sea quieted, becoming as flat as a country pond. The Scorpion canoe floated peacefully upside down. One by one, the survivors swam to it and clung, panting, to its sleek hull. There were seven of them: Smee and the six other men who'd been with Hook. But Hook himself was gone.

And so were all of the boys.

ᴛINK'S ᴊEARCH

ᴛINKER BELL SHOT ACROSS the surface of the sea, a streak of golden light, flying faster than any bird ever had.

But not fast enough.

She had kept her promise to Peter: she had observed the brutal, one-sided battle; she had watched as the Mollusks were driven back to their village and forced to surrender. Then she had flown back to the boys' hut to discover—to her horror—that Peter and the other boys were gone.

She flew up high, frantically searching for them, but the jungle canopy blocked her view. She then flew lower and darted from tree to tree, asking the birds and monkeys where the boys had gone. The birds, as usual, were useless—*idiot birds!*—but the monkeys told her that the pirates had come and taken the boys in the direction of the beach.

Tink zoomed to the beach and saw a mark in the sand where one of the Scorpion war canoes had been dragged back into the water. Soaring high into the sky for a better view, she quickly spotted it: a dark shape on the blue water, already growing small in the distance. In an instant she was flying toward it, and in the next instant she saw that something was wrong. The canoe suddenly veered to the left, then rose straight into the air. Then, in a sickening moment, it turned sideways, spilling its occupants into the sea.

Tink was almost there now, swooping low, skimming the water. Her heart leapt when she saw figures flailing in the water—*Peter?*—but then ached when, zipping from head to head, she saw that they were all pirates.

Where was he?

Tink zigzagged frantically above the overturned canoe and the pirates, searching for the familiar head of tousled red hair. Back and forth she shot, again and again and again, until finally, with an anguished burst of bells, she accepted the horrible truth.

Peter was gone.

CHAPTER 19

*H*ELPLESS

*F*IGHTING PRAWN LAY FACE DOWN in the dirt, a Scorpion
warrior standing over him, spear point just touching his
back. Around him, the rest of the Mollusk warriors were
also lying on the ground, disarmed, powerless. They
could do nothing but watch with growing rage and
frustration as the Scorpions herded the tribe's terrified
women and children into the clearing in front of the compound.

The fright turned to horror when, one by one, the
Scorpions began separating the mothers from their children,
the mothers wailing as scowling, red-painted men yanked
their screaming children from their arms.

Fighting Prawn looked up in fury at the chief of the
Scorpions, who was standing a few feet away, supervising. He
was a man of about Fighting Prawn's age, with graying hair
and a necklace of shark's teeth.

"What kind of warriors are you who take *children?*" Fighting Prawn shouted.

The Scorpion chief did not understand the Mollusk language, but he understood Fighting Prawn's tone. He grunted and spat a gob of saliva that landed on Fighting Prawn's bare back. Fighting Prawn, enraged, started to rise, but stopped when he felt the spear tip cut into his flesh. He looked over his shoulder and saw that the warrior standing over him would be more than happy to impale him. In despair, he sank back to the dirt.

The Scorpions, having separated the children, were now tying them together at the waist by ropes made from vines, forming a long line. Fighting Prawn's heart sank as he spotted his own daughters in the line.

When the children were all tied, the Scorpions began shouting at them, in words they did not understand, to move. Some of the children tried to run to their mothers, only to be struck by the Scorpions and shoved roughly back into line. Prodded by their captors, the children began to move into the jungle.

Fighting Prawn heard a shout behind him and twisted around to look. One of his warriors, unable to bear the sight of his children being led away, was getting to his feet. Two Scorpion guards were moving toward him, spears drawn, clearly intending to kill him.

"Get down!" Fighting Prawn shouted at the warrior. "You

must stay alive to fight for your children when the time comes!"

Reluctantly, the warrior lay back down. But the look he gave Fighting Prawn made it clear that he doubted he would get a chance to fight.

Is he right? Fighting Prawn wondered. *Have I betrayed my people?* His mind raced, searching for a plan, something that would give him hope. But there were *so many* Scorpions, and they were such skilled fighters. . . .

His mind swirled with horrible thoughts as he watched the last of the children disappear into the jungle. Helpless, and very nearly hopeless, he pressed his face into the dirt so his people would not see his tears.

CHAPTER 20

$\mathcal{P}$ETER'S $\mathcal{P}$ROMISE

"$\mathcal{P}$ETER," SAID JAMES. "Wake up. Please, Peter. Please wake up."

Peter moaned. His eyelids fluttered, then opened. Above him hovered the anxious faces of James, Prentiss, Thomas, and Tubby Ted.

"He's alive!" said Prentiss.

Peter shivered. He was lying on something hard that felt like metal. He was cold and soaking wet. The air was dank, smelling of the sea and human sweat. He heard water rushing nearby. He tried to sit up, but he was too weak.

"Where are we?" he said.

"It's some kind of ship," said James.

Peter strained to lift his head. He was in a long, low-ceilinged room with curved walls; it was quite dim, illuminated by a lone lantern swaying in the distance. He saw a row of metal bars—he and his mates were in a cell at one end of the long room. Toward the center, beneath the lantern, he could make out the figures of men in red uniforms. He looked for portholes and saw none. He tapped the floor—it *was* metal. This was like no ship he'd ever been on.

"But how . . . how did we get here?" he said.

"There were these *things*," said Thomas.

"Like giant snakes," said Prentiss, shuddering. "With suckers!"

"When the boat went over, they grabbed us, pulled us down, and put us in here," said James.

"I thought I was going to drown," said Thomas. "I was underwater and getting sucked deeper and deeper. Nothing but water and more water . . ."

"Then a door shut," said James, "and the water went away somehow, and those men put us in here."

"What about the pirates?" said Peter.

"I don't know what happened to them," said James, "except for . . ." He nodded nervously to his right. Peter looked that way and saw that there was another cell next door. Sitting on the floor of that cell, glaring balefully back at him, not eight feet away, was Hook, although his name no longer fit him. Someone had taken the bent sword off his left arm, leaving an empty sleeve tied in a knot at the end.

The two locked eyes for a moment, then Peter turned back to James. Lowering his voice, he said, "Has he said anything?"

"No," whispered James, glancing at Hook. "He just sits there staring at you."

"And Tink?" said Peter, a trace of hope in his voice.

"Haven't seen her," said James. "Sorry."

"What about *them?*" Peter whispered, nodding toward the men in the distance.

"I tried to talk to them," said James, "but they don't answer."

"They've given us nothing to eat," said Ted.

"Help me up," said Peter, struggling to rise.

"Peter, no," said James. "You shouldn't . . ."

"Help me up."

"All right," said James, taking Peter's arm and helping his friend to his feet. Peter clung to the bars of the cell door, fighting off a wave of dizziness. Then he called out to the men sitting under the lantern.

"Hello!" he said. "Hello! May I speak with you, please?"

The men looked over. One of them, thin, with a full beard and dark, piercing eyes, stood and took a few steps toward the cell, squinting and frowning into the gloom. When he realized that it was Peter calling, his eyes widened and he shouted something in a strange language. One of the other men stood and walked to a metal door at the far end of the room. He rapped twice, then walked hastily back to the group under the lantern, clearly eager to get away from the door.

The door swung open. The men turned away and looked down. A dark shape oozed into the room.

Peter gasped. *Impossible!* He felt the other boys moving close to him.

"What's *that?*" whispered Prentiss.

Peter felt his skin crawl, understanding now what had caused the dread he'd experienced in the canoe.

"It's all right," he said quietly.

"But what *is* it?" said James.

Peter had no quick answer for that, so he remained silent, feeling his mates crowd even closer to him as Ombra glided toward the cell. The dark shape passed the uniformed men, paused, and with a voice that Peter had hoped he'd never hear again—a voice like a dying moan from a deep well—said something in a language Peter did not understand.

One of the men, shoved forward by the others, unhooked the lantern with a trembling hand and reluctantly followed the dark shape. Ombra stopped at the boys' cell, directly in front of Peter, who took an involuntary step back, the other boys crowding behind him. Ombra stood still, presumably looking at Peter, though there was no face visible in the capelike form, just the two dimly glowing red orbs. Then he spoke, in a hideous groan that made Peter flinch despite himself.

"You hoped you were rid of me."

Peter said nothing.

"You were never rid of me, Peter." Ombra turned to the man with the lantern. "Bring it closer," he ordered.

The man brought the lantern forward. Flickering yellow light spread through the cell. Ombra—half-turned away from the light—glided toward the cell's bars. Peter stepped back and opened his arms to push the boys away from Ombra.

"Don't let him touch your shadow!" he said.

Too late. Swiftly, like ink flowing, Ombra oozed through a gap in the bars and into the cell. Peter stumbled backward with Prentiss clinging to him; Thomas and Tubby Ted ran to the far corners of the cell, cowering, their backs to the bars.

James did not move. Peter looked down and saw that his friend's shadow was gone. He had been Ombra's prey.

James stood alongside the dark shape, his expression vacant. He turned to look at Peter with lifeless eyes. Then he spoke, not in his own voice, but in Ombra's wheezing groan.

"Your friend is very loyal to you," said Ombra/James.

"Let him go," said Peter. "He's done nothing to you."

"He has not," said Ombra/James. "But *you* have. So this is a warning to you, Peter. If you disobey me on this voyage, if you make trouble, if you seek to escape, your friends will suffer. You know I can make them suffer."

As he spoke, Ombra/James raised his right hand, dug his fingernails viciously into his own cheek, and raked his face. Parallel trails of blood began to ooze from the wounds.

"Stop!" shouted Peter, grabbing at James's arm. "Please, stop!"

Ombra/James put his bloody hand down and regarded Peter impassively.

"So there will be no trouble?" he groaned.

"No," said Peter.

There was a flicker of movement on the floor; Peter looked down and saw the dark shape of a shifting shadow slither the two feet from the base of Ombra's capelike form to James's feet. James groaned and collapsed to the floor, where he slapped his hand to his wounded cheek and cried out in pain. Ombra's voice groaned again, this time coming from the cape.

"We have an understanding," he said. He turned and seeped back through the bars. Peter approached James, but as he did, he felt an odd tugging sensation at his feet. He looked down to see his own shadow, which should have been slanting *away* from the light of the lantern, bending and curving, as if trying to reach *toward* it—or, Peter realized, toward Ombra. A moment later, the dark thing was gone, gliding back to the far end of the vessel. As the man with the lantern turned to follow him, Peter's shadow returned to normal.

Peter dropped to his knees next to James, who was covering his bleeding face with his hand. James looked at Peter, eyes wide with confusion and fear.

"What happened?" he said.

"It's all right," said Peter. "You're all right now." He glanced over his shoulder at Hook's cell. The pirate was standing against the far wall, his eyes following the dark form of Ombra as it disappeared into the distant gloom. Hook's eyes flickered to Peter, and in the instant before he looked away again, Peter saw that the once-fearsome pirate was quite terrified.

Kneeling over James, Peter struggled to sort out the troubling questions swarming through his mind. How could Ombra still exist when he had been shattered into a thousand pieces of shadow? Why had that not killed him? Where was Ombra taking him and his mates? What would happen to them? And—most puzzling of all—why had Ombra used James to threaten him? Why had he not simply taken *his* shadow, as he easily could have? Peter recalled his struggle with Ombra at Stonehenge and wondered—was it possible that Ombra was *afraid* of him? And what had caused the odd behavior of his own shadow?

As he comforted James, he heard Ombra's awful voice in his mind, over and over: *You were never rid of me, Peter.*

CHAPTER 21

No Time to Lose

MOLLY WAS AWAKENED by two taps on the door of her tiny cabin.

"Yes?" she said sleepily.

"We've sighted the island," said her father.

Instantly, Molly was wide awake, hunting for her shoes by the dim light filtering in through the lone porthole. "I'll be right there," she said.

"I'll be on deck," came the curt answer, followed by the sound of receding footsteps. Leonard had been civil but distant toward his daughter since she and George had been discovered as stowaways.

At least he woke me, thought Molly. She finished putting on her shoes and went to George's cabin, pounding on the door until a grumpy voice answered.

"What?"

"We've reached Peter's island," she said.

"How lovely for young Peter."

Molly smiled at George's annoyance. She would never admit it, but she quite enjoyed the fact that George was jealous of Peter.

"Fine, then, George Darling," she said. "If you're not interested, you can stay in your smelly little cabin. I'm going on deck."

"Hang on! I'm coming."

When Molly and George reached the deck, the rising tropical sun was a reddish-orange ball on the horizon. The sticky sea air was already warm; soon enough the day, despite the steady breeze, would be blazing hot. Molly and George found Leonard Aster on the quarterdeck with the captain of the *Michelle*, a stocky, solid man named Stavis. Dead ahead but still distant was Mollusk Island, its jungle-covered volcanic peak rising steeply from the sea.

Molly stared at the island, remembering the tumultuous time she and Peter had spent there after being shipwrecked in a storm and washed ashore, along with a trunk of starstuff. In their efforts to protect that priceless cargo, she and Peter had somehow managed to overcome greedy pirates, angry natives, and Slank, a brutal agent of the Others.

As Molly gazed at the island, her father studied her. He, too, was remembering her bravery. When he spoke to her, his voice carried a warmth that had been missing for days.

"It will be good to see Peter again," he said.

Molly smiled and nodded. "It will. Though he may not be happy to see us when he learns we've come to take him back to London."

Leonard's expression became serious. "I agree," he said. "And I'm counting on you to help me convince him that he's in grave danger and must come with us. *Will* you help me, Molly?"

"I thought I wasn't to be allowed on the island," said Molly.

"You won't be," her father said firmly. "But I'm sure Peter will want to see you. Which means he'll have to visit the ship."

"Father!" said Molly. "You'd use me as bait to trap him?"

"If I have to, yes," said Leonard. "For his sake and ours, we can't risk letting him stay here, where the Others could get him. You understand that, Molly?"

Molly nodded glumly. She hated the thought of deceiving Peter, but she knew her father was right.

"Who else lives there?" said George, looking at the island.

"There's a tribe of natives," said Molly. "The Mollusks."

"*Mollusks?*" said George.

"Yes, Mollusks," said Molly. "The chief is named Fighting Prawn."

"Fighting *Prawn*," snorted George. "You're joking."

"I wouldn't laugh if I were you," said Molly. "They're quite fierce."

George looked at Leonard Aster, who nodded and said, "Not to mention the fact that Fighting Prawn detests the English."

"Would they attack us?" said George, suddenly less amused.

Molly and her father exchanged a look.

"I think we'll be safe enough," said Leonard. "Fighting Prawn owes his life to Peter and knows we're Peter's friends."

"Unless, of course, we try to kidnap Peter," said Molly.

Leonard frowned. "Good point," he said. "Let's hope it doesn't come to that."

They fell silent, watching as Mollusk Island grew steadily larger off the bow. When it was about three miles away, Captain Stavis ordered the sails reduced and, with help from Leonard, guided the ship through a series of reefs into a bay fringed with a white-sand beach. They dropped anchor in twenty feet of water, about two hundred yards from shore. When the anchor was set, Stavis ordered the crew to lower a rowboat. Leonard climbed down a rope net to the boat. He was unarmed. As he prepared to push off from the *Michelle*, Stavis called down, "Are you certain you don't want some men to go ashore with you?"

"Yes," replied Aster. "The Mollusks know me. I want them to see there's no threat."

He pushed off from the *Michelle*. As he rowed, Leonard glanced frequently over his shoulder at the island. He saw no sign of life on the beach, human or otherwise. This troubled him. Surely the Mollusks had seen the ship approaching. They were very protective of their island; why hadn't they come to the beach to confront the visitors?

When he was halfway to shore, he heard a splash beside him. He turned and saw, poking out of the water, a sleek silver gray shape topped by intelligent eyes and a permanently smiling mouth.

"Ammm!" exclaimed Leonard, delighted to see the porpoise who had long served as a staunch ally of the Starcatchers. Switching to the porpoise's language, Leonard began making a series of clicks and whistles, speaking carefully, as he was a bit rusty. He had barely begun the traditional porpoise salutation—loosely translated to English, it means "It is pleasant to hear your noises again"—when Ammm interrupted him with a burst of chittering sounds so rapid that Leonard understood only one word: Go.

Go? Aster asked, in Porpoise.

Go now, the porpoise answered. Bad men. Go.

Leonard was about to speak again when he heard shouts from the ship. He looked up and saw Captain Stavis and his crew yelling and pointing frantically toward the island. He whipped his head around and gasped. The once-empty beach now swarmed with activity, as howling men, their faces and chests painted red—hundreds of them, it appeared—poured from the jungle, dragging long canoes.

142

Immediately, Leonard turned the rowboat around and began rowing hard back toward the *Michelle*. Aboard the ship, Stavis had his men taking in anchor line and raising sail, readying for a quick departure.

But would it be quick enough? Aster saw that the first canoe was already in the water, with men leaping in, grabbing paddles, and skillfully propelling the sleek craft through the surf with astonishing speed. Leonard feared that even with its head start, the rowboat would be overtaken by the canoe, which . . .

. . . *which was capsizing!* It happened so fast that Leonard's eyes could barely follow it, but as the canoe was spilling its occupants into the sea, he caught a glimpse of two powerful green tails and two heads of blond hair. He smiled grimly and said a silent thank-you to the Mollusk Island mermaids. A second canoe went over, and then a third. The mermaids had bought the little rowboat time to reach the ship.

As he approached the *Michelle*, Captain Stavis leaned over the rail and shouted "Leave the rowboat!" Leonard complied, jumping from the boat to the netting and clambering up the side of the *Michelle*. The ship was already moving, but agonizingly slowly. The canoes were coming fast, the paddlers howling.

"Mr. MacNelly, is the stern chaser ready?" Stavis yelled.

"Aye!" came a voice from below.

"I want grape," the captain hollered.

"Grape it is, Captain!" shouted the voice.

"Fire on my command," shouted Stavis, watching the canoes draw closer, closer . . .

"Ready," called Stavis. "Fire!"

BOOM. The stern-mounted cannon, packed with "grape"—small iron balls—sent a lethal hail flying across the water. The first three canoes stopped instantly as the paddlers fell backward, most of them wounded, some of them screaming. The other attackers immediately slowed their canoes, not eager to meet the same fate.

"Reload!" shouted Stavis. But there was no need to fire the cannon again; the *Michelle* was picking up speed, and the attackers had apparently lost their appetite for the chase. The ship would escape.

Leonard made his way to the quarterdeck, where he got a relieved hug from Molly, then turned to Stavis. "My compliments, Captain," he said. "That was a fine piece of seamanship. I apologize for the loss of the rowboat."

"Thank you, Lord Aster," said Stavis, "and never mind the boat. I'm glad that's all we lost. If not for that . . . was that a *dolphin?*"

"A porpoise, actually," said Leonard, winking at Molly.

"Ah," said Stavis. "Well, it's a good thing it came along. If you hadn't stopped to look at it, those savages would have had you. It's almost as if the porpoise was warning you!" The captain grinned at the absurdity of that.

"Yes," said Leonard, with another wink at Molly. "Almost."

"I thought you said the Mollusks wouldn't attack," said George.

"Those weren't Mollusks, were they, Father?" said Molly. "The red paint . . ."

"No," said Leonard, "they weren't."

"They're Scorpions, I believe," said Stavis, looking back toward the receding canoes. "You can tell by those scars on their shoulders. The red paint, too. A bad lot, the Scorpions. Very bad lot. We're lucky to be out of their hands. Very lucky."

"But what about Peter?" said Molly, looking back at the island. "We can't leave him back there."

"I hate to say this, miss," said Stavis, "but if your friend has been captured by the Scorpions . . ." He shook his head.

"Father," said Molly. "We *must* help Peter. We can't leave him on that island."

"And we won't, Molly," said Leonard, frowning. "But we can't go ashore until we have some information."

"But how will we . . ."

Molly stopped as her father gave her a significant look and a subtle nod toward the water.

"Oh," she said. "I see."

"See what?" said George.

Molly pulled George aside and whispered, "Father's going

to talk to Ammm and find out what's happened on the island."

"Who's Ammm?" said George.

"Perhaps," said Leonard, before Molly could answer, "we should continue this discussion below." He instructed Stavis to keep the ship within sight of the island, then went down to his cabin, followed by Molly and George.

"Who's Ammm?" repeated George when the door was closed.

"He's the porpoise Father was speaking to," answered Molly.

"Ah," said George, who knew from firsthand experience that Starcatchers sometimes spoke with animals. "What did he say?"

"Only that there were bad men, and I should go," said Leonard. "But I'm certain he has more to tell us. I'm also certain he's following the ship. He'll stay out of sight until nightfall, when we can speak without being seen by the crew."

"That's all we're going to do?" said Molly. "Sail back and forth for the rest of the day?"

"I'm afraid it's the best we can do," said Leonard.

They passed a long, uneventful, and thoroughly unsatisfying day staring at the island as the ship tacked back and forth, back and forth. When sunset finally came, Leonard had Stavis order the crew belowdecks, except for Stavis himself, who took the helm and stared straight ahead, studiously ignoring whatever went on behind him. Leonard, Molly, and George stood along the rail at the stern of the ship, staring at the frothing white moonlit trail of the ship's wake on the dark water, waiting.

And then Molly heard it. Not squeaks or whistles—bells.

"It's Tinker Bell!" she exclaimed.

She pointed off toward the left, where a streak of green-gold light, reflected as a zigzagging lightning bolt on the rippling sea, was shooting toward them from the direction of the island. In a few seconds, Tink reached the ship and landed on Leonard's shoulder, from which perch she delivered a burst of bells several minutes long directly into his ear. Leonard listened intently, his expression growing somber. He was among the very few people in the world—Peter was another—who could understand Tink.

Molly, to her great frustration, was not.

"What's she saying?" she demanded.

Tell her to shut up, said Tinker Bell.

"She asks that you let her finish," said Leonard.

Tink emitted another long burst of bells while Leonard listened intently and Molly tapped her foot impatiently. Finally Tink finished, and Leonard said, "How long ago?"

A short burst.

"Oh dear," said Leonard.

"*What?*" said Molly, unable to restrain herself.

"Well, to begin with," Leonard said, "Peter's not on the island."

"What?" said Molly. "But . . ."

Leonard raised his hand. Molly closed her mouth. Leonard continued: "There was an attack early yesterday. This Scorpion tribe overwhelmed the Mollusks. During the battle, that pirate, the one called Black Stache . . ."

Tink interrupted; Leonard listened, then nodded.

"Apparently, since his encounter with Peter, the pirate goes by the name Captain Hook. In any event, during the battle, this Captain Hook and some of his men managed to capture the boys. Tink didn't see it happen, but the monkeys told her that the pirates took the boys to the beach, stole one of the Scorpions' canoes, and set out to sea."

"Why didn't Peter fly away?" said George.

More bells from Tink.

"Peter is sick," said Leonard. "He was wounded by a poisoned arrow, and he's unable to fly."

"Oh my," said Molly. "This is *awful*."

"I'm afraid it gets worse," said Leonard. "The canoe was overturned, and Peter and the other boys were . . ." Leonard hesitated and looked at Tink, who chimed a few notes.

"Were *what?*" said Molly.

"We don't . . . that is, Tink doesn't know for certain. When she got to the overturned canoe, only pirates were left on the surface. The boys were gone."

"Oh *no*," said Molly, covering her mouth with her hand and looking down at the black water. "Then we're too late."

"Perhaps not," said Leonard.

Molly looked up with tear-flooded eyes. "What do you mean?"

"There was something underwater when this happened," said Leonard. "Something very large. Tink didn't see it, but there were dolphins nearby. They told Ammm there was . . . It's quite strange, actually. . . ."

"Was *what*, Father?"

"An iron whale," Leonard said.

"An iron *whale?*" said George.

"That's how they described it to Ammm: an iron whale. And it was being pulled by . . ." Leonard turned to Tink, who emitted some odd-sounding chimes. "I suppose the best translation is 'monsters,'" Leonard said.

"Monsters," said Molly.

"Sea serpents pulling an iron whale," said George. "I think the dolphins got into the grog."

"It must be some sort of underwater ship," said Leonard. "But the important thing is this: the dolphins say they could hear human voices inside the ship."

"So Peter could be in there," said Molly. "Alive."

"We must hope so," said Leonard.

"Where is this wh . . . this underwater ship now?" said Molly.

"It left here more than a day ago," said Leonard. "It's moving very swiftly—far faster than any ship can sail. Tink says Ammm has been tracking it using a sort of relay system—dolphins and porpoises and the occasional gull. Ammm also sent a message back to England to tell us what had happened; he and Tink had planned to wait for us here. It's very fortunate that we were already en route—though we've still lost valuable time. We'll begin our pursuit immediately. Ammm and his friends will guide us. Tink says they will . . . ah, here they are now."

Leonard nodded toward the water. Molly and George looked down and saw the sleek smiling face of Ammm poking up through the ship's wake, along with four other porpoises.

"Ammm!" cried Molly. She immediately shifted to porpoise language, chittering and squeaking a heartfelt greeting. Ammm responded with equal warmth, concluding with the question: *Are your teeth still green?* Molly, despite her worries, managed a laugh.

"Sir," George asked Leonard. "Have you any idea where the underwater ship is going?"

Leonard looked grave. "From what Tink tells me, the destination appears to be Rundoon."

"So the Others have Peter," Molly said softly. "And he's wounded."

"Yes," said Leonard. "And we have no time to lose."

KING ZARBOFF THE THIRD

PETER WAS FINDING it harder to breathe. The air inside the vessel, which had never been fresh, was now positively foul, stinking of the sweating bodies of men and boys confined for . . . *How long?* There was no way to tell, really. Peter had lost track of the hours as he'd drifted in and out of a restless sleep on the hard floor of his cell, surrounded by the sprawling forms of the other four boys. They had not been given anything to eat or drink. A few times they'd called out to the soldiers, asking for water, but their pleas had been ignored.

At least Ombra has left us alone, thought Peter.

With effort, he raised his head and looked through the bars into the next cell, where he saw Hook slumped against the far wall. The pirate's face was shrouded in shadow; Peter couldn't tell if Hook was asleep or staring back at him. Peter turned and looked toward the center of the room, where, beneath the swaying lamp—dimmer than it had been earlier—the soldiers reclined on benches and lay on the floor, apparently asleep.

Peter rested his head, staring up into the gloom, listened to the water rush past the hull of this strange ship. Once again he drifted off into a half-sleep . . .

Perhaps an hour later—perhaps six—Peter felt a nudge.

"Peter!" whispered James. "Wake up!"

"What?" said Peter.

"We've stopped," said James.

Peter listened: the sound of rushing water had been replaced by that of waves lapping against the hull. It was accompanied by a gentle rocking motion. He felt a heavy *thump* as the vessel settled against something—a wharf? This jostled the other boys awake. Hook was on his feet, as were the soldiers. Peter heard a dull tapping on the hull from the outside. A section of the ceiling slid open. Brilliant sunlight blazed into the vessel, forcing the occupants to shield their eyes.

That will keep Ombra in his room, thought Peter, remembering how much the shadow creature hated light.

The soldiers positioned a ladder against the opening, then came over, drew their curved swords, and unlocked the cells. They barked orders, which neither the boys nor Hook understood, but it was clear from their gestures that it was time to go. Peter, still quite weak, leaned on James as he shuffled out of the cell. One of the soldiers pushed James away and tied a rope around Peter's waist, tying the other end to his own waist.

"Looks like they don't want you flying off," said James.

Peter managed a wan smile. "Even if I wanted to," he said, "I don't think I could."

Prodded by the soldiers, the boys and Hook moved to the ladder and climbed out, blinking in the brilliant sunshine. They got their first look at the strange vessel they'd been traveling in. It rode low in the water next to the wharf. Hook, the veteran seaman, stared in puzzlement at its sleek metal form, devoid of masts or sails, unlike any ship he'd ever seen. Then, pushed forward by their guards, the prisoners walked down the gangway to the wharf, where they were met by more soldiers clad in red tunics.

Peter looked around, trying to get his bearings. They were in a harbor, with a few ships docked nearby—the air smelled impossibly good. Peter recognized one of the ships: *Le Fantome* had carried Ombra to London from Mollusk Island, with Peter and Tink as stowaways. Beyond the harbor was an arid, brown, rocky coast, dotted with the occasional palm; above that rose a city, a jumble of twisting streets and dusty sun-baked buildings.

The soldiers gathered curiously around the prisoners, particularly interested in Hook, with his tattered clothes and flamboyant moustache. An officer barked an order, and the prisoners were herded off the wharf and onto a large wagon hitched to a pair of white horses.

Surrounded by soldiers, the wagon rumbled off the wharf and up the road into the city. As it made its way along narrow dirt streets crowded on each side by tumbledown homes, people clad in light-colored robelike garments emerged to watch. A few children tried to run alongside the wagon but were driven off by shouts and vicious kicks from the wagon guards. The older citizens glared but kept their distance. It was clear that there was no love lost between the residents of the city and the soldiers.

The wagon pushed through a crowded market street where the excited babble of many voices engaged in heated bargaining was replaced by silence as the wagon rolled past, the target of a hundred stares. On either side, almost close enough for Peter to touch, were stalls from which merchants sold all manner of goods—rugs, lamps, robes, ropes, pottery, knives, jewelry, cheese, dates, flatbread, and many other foods that the boys did not recognize.

"I'm hungry," said Tubby Ted, mostly to himself.

The wagon turned a corner, emerging from the cramped and crooked dirt street onto a broad, straight, stone-paved avenue. It led to an impressive gated archway in a high stone wall, beyond which stood a gigantic building that dwarfed the puny hovels that made up the rest of the city. It was a hulking structure from which sprouted a forest of turrets and sharp-tipped spires that pierced the deep blue sky like daggers.

The wagon rumbled along the stones to the iron gate, which was guarded by more red-jacketed men armed with swords. The guards swung open the gate to let the wagon pass, then they heaved it closed. The prisoners were now in a large courtyard inside the castle wall. The wagon pulled up to a massive door flanked by still more soldiers. The door was opened; the guards prodded the boys and Hook to get off the wagon and enter.

They found themselves in a gigantic entry hall, likely the largest room any of them had ever stood in, with a vaulted ceiling higher than a ship's mast. Windows set high in the side walls sent shafts of sunlight slanting across the vast, empty space. The prisoners were led along the length of this hall to two large doors decorated with a gold Roman numeral III.

A huge man, clad in a black robe and carrying a sword in his sash, stood in front of the doors. As the prisoners and their guards approached, he raised his right hand, folding his thumb over his little finger, with the other three fingers sticking up. He bellowed a phrase that ended with something Peter thought he recognized, though he couldn't quite remember from where. The soldiers responded by raising three fingers and repeating the phrase. Then the huge man rapped thrice on the doors, which swung open as a pair. Peter felt the rope around his waist being untied; then, along with the other prisoners, he was shoved inside. The red-clad soldiers remained outside. The doors closed with an echoing bang.

The prisoners didn't move, for at first the room appeared pitch black. But as Peter's eyes adjusted, he saw the faint flicker of torches up ahead. The room felt quite large, though he could not make out walls or ceiling, only the torch-lit gloom giving way to blackness beyond. Imposing black-robed figures stood to either side. Peter's eye caught the gleam of torchlight reflecting from their swords. These men stepped closer and shoved the prisoners forward. Peter went first, followed by the other boys, and finally, Hook. Peter saw now that the torches occupied four corners of a raised rectangular platform, which was surrounded by a dozen or so shadowy figures, large and small. At the center of the platform was a large chair—a throne, judging by its grandeur. Next to the throne a dark, bulky, twisting shape was coiled like a pile of thick rope.

A man in a long white robe occupied the throne. He had a round face framed by a long, unkempt, black beard.

His deep-set eyes glittered in the torchlight as he examined the prisoners, his gaze lingering longest on Peter and Hook. Then he turned his head and addressed a figure standing in the shadows. "Tell them," he said, speaking English with an accent that Peter did not recognize.

"Yes, Your Highness King Zarboff the Third!" came the answer in a high-pitched voice. A boy stepped forward, his right arm raised in the three-finger salute. Peter gasped: *he knew this boy.* He'd been a schoolmate of Peter's at St. Norbert's.

James recognized him as well. "It's Slightly!" he said, using the boy's nickname from St. Norbert's. His real name was Edward Slight.

"Slightly, what are you—" Peter began, shutting his mouth when he saw the warning—and the fear—in Slightly's eyes.

"You are in the presence of His Highness King Zarboff the Third," said Slightly, again raising three fingers. "You will address him as Your Highness King Zarboff the Third, and whenever you say his name you will raise your right hand with three fingers up, like this."

"Tell them to do it," said the king.

"His Highness wants you to do it," said Slightly.

"Do what?" said James.

"Make the salute," said Slightly.

"Now?" said James.

"Yes," said Slightly, his tone urgent. *"Now."*

Slowly, the five boys raised their right hands and held up three fingers each. Hook, glaring at Zarboff, kept his arms at his side. Zarboff regarded the pirate for a moment, his face expressionless, then said something in a language Peter did not understand. Immediately two of the black-robed men grabbed Hook and forced him to his knees. A third man grabbed Hook's right arm and placed it on the throne platform, with the palm pressed down and the fingers spread. A fourth man stepped forward and drew his sword, holding its gleaming edge just above Hook's hand.

"Explain to him," said Zarboff.

"If you don't make the salute," said Slightly, "His Highness will take your thumb and little finger—then you will have no choice but to give the three finger salute."

Hook stared at the blade hovering over his hand. "All right," he said.

Zarboff nodded, and the soldiers released Hook, who stood and then slowly raised his hand in the three-finger salute.

"Good!" said Zarboff brightly, as though they were having tea. He pointed at Peter. "You are the one called Peter, yes?"

"Yes," said Peter.

"You can fly, yes?" said Zarboff.

"Yes."

"Show me," said Zarboff.

"I'm not sure that I can," said Peter. "I was injured by an . . ."

"SHOW ME!"

As Zarboff's command echoed through the room, black-robed men moved toward Peter.

"You'd better show him," said Slightly.

"All right," said Peter. He strained upward. Ordinarily, such an effort would have sent him shooting skyward. But in his weakened state it served only to make him feel a bit lighter. He strained again, feeling the blood pounding painfully in his forehead, but his feet did not leave the ground.

Zarboff said something in his own language. One of the black-robed men drew his sword.

"If you really can fly," said Slightly, his voice low but urgent, "you had better do it right now."

The swordsman stepped closer. Peter, eyes tight shut, took a deep breath and heaved upward with all his strength. Slowly, painfully, he began to rise—six inches, then a foot, then three feet, then six. He hovered there, his body clenched in pain, his face glistening with sweat, for fifteen seconds. Then he dropped to the floor, stumbling as he landed, so that James had to grab him.

Zarboff clapped his hands, delighted.

"You will teach me," he said.

Peter, trying to catch his breath, did not answer.

"I said, *You will teach me,*" said Zarboff.

"Tell him you will teach him," whispered Slightly.

"Yes, Your Majesty," gasped Peter. "I will try to teach you. But there's . . . I mean, to fly you must have . . ."

"Starstuff," said Zarboff.

Peter's head snapped up. Zarboff was grinning.

"I will have starstuff," he said. "All the starstuff I need. You will find it for me."

Peter frowned. *What was he talking about?*

"Yes, flying boy," said Zarboff, smiling at Peter's puzzlement. "You will help us. And to make sure you don't fly away, I will keep your friends here. They will be my servants. This is a great honor." He looked at Slightly. "It is a great honor, yes?"

"Yes, Your Highness King Zarboff the Third!" said Slightly, giving the salute.

"Bring the others forward," said Zarboff.

Slightly gestured, and five small figures stepped into the torchlight. They were boys, and Peter knew them all—three about his age, known at St. Norbert's as Curly, Tootles, and Nibs; and two younger ones known as the twins. Their faces reflected the same fear Peter saw in Slightly's eyes.

Zarboff, addressing Peter, said, "These servants will teach your friends what they must do. If they learn well, they will have the honor of serving me. If they do not, they will have the honor of feeding Kundalini."

At the sound of that name, the twins whimpered.

"Kundalini is not hungry now," said Zarboff. He reached down and touched the dark shape next to his throne. The shape moved, and slowly a triangular head rose, the torchlight reflecting from two yellow eyes. Peter had seen snakes

before; there were many on Mollusk Island. But he had never seen one half as massive as this.

"He ate a pig not too long ago," said Zarboff, his fingertips gently, lovingly stroking the snake's head. "He will not be hungry for a few days. If you and your friends behave, his next meal will be another pig. If not . . ."

Zarboff nodded toward Slightly and the other servant boys, all of whom were staring at the snake in terror. "They have seen what happens when a servant displeases me. It is not pleasant for the servant, although Kundalini likes it very much. He takes so long, it is as though he enjoys hearing the screams."

Zarboff, still stroking the huge snake, smiled at Peter, his teeth bright white in the torchlight. "So you and your friends will cooperate, yes?"

"Yes," said Peter hoarsely.

"Yes, *what?*" said Zarboff.

"Yes, Your Highness King Zarboff the Third." He lifted his hand weakly, holding up three trembling fingers.

CHAPTER 23

THE JACKAL COMMANDS

OMBRA GLIDED SILENTLY ACROSS THE SAND, beneath the night sky. Ahead of him there were sporadic movements and rustling sounds—the scuttling and slithering of spiders, snakes, and other night hunters fleeing the path of the swift-moving, cold, dark shape.

Ombra traveled alone. He had left the sea pod after dark and skirted Maknar, choosing to cross the open desert rather than take the road. Now the head of the Jackal lay before him, its huge stone form looming in the starlight. Ombra glided up the steps and into the dark hole beneath the giant teeth that framed the entrance.

He descended the narrow, deep stairwell, the air growing colder and more stale with each landing. He arrived finally at the underground chamber; it was, as always, pitch dark. Ombra swept to the center of the chamber and stopped, waiting as the beings in the blackness around him merged with him and he with them, so their thoughts could inter-mingle.

We have the Watcher boy, Ombra thought.

Where is he? thought the beings.

At the palace.

Why did you not bring him here?

He is injured. But he is gaining strength.

We will need the boy soon. He must be ready.

I will see that he is ready.

Will he cooperate?

We have his friends. The boy is loyal to them. He will do as we instruct him, to keep them alive. And we have another prisoner, a pirate. The boy fears him. He may also be useful. I am certain that the boy can be made to cooperate.

You must be certain. There is little time left, and the boy is essential. You failed once to control him and placed the plan in jeopardy. You must not fail this time.

I will not fail. I will control the boy.

Understand that you will not get a third opportunity. If you fail, you will be sent to the Brightness.

Ombra did not respond. There was no need: the other beings could feel his fear.

As soon as the Watcher boy is strong enough, you will bring him here.

I will bring the boy here.

That is all. Go.

Ombra separated himself from the beings, moving back up the stairway and out into the desert night. He began to glide toward the palace spires rising in the distance. Just ahead, a large spider emerged on thick hairy legs from a hole in the sand. It sensed Ombra's approach and tried to retreat into its hole. Too late; the dark shape was upon it, then past it, leaving behind a dead, cold carcass on the sand. Ombra took no notice. His thoughts were on the palace ahead and the boy who would determine his fate.

CHAPTER 24

THE MAN IN THE WHITE ROBE

MOLLY AWOKE TO FIND that the ship had docked. Through the porthole of her cabin, she saw that they were tied to a busy wharf, bustling with sun-browned men clad in loin-cloths and turbans. The men shouted in an unfamiliar tongue as they loaded and unloaded cargo ships with odd shapes and strangely rigged sails.

Molly squinted against the brilliant sun. She saw palm trees like those on Peter's island and a port city of baked-mud houses painted a blinding white. Donkeys laboring under towering burdens, sometimes larger than the poor animals themselves, trudged slowly up narrow streets, which they shared with ox-drawn carts and a jostling mass of human-ity—scores of barefoot, chattering children and sandal-clad men and women in flowing robes.

Many of the women, Molly noted with amazement, were carrying huge baskets balanced on their heads. But it was the sight of the majestic creatures next to the wharf that made her gasp with delight. She dressed quickly and ran to the big stern cabin, where she found her father busy disguising himself as a native. He had donned a long white robe and daubed his face with brown boot polish. He was now wrapping his hair in a turban.

"How do I look?" asked Leonard.

"Positively nomadic," answered Molly. "Are those *camels* out there?"

"Indeed they are," answered her father. "And I'm to ride one of them."

"Is this Rundoon?" said Molly.

"No, we wouldn't be safe there. This is Ashmar, just across the border to the west. The prince of Ashmar is an ally. I will pose as a carpet merchant and cross the border after sunset."

"To find Peter," said Molly, no longer smiling.

"Not quite yet. But soon, yes. Do you remember Bakari?"

Molly frowned for a moment. "The man from Egypt," she said.

"Yes," said Leonard. "That's the one." Bakari was a Starcatcher based in Egypt; he had warned the Starcatchers in England to "Beware the shadows"—the first they had heard about Ombra.

"I'm to meet him here," Leonard said. "Our friend Ammm arranged it. Bakari has contacts in Rundoon. He will help us to find Peter and perhaps also find out what the Others are up to." He finished wrapping the turban and turned to face Molly.

"Well?" he said.

"Splendid!" said Molly. "Even I wouldn't recognize you. May I go see your camel now?"

Leonard frowned. "I'm sorry, Molly, but I can't allow that. Agents of Rundoon are surely watching this port. You and George must remain belowdecks. You must not be seen."

"But, Father!" she protested.

"Absolutely not, Molly. If word got back to Rundoon that an Englishman and his daughter had arrived by ship . . . well, we would be in great danger."

"So we're prisoners, George and I?"

"May I remind you," said Leonard, with just a touch of anger in his voice, "that you and George should never have boarded this ship in the first place?"

Molly reddened and looked down. Leonard let his reprimand hang in the air for a moment, then put his hand on his daughter's shoulder. In a much softer voice, he said, "It's for your own good, Molly. This place is very unsafe. If anything happened to you, I could not forgive myself."

Molly looked up, her face somber. "But what about you, Father? Isn't it unsafe for you as well?"

"I'll be careful, I promise." Leonard's eyes twinkled. "Besides, I'll have help." He nodded toward a small, ornately carved wooden box on his writing stand.

Molly looked at the box, puzzled. "I don't understand," she said.

Leonard tapped lightly on the lid. "Is everything all right in there?" he asked.

The box emitted a muffled, discordant clattering of bells.

No, Tink was saying, *everything is not all right, because I am inside this stupid box.*

"Only a bit longer," said Leonard. "We don't want the crew seeing you, now, do we?"

"Tink is going with you?" said Molly, with just a hint of jealousy.

Of course I am, you silly goose.

"What did she say?" asked Molly.

"She says she's sorry you can't join us," said Leonard.

Hours later, as the late-afternoon sun beat down on the *Michelle*, Molly and George watched through a porthole as the tall, white-robed figure of Leonard Aster descended the gangway to the wharf, carrying the small wooden box containing Tink. Leonard was met there by a stocky man with a thick black beard—Bakari, Molly assumed. He, too, wore a white robe, but his was stained and worn, as though he had been traveling. He led Leonard to a pair of kneeling camels.

The two men mounted the animals, a process that brought a smile to Molly's face. Her father, an accomplished horseman, nearly slipped off the unfamiliar wooden saddle as the camel abruptly rose to its feet. But he managed to hang on, and in a few moments the two riders were moving.

Molly and George watched them start up the narrow street. Immediately, they were surrounded by barefoot children, holding their hands up toward the camel riders and beseeching them for coins, food, anything.

Then something else caught Molly's eye: two men emerged from behind a building on the wharf. They were not dockworkers, and their full attention seemed to be on the two camel riders. The men started up the dusty street at a near trot, much faster than anyone else moved in this heat.

"Do you see those two?" said George.

"I do," said Molly.

"I don't like the look of them."

"Nor do I. Father said there were agents about. That's why we're supposed to stay belowdecks, so they won't see us. And why Father is in disguise."

"By the look of things," said George, "his disguise isn't working."

Molly nodded in grim agreement. The two men were trotting close behind the camels now. It was obvious: they were following her father and Bakari.

"Do you think we should try to warn your father?" said George.

"He said under no circumstances were we to leave the ship," said Molly. "We're to wait here until he comes back."

"Yes, but that was when he thought he wouldn't be found out," said George. "If they know he's here, then—"

George didn't finish the thought, but he didn't need to; Molly had been thinking the same thing. *Maybe he won't come back.*

She looked at George, her expression telling him all he needed to know.

"So," he said, "I guess we'll be leaving the ship, after all."

CHAPTER 25

BAD THINGS

PETER PEERED OUT THROUGH THE CELL BARS, looking in both directions to make sure there were no guards nearby. Then he stepped back to the center of the cell, exhaled, and rose slowly off the floor. He made his body horizontal and floated up to the ceiling, then became vertical and drifted gently back to the floor. He allowed himself a small smile.

James smiled, too, although the effort made him wince because of the still-raw wounds Ombra had caused him to inflict on his own face.

"Feeling better?" said James.

"Yes," said Peter. "Much. Another day and I'll be as good as new."

"Fat lot of good that will do," said Tubby Ted, sprawled in the corner of the cell he had made his own. "Flying won't help if they never let us out of here."

"We'll see about that," said Peter. He tried to sound

confident, but Ted had a point: the boys were being held in a dungeon deep inside the palace. The iron cell bars that contained them looked out on a dim, torch-lit corridor with guards posted at either end. The only other opening in the cell was a small barred window at the top of the back wall. This window looked out on the palace courtyard, a vast space surrounded by a high stone wall with guard towers evenly spaced along the top. Inside the wall were two odd-looking, freestanding towers perhaps fifty feet high, tapering at the tops to sharp points. These were a dull reddish color, unlike any stone Peter had ever seen.

The boys had been given rough, itchy, camel-hair blankets to sleep on, and the two nights they'd been there had been far from restful. There were no beds, so they had to lie on the cold stone floor.

And then there were the monkeys—a half dozen of them housed in a nearby cell. The boys couldn't see them, but they could certainly smell and hear them. At odd times—sometimes in the middle of the night—they would erupt in a loud chorus of shrieks and gibbering that made sleep impossible. Peter wished he had Tink with him; she could talk to monkeys.

The boys had not yet left the cell. The door had been opened only twice, both times to allow a man—a doctor, apparently—to come in and examine Peter. The only other visitors were Slightly and Tootles, who brought food twice a day, passing pots through the cell bars. It was an unfamiliar cuisine—round, flat bread and strange-tasting pastes in small earthen pots. At first only Tubby Ted would eat anything other than the bread. But by the second day the boys' hunger got the better of them, and they wolfed it all down.

The food delivery was supervised by guards, but they did not speak English, so Peter used the opportunity to get information from Slightly, who had picked up some of the Rundoon language. Because of this, he was able to eavesdrop on King Zarboff's conversations. This morning he had brought disturbing news.

"A strange man came last night to see Zarboff about you," he said. "If it *was* a man. Very strange."

"What did he look like?"

"That's the thing: I never actually *saw* him. He was more like a cape with a black ghost inside. And the way he moved . . . it gave me the frights, I don't mind telling you. Even Zarboff seemed scared of him, and Zarboff ain't scared of nobody. I swear even the *snake* was afraid of him."

"He's called Ombra," said Peter in a whisper. "You'd best stay away from him."

"Believe me, I will. But it's you he's interested in. Heard him ask if you're healthy enough yet."

"Healthy enough for what?"

"He mentioned the Jackal," said Slightly, with a look that told Peter this was not a good thing.

"A jackal? That's some kind of animal, right?"

"Not this Jackal. It's said to be out in the desert somewhere, along with the other tombs and temples. I never went there, mind you, and never want to. People say bad things happen out there. Zarboff went once and came back with a look of death on his ugly face."

"Why am I supposed to go there?"

"Dunno."

Peter was silent for a moment. "What about my mates?" he said.

Slightly's eyes swept over James, Prentiss, Thomas, and Tubby Ted, all busily eating.

"I'm to train them," he said. "They're going to help me and the other boys work for Dr. Glotz."

"Who?"

"Dr. Glotz works for Zarboff. Calls himself a scientist. He uses us as workers because he don't speak Rundoon. Those are his monkeys making all that racket."

"What are the monkeys for?"

"For Glotz's experiments."

"What experiments?" said Peter.

But before Slightly could answer, the conversation was halted by a guard, who shouted something and clouted Slightly on the head. He said something in Rundoon that Peter didn't understand; but the message was obvious: *Shut up*. The boys finished eating in silence, then passed the empty pots back through the cell bars. Peter decided to risk asking Slightly one last question. He did so in a faint whisper.

"Did Zarboff say I was healthy enough to go to the . . . the tomb?" he asked.

Slightly nodded somberly. "Tonight," he said.

———◦•◦———

Five hours later, darkness had fallen and the boys were asleep—all except Peter, who sat against the cold stone wall, waiting and listening.

Footsteps approached. Two guards. They opened the cell door, and the boys stirred. The guard gestured to Peter, who rose and walked out. James looked up but didn't say anything. The guards closed the door and, one in front of Peter and one behind, marched him through a maze of dim corridors, then up a steep flight of steps to a heavy door. The lead guard opened the door and shoved Peter outside and into the waiting arms of four soldiers. Next to them was a horse-drawn cart with a robed man sitting in the driver's seat, his back to them.

Two of the soldiers held Peter, gripping him so tightly that his arms hurt. The other two put a heavy metal ring with a chain attached to it around his neck. It felt cold against his skin. A lock clicked shut. The soldiers lifted Peter into the cart and locked the other end of the chain to a metal ring bolted onto the cart. They checked to make sure the lock was properly closed and the chain secure. Then they stepped away from the cart. The robed man flicked the reins, and the cart rumbled into the darkness.

In a few minutes they had left the city and were moving across the starlit desert. The air was alive with sounds and smells that were strange to Peter. Finally, he saw something in the distance—pointed ears, then a giant head. It looked like an animal poised to strike as it rose out of the sands. The Jackal. Peter remembered Slightly's words: *People say bad things happen out there.*

They approached the mouth, its huge teeth framing the entrance. The cart stopped. The robed man did not turn around. They sat there, unmoving for a minute, two minutes, three. Peter could not take his eyes off the gaping mouth of the Jackal.

Suddenly the horse began to dance nervously sideways, whinnying. Peter felt the air go cold. He turned slowly, not wanting to face what he knew would be there.

"Step down," groaned Ombra.

Peter climbed out of the cart. Ombra flowed toward him. Peter stepped back; the chain attached to his neck went tight and stopped him. Ombra oozed past him to the cart, and Peter heard a metallic sound. The other end of the chain was no longer attached to the cart, but instead was somehow connected to Ombra himself, disappearing into his black form.

"You will follow," groaned Ombra, and he began gliding toward the Jackal, pulling the chain. Peter resisted for an instant but immediately stumbled forward as he was yanked by what felt like immense strength. He was forced to half trot to keep up as Ombra moved silently across the sand toward the Jackal.

They entered the open mouth, walking down a giant stone tongue. The dim starlight gave way to darkness, then utter blackness. Peter fought to control the fear rising in him as Ombra dragged him relentlessly forward.

Ombra stopped. Peter jerked awkwardly backward to avoid bumping into the hideous *thing* leading him.

"We will descend steps," said the groaning voice, much too close.

Peter felt the tug of the chain again. He shuffled forward, putting his hands out. He touched a cold stone wall. He slid his toes forward until he felt a step, then started down. He had never experienced such utter, disorienting blackness. He counted twenty-seven steps before they arrived at a landing. The chain tightened, and he was pulled down another flight of steps. He could sense Ombra just in front of him, the only sound the clinking of the chain.

Down they went, down and down—seventeen more steps—Peter utterly blind and increasingly unable to control his mounting dread. Down and down and . . .

"Stop," said Ombra, sounding farther ahead all of a

sudden. His groaning voice echoed, suggesting a larger space. Peter waited in the blackness, barely breathing. He heard a new sound, like whispering—many low voices whispering. And then . . .

Peter.

Peter jumped at the sound of the voice. It was like Ombra's cold moan, but it was stronger, and it seemed to come from everywhere at once—ahead of him, behind, above—as if from the darkness itself.

Peter, the voice said again.

"Yes?"

Do you know why you are here?

"No." It wasn't exactly a voice, he realized. It was more like he was thinking what was being said to him.

You are here because you are a Watcher.

"I don't know what that means."

You have powers, and you will use them to show us where the starstuff falls.

"But I don't know where any . . ."

You will show us. You are a Watcher, as your father was.

Peter took a staggering step backward, as if he had been struck. The chain clattered. *"My father? You know my father?"*

Your father helped us. He did so to keep you alive. You will help us now, to keep your friends alive.

"But I don't know what you're talking about! How can I help you if I don't . . ."

When the time comes, you will know. You will feel the Fall and you will take us there. If you fail to help us, your friends will die. Do you understand?

"Where's my father now? Can I—"

Do you understand? The voice inside him was so loud that Peter clutched his head in pain.

"Y . . . yes," Peter said. But he didn't understand anything.

If you fail, repeated the voice, *your friends will die.*

CHAPTER 26

CAP'N SMEE

THE LINE OF MOLLUSK CHILDREN, bound together by rope tied to their waists, trudged along the jungle path. They were herded by scowling Scorpion warriors, who shouted at the children in a tongue they did not understand, shoving them, jerking them brutally to their feet if they fell. Some of the children were crying; some were too shocked to cry, and moved numbly forward with vacant faces.

Shining Pearl, daughter of Fighting Prawn, was neither crying nor numb. She was watching the Scorpion warriors and studying the rope that bound her to the boy in front of her and the boy behind. The rope formed simple slipknots around their waists. The knots were drawn tightly now, but Shining Pearl thought she could free herself. *If the rope goes slack, even for a few seconds. . . .*

She knew this path well, far better than her captors did; she had learned its twists and turns during endless

games of chase. Just ahead, it took a long bend to the left.

The closest Scorpion warrior was about fifteen yards ahead of her. Shining Pearl kept an eye on him. In a moment, because of the bend in the path, he wouldn't be able to see her.

"Ssss!" she hissed softly, calling to the boy in front of her, whose name was Green Stone. He glanced back, stumbling as he was dragged forward by the rope connecting him to the girl just ahead.

Shining Pearl held her finger to her lips, then beckoned for Green Stone to edge back toward her. He pointed to the taut rope pulling him forward. Shining Pearl leaned back for an instant, tugging him, and he nodded to show he understood. She held up her hand to make sure he waited for a moment. Again, he nodded.

Finally the path began its slow curve. The warrior disappeared around the bend.

"Now!" she hissed.

Green Stone dug in his heels, nearly pulling the girl ahead of him off her feet. The rope behind him slackened for just an instant, and in that instant, Shining Pearl pulled the slipknot open, sucked in her stomach, and lifted the loop over her head. She dropped to the path, rolled under a giant leaf, and watched as the rope pulled taut again, leaving a gap where she had been.

Praying that the Scorpions wouldn't notice that gap,

Shining Pearl lay perfectly still until the line had passed and the callused feet of the last Scorpion warrior had disappeared around the bend. She lay still a few minutes more to be sure, listening as the cawing and jeering of the jungle birds finally returned. On hands and knees, she crept deeper into the jungle, staying away from the paths.

For the moment, she was safe. But where should she go? The Scorpions were swarming around the village; if she stayed on this side of the island, she would surely be caught. That left the other side of the island.

The pirate side.

What about the pirates? she wondered. *Had the Scorpions attacked them, too?* The more she thought about it, the more unlikely it seemed. The Scorpions would have used all their force to defeat the Mollusks. They might not even know that the pirate camp existed.

Would it be safer on that side of the island? It was a very dangerous place: the pirates were cutthroats, and as if *they* weren't bad enough, Mister Grin, the giant crocodile, was usually lurking near their camp, hoping to make a meal of Captain Hook. Fighting Prawn had told Shining Pearl many times that she must never cross the mountain to the pirate side.

But her father was helpless now—the entire tribe was, except for Shining Pearl. Of all the Mollusks, she alone could act. And the more she thought about the situation, the clearer it became: if she had any hope of fighting back against the Scorpions, she would need the help of the ruth-less men on the other side of the mountain.

Shining Pearl took a deep breath. Then she began to climb.

Smee stood on the beach, gasping and dripping seawater. The other six pirates stood five yards away, also dripping, staring at Smee, waiting.

They were lucky to be alive. After watching Hook and the boys disappear into the churning, bubbling water, Smee and the others had clung to the overturned canoe, lifting their legs as high as they could, terrified that at any moment they, too, would be sucked below.

Instead, the sea had quieted, and the canoe had drifted from the spot. The pirates had talked about swimming back to the beach where they had stolen the canoe, but they were not good swimmers, and this side of the island was crawling with red-painted, spear-carrying warriors. So they had clung to the canoe, hoping for the best. Their hopes were rewarded as the current carried them, slowly, around the north side of the island, bringing them close enough to a point where, with much flailing and sputtering, they were able to swim to shore.

Now, on the beach, the other pirates were all looking at Smee. It bothered him, facing five and a half pairs of eyes (one of the men wore an eye patch).

"What are you looking at?" Smee said.

"We're looking at you," said one of the men, whose name was Hurky.

"I can see you're looking at me," said Smee. "But *why* are you looking at me?"

"We're waitin' for orders," said Hurky.

"Ah," said Smee. He resumed gasping. Then he frowned. "Wait a minute," he said. "Orders from who?"

"From you," said Hurky.

Smee was so taken aback by this that he literally took a step back. "From *me?*" he sputtered. "I don't give orders. *Cap'n* gives orders."

"Smee," said Hurky. "If the cap'n is givin' any orders right now, it's to a fish. He's gone, Smee. You was first mate. You're next in line. You're the actin' cap'n now. So we're waitin' on your orders."

The other five men nodded in agreement and continued to stare expectantly at Smee. He could feel the weight of all eleven eyes. He rubbed his bare forehead with both hands. He was trying to think, but thinking was the one thing Smee had always found hardest to do. He had spent most of his life doing it as little as possible.

"Cap'n Smee," said a voice. *Cap'n Smee.* It sounded bizarre to Smee. He peeked out between his hands; he saw the voice had come from a man named Boggs.

"What is it?" he said reluctantly.

"I was thinking," said Boggs, "that it might be a good idea to go to the fort."

"The fort?" said Smee.

"Aye, Cap'n. The fort."

Smee frowned, thinking about it. "The fort," he said.

"Aye, Cap'n."

"We should go to the fort," said Smee.

"So that's your order then, Cap'n?" said Hurky.

"What is?" said Smee.

"That we should go the fort," said Hurky.

"Yes," said Smee. "I believe it is. Follow me, men."

He began walking. The men hesitated.

"Cap'n Smee," called Hurky.

"What?" said Smee, stopping.

"The fort is the other way."

"Ah," said Smee. He turned around and started walking in the opposite direction.

"Follow me, men," he said again.

And one by one, the men fell in behind, following Acting Captain Smee.

CHAPTER 27

A Desert Conversation

Leonard Aster was getting used to the camel. Unlike a horse, it had a swaying, side-to-side gait that was surprisingly comfortable. And he was learning to control it, thanks to Tink, who could speak a little Camel.

He says you're pulling too hard on his nose, she told Leonard.

"Please tell him I'm sorry," said Leonard, easing up on the reins, which were attached to a wooden peg inserted into the camel's nostrils. The camel emitted a snorting sound.

He says thank you, said Tink. *His name is Azerraf.*

"Please tell Azerraf he is welcome," said Leonard.

Bakari looked on in amusement.

"I've never heard anyone speak so politely to a camel," he said.

"Well I certainly don't want to irritate him," said Leonard, smiling. "It's a long way to the ground."

The two riders had said nothing of importance as they made their way out of the streets of Ashmar. Now they were east of the city on the desert road to the Rundoon border; Tink had been released from the confinement of the box, and the men felt it was safe to talk. Just in case, Bakari twisted in his saddle and looked back: in the distance, perhaps a mile behind, he saw two men, also on camels. Other than that, they were alone. Still, Bakari lowered his voice.

"We have an informant in Zarboff's palace," he said. "A guard who detests Zarboff and will tell us what he sees in exchange for gold. He says the boy and his friends are being held in the palace dungeon."

"Is Peter all right?" said Leonard.

"He was quite sick when he arrived, but he's doing better. The palace doctor has been attending to him."

"Does our informant know why they want Peter?"

"No. Only that they want to get him healthy soon. And that last night he was taken to visit a place in the desert near Maknar, a tomb called the Jackal."

"A tomb?"

"Our man says it's an evil place inhabited by living shadows."

Leonard was staring at Bakari. "Living shadows," he said.

"Yes," said Bakari. "Like the one that attacked my group in Egypt, and you in England. Our man said one of these shadow creatures came to the palace to speak with Zarboff."

"What did they talk about?"

"Our man couldn't hear their conversation. But he did hear Zarboff address the shadow creature as Lord Ombra."

Leonard looked stunned. "He's the one who followed us to England," he said. "I thought he'd been destroyed at Stonehenge."

"Evidently not," said Bakari. "According to our informant, it was this Ombra who brought the boy and the others from the island, on—this sounds odd, but our man insists it's true—some kind of underwater ship."

Leonard nodded. "I'm aware of that ship," he said. "We reached the island not long after it left."

"Do you have any idea why the Others and these shadow creatures have gone to so much trouble to get the boy?" said Bakari.

"I'm afraid I do," said Leonard. "I think they're going to use him to locate the next starstuff Fall."

It was Bakari's turn to look stunned. "How would he do that?"

"I believe Peter has an unusual ability," said Leonard. "I don't know how it works, and I suspect he doesn't know, either. But I believe it's the same ability that his parents, or at least his father, had." He told Bakari what Molly and George had learned in Oxford about the mysterious Mr. Pan, who had used newspaper notices to alert the Starcatchers about falling starstuff, until he and his wife had disappeared, leaving a son named Peter.

"What do you think happened to them?" said Bakari.

"I believe the Others got them and brought them here to Rundoon," Leonard said. "I believe the Others used them to locate starstuff Falls. That's why we stopped getting the warnings. That's how the Others got to the Scotland Fall ahead of us."

"But you got that starstuff back," said Bakari.

"Precisely," said Leonard. "It was a huge amount, and the Others wanted it very badly. Now, I believe, they intend to use Peter to get more."

"Why can't they use his parents again?"

"Something must have happened to them. In fact, it probably happened not long after the Scotland Fall, because the Others arranged to have Peter put on the boat that was supposed to bring that batch of starstuff to Rundoon. But that boat never got here—thanks to Peter and Molly. And now the Others are after more starstuff. They have something in mind, something big, something to do with these shadow creatures. Whatever it is, it's why they brought Peter here, I'm sure of it. And it's why we must get him out of there before the next starstuff Fall."

"It won't be easy," said Bakari. "The dungeon is deep inside the palace complex and heavily guarded."

"What about your inside man?"

"He can get us through the main palace gate," said Bakari. "But beyond that we're on our own. It won't be easy—Zarboff has guards everywhere."

I can get past the guards.

"What did she say?" said Bakari.

"Tink says she can get past the guards. I have no doubt she can. The trick will be for *us* to get past them and somehow get Peter out. We must find a way to do that. We can't let him stay in there."

The two men rode on in silence, their thoughts on the difficult task facing them and their eyes on the desert road ahead.

Neither of them noticed that what had been two camel riders behind them was now only one. And that the one was drawing steadily closer.

CHAPTER 28

JAMES'S PROMISE

THE CLINK OF THE LOCK and the creak of the iron cell door woke James. He watched with half-open eyes as two guards shoved Peter into the dark cell. Peter slumped to the floor, his back against the wall. The other boys remained asleep.

"Are you all right?" whispered James.

"Yes," whispered Peter. "I'm fine."

He didn't sound fine to James. "Where did they take you?"

"To that tomb thing Slightly talked about," whispered Peter. "The Jackal."

"Why?"

Peter started to answer, then stopped himself. He had more questions in his mind than answers. The one thing he did know was that if he didn't help the Others find the starstuff, they said they would kill his friends. But he didn't want to tell James that.

"I don't really know," he said finally.

"But what did . . ."

"James," said Peter, cutting his friend off, "I'm too tired to talk right now."

"All right," said James, although it clearly wasn't all right. "Good night, then." He rolled sideways away from Peter, wrapping himself in his blanket.

Peter lay down and pulled his own rough blanket around him. The two boys were just a few feet apart in the darkness. Minutes passed.

"James," whispered Peter.

"What?"

"I won't let anything happen to you and the boys."

"I know you won't, Peter. But can't I help? Can't I do something?"

"Yes," said Peter. "You can help by comforting the others if . . ."

"If what? Peter, what's going to happen?"

"I don't know. But promise me you'll be the leader, if you have to. You'll watch after the others."

"I . . . promise," whispered James.

"Good. Now, it's very late, and we need to sleep."

"All right," said James.

The cell fell silent. But neither James nor Peter slept.

CHAPTER 29

Urgent News

*I*N A HUGE, DOMED CHAMBER decorated with golden drapes, King Zarboff was soaking in a gleaming copper bathtub big enough to hold a horse. Zarboff, a substantial man who filled most of the tub, sloshed the foaming water over the edge when he moved. Four servant boys, including Slightly, stood by with jugs of hot water to keep the temperature exactly to the king's liking. From time to time the boys glanced nervously toward a large straw basket at the foot of the tub; inside it was Kundalini, the king's pet snake. The boys were all thinking of the time when one of the servants had poured a bit too much hot water into the king's bath. . . .

The bath-chamber door opened. A guard entered.

"Your Highness King Zarboff the Third!" he said, giving the three-finger salute.

"How dare you disturb my bath?" Zarboff snapped.

"There's a visitor to see you," said the guard, his voice

quavering, eyes darting to Kundalini's wicker basket. "He claims to carry urgent news from the port of Ashmar."

"It had better be urgent," growled Zarboff. "Send him in." He waved his hand at the young servants, dismissing them.

The boys followed the guard out. Slightly was last in line—but he didn't leave the chamber. At the door, he glanced around quickly to make sure the king wasn't looking, then ducked behind one of the enormous golden drapes.

A few moments later the guard returned, followed by a man who showed signs of having ridden hard across the desert—his clothes full of sand and dust, his turban discolored by sweat and dirt.

"Your Highness King Zarboff the Third!" he said, saluting. "My name is Jibran. I am the son of . . ."

"I don't care who you are," said Zarboff, lathering his left foot. "What is your urgent news?"

"A ship," said Jibran. "It arrived in Ashmar this day."

"Many ships arrive in Ashmar."

"This ship carried Englishmen."

Zarboff paused while washing his toes and looked at Jibran. "How do you know this?"

"I saw the ship, Your Excellency. I was there, in Ashmar. I have ridden here to bring you this news."

"What else?"

"An Englishman disguised himself and left the ship,

where he joined another—a man I recognized. His name is Bakari."

Zarboff's foot splashed back into the tub. "Bakari? You are certain?

"Yes, Your Highness."

"And where are they now, these men?"

Jibran shifted nervously, swallowed, then said, "Your Highness, it is my understanding that this information is quite valuable. And as I am a poor man and have risked much to bring this news to Your Highness, I was wondering if there might be, that is, if Your Highness could possibly . . ."

"You seek a reward," interrupted Zarboff, his voice unusually soft.

Emboldened by that softness, Jibran said, "It seems only right, Your Highness."

Zarboff stared at Jibran for several seconds. Then he smiled. This was also unusual.

"All right, then," he said. "You shall have your reward." He gripped the sides of the tub and began to lift himself, shouting, "Towels!"

Instantly, the servant boys, who had been waiting out-side, scurried in carrying huge swatches of gold-dyed cotton. As they passed, Slightly ducked out from behind the drapes and joined them. They wrapped Zarboff in the towels and helped him fit his large, hairy feet into gold-embroidered slippers.

"Guard!" bellowed Zarboff.

"Yes, Your Highness!"

"Fetch Lord Ombra," said Zarboff.

The guard went pale. "Yes, Your Highness," he said. He turned and trotted from the chamber.

Zarboff turned back to Jibran. "When Lord Ombra arrives, you will tell us all you know."

"Yes, Your Highness," said Jibran. "And . . . the reward?"

"Oh yes," said Zarboff, smiling again. "You will get exactly what you deserve."

CHAPTER 30

*F*RANKLIN

*A*S THEY NEARED THE HEART OF MAKNAR, Leonard and Bakari dismounted from their camels and led them by the reins through the crowded streets. Activity swirled around them: men and women shouting and bantering, bargaining for all manner of goods. The sweet smell of incense and the musky odor of burning rope filled the air. Rug merchants sat cross-legged next to their colorful wares, sucking on tubes that ran to bubbling hookahs from which tobacco smoke rose like gray rope. Barefoot children ran past in packs, laughing and chasing one another in a game as timeless as humanity itself.

From just ahead came a mournful, haunting melody. A crowd was gathered around a snake charmer, who was playing a flutelike instrument, drawing a cobra from a wicker basket. The cobra swayed back and forth, apparently moving in time to the tune. Then it became motionless as the snake charmer leaned forward and, to gasps from the onlookers, kissed the top of the cobra's head. The crowd applauded, some people tossing coins.

The afternoon was turning into evening, although to Leonard, unused to the desert, the heat still felt brutal. Finally the sun winked good-bye on the horizon. As darkness fell, the streets began to empty. Leonard and Bakari found a deserted square, and Leonard, apparently speaking to the air, said, "All right, Tink."

It's about time, said Tink, poking her head out of a fold in Leonard's turban.

Bakari pointed to a group of spires looming in the distance, turned reddish gold by the last rays of the sinking sun.

"Zarboff's palace," he said.

"How do we go in?" said Leonard.

"Our man guards a door on the east wall," said Bakari. "It's near the palace kitchen. We'll enter that way."

"All right, Tink," said Leonard. "We'll be near the kitchen. You need to find Peter, then come find us and lead us to him. Can you do that?"

Of course I can, said Tink, and then she was flying, a streak of light in the night sky.

"She thinks she can do anything," said Leonard, watching the streak disappear over a building.

"I hope she's right," said Bakari, as the two men began trudging toward the palace.

Tink had seen only one city other than Maknar—London. The two places could not have been more different. London was clouds and rain and cold. Here, even in the dusk, she could feel the waves of heat wafting upward from the parched streets and sun-baked buildings.

She sensed something hurtling toward her and veered sharply left. It was a swarm of huge dragonflies, nearly the size of Tink herself.

Watch where you're going! she chimed. They ignored her. This did not surprise Tink: most insects, in her experience, were very stupid.

She resumed flying toward the palace now looming ahead, its towering walls elaborately decorated with mosaic depictions of epic battles. She swooped high over the near wall, unobserved by a guard in the watchtower directly below. The instant she was inside she felt it—an unmistakable flutter in her tiny heart . . . *Peter.*

He was here. But where, exactly? The palace complex was enormous—dozens of buildings, hundreds of windows, and many, many rooms. Tink flew across a huge courtyard with two odd-looking, sharp-pointed towers. Ahead, she saw a line of gray doves standing on the peak of a steep-angled tile roof. *Birds, at last.*

Tink settled next to the doves, who regarded her curiously.

Hello, she said.

Hello, said the nearest dove, in a thick accent that Tink barely understood.

I'm looking for a boy, said Tink, speaking slowly. *Boy.*

The dove studied Tink for a moment, then said, *Girl.*

I know I'M a girl, said Tink, trying to remain patient. *I am looking for a boy. Do you understand? Boy.*

The dove turned and consulted the other doves, speaking quickly in sounds Tink could not follow. Then it turned back to Tink.

Girl, it said.

Idiots! said Tink, losing her temper.

Girl, replied the dove.

With a *hmph!* of contempt, Tink launched herself from the roof and began a circuit of the courtyard, hovering in front of each window so she could look inside. It was slow going, and after only a few dozen windows—all looking into empty rooms—her patience had worn thin. At this rate it would take her all night to . . .

What was that?

It echoed across the courtyard, coming from well below where she was flying, a screeching sound Tink knew well from the thick, teeming jungles of Mollusk Island.

Monkeys.

Finally, an intelligent creature! Tink tucked her arms in and threw herself into a steep dive—down, down, down into the shadowy courtyard. Just before the ground she leveled off, swooping along a line of barred windows, listening. She thought she felt Peter's presence closer now, but could not tell precisely where . . .

There it was again, the screech. She shot to the window from which it had come. Cautiously, she poked her head through the bars, wrinkling her nose at the pungent monkey smell.

Hello, she said in monkey. *I'm looking for a boy.*

I'm a boy, said a monkey voice. *And I'm looking for a banana.*

I haven't got any bananas, said Tink.

Neither have I, said the monkey. *That's why I'm looking for one.*

The monkey approached the window; Tink saw that he was quite young. Behind him she saw a dozen or so other monkeys of various ages sprawled around the cell, most of them asleep. The young monkey climbed up to the bars. *Who are you?* he said.

I'm Tinker Bell. Who are you?

My name is Franklin. You speak monkey quite well for a bird.

I'm not a bird, said Tink, a bit huffily. *I'm a bird-woman.*

Good, said Franklin. *The birds around here are idiots.*

Tink, who was of bird ancestry, ordinarily would have defended the species, but in this case she agreed with the

criticism. And she needed Franklin's help. So all she said was, "I'm looking for a boy human."

Which one? said Franklin. *There are lots of them around here.*

Tink's hopes rose. *This one is named Peter.*

Franklin frowned, rooted around in his chest fur, extracted a bug, examined it for a moment, then popped it into his mouth. *I've heard that name,* he said, chewing.

When? said Tink. *Where?*

From the cage that way, said Franklin, pointing. *They have humans there.*

Thank you! said Tink, turning to go.

Be prepared, said Franklin. *They smell awful.*

But Tink was already gone, darting along the wall and in through the next barred window, where she found . . .

Captain Hook!

The pirate lay on the floor, snoring. Tink noticed his hook was gone: in its place was the wrapped stump of his forearm. Tink sneered at Hook defiantly but kept her distance, just in case. She darted through the bars into the next cell, which was a bit larger. On the floor were five sleeping forms wrapped in foul-smelling blankets. Heart pounding, her glow the only light in the cell, Tink darted from one body to the next. The first was James, the second Prentiss.

Of the third, all she could see was the tangled, untamable mass of red hair so familiar to her—the place where, except for these past few horrid days, she had slept every night since she was brought into existence. With a gentle chime, Tink settled onto the unruly mop—knowing that she would soon have to leave and find Leonard, but utterly thrilled that her beloved Peter appeared to be all right, and that she, for at least this moment, was home.

CHAPTER 31

JIBRAN'S REWARD

JIBRAN AVERTED HIS EYES as Zarboff, still dripping from his bath, dressed himself with the help of the servant boys, in a gold turban and purple robe. When he was done, Zarboff said, "Rat!"

One of the boys ran out and returned moments later holding a fat, wriggling rat by its pink tail. Zarboff took the rat and carried it to Kundalini's wicker basket. He held it over the basket and whistled a strange little tune with a haunting melody.

Jibran's jaw went slack as Kundalini's enormous head rose from the basket, torchlight glinting from the snake's scales. An impossibly long tongue flicked out toward the squirming rat; huge jaws opened like a trapdoor. Zarboff dropped the rat. With a movement almost too quick to see, Kundalini snatched the doomed animal out of the air. His jaws snapped shut. The rat was now a bulge in the snake's throat, wriggling for a few more seconds, then still.

Jibran tried to swallow, but his throat was too dry.

The snake's massive head rose higher, toward Zarboff's hand, his flicking tongue looking for more.

"That's all for now, Kundalini," said Zarboff. "Perhaps there will be another treat soon." He gave Jibran a look that made the man's blood run cold.

In a moment, it ran colder still, as Ombra glided soundlessly into the chamber. Jibran started to back away from the dark form but stopped when its head—or the place where its head should have been, turned toward him. Jibran saw no face, only what looked like two glowing coals. He could not move; he could barely breathe.

Zarboff dismissed the boys with a wave. They left quickly, including Slightly, who had no desire to remain in the room with Ombra.

The door closed. Jibran stared at Ombra.

"Lord Ombra," said Zarboff, "this is Jibran. He has news of English visitors who arrived by ship in Ashmar. He wishes to be paid for this information."

"Does he?" said Ombra, in a voice that sounded like the moaning desert wind, a voice that made Jibran drop to his knees, whimpering in fear.

"Please," he said. "I will tell you. There is no need to pay me."

"No," said Ombra, moving forward. "There is not."

As the dark shape glided toward him, Jibran tried to

scream, but no sound came from his throat. He raised his arms to protect himself from the blow he expected. But instead of striking him, Ombra slithered to Jibran's right, to the place on the stone floor where the torchlight cast the kneeling man's shadow. Jibran watched his shadow stretch like a falling drop of water, reaching as if with a will of its own toward Ombra's dark shape, flowing into it, and then . . .

Jibran slumped, his arms falling to his sides, his face slack, vacant.

Ombra was still for a moment. Then Jibran's shadow flowed back, reattaching itself to the man. He slipped sideways to the floor, moaning. Ignoring him, Ombra turned toward Zarboff, who shivered in his purple robe, feeling an unpleasant chill as he saw the glowing orbs in the dark hood.

"This man saw Lord Aster," Ombra groaned. "Aster and Bakari were on the road to Maknar; they are probably already here. You will order your men to seal the palace immediately. You will double the guard on the prisoners. I will go to the dungeon now."

With that, Ombra was gone, flowing from the chamber with astonishing speed, like windblown smoke.

Zarboff also moved quickly, for a man unused to haste.

"Guards!" he called, waddling to the doorway. Reaching it, he turned, remembering Jibran. The informant was still lying on his side, moaning, disoriented by his encounter with Ombra.

Zarboff looked toward the wicker basket and whistled the odd little tune. Immediately, the massive head of Kundalini appeared. It moved back and forth, tongue flicking, sensing the air. Then the snake began to move, flowing out of the basket with an easy, eerily smooth movement that belied its enormous size. In no hurry, the snake undulated across the floor toward Jibran.

Zarboff hesitated, wishing he could stay, then reluctantly closed the door.

CHAPTER 32

THE BATTLE
IN THE DUNGEON

"TINK!" SAID PETER, blinking awake in the dark cell. "You found me!"

Well, of course I did, said Tink, settling into Peter's outstretched hand, pleased by the joy on his face.

"But how did you . . ."

No time to explain. Wake up the others and tell them to get ready. I'll be back soon with Lord Aster to get you out of here.

"Lord Aster! How . . ."

No time. Do you know where the palace kitchen is?

"No."

Never mind. I'll find it. Just be ready.

Before Peter could respond, she was gone, a blur of green-gold light streaking through the barred window into the courtyard.

Tink rose to a hundred feet, looking around for a sign that would indicate a kitchen—a plume of smoke, perhaps, or barrels of food. She saw neither of those, but something did catch her sharp eyes—small dark shapes scurrying along the edge of a wall below. Rats.

Tink swooped toward the shapes, trying to remember her rodent vocabulary. She landed in front of the lead rat, a big fellow who stopped abruptly and raised himself up on his hind legs, snarling.

Move, bird, he said.

Tink, pleased that she understood the rat but not at all happy with his tone, said, *I'll move when you tell me where the kitchen is.*

The rat blinked, apparently not understanding.

Food, said Tink. *Where is the food?*

Instantly the rat dropped to all fours, baring needle-sharp teeth. Behind him the other rats, a half dozen of them, did the same.

Our food, said the big rat. *OUR FOOD.* With an ugly screech it lunged toward Tink, who, hurling herself upward, barely escaped its snapping jaws. Trembling, she shot upward, leveling off when she was well out of reach. The rats watched her for a moment, then resumed scurrying along the wall.

Keeping well above and behind, Tink followed the rats around a corner, then to a low stone building with a series of chimneys on the roof. The rats scurried along the side of this building to an old wooden door with a wide crack near the bottom. One by one, they squeezed through the crack.

The kitchen, Tink thought. Zooming low, she shot around a corner of the building. Her heart swelled with relief when she saw two figures, one tall and one short, standing in front of it.

"Tink!" said Leonard. "Did you find Peter?"

Yes, said Tink. *This way. Hurry.*

With Tink darting impatiently ahead, Leonard and Bakari trotted along the wall, then across the courtyard to the low windows of the dungeon cells. Peter was waiting for them, his face pressed against the bars, smiling at the sight of Molly's father. Behind him, looking sleepy, stood James, Prentiss, Thomas, and Tubby Ted.

Leonard dropped to his knees. "Peter," he whispered through the bars. "Are you all right? Can you walk?"

"Yes, sir," said Peter. "Thank you for . . ."

"We're going to get you out," interrupted Leonard. "Which way is the entrance to the dungeon?"

Peter frowned, remembering the night the prison guards had taken him out. "That way," he said, pointing to Leonard's right. "But there's guards." As he spoke, the sound of men shouting echoed across the courtyard.

"We'll hurry," said Leonard, rising to his feet. "Be ready, Peter."

Leonard and Bakari, with Tink zipping ahead, ran to the

right along the dungeon wall to a massive wood door, criss-crossed with bands of iron. Bakari tried the handle; the door swung open.

The echoing shouts were louder now.

Stepping through the doorway, Leonard and Bakari found themselves in a small room with two red-coated palace guards—both sound asleep. Tink fluttered above them, then pointed to a metal ring glinting from her glow.

Keys, she chimed softly.

The shouts in the courtyard were now very loud.

Carefully, Bakari unhooked the ring of keys from the hook on the sleeping guard's belt. Then, with Tink leading, they raced down a torch-lit corridor leading left, back toward Peter's cell. They passed a dozen empty cells, then one filled with small dark shapes. Leonard stared.

Monkeys, said Tink in his ear. *The next cell is Hook's, and then . . .*

But before she could finish, there were angry roars from behind. Bakari and Leonard whirled to see the two guards they had left sleeping—apparently awakened by the shouts outside—charging toward them with swords drawn. Leonard and Bakari drew their own swords, and in a moment the stone corridor rang with the clash of steel on steel, swords flashing in the torchlight. Leonard and Bakari were excellent swordsmen, but time was against them; the sound of the battle was sure to bring more guards.

Leonard heard an urgent chime in his ear.

Close your eyes! said Tink. *Tell Bakari!*

"Bakari!" shouted Leonard. "When I count to three, drive him back, then close your eyes!"

"During a *sword fight?*" said Bakari.

"Trust me!" said Leonard. "One, two . . . NOW!"

Leonard and Bakari both thrust their swords violently, driving their opponents back; they then closed their eyes, Bakari quite reluctantly. In the next instant the once-dim corridor flashed with a white light more brilliant than the midday desert sun. Tink, having used all her energy, dropped to the floor. The two guards screamed, covering their eyes—too late, as they were temporarily blinded. When the brightness was gone, Leonard opened his eyes and stepped quickly between the helpless guards, raising his sword, hilt-first, and quickly clubbing them both unconscious.

"Come on," he said to Bakari, turning to run along the corridor. He passed a cell where the tall, thin figure of Hook stood in the shadows. Then, at last, he came to the cell where Peter was waiting with his mates.

"All right, boys," Leonard said. "We'll have to move quickly now." He looked over his shoulder at Bakari, who was standing ten feet away, next to a torch.

"Bring the keys!" said Leonard.

Bakari did not move.

"For heaven's sake, man!" said Leonard. "Hurry!"

Bakari did not move.

"Lord Aster," said Peter.

"What?"

Peter was pointing toward Bakari's feet. "Look."

Leonard looked, and his blood ran cold.

Bakari had no shadow.

There was shouting in the corridor now, the sound of many men running, coming closer.

Leonard raised his sword, pointing it at Bakari's chest.

"Give me the keys," he said.

Bakari opened his mouth, but instead of Bakari's voice an awful groan came out.

"Go ahead, Lord Aster," it said. "Stick your sword into your Starcatcher friend. Do you think I care?"

Leonard hesitated, then lowered his sword, his shoulders slumping. Ombra emerged from the shadows, and now the groaning voice came from his own dark shape.

"A wise decision, Lord Aster," he said. Moments later, thundering feet announced the arrival of a dozen guards; Leonard was now hopelessly outnumbered. On Ombra's orders, the guards disarmed him, then shoved him, along with the slack-faced Bakari, into a vacant cell next to the boys'.

"Now that you both are comfortable," groaned Ombra, "I will return your associate's shadow. I need no longer burden myself with it, as it has given me all I need to know." A shadow emerged from under his robe, and as two terrified guards leapt out of the way, it slithered across the floor and into the cell. It attached itself to Bakari, who groaned and slid to the floor.

As Leonard was helping the disoriented Bakari to his feet, King Zarboff, surrounded by his personal guards, entered the corridor, huffing from the exertion of crossing the courtyard.

"Lord Ombra," he gasped. "My men have sealed the palace. It is impossible for the Starcatchers to get inside."

Zarboff felt a chill as Ombra looked at him, then groaned, "The Starcatchers are here."

Zarboff stared at Leonard and Bakari. "But that's not possible!" he sputtered. "How did they get in?"

"They were admitted by an accomplice, a member of your palace guard," said Ombra.

"Who is this traitor?" roared Zarboff. "I will feed him to Kundalini one piece at a time!"

"I will give you his name," said Ombra. "But first you must dispatch a group of your best men—ten should be sufficient—to the port of Ashmar. Have them wear civilian clothes and travel unobtrusively. They are to board a French ship called the *Michelle*."

"No!" said Leonard, lunging to the cell bars.

Ombra ignored him, continuing to speak to Zarboff. "On the ship is Lord Aster's daughter, whose name is Molly."

Now Peter was gripping the bars of his cell, staring at Ombra.

"Your men are to seize this girl," said Ombra, "and bring her here."

"You don't need my daughter, Ombra," said Leonard. "You have me."

"Your gallantry is touching," said Ombra. "But the girl has already caused me far too much trouble. She is a Starcatcher; the more of you in captivity, the better." He turned to Zarboff. "Dispatch your men to Ashmar at once. I will see you in your chambers."

Zarboff, who disliked taking orders but had no intention of contradicting Ombra, huffed from the room, trailed by his personal guards.

"Ombra," said Leonard. "Whatever you're planning to do here, I give you my word that I will not interfere if you will leave my daughter alone."

Ombra turned to face Leonard, the red spheres in his hood-shape glowing brightly.

"You amuse me, Lord Aster," he groaned, "talking as though you *can* interfere, when in fact you are helpless. I will do as I please with your daughter and this boy and you. The only reason you are alive right now is that I expect to enjoy your reaction when you see the undoing of everything you Starcatchers have done for thousands of years."

"What are you talking about?" said Leonard.

"You will see," groaned Ombra, "soon enough." He turned to the guards and said something in the Rundoon language. Then he glided away down the corridor, leaving Leonard and Peter staring at each other through the bars.

"What does he mean?" said Peter. "What's he going to do?"

"I don't know," said Leonard. "I . . ."

He was silenced by a guard who banged against the cell bars, shouting. Neither Leonard nor Peter understood him, but it was clear he did not want them to talk. Peter and Leonard stood looking at each other for a few more seconds. Each saw despair in the other's eyes. They were trapped and helpless, and Molly was in danger. *Molly was in danger.*

Leonard shifted his gaze to look after Bakari. Peter turned and walked to the back wall of his cell, slumping to the floor. James started to say something to him, but a shout from a guard cut him off. There would be no more talking. Under the vigilant eyes of the guards, the prisoners sat silent, each in his own world of helplessness and hopelessness. In time, as the slow minutes ticked past, the prisoners dozed, and the only movement in the dungeon was the flickering of the torch flames . . .

. . . and one other thing. Down the dim corridor, a few yards from where the sleepy guards watched over their sleeping captives, a tiny glowing form was climbing, inch by agonizing inch, up the wall toward a window. She was exhausted and had to pause often to rest. But at last she reached the window opening and pulled herself through the bars to the narrow ledge outside. There she rested for a half hour, trying to regain her strength, knowing that each passing minute increased the danger.

Finally, she rose on wobbly legs, set her wings vibrating, and leapt forward. She dropped almost to the ground before she found the lift she needed, then slowly began to rise, up and up, above the palace complex and over the wall, hovering there, studying the stars to get her bearings. Then, hoping for a favorable wind, she set off, a tiny bright speck in the unspeakable vastness of the desert night.

CHAPTER 33

The Alliance

Fighting Prawn, on bleeding knees, once again raised the heavy stone over his head and once again slammed it down. He grimaced as the stone struck the hard lava, blasting a cloud of stinging rock chips into his face. He wiped the sweat and dust from his eyes, glancing around to see how his men were doing, keeping an eye out for the Scorpion guards.

He and his warriors were toiling deep under the mountain inside a twisting tunnel left by escaping lava. It was as if a giant worm had dug its way to the surface a thousand years before. The tunnel air was stale and smoky from the sputtering torches, their flickering light causing the workers' shadows to dance on the dark walls.

The men were forced to work without food or water. If a man stopped pounding rock, Scorpion guards would kick and whip him. Hour after hour, the workers pounded their stones against the jagged lava rock, breaking off chunks, which were hauled out in baskets by the Mollusk children—for what purpose, Fighting Prawn did not know.

There were pirates down there, too, forced to work alongside their former Mollusk enemies. Fighting Prawn had managed to speak to one briefly, before the guards stopped him.

"They didn't get all of us," the pirate had whispered. "There's some that got away. Maybe there's hope for us."

Fighting Prawn only shook his head. What could a handful of pirates do against the Scorpions? He thought about trying to lead an uprising, but his men had no weapons other than the stones, which would be of little use against the spears and knives of the guards. Besides, his men were hungry and exhausted; many were bleeding from cuts inflicted by the sharp rocks or the Scorpions' blows. Fighting Prawn knew they could not hold out much longer.

He worried, too, about the children, forced to drag the heavy baskets, shoved and kicked by the snarling guards. He had caught one heartbreaking glimpse of his youngest daughter, Little Scallop, but had not yet seen Shining Pearl. He knew Shining Pearl could be headstrong. He hoped she hadn't gotten into trouble with the Scorpions.

＊

Shining Pearl crept toward the murmur of men's voices. She was hungry and soaking wet. A steady rain fell; water dripped from every leaf, turning the ground into slippery black muck. Everything smelled of rot and decay. Shining Pearl wished she were home in the village, surrounded by her family, with a warm fire burning and the smell of cooking fish on the wind.

Close to the voices now, she gently drew an enormous leaf out of the way and saw a group of seven men—pirates—crouched in a clearing. She hesitated, then took a breath and stepped bravely forward.

"Hello," she said, using the English she had learned from her father.

Six of the seven men leapt to their feet, drawing knives. The seventh pirate, a little round man, fell over backward.

"It's a girl!" said one of the men.

"It's one of them local savages," said another, stepping forward. He grabbed Shining Pearl by the arm and leaned his face in close to hers. His grip was painful; his breath was awful. "What're you doing on this side of the island, missy?" he said.

"I . . . I . . ." Shining Pearl stammered.

"You *what?*" said the pirate, shaking her arm.

"Here, now," said the round little man, struggling to his feet. "She's just a girl. She ain't done nothing. Let her go."

To Shining Pearl's surprise, the man holding her arm said, "Aye, Cap'n Smee," and released her. Evidently this little man, Smee, was in charge.

"Here now, little girl," he said. "What *are* you doing here?"

"I'm hungry," she said. She thought, *And I'm lonely*, but didn't say it.

"We're all hungry," muttered one of the men.

"Quiet!" snapped Smee. Shining Pearl could tell by the look on the faces of the other pirates that they were taken aback by his tone. He turned back to Shining Pearl and said, "Where's your family, little girl?"

"They . . . they . . ." Shining Pearl put her face into her hands, sobbing. She was furious at herself for breaking down, but she couldn't help it.

Smee put his hand on her shoulder.

"Go ahead," he said. "It's all right."

"They took my family," she sobbed. "The Scorpions took them all. I ran away, but there's nowhere to go. I can't go back to the village. Those horrible men . . ." She sobbed some more, her shoulders quaking.

"There, there," said Smee. "You can come with us, to the fort."

This brought grumbles from the other pirates.

"We've got enough troubles already," said the biggest of the men. "We don't need no girl slowing us down."

Smee faced the men. "I'm acting cap'n," he said. "And I say she comes with us to the fort."

The men glared back; Shining Pearl could tell they were on the verge of rebellion. She cleared her throat.

"You can't go to your fort," she said.

All eyes turned to her. "Why not?" said Smee.

"The Scorpions are there, too," she said.

"How do you know that?" said the big man.

"I've just come from there," said Shining Pearl. "The Scorpions found your fort and they captured the rest of your . . . pirate friends."

"How come they didn't capture *you?*" said the big man.

"They did, when they came to our village. But I escaped into the jungle and headed to your fort, thinking . . ."

"Yes?" said Smee. "Thinking what?"

"Thinking maybe we could help each other."

The pirates snickered—all but Smee.

"But if you was already over at the fort," he said, "how did you get here so quick?"

"I know this island," said Shining Pearl. "I know all the paths and the hiding places. I know it a lot better than the Scorpions do." One by one, she looked each pirate in the eye. "And better than any of *you* do."

The men scowled and exchanged glances.

"All right, then," said Smee. "Seems to me it's a good thing that . . . What's your name, little girl?"

"Shining Pearl."

"Seems to me," continued Smee, "it's a good thing Shining Pearl found us. Seems to me maybe we *can* help each

225

other out." He looked around. "Any of you men want to argue?"

None of the men spoke.

"All right, then," said Smee. "Shining Pearl, welcome to the crew."

CHAPTER 34

THE BORROWED CAMEL

MOLLY AND GEORGE found it more difficult than they expected to get off the *Michelle*. Leonard Aster, well aware of Molly's tendency to take matters into her own hands, had left orders with Captain Stavis that the two children were to be watched closely, and Captain Stavis had relayed these orders to the crew.

But sailors being sailors, and a port being close at hand, it was not long before the crew became distracted. By the second evening, Molly and George, having waited impatiently all day, saw their chance to sneak off. As darkness fell, with the crew dozing after a bit too much food and grog, they sneaked onto the ship's deserted main deck and tiptoed down the gangway to the dock.

Once ashore, they ducked behind a huge pile of traps next to a stone building; the traps reeked of dead fish.

"Now what?" whispered George.

"One thing for sure," said Molly. "We must get away from these awful traps."

"We can't go 'round in these clothes," said George. "We need robes, like the one your father wore."

Molly nodded. "I saw laundry lines from the ship, by a big house up that way. We can borrow some robes."

"*Borrow?*" said George.

"Desperate times," said Molly, "call for desperate measures."

"What does that mean?" said George.

"It's an expression my father uses: it means sometimes you have to borrow a robe," said Molly. She reached into the pocket of her dress and pulled out some coins, the last of the French money her mother had given her. "Besides, we'll leave this as partial payment. Come on."

The streets were nearly empty, as most of Ashmar was having supper; nevertheless, Molly and George kept to the narrow alleys as they moved away from the harbor and up a hill, their mouths watering as the aroma of cooking wafted out of every house they passed.

"There," Molly whispered. Just ahead was a whitewashed stone house, much larger than its neighbors, with a fine view of the harbor. Along the side of the house was a clothesline, on which hung a half dozen white robes. Next to the clothesline, kneeling in a patch of dirt and contentedly chewing its cud, was a camel.

Molly and George looked around. The street was deserted. With nightfall now complete, they crept in darkness around the side of the house, took the two smallest-looking robes off the clothesline, and put them on. George's fit fine; Molly's was too large, but she rolled and tucked it until it was serviceable. When they were dressed, Molly put the coins on a stone next to the clothesline and whispered, "Let's go."

George didn't move. He was looking at the camel.

"Why don't we borrow this as well?" he whispered.

"Are you *insane?*" hissed Molly.

"Molly, we've got to go miles across the desert," George said. "On foot it could take us forever."

"But we don't know how to ride a camel."

"It's got a sort of saddle," said George, eyeing the wooden contraption strapped to the camel's back. "How different can it be from a horse?"

Molly frowned. She didn't like the idea of taking a camel—*stealing* was the word for it, she knew—but they *were* desperate. She had to find her father and Peter.

"All right," she said.

Quickly, George untied the camel. Then he and Molly climbed into the saddle, wedging themselves in, George in front and Molly in back. George dug his heels into the camel's sides and said, "Up!"

Slowly, the camel turned its head and looked back with

an expression of what appeared to be annoyance. It turned its head forward again and resumed chewing its cud.

"Fine bit of horsemanship," said Molly.

"I suppose you can do better," said George.

"I'm not the one who said he could ride a camel," said Molly.

George, irritated now, brought his legs out farther and kicked the camel hard. This time the camel, rather than turning around, raised its head and emitted a loud, unhappy, gurgling sound. From inside the house came a shout.

"Someone's heard us!" said Molly.

George kicked the camel again; the camel responded with another protest, this one even louder.

Now Molly and George heard several shouting voices and running feet.

"They're coming!" Molly said. "We've got to get out of here!"

Molly struggled to get out of the saddle, hampered by her bulky robe and the tight quarters. George, determined to dominate the camel, kicked it yet again. "Up, you mangy beast!" he hissed. This time the camel whirled its head around and spit at him. George leaned violently backward, knocking his head into Molly's. A wad of camel spit sailed past.

"Ow!" she said. "George, *let me out of this saddle!*"

Just then, four men, two holding swords, burst around

the corner of the house. Catching sight of George and Molly, they charged toward the camel, shouting angrily, their faces filled with fury. Now George and Molly were both trying frantically to climb out of the saddle, but they and their robes were too entangled. Molly thought about using the starstuff in her locket but could not get to it in time. They had no chance to escape—the first shouting man was almost upon them, drawing back his sword, and . . .

. . . and stopping short as a brilliant streak of light flashed in front of him, inches from his eyes. The man jerked backward abruptly, causing the second man to run into him, and the third and fourth to run into both of them. The men went down in front of the camel in a clattering, shouting heap.

"Tink!" shouted Molly.

Tink responded with a burst of chimes that Molly did not understand. It wasn't aimed at her, anyway; Tink was saying something to the camel. Instantly, the beast got up, the sudden motion almost pitching George and Molly out of the saddle. But they hung on as the camel, urged on by Tink, got to its feet and lurched forward toward the street. One of the fallen men managed to lunge at the camel as it passed. He grabbed Molly's leg, jerking it down and back. Molly screamed in pain. George lashed out and kicked the man's head; he grunted and let go. The camel reached the street and turned right. George clung to the saddle and Molly to George, as the camel, responding to Tink's chimes, went from a trot to a gallop. From behind, they heard the sounds of angry voices and running feet. Neither looked back. The sounds receded.

In minutes they were at the edge of the city and then on a road going into open desert. The camel slowed down to a swaying walk. The night closed around them.

"Are you all right?" said George.

"Yes," said Molly, though her leg throbbed. "I'm fine." She leaned around George and spoke to Tink, who now sat atop the camel's head between its floppy ears, looking forward.

"Thanks, Tink," she said. "You found us just in time."

Tink turned and, with an expression that was slightly less disdainful than the one she usually used toward Molly, chimed a response. Then she chimed again, and again, more earnestly.

"What is she so worked up about?" said George.

Molly shook her head. "I can't understand bell-speak," she said. "But I think I recognized one bit. It's Peter she's worried about." She looked out at the vast darkness of the desert. "And it's Peter she's taking us to."

CHAPTER 35

THE NIGHT CARAVAN

THE BOYS AWAKENED to the sound of the cell door opening. Peter blinked his eyes open and saw at least a dozen guards gathered in the corridor. He looked out the window; it was still night.

"What's happening?" whispered James.

"I don't know," said Peter as several of the guards entered the cell, shouting and gesturing for the boys to stand. One of them kicked the still-sleeping form of Tubby Ted.

"Ow!" he said, then "Ow!" again as the guard yanked him to his feet. "What are they doing? It's dark out! Wh . . . OW!"

A clout on the ear silenced Ted, who was herded into the corridor along with the other boys. Peter exchanged concerned glances with Leonard Aster and Bakari, who, awakened by the noise, stood in their cell watching. Hook was also awake; as usual he brooded silently in the shadows of his cell.

The guards organized the boys into a line, then moved them forward to the monkey cell, where they stopped. A guard unlatched the cell door and another guard, looking none too happy, slipped inside the smelly cell, holding a stick with a loop of rope at the end of it. The monkeys screeched and leapt about, avoiding the guard. He seemed to be after a specific one, and with considerable effort, he finally managed to ensnare it, getting the loop around its body and then quickly pulling it taut. He carried the monkey, shrieking and squirming, out of the cell and got it into a cage, which was quickly closed. Two guards picked it up.

The little convoy—boys, guards, and caged monkey—moved forward a few more yards, then stopped again, this time at what appeared to be a locked storage room. Two of the guards went inside and emerged a minute later. Peter gasped when he saw what they were carrying: suits made of golden mesh.

Peter had seen this kind of suit twice before: the first time had been on Mollusk Island, when golden-garbed Starcatchers handled the starstuff that Peter and Molly had managed to rescue from the Others. The second time had been at Stonehenge—Leonard Aster had worn such a suit to protect himself from the same starstuff when he brought it to the Return. Peter knew the suits were for handling starstuff. But for whom? And more important: where?

The guards barked, and the parade started moving again,

down the dungeon corridor and then out into the clear desert night. Just as Peter was about to step through the doorway, one of the guards tied a rope around his waist, knotting it tightly, then secured the other end around his own waist. Peter would not be flying anywhere.

The parade crossed the vast, empty courtyard, passing one of the odd-shaped metal towers, its sharp point thrusting toward the star-filled sky. A thought occurred to Peter, and he looked around to confirm it: there had been two such towers. Now one was gone.

But he had no time to ponder that mystery as they were going through a massive gate, and his attention was drawn to the sight awaiting them outside the palace compound. It was a strange caravan. At the front were four horses, each ridden by a soldier with a sword at his side. Behind them was a large open carriage, drawn by two horses. The carriage was opulently decorated, on its floor was a fabulously ornate carpet decorated in gold thread; on this carpet was a throne. And on this throne sat His Majesty King Zarboff the Third. Next to him was the large basket in which he kept his snake, Kundalini.

Behind the king's carriage was a camel with a sort of platform strapped to its back; on this platform, secured by chains, was a large chest made of wood, with metal hinges and fasteners that gleamed yellow in the starlight. Peter assumed that they were gold and that the chest was lined

with gold as well; the chest, he was sure, was designed to hold starstuff.

Behind the camel was a flatbed wagon drawn by four more horses. Most of the wagon bed was taken up by a large cage. The guards shoved the boys toward this cage and made them climb into it. Once Peter, the last to enter, was inside, the guard untied the rope around his waist and padlocked the cage shut. The monkey's cage was placed on the back of the same wagon, along with the gold suits. The guards formed ranks behind the wagon. Some commands were shouted, and the caravan began moving.

The only sound on the deserted streets of Maknar was the clopping of horses hooves and the rumbling of wagon wheels. The boys stared out through their cage bars, watching the city give way to the open desert. Peter recognized the road; he'd been on it before. He kept his eyes trained forward, and after a short while he saw it—the pointed ears and massive head of the Jackal. Squinting, he saw another shape rising in the starry sky, perhaps a hundred yards beyond the Jackal—a sleek, sharp-pointed shape. He stared until he was sure of what it was—the tower that had stood with its twin in the palace courtyard. *How had it been brought here?* Peter wondered. *And why?*

The caravan reached the mouth of the Jackal and stopped. The boys stared fearfully into the gaping darkness between the huge teeth; the guards avoided looking at it.

They waited several minutes, and then out of the blackness of the Jackal's mouth came the even blacker form of Ombra. The horses snorted and danced uneasily; the monkey whimpered and cowered in its cage. Ombra glided silently to the front of the caravan and slithered into the royal carriage with Zarboff. The king waved his hand, and the caravan moved again, covering the short remaining distance to the place where the needle-shaped iron tower rose into the sky.

At the base of the tower were a dozen or so figures working by the light of lanterns hanging from poles in the sand. Among the figures, Peter recognized Slightly and the other slave boys.

"Keep the powder away from the lanterns!" a man shouted in heavily accented English. *"Away from the lanterns!"*

Beyond the tower, Peter saw three huge wagons hitched together into a train; these in turn were hitched to a team of eight horses. This, Peter realized, was how the tower had been hauled out here; he still had no idea why.

The caravan stopped. The guards unlocked the cage and gestured for Peter—and only Peter—to get out. As he climbed through the cage door, two of the guards grabbed his arms and lifted him out, gripping him painfully hard. He felt the desert air grow colder and turned to see Ombra gliding up with Zarboff trailing behind, and behind him two guards straining under the weight of the basket containing the king's enormous snake.

Ombra stopped in front of Peter. "We will need your powers of flight," he groaned. "So we are going to order the guards to release you. You will do exactly as we say. You will not attempt to escape."

Zarboff stepped forward. "If you in any way disobey us, if for any reason you fail to return, I will put Kundalini into the cage with your friends." He beckoned to the men carrying the basket. They set it on the sand next to the cage. As the boys stared in horror, Zarboff whistled his odd tune, and the massive head of Kundalini rose from the basket, its tongue flicking out as if tasting something.

"It would take him some time to eat them all," Zarboff said. "I don't know which would be worse—to be the first meal, or the last." He laughed, enjoying the effect his words had on the boys in the cage, who, except for James, were now sobbing.

"Stop," Peter said to Zarboff. This clearly surprised the king, who was unused to taking orders from anyone, let alone a boy. "I promise I won't try to escape."

Zarboff, angry, was about to say something about Peter's tone, but Ombra cut him off.

"The boy understands the situation," he groaned. "Come."

Zarboff closed his mouth, but his expression told Peter that their discussion was not over.

They walked toward the tower, the guards following, carrying the monkey cage. As they drew close, Peter saw that the tower was standing next to wooden scaffolding, which went about two thirds of the way up. On the scaffolding were winches attached to ropes and pulleys, like a ship's rigging. Clearly, this was how the tower had been raised upright. Peter saw that four large, rectangular metal plates had been attached to the base of the tower on what looked like hinges. There was a large opening between two of these plates. Slightly and the other slave boys were carrying buckets from a wagon to this opening. One by one, each boy dumped the contents of his bucket into the hole and then went back to the wagon for more.

Supervising this activity was a man with a high-pitched voice, shouting orders in an accent unfamiliar to Peter. The man was tall and very thin; he had white hair that stood out from his head like a cloud. His deep-set eyes, hidden by shadow, looked like holes drilled into his skull.

"Where is Albert?" he said, as Peter and the others approached. "Did you bring Albert?" If the man was in any way intimidated by Ombra or Zarboff, his voice did not betray it. "Ah!" he said, catching sight of the caged monkey. "Albert! Good! And this must be the flying boy." He leaned close, studying Peter with a gaze so intense it made Peter look down. "It's Peter, yes?"

Peter nodded.

"I am Doctor Viktor Glotz," said the man. "You are going to find the starstuff Fall for us."

"But . . . I don't know how," said Peter.

"I will tell you," said Glotz. He pointed to the metal tower. "This," he said proudly, "is a rocket. Do you know what a rocket is?"

Peter looked doubtfully at the tower. "Like fireworks?" he said.

Glotz snorted. "Fireworks," he said, "are children's playthings. They reach an altitude of a few hundred feet at most. This rocket, *my* rocket, can go, *will* go, high above Earth. Higher than the highest clouds."

Peter looked even more doubtful, his eyes sweeping up the tall, obviously heavy tower.

"You do not believe me?" said Glotz, his voice getting louder. "You think it is impossible? That is what they said in Russia. They said Viktor Glotz was a madman. Fools! They will see! They will see who is a fool! They—"

"Dr. Glotz," interrupted Ombra. "I presume your preparations are complete."

"We are on schedule," said Glotz, calming down. "We will launch"—he pulled out a pocket watch, squinting at it by the lantern light—"in two hours and twenty-six minutes, a few minutes before dawn."

"And you're certain it cannot be sooner?" said Ombra. "It cannot take place in darkness?"

"No," said Glotz. "I have calculated and recalculated. If we want the Fall to occur near here, we must do it exactly according to the schedule. Otherwise, I can't say where the starstuff will come down. It could be in Scotland again."

Peter listened openmouthed. "You made that happen?" he blurted out. "*You* made the starstuff fall in Scotland?"

Glotz smiled. "Yes," he said. "I made it fall in Scotland. And in a few hours, I will make it fall here."

"But I thought . . ." said Peter, "I mean, the Starcatchers said nobody knew when, or where, or . . ."

"The Starcatchers," said Glotz, his voice dripping contempt, "are fools. They have never understood what they were dealing with. For centuries they had access to power, unimaginable power, the power of the universe itself. And what did they do with it? They sent it back! *They gave it away.* Well, they had their opportunity, and now I have mine." Glotz glanced at Ombra and Zarboff, then corrected himself: "I mean, *we* have ours. And we will not waste the opportunity."

"What will you do with the starstuff?" said Peter.

Glotz smiled and said, "We will use it to get more." Seeing Peter's puzzled look, he pointed to the tower. "This rocket," he said, "will carry a small amount of starstuff into the sky. You can see it up there, near the top."

Peter looked up and saw that just below the place where the rocket began to taper to a point, there was a seam in the metal; light was shining through the seam, the yellow-gold light of starstuff.

"It is all we have left," said Glotz. "And it is not much. But my calculations show that it will serve its purpose. Two purposes, actually. One, it will lift the rocket, with help from the fuel these boys are putting in it now." He pointed to Slightly and the others, still methodically dumping their buckets into the opening.

"Then," continued Glotz, "when the rocket reaches maximum altitude, Albert"—Glotz pointed to the monkey cage—"will pull the lever that opens the hatch, releasing the starstuff into the sky. That will cause a disruption. And that, in turn, will cause more starstuff to fall. Quite a large amount of starstuff, if my calculations are correct. And I am quite sure they are." Glotz beamed, pleased with his genius.

Peter frowned. "Albert? The *monkey* will open the hatch?"

"Yes," said Glotz, still beaming. "*And* he will steer the rocket! I have trained him both to navigate and operate the controls. We tried using humans, but they were unreliable."

"What happens to the monkey after the starstuff is released?" said Peter.

Glotz waved his hand.

"We have more monkeys," he said.

"But what—" Peter began.

"Enough," interrupted the low wheeze of Ombra. "Dr. Glotz, you will complete your preparations. There must be no problems."

"There will not be, Lord Ombra," said Glotz. "I assure you of that." He turned to Peter. "When we finish preparing the rocket," he said, "I will give you your instructions."

The remaining preparations took the better part of two hours. Under Glotz's watchful eye, Slightly and the other slave boys finished loading the fuel. Next Glotz climbed the wooden scaffold with two of the boys. Using a winch, they hauled the cage containing Albert the monkey up to a platform next to a small hatchway near the top of the rocket, above the glowing starstuff. Glotz put the monkey inside, closed the hatch, then descended with the boys.

The soldiers then attached ropes to the scaffolding and used horses to drag it away from the rocket, which now stood alone. When they were finished, Glotz called, "Get the fuse!"

Slightly and the boy called Tootles went to the fuel wagon and returned carrying a coil of what looked like black rope. Glotz took this to the base of the rocket and carefully inserted one end into a small hole. Then he backed away, uncoiling the fuse, cutting it at a length of ten feet. Meanwhile the soldiers moved all of the animals and wagons behind a sand dune. Peter stood near the cage that held his friends. None of the boys spoke.

The first faint hints of pink were now appearing in the eastern sky. Ombra conferred briefly with Glotz and Zarboff, then glided off in the direction of the Jackal. Peter knew he would not let daylight catch him outdoors. When he was gone, Glotz beckoned Peter over.

"In two minutes," he said, "I will light the fuse. When I do, things will happen quickly, so you must be ready. The rocket will ascend. You will see bright lights in the sky. Then the disruption will occur, and the starstuff will fall. I do not know exactly where, but it will be close, within fifteen miles. You must fly to it, confirm the location, and return here immediately with directions, so we can retrieve it. Do you understand?"

"But how will I find it?" Peter said. "How will I know where it is?"

"You will know," said Glotz, "just as your parents knew."

Peter, stunned, took a staggering step back. "You *knew my parents?*" he said.

"Of course," said Glotz. "They were here in Rundoon for years. You didn't know that?"

"Where are they now?" said Peter. "Are they still alive?"

Glotz waved his hand dismissively, exactly as he had when talking about the monkeys.

"There is no time for talking," he said. "It is almost time to light the fuse."

Peter, his mind swirling with questions, watched as Glotz, with his pocket watch in one hand and a match in the other, squatted on the sand next to the fuse. He said something to himself in a strange-sounding language. Then he struck the match and touched it to the fuse. It flared to life, sending out a shower of sparks that crept toward the waiting rocket.

Glotz walked quickly away from the rocket, to where Peter was standing.

"Now, boy," he said to Peter, "it is up to you."

CHAPTER 36

Pursuit

𝒯HE RIDERS WERE GAINING.

Tink heard them first, long before Molly or George would have. This was hours after they had fled Ashmar. They were crossing the desert under the billion-star night sky, the camel moving at a leisurely swaying walk, when suddenly Tink leapt up from her spot on the camel's head and took off flying in the direction from which they'd come. She zoomed back a few minutes later and chimed something urgent-sounding into the camel's ear. Immediately, the camel lurched forward into a gallop, nearly sending Molly and George spilling out of the saddle.

"What is it?" George shouted, clinging to the saddle. "What's happening?"

"Tink must have seen something back there," said Molly, trying to look behind her without falling off the jouncing camel. It took her several tries, but finally she caught sight of them coming over a rise, four tall silhouettes against the star-lit sky.

"Oh dear," she said. "There are men on camels galloping after us."

George looked back. "They're probably the men whose camel we borrowed."

Molly nodded. The two of them hung on as the camel raced forward into the night, urged on by Tink. From time to time, Molly glanced behind her. Each time she did, the pursuers appeared to be closer.

CHAPTER 37

THE HEAVENS EXPLODE

PETER AND THE OTHERS watched as the sparking, sputtering flame crawled along the fuse. It reached the rocket and crawled up the side, disappearing into the hole.

For a moment, nothing happened. Peter wondered if the fuse had gone out.

And then all thought was driven from his mind as the desert exploded with a roar that sounded and felt like a thousand thunderclaps all at once, and a brilliant light that left him temporarily blind. When he could see again, he barely believed what his eyes showed him: the rocket, which had seemed so massive, so immobile, was shooting into the sky like an arrow with a fiery tail, growing smaller each second.

He felt a hand grip his shoulder and turned to see Glotz looking down at him, his face flushed with excitement.

"Be ready," Glotz said.

"What on earth is that?" said Leonard Aster. He had been awakened by a rumbling sound in the distance, like thunder, although it couldn't have been thunder, not on this cloud-free desert night. He and Bakari were now standing by the tiny window of their cell, watching a bright streak of light ascend into the sky a few miles away.

"It's like a shooting star," said Aster. "But it's going in the wrong direction."

Bakari frowned. "That reminds me," he said. "I had a report from one of our people in Rundoon concerning—"

But before he could finish his sentence, the heavens exploded.

Suddenly, the entire sky was red, from horizon to horizon, and then an iridescent purple, and then the brilliant blue-green of a sunlit tropical lagoon, and then red again, the colors not blending but changing one into the other in an instant. At the launch site the boys cried and the soldiers cowered and the horses whinnied and reared in panic. King Zarboff got on hands and knees and crawled underneath his carriage.

Glotz, standing next to Peter and staring at the spectacle in the sky, was delighted.

"Exactly as I calculated," he said. "The Fall is taking place very near us. Can you feel anything yet?"

"No," said Peter. "I . . ."

At that instant, the heavenly colors suddenly disappeared, as if a giant candle had been snuffed. The sky was all star-studded blackness, with the edge of dawn just barely appearing in the east. A moment later, Peter stagger-stepped backward as he felt an invisible wave of heat—not hot air but a surge of warmth that went into him, through him, taking his breath away.

"Now you feel something, yes?" Glotz said eagerly.

"Yes," gasped Peter.

King Zarboff had crawled out from under the carriage and was waddling over.

"Does he feel it?" the king asked.

"Yes," said Glotz.

"Where?" Zarboff shouted at Peter. "Where did it fall?"

"Give him a moment," said Glotz quietly, his eyes on Peter. "He will find it."

"He had better find it," growled Zarboff.

Peter inhaled, trying to get his breath back. He could still feel the warmth, but now it was only on one side of him, his right side. He felt as though his skin was burning; he wondered how Glotz and Zarboff could not feel it.

Glotz was watching him closely.

"Which way is it?" he said. "Which way is the Fall?"

"That way," said Peter, pointing to the right.

"Good, good," Glotz said. "We will start moving that way. You will fly ahead and locate the exact spot. It will be easy for you to see when you get closer. But you must not get *too* close. You must locate the Fall and fly back immediately to tell us where it is. Do you understand?"

"Yes," said Peter.

"If you are not back within an hour," said Zarboff, "I will put Kundalini in the cage with your friends."

"But what if I . . ." began Peter.

"Find it!" thundered Zarboff. "Now!"

Peter took a step and launched himself into the slowly brightening sky. He rose about fifty feet and hovered for a moment, looking down at the cage containing his friends. He could see their pale faces looking up at him through the bars. He gave them what he hoped was an encouraging wave, then made his body horizontal and began swooping over the desert toward the source of the heat.

———◆———

The four pursuers were quite close now. Molly and George could hear their shouts and, when they turned around, see the fury on their faces.

Molly glanced at the sky. The strange lights were gone. She had never seen anything like them, nor had George, who was an amateur astronomer. The lights had energized

Tinker Bell, who had pointed at the sky and chimed a series of excited statements, giving up in disgust when it was clear that Molly and George did not understand her.

The pursuers had also reacted to the lights, slowing down to point at the sky and yell to each other. For a moment Molly hoped that they would abandon the chase, but when the lights stopped, they resumed galloping at full speed. They were excellent riders, and they gained steadily. Molly saw now that each of the men had a sword. She wondered what they did in this country to camel thieves.

The men drew closer, closer. Tink chimed constantly to the camel, but it was clearly overmatched. Molly was reluctant to turn around now, for fear that the next time she did, the men would be upon them. Ahead, the desert stretched endlessly into the empty distance, offering no help, no safety. The pursuers' shouts grew more excited; they had their prey almost in hand, and they knew it.

Molly felt something. It was a sensation of warmth at her throat—quite intense, almost painful. Her hand went under her robe, to her neck, to . . .

The locket. She pulled it out; it was glowing. Tink was fluttering in her face, chiming something over and over.

"Look out!" George yanked Molly forward. She felt something brush against her hair. She turned and saw one of the camel riders, who had drawn even with her and George. It was his sword she had felt; he was drawing it back for another strike. And he would have struck Molly this time, had not Tink, who made up in speed what she lacked in size, delivered a kick to his nose that made him yelp in pain and veer sideways, his blade harmlessly slicing the air.

But he was coming right back, and his cohorts had now drawn alongside Molly and George as well. Tink was in Molly's face again, chiming something and gesturing frantically toward . . .

The locket! Of course! As Molly fumbled with the clasp while she balanced on the bouncing saddle, Tink bought her some time by zipping back and forth among the camel riders, fluttering in their faces and making a sound that their camels apparently found upsetting. But she could not stop all four at once, and it would not be long before one of their swords found its mark.

Molly finally got the locket off her neck. "George!" she said. "Lean sideways!"

"Why?" said George, eyeing the angry swordsmen on either side.

"Do it!" shouted Molly, giving George a hard sideways shove with her left hand. George wisely obeyed, leaning out of the way. With her right hand, Molly flicked her locket open and dumped its contents onto the camel's neck. Molly had not opened the locket since she had retrieved it months ago from under the bed in her room: it had wound up there during a struggle on the awful night when Ombra had kidnapped her mother. Thus, Molly did not know how much starstuff the locket contained. And she had no idea how much starstuff it took to make a camel fly. As she watched the glowing golden stream pour onto the camel, she desperately hoped it was enough.

There were shouts from both sides, as the four pursuers, organized now, all lunged toward George and Molly at the same moment, their swords flashing out and striking . . .

. . . air.

One of the riders had thrust so hard that he fell sideways off his camel. The other three could only gape as Molly and George rose swiftly out of their reach on the back of what was, at that moment, the happiest camel there had ever been.

—◦—

Peter flew as fast as he could, which was very fast indeed. He had not flown for what seemed like weeks, and despite the unhappy circumstances, it felt good to once again have the wind streaming past his face and to see the ground racing beneath him.

The fallen starstuff pulled him. He couldn't see it yet, but he knew it was there because of the warmth, and also because he just *knew*. He swooped down to gain still more speed, then soared up high, coming over a huge dune that overlooked a valley.

And there it was.

He couldn't actually see it, any more than he could see the sun at midday; its light was too bright to be viewed directly. But the fallen starstuff was there at the bottom of the valley, filling it with brilliance, turning the sand into gold for a mile and more in every direction. Peter leaned and turned left in a long graceful curve, getting his bearings, making sure he would be able to lead Glotz and Zarboff to this place.

As he headed back toward the caravan, Peter tried to think only about James and the others. He was doing this for them; he *had* to do this for them. He tried not to think about the price that would be paid for saving his friends—the unimaginable glowing power in the valley behind him, which was about to be turned over to Glotz, to Zarboff, to the Others.

To Ombra.

Peter tried not to think about it, but it wasn't easy.

CHAPTER 38

CINK'S IDEA

"HOW LONG DO YOU THINK we should stay up here?" said George.

"The starstuff will wear off in time," said Molly.

"I know," said George, looking down a bit nervously at the desert far below. "I'm just wondering what will happen if it wears off too quickly, with us all the way up here. We've left those men far behind; perhaps we should descend." To the camel, he said, "Down! Down, camel!"

The camel paid no attention. Tink, sitting between the camel's ears, turned, and with an annoyed look, said something to George which he did not understand, but which definitely did not sound complimentary.

"I think Tink is guiding the camel someplace," said Molly.

"I wish she'd tell us where," said George.

Tink made an exasperated face, then looked forward again.

They flew in silence for ten more minutes, then Molly, looking down, said, "I think it's wearing off."

George looked; she was right. The camel was descending—not too rapidly, but rapidly enough to make both George and Molly a bit nervous. The camel's stomach was also making unhappy sounds. Tink began chiming into the camel's ear. In response, it turned its head a bit to the right, putting them into a gentle turn. More chimes, and the camel straightened; Molly and George could see that they were going to come down near the top of an exceptionally large dune. From beyond the dune, Molly saw a glow in the sky— a light even brighter than the fast-rising desert sun. At the same time she saw it, she felt it.

"Starstuff," she said.

"What?" said George. "Where?"

"Ahead, there, that glow," she said. "It's starstuff. A lot of it."

"How do you know?"

"Believe me: I know."

The camel, making odd noises, descended quite rapidly now. As it neared the dune, Tink urgently chimed something to it, and it leaned its head back hard, groaning with the effort. The descent slowed just enough, and the camel landed on the sand, stumbling a bit but maintaining its balance. As soon as it stopped, it went down on its knees and emitted a sigh that suggested it did not intend to rise anytime soon.

That suited George and Molly; they quickly extricated themselves from the saddle and climbed down to the sand.

Molly immediately set off up the dune, Tink alongside her. When they reached the crest, Molly gasped and shielded her eyes from the brilliant glow. She turned around, waving George away.

"It's here, in this valley," she said. "There must be a massive quantity of it. We can't get any closer."

"Do you suppose that's why we saw those lights in the sky?" said George.

"Must be," said Molly. "It must have just fallen. All these years I've heard of starstuff Falls, and how much effort the Starcatchers have gone to, trying to find it. And now here it happens just a few miles from me."

"And from the capital of Rundoon," said George.

"Yes," agreed Molly. "Quite a coincidence, this happening here."

"You don't really think it's a coincidence, do you?"

"No," said Molly. "Of course I don't. I think the Others made it happen somehow." She frowned. "Which means soon they'll be along to collect it."

"Can we collect it first?" said George.

"No," said Molly. "We'd need special suits, gold ones, like the one Father had at Stonehenge. Nobody can get anywhere near that much starstuff. Except Peter, of course. He has survived it. But nobody else could."

Tink was in Molly's face now, chiming something.

"I'm sorry, Tinker Bell," said Molly. "I don't understand you."

Tink, rolling her eyes, did a slow pantomime. She pointed at herself, then she pointed over the crest of the dune toward the glow. Then she pointed at the empty locket around Molly's neck.

"I'm sorry, Tink, I don't . . ."

Tink impatiently repeated the pantomime; this time, at the end, she took hold of the locket and tugged on the chain.

"She wants your locket," said George.

"Yes," said Molly, "but wh . . . Ah, I see. She's saying she can fly to the starstuff. It won't hurt her."

Tink nodded encouragingly and tugged on the locket again.

"Ah!" said Molly. "She wants to refill my locket with starstuff."

Tink beamed.

"All right," said Molly, unclasping the locket and handing it to Tink. "I suppose it can't hurt. But I'm not sure what good it will do us. You can take only a tiny amount; there will still be . . ."

But Tink, clutching the locket in her tiny hands, was already gone.

CHAPTER 39

An Ugly Smile

Peter, flying well above the dunes, saw a line of dark dots crawling across the endless sand. The caravan! He angled his body downward. Two minutes later he was alighting next to the cage that held his friends.

Zarboff occupied the throne set atop the carpet in his carriage. A guard stood next to him, holding an umbrella to protect the king from the sun. Aside from the throne, there was nowhere to sit in the carriage, so Viktor Glotz lay sprawled on the carpet. He leapt up when Peter landed.

"Did you find it?" he asked eagerly.

"It's that way," Peter said, pointing.

"How far?" said Zarboff.

Peter thought about it. "Eight miles," he said. "Or nine. You'll follow this valley between the dunes."

"Good," said Zarboff. He clapped his hands and barked an order in the Rundoon language. Peter felt strong hands grab both of his arms. Two soldiers dragged him roughly toward the wagon carrying the cage that contained James and the others.

"You don't need to do this," Peter shouted to Zarboff. "I made a promise, and I'll keep it! I won't try to escape."

"No," said Zarboff. "You won't."

The guards opened the cage door and shoved Peter inside. The door clanged shut. James, Thomas, Prentiss, and Tubby Ted barely acknowledged Peter; they looked hot, tired, listless.

"They've given us no water," said James. "None at all."

Sitting in the back of the wagon, next to the pile of golden suits, were Slightly and the other slave boys, looking not much better than the boys in the cage. Peter and Slightly exchanged a look; Peter thought he detected pity in the other boy's face. Peter started to say something, but Slightly, nodding toward the guards, shook his head.

Orders were shouted, and the caravan started up again, moving slowly across the desert, toward the starstuff. From his shaded throne in the front, Zarboff turned around and looked back. His eyes found Peter's. Then he reached out his hand and, smiling an ugly smile, patted the basket containing his snake.

CHAPTER 40

A Voice in the Sky

Whatever Tink was doing with Molly's locket, it was taking her quite a while. George and Molly grew increasingly hot and thirsty as they sat on the sand, trying to get some shade from the camel.

"What do we do when she gets back?" said George. "Make the camel fly again?"

"I don't know," said Molly. "We need to find Maknar, because that's where Father was going, and that's where Peter is. But I don't know how far it is, or which direction. I'm hoping Tink will take us there."

"What about the starstuff?" said George, nodding toward the glow at the crest of the dune, still brighter than the desert sun.

"We need to tell Father about that," said Molly. "He'll want to . . . Here comes Tink!"

Tink was streaking over the crest of the dune, clutching

the locket, which she dropped into Molly's waiting hands. The locket felt warm; Molly could sense the power it contained.

"Thank you, Tink," she said. "Now we need to get to Maknar as qu—"

Tink interrupted with a burst of chimes, shaking her head urgently.

"What?" said Molly. "You don't want us to go to Maknar?"

Tink nodded vigorously.

"But why not?" said Molly.

Tink pointed toward the crest of the dune. She made a soft chiming sound, pointed to her own heart, and then pointed to Molly's heart.

"Oh," said Molly. "I see."

"What is it?" said George.

"It's Peter," said Molly, her face brightening. "He's close."

———⋅◆⋅———

They were within two miles of the starstuff now; Peter could feel it and could see the radiant glow ahead, turning the blue sky nearly white. The caravan had skirted around the huge dune from which he had viewed the starstuff Fall; it now towered over them, to the right. Ahead, in the valley, lay the starstuff.

The caravan kept moving until the glare became too

bright for it to continue. There it stopped, and under Glotz's supervision, the soldiers unstrapped the gold-hinged chest from the camel and lowered it to the ground. Glotz then came back to the wagon carrying the boys, both caged and uncaged.

"Put on the suits," he said.

With no enthusiasm, Slightly and three of the other slave boys picked up the gold-mesh suits and began putting them on. One suit was considerably larger than the others; Glotz put this on himself. He checked the boys' suits to make sure that they had their headpieces fastened tightly, with no open seams at their necks. They now looked like strange golden beings, their faces covered with fine gold mesh.

"You will keep your suits on until I tell you to remove them," said Glotz. "If you remove them any sooner, you will die. Do you understand?"

The four gold-covered heads nodded.

Glotz led them over to the trunk, which was sitting on the sand next to the camel. Glotz unlatched it and opened the lid; Peter could see that, as he suspected, the trunk was lined with gold. Glotz reached inside and lifted out two small golden shovels. He inspected these, nodded, and put them back into the trunk.

"Pick it up," he said to the boys. They lifted the trunk, grunting at the formidable weight.

"Oddly enough, it will be lighter once it is full," said

Glotz, chuckling at his own statement. He turned toward Zarboff and said, "We should be back within the hour."

Peter watched through the bars until the tall, gleaming figure of Glotz disappeared into the brilliant glow of the valley, with the golden-garbed boys trudging behind, carrying the chest. His attention then shifted to Zarboff, who was directing his men to remove the throne and carpet from his carriage and carry them back toward the wagon. They unrolled the carpet onto the sand next to the cage containing Peter and the others, and they set the throne down on top of it, facing the boys. Zarboff then sat on the throne. The guard with the umbrella stood behind, shading him.

Zarboff looked at the boys for a few moments, his eyes lingering on Peter. Then he clapped his hands and said something in the Rundoon language. Two soldiers trotted over to the king's carriage. As the boys watched in horror, they picked up the big basket and carried it over to the carpet, setting it next to the king. He reached out his hand, resting it on the basket lid, gently drumming his fingers, clearly enjoying the look on the boys' faces.

Then he began to whistle. The basket lid lifted.

Peter, struggling to sound calm as the enormous head emerged from the basket, said, "You told me if I came back, you wouldn't hurt my friends."

"No, stupid boy," said Zarboff. "I said if you *didn't* return, I would feed your friends to Kundalini. And I would have. It just so happens that I planned to do the same thing whether you returned or not."

"But that's not fair!" pleaded Peter.

"Fair?" sneered Zarboff. "Do you think it matters to me what is *fair*?"

The snake eased out of the basket, its massive head sliding across the carpet toward the cage. James, Prentiss, Thomas, and Tubby Ted backed against the far wall of the cage. Peter's mind raced, looking for arguments.

"If you kill me," he said, "you won't have anyone to find the starstuff."

Zarboff smiled. He gestured toward the glow in the sky. "You've already told us where to find it. And have no fear: we will use that starstuff to get even more—all we want— more starstuff than the Starcatchers ever dreamed of. We don't need you anymore."

The snake's tail slipped out of the basket now; its long, thick body slithered easily across the carpet. It raised its head to the cage bars, flicking its tongue toward Peter's bare legs. Peter jerked backward, away from the probing tongue.

"I think Kundalini likes you," said Zarboff. "Perhaps if you're lucky he will eat you first and spare you the agony of seeing your friends consumed."

The snake, trying to get to Peter, pressed against the cage bars, but its head was too large to fit through. Zarboff barked some orders, and three soldiers came running over. One of them, keeping a wary eye on Kundalini, opened the cage door; the other two stood next to the opening with swords drawn, to prevent the boys from escaping.

The soldiers stepped back as Kundalini thrust his massive head through the opening. Peter backed against the far wall of the cage with the other boys. They watched in horror as the snake entered the cage. Prentiss screamed. Zarboff, seeking a better view, rose from his throne and stepped forward.

Neither Zarboff nor his soldiers, intent on watching the drama in the cage, saw what Peter saw: a shadow flying toward them across the sand. None of them looked up until the sound came from overhead—the sound of a young man and a young woman shouting. Peter thought the voices sounded familiar. He glanced up, but in the glare of the sun he couldn't see anything more than a dark, flying shape. Quite a *large* flying shape, in fact.

Some of the soldiers looked up, too. They began shouting and pointing as they realized that the flying shape was, impossible though it seemed . . . a camel.

For a moment, Kundalini was forgotten, as all faces turned skyward, including the face of King Zarboff the Third, whose mouth fell open in amazement. This was unfortunate for him, for it was at exactly that moment that the flying camel, on Tink's chimed command, released a long pent-up load of camel dung, which fell directly and massively onto His Royal Highness's upturned face. He roared in rage and began to stagger around blindly, screaming for someone to wipe his face; his men raced to help him but were hindered by the flying camel, which was making low swoops back and forth across the area, continuing to emit dung bombs.

"Tink!" shouted Peter, hearing the familiar bells. She answered with a chime and swooped down to him, darting through the cage bars and dropping something into his hand. He looked down: it was Molly's locket. Tink was at his ear, chiming as loud as she could.

The snake!

Peter looked and saw that Kundalini, who was not going to be distracted from a tasty meal by a flying camel, was only inches away, preparing to wrap its first deadly coil around Peter.

Peter flipped open Molly's locket. His hand was instantly enveloped in a radiant sphere of golden light. He reached down and poured some starstuff onto Kundalini's head. The effect was immediate: the huge snake reared back like a snake charmer's cobra and began to rise with a spiraling motion. In a moment its entire body had lifted off the floor of the cage. The head turned slowly until it found the still-open cage door, and then it spiraled out of the cage. The appearance of a flying snake had the effect of further disconcerting the soldiers, who were still dodging the flying camel while trying to assist their king, who was wandering blindly into the desert, screaming for somebody to wipe his face.

With Kundalini gone, there was nothing between the boys and the open, unguarded cage door. Peter grabbed the still-stunned Prentiss and Thomas and shoved them toward the opening; James did the same for Tubby Ted. The boys clambered out and jumped from the wagon onto the carpet where Zarboff had been sitting on his throne. Peter looked around: the soldiers were all preoccupied with the swooping camel, the flying snake, and their highly irate king. But the moment would not last. They had to get out of there. But how?

"Get them!" screamed Zarboff. The king was pointing at Peter and the others. Soldiers were running toward them.

Peter looked down at Molly's locket. And the carpet.

The carpet.

With a flick of his wrist, Peter dumped the locket's contents onto the carpet. In the next second, it was six feet off the ground and rising so fast that all the boys, even Peter, lost their balance and fell.

"Help!" yelled Ted, who was falling off the edge. Peter lunged and grabbed him, managing to pull him back onto the flying carpet just as a soldier's sword sliced the air where his legs had been. Soon the carpet was well out of reach, rising weightlessly, balloonlike, into the desert sky. They passed by the sinking Kundalini and left behind the furious, frustrated screams of His Royal—and currently quite smelly—Highness King Zarboff the Third.

"Hello, Peter!" called a voice, a very familiar voice, one that made Peter's stomach flutter in a way that was not at all unpleasant. Peter looked up and saw her, looking quite self-assured on the back of a flying camel, and such was the joy in Peter's heart that he even managed to muster a lukewarm fondness at the sight of George.

"Hello, Molly," he called back.

"I suppose we should get out of here, before we start to come down," she said.

"Yes," said Peter. "I suppose we should."

They stared at each other for a few more seconds, which was longer than Tink could tolerate.

I'm the one who rescued you, remember? she chimed unnecessarily loudly into Peter's ear.

"Of course, Tink," said Peter, still looking at Molly.

"What did she say?" said Molly.

"She says it's wonderful to see you again," said Peter.

CHAPTER 41

OASIS

*T*HE CARPET WAS DESCENDING—and sagging in the middle—as the starstuff wore off. Behind the carpet, the camel
carrying Molly and George was also rapidly losing altitude.

Peter, shielding his eyes from the glare of the sun,
scanned the horizon. Far in the distance he could see the
spires and sprawl of Maknar. Otherwise there was nothing
but an endless sea of sand.

Then he spotted it—a patch of green in the vast expanse
of desert.

"To the right!" Peter shouted. Holding the edges, he and
the other boys leaned right, steering the carpet. They didn't
have quite enough lift to make it to the oasis and came down
a bit short. Behind them, the camel—now an experienced
flyer—landed without so much as a stumble.

The noonday sun had turned the sand to fire; the boys had
not had a drop to drink for hours. So when Peter pointed to

the palm trees and said, "Water," the race was on. In a minute, James, Tubby Ted, Prentiss, and Thomas were plunging their heads into a small pond in the shade of a towering palm.

Peter was thirsty, too, as were George and Molly. But instead of racing to the oasis, the three of them stood in an awkward triangle on the blistering sand. They had not seen each other since London, the day after that terrifying night at Stonehenge. They had much to say to each other, but nobody knew how to start.

Molly broke the silence, stepping forward and giving Peter a hug, which made his face even redder than the sun already had.

"I'm so glad we found you," she said.

"I'm glad you did, too," said Peter. "Thanks." He straightened up, making himself as tall as he could, although he was no longer as tall as Molly, and never would be again.

I'm the one who found you, noted Tink, landing possessively on Peter's head.

Peter, ignoring her, turned to George. They shook hands awkwardly.

"Thanks to you as well, George," said Peter.

"It was nothing," said George.

That's true, said Tink.

"Be quiet, Tink," said Peter. He turned back to Molly. "Molly, I've so much to tell you. Your father—"

"Where is he?" said Molly.

"In Zarboff's dungeon," said Peter. "He was brought in with another man."

"Bakari," said Molly, her face falling. "This is awful."

"It's worse than you know," said Peter. "First of all, Ombra is still alive. And he's here."

"But how can . . ."

"I don't know," interrupted Peter. "But he's definitely here, along with others like him, and they're controlling Zarboff and the Others. They're after starstuff, Molly, but they don't just wait for it to fall. They can *make* it fall. They made it fall last night."

"The lights in the sky," said Molly softly.

Peter nodded.

"How did they make it fall?" said George.

"They sent up a rocket," said Peter.

"A *what?*" said George.

As George and Molly listened with growing amazement, Peter told them about Viktor Glotz and the huge, monkey-piloted rocket. George had many questions about the rocket, which Peter answered as best he could. When he was finished, Molly said, "So they send up starstuff to bring down *more* starstuff?"

"Yes," said Peter. "They call it a . . . a Disruption. And when they collect the starstuff they've just brought down, they plan to send it up in another rocket—they've one left— and it will . . ." He hesitated.

"It will what?" said Molly.

"Glotz said it will change the universe," said Peter.

"That's nonsense," said George.

"Well, it's what he said," snapped Peter.

"Then he's insane," said George.

"Is he?" said Molly. "Seems to me his plan to make starstuff fall wasn't insane."

George reddened. Peter enjoyed that sight, but only for a moment. "Anyway," Peter said, "whatever they plan to do with the starstuff, they have it now, thanks to me."

"What do you mean?" said Molly.

"I mean," said Peter, "I led them right to it." He told Molly how Zarboff had threatened to kill his mates with the snake if he refused to cooperate. He spoke with his face down, unwilling to look Molly in the eye. When he was finished, she put her hand on his forearm.

"Don't blame yourself, Peter," she said softly. "You had no choice."

Peter nodded. "The odd thing is," he said, "they *knew* I would be able to find the starstuff. They—Ombra—brought me here from the island just to find it for them. They said they used my parents for the same thing. I never even knew who my parents were, or whether they were alive. And they were *here*, Molly!"

Molly and George exchanged a significant look.

"What is it?" said Peter. "Do you know something about my parents?"

"Yes," said Molly. Peter listened intently, his eyes locked on hers as she told him what she had learned on her trip with George to Oxford—the notices placed in the newspaper by the mysterious Mr. Pan; the disappearance of Pan and his wife at the same time that Peter, as a baby, was placed in St. Norbert's Home for Wayward Boys.

"Pan," said Peter. "That's my name, then? Peter Pan?" Nobody at St. Norbert's had ever told him that.

"Yes," said Molly.

"And my father . . . my parents . . . they worked with the Starcatchers?"

"Yes," said Molly again. "They warned us when the starstuff was going to fall. Somehow they could predict it. The Others brought you here because they knew you could, too."

"But I *didn't* predict it," said Peter. "I only felt it after it fell."

Molly thought about that for a moment, then said, "Well, somehow you have a special connection to the starstuff, as your parents did."

"The Others forced my parents to help them," said Peter bitterly. "And now they've forced me to do the same thing. Thanks to me, they have all the starstuff they need for whatever they have planned."

"This Glotz fellow," said George. "Did he say when they were going to send up the last rocket and . . . change the universe?"

"Yes," said Peter, thinking back. "He said something odd, about a . . . shower. In two days, he said."

"The Leonid shower!" said George.

"What's that?" said Molly.

"A huge meteorite shower," said George. "It happens only once every thirty-three years. I believe it peaks after only a few nights. That must be when this Glotz fellow intends to send up the rocket."

"Then we must stop him," said Molly.

"How?" said Peter.

"First, we must get Father and Bakari out of that dungeon," said Molly.

"That won't be easy," said Peter.

"Well, we must," said Molly.

She likes to give orders, observed Tink.

"Yes, she does," agreed Peter.

"What did she say?" Molly asked suspiciously.

"She said you look thirsty," said Peter. He gestured toward the oasis, with its beckoning pool of shaded water. The three of them began walking that way. Tink, riding on Peter's head, cocked her head, then took off and flew high into the sky. She returned a minute later, landing on Peter's shoulder with a brief burst of bells. He nodded to her, then turned back to Molly, who was outlining her plan.

"Before we get to Maknar," she was saying, "you and the other boys will need robes."

"We've no money to buy them robes," said George.

"No," said Peter, "but we have a very fine carpet." He grinned. "A carpet fit for a king, in fact. I'm sure we could trade it for robes."

"Who are we going to trade with out here in the middle of the desert?" said George.

"The caravan," said Peter.

"What caravan?" said George.

"The one on the other side of that dune," said Peter, "approaching the oasis now." He winked at Tink.

In half an hour's time they had traded King's Zarboff carpet to the caravan merchants for five robes, some bread, and skins for carrying water. It was clear from the eagerness with which the merchants had accepted the trade that the children were getting a terribly unfair bargain, but they were satisfied. And so, as the afternoon sun burned in the desert sky, seven robed figures—and one camel—began trudging across the sand toward the spires of Maknar.

CHAPTER 42

QUESTIONS

LEONARD ASTER HEARD IT COMING: a wheezing sound in the dungeon passageway. He'd been up all night worrying, awaiting the return of Peter and the boys. The barred hole in the dungeon wall allowed little light to penetrate their gloomy cell, but by his reckoning it was now broad daylight outside.

Too long . . .

He leaned down and shook awake the dozing form of Bakari.

"Wake up," he whispered. "Ombra is coming."

As Bakari quickly rose, the dark shape glided into view, stopping in front of the cell. The air grew colder; the groaning voice spoke.

"Good morning, Lord Aster," said Ombra. "I trust you slept well."

"Where are the boys?" said Leonard.

"That is precisely what I am here to find out," said Ombra.

"What are you talking about?" said Leonard. But before he could answer, Ombra had stretched taller and thinner. He slipped through the cell bars, moving toward Leonard's shadow on the stone floor. Leonard took a step back, but Ombra was too quick, and there was no escaping it: Ombra touched his shadow. The last thing Leonard felt was intense cold, starting at his feet and quickly sweeping up through his body, as if his blood were turning to ice.

The next thing he knew, he was lying on the floor.

"Are you all right?" asked Bakari, kneeling over him.

"Yes," said Leonard, struggling to get up. "What . . ." He stopped, seeing that Ombra was still in the cell, standing in its darkest corner, away from the dim light seeping through the window.

"My apologies for your discomfort, Lord Aster," groaned Ombra. "I needed to find out if you have been in touch with your daughter."

"Molly? Where is she?"

"I do not know at the moment. When Zarboff's men reached the ship, she was gone. And then early this morning above the desert, a young lady appeared on a flying camel."

Leonard smiled despite himself. "Molly," he said.

"I assume so," groaned Ombra. "I was not there, but she fits the description given by the soldiers. She was with a young man. They caused some confusion, during which they managed to liberate the flying boy and his friends."

"They escaped," said Leonard, relief sweeping through him.

"Yes," groaned Ombra. "But it makes no difference now. We have the starstuff we need to carry out our plan."

Leonard's smile faded.

"I assume," groaned Ombra, "you saw the celestial display early this morning?"

Leonard nodded. "Rather impossible to miss. Starstuff, I assume. But how could it fall here in Rundoon? What kind of coincidence could—"

"No coincidence at all," groaned Ombra. "We caused it. A rocket constructed by a scientist, Dr. Viktor Glotz. "

"He *caused* a starstuff Fall?" said Bakari.

"Yes," wheezed Ombra. "It has taken years to perfect the technique—years we have spent patiently waiting. But now . . ." He stepped slightly out of the shadows. "Now we have a great deal of starstuff. Now we are ready."

"Ready for what?" said Leonard. Ombra's hood turned toward him. He saw the eyelike spheres glowing red in the gloom; he felt the chill deepen.

"I have a question for you, Lord Aster," Ombra groaned. "Do you know what starstuff is?"

"No," said Leonard. "Only what it can do."

"Do you wonder why it falls to Earth?"

"Of course."

"I will tell you," said Ombra. "I do not have to, of course. But we have time, and I am eager to see your reaction when you grasp the *scale* of what is going to happen. You Star-catchers are but a very small part of a very large struggle—a struggle as immense as the universe itself. Tonight that struggle will end." The red orbs inside the hood flashed even brighter. "Everything will change, forever."

The red orbs glowed brighter. The cell grew still colder.

"Everything," repeated Ombra. "Forever."

CHAPTER 43

SHINING PEARL'S IDEA

SHINING PEARL CROUCHED at the entrance to the cave, peering out through the rain. Behind her, the pirates sat in the dirt, exhausted, wet, hungry, miserable.

"D'you see anything?" whispered Smee.

"No," whispered Shining Pearl. "I think they're gone."

"Now what?" said one of the men.

It was a good question. The Scorpions seemed to be everywhere, patrolling in groups of four or five men, scouring the island's jungle hillsides and valleys. Twice in the past sleepless day the pirates had come very close to being spotted; they would surely have been caught by now, had it not been for Shining Pearl's intimate knowledge of the island's geography. But they could not run forever. Sooner or later, the Scorpions would find them. The pirates understood this now; Shining Pearl could see it on their faces. She judged that now was the time to tell them about her idea.

"We have two choices," she said.

They were all watching her.

"We can keep running," she said. "There are other caves. If we're careful, moving by night, keeping quiet, we might be able to avoid them for a while longer."

The men looked around at the dank, dark cave.

"What's the other choice?" said the pirate named Hurky.

Shining Pearl took a deep breath. "We attack them," she said.

Hurky laughed, a harsh bark. "*Us*, attack *them*?"

"Yes," said Shining Pearl.

"But," said Smee, "we don't have . . . that is, what would . . . I mean . . . How?"

"Do you have any clothing belonging to Captain Hook?" said Shining Pearl.

Smee frowned. "I b'lieve the cap'n's old pants is back at the fort. I made him a new pair from sailcloth, but I was going to patch his old ones." He frowned more deeply still. "But what does the cap'n's pants have to do with attacking them Scorpions?"

Shining Pearl explained her plan. When she was done, the pirates sat quietly for a moment. Hurky broke the silence.

"Seems to me," he said, "that it probably won't work."

The men nodded.

"But it also seems to me," said Hurky, "that it's better

than spending the rest of our days hiding in caves, waiting for them to kill us."

The men nodded again. They turned to Smee, who looked back at them, puzzled, until it dawned on him that a decision had been made and that it was up to him as acting captain to express it.

"All right, then," he said to Shining Pearl, "let's carry out your plan."

CHAPTER 44

A LEAK IN THE UNIVERSE

"THE FIRST THING YOU MUST UNDERSTAND," groaned Ombra, "is that humanity is an accident. You, who think you are the center of creation, are in fact here because of a flaw in the cosmos."

"I have no idea what you're talking about," said Leonard.

"No," said Ombra, "you would not. You humans are so involved with the details of your tiny lives that you never notice the immense struggle beyond this insignificant speck you call the world."

"Then perhaps you will be so kind as to enlighten me."

"I will try," groaned Ombra, "though it will be difficult for you to comprehend, given the limitations of human thought and language. To put it as simply as I can: there are two conflicting sides in what you call the universe. On one side is creation, being, light; on the other side is destruction, nothingness, darkness."

"And you are on the side of darkness," said Leonard.

"I am not only on the *side* of darkness," groaned Ombra. "I *am* darkness."

"And the Others?" said Bakari.

"The humans that you call the Others are unimportant. They do what I wish them to do, without knowing why. Like you Starcatchers, they are pawns in a game they do not understand."

"If we're so insignificant," said Leonard, "then why are you here, interfering in our affairs?"

"I will explain," groaned Ombra. "But you must first understand some history. The struggle between light and darkness has gone on since the beginning of what you call time. It was going on before there *was* time, though I do not expect you to know what I mean by that. What you need to know is this: for the past several billion of your years, light has been winning the struggle. The side of existence, of being, is expanding. The side of nothingness, of darkness— my side—is retreating. We have survived in pockets, in voids of darkness; one such void is . . . not far from here. But we are losing. We are being driven back everywhere, by a force we cannot match."

"Starstuff," said Bakari.

"Yes," said Ombra. "Starstuff. It flows outward across the universe from a point called the Beginning. Where there was nothing, it creates something. It leaves stars in its wake, galaxies, structures bigger than galaxies, and structures bigger than those. Along the way it also leaves incalculable quantities of smaller, random clots of matter and gas—comets, asteroids, rocks, dust particles—and planets. There are untold millions of planets about the same size as your Earth, did you know that, Lord Aster? I see by your expression that you did not. You humans believe you are unique. And in a sense, you are correct. Because of all these untold millions of planets, yours alone is located near the flaw."

"What flaw?" said Leonard.

"In the starstuff conduit," said Ombra. "It passes very close to Earth. You cannot see it; it does not exist in the same way that ordinary matter exists. But it is there nonetheless, carrying starstuff from the Beginning to the remote reaches of the universe, as an aqueduct carries water. But there is a flaw, and sometimes it causes a leak in the aqueduct. This is known as a Disruption, and when it occurs, a tiny quantity of starstuff escapes and enters your reality."

"A starstuff Fall," said Bakari.

"Yes," said Ombra. "It has been falling here for quite some time. That is the reason life came to exist on this barren rock in the first place. That is the reason this life acquired intelligence. You humans, and what you call your civilization, are here because of a leak in the plumbing of the universe."

"And is that why you've come?" said Leonard. "To retrieve this leaked starstuff?"

"No," said Ombra. "We have come for far more than that. But to understand it, you will need to indulge me for a bit longer."

Leonard nodded.

Ombra continued: "As humans gained in intelligence, they began to understand the power of the starstuff. Some humans wanted to use it to dominate; other humans wanted to prevent them from doing so. This led to the struggle between the Others and you Starcatchers. This struggle went on for thousands of years before it was noticed."

"Noticed by whom?" said Leonard.

"By my enemies," said Ombra. "By the powers of light. Their attention had been focused elsewhere in the universe, on their struggle against my side, against darkness. When they finally saw what their starstuff Falls on Earth had caused—the development of intelligent life and the conflict between the Starcatchers and the Others—they felt responsible and decided to intervene. Had my side been in control, we would have simply eliminated your troublesome planet. But the powers of light choose not to destroy life."

"Good for them," muttered Leonard.

"As you will see in a moment," said Ombra, "it is *not* good for them. But to continue: the powers of light felt responsible for you humans and chose to set up a mechanism to prevent you from using the starstuff to destroy yourselves. That mechanism was the Watchers."

"Watchers?" said Leonard, exchanging a glance with Bakari.

"Yes," said Ombra. "Watchers are beings with certain abilities, including the ability to sense an impending Disruption. These Watchers were put here on Earth, in very small numbers, to warn the Starcatchers, so you could retrieve starstuff Falls before the Others could get to them. Centuries ago the Watchers showed your ancestors how to return the starstuff. Your ancestors passed this knowledge along to you, as I learned during our unpleasant encounter at Stonehenge, when you were able to return the starstuff that we retrieved, and that you Starcatchers managed to get away from us."

"We barely got it back," said Leonard. "We were never warned about that Fall."

"No," said Ombra. "*We* were warned. For the past twelve years, the only Watcher on Earth has been working for us."

"Peter's parents," said Leonard.

"Very good, Lord Aster," groaned Ombra. "But not both his parents. Only his father. He made a mistake, unusual for a Watcher. He fell in love with an ordinary human. He married her. They had a child. That gave us the control we needed. To save his wife and child, he had to work for our side, the shadows."

"But," said Bakari, "didn't your enemies—the powers of light—notice that they lost their Watcher twelve years ago?"

"No," said Ombra. "As I have said, their attention is focused elsewhere in the universe, and twelve years is nothing in the time span of this struggle. The powers of light have no reason to believe anything is wrong on Earth. And when they discover the effects of what we're about to do, it will be far too late."

"What do you intend to do?" said Leonard softly.

"At last," groaned Ombra, "we come to the present. You have no doubt noticed the tall metal structure in the courtyard outside."

Leonard and Bakari nodded.

"A rocket, designed by Dr. Glotz. He is quite intelligent, for a human; we have enhanced this intelligence by exposing him to controlled doses of starstuff. Since this exposure, he has been using his talents to exploit the flaw in the conduit. He has made remarkable progress. He developed a means to send up a rocket containing a small quantity of starstuff, thereby causing a Disruption that brings down a larger quantity. That is how he caused the Scotland Fall. More recently he has learned to control the location of the Fall, as he did this morning. That starstuff was located for us by the Watcher's son, Peter, who apparently has inherited at least some of his father's powers. It is a very large quantity of starstuff we now have in our possession. Tonight, Dr. Glotz will send it up in the rocket, to be released at precisely the right moment during the Leonid meteor shower. You will want to be looking out your cell window when it happens. Dr. Glotz assures me that it will be quite spectacular. But there is another reason why you should watch, Lord Aster."

"Why is that?"

Ombra's eyes glowed brightly in the cell gloom.

"Because," he said, "it is the last thing that you, and all other humans, will ever see."

The cell was silent for a moment.

"I don't understand," said Leonard.

"You will never understand," said Ombra. "As I said, the limitations of your language—and, with all due respect, your minds—render the concept beyond your grasp. I will leave it at this: if Dr. Glotz is correct—and I am confident that he is—the extreme, sudden shock to the starstuff flow caused by the rocket tonight will cause it to reverse, like a wave hitting a wall. The result will be an immediate stop to the expansion of the universe. It will actually begin to contract. This Reversal will happen with inconceivable swiftness. In less than a moment, all light and all it has ever created, will be gone. All of it—from the tiniest mote of dust, to your precious Earth, to the galaxies themselves—all gone back to before the Beginning. Before time. In their place: timelessness and nothingness. And we will rule in darkness, as we once did. Forever."

Leonard and Bakari stared at the red orbs for several long moments. Bakari broke the silence.

"Why are the Others helping you, if it will cause their deaths?" he said.

"The Others are humans: ignorant fools," said Ombra. "Zarboff knows only that there will be more starstuff. He does not think beyond that."

"But surely Dr. Glotz knows what he is bringing about," said Leonard.

"He trusts his theories," said Ombra. "But he cares only about one thing: that in his last instant of existence, before the Reversal, before everything becomes nothing again, he will have proved his theory correct."

"He's insane," whispered Leonard.

"That hardly makes him unique among you humans."

Again the cell was silent. When Leonard spoke again, his voice was hoarse.

"You won't win, you know," he said.

He felt the red orbs gazing intently at him. He forced himself not to look away.

"And why is that, Lord Aster?" Ombra said.

"Because," said Leonard, "light overcomes darkness. A tiny match can illuminate the darkest room. As long as there is some light somewhere in the universe, you can be defeated."

"But that is precisely the point, Lord Aster," groaned Ombra. "What if there is no universe?"

Ombra kept his gaze on Leonard, as if awaiting a

response; Leonard had none. Finally Ombra turned and oozed back through the cell bars. Then he was gone, disappearing into the dungeon gloom, leaving Leonard and Bakari to look out the window at the bright desert day.

Perhaps the last day ever.

CHAPTER 45

DOOMED

*I*T TOOK THE CHILDREN HOURS to reach Maknar—hot, thirsty hours, with the city beckoning in the distance, a mosaic of sunbaked huts, hunchbacked palms, and the glinting spires of Zarboff's palace. The sea of sand played tricks on their eyes: sometimes, as they trudged forward, the city seemed to move farther away, like a desert mirage of shimmering blue water.

But finally they were standing in a bustling marketplace, doing their best to look inconspicuous in their newly acquired robes. Around them swirled the sounds of people bargaining, and a hundred scents—acrid sweat, sweet incense, coconut, spices. The camel, which had carried Tubby Ted, Prentiss, and Molly most of the way, let out a strange humming noise. Thomas led it to a water trough, from which it drank thirstily.

"What now?" James said. He intended the question for Peter, but it was Molly who answered.

"We must go to the palace," she said, "and free Father."

And be caught immediately, like a big stupid fish, observed Tink, who was hiding under Peter's robe.

"What'd she say?" asked Molly.

"She said the palace is heavily guarded," said Peter. "We can't just go barging in there, Molly."

"Well, we can't just stand here, either," said Molly. "People are starting to notice us."

This was true: even in the colorful chaos of the market, their group was drawing curious looks.

"All right," said Peter. He gestured for the group to gather, whistling to Tubby Ted, who was wandering toward the food stalls. When they had all huddled together, Peter spoke, his voice low.

"As I see it," he said, "we need to do two things. We need to free Lord Aster and Bakari. Then we need to get all of us out of here. We need a ship."

"We came by ship to Ashmar," said Molly. "But that's another long trip across the desert. I doubt we'd make it if we were being chased."

Peter nodded. "There are ships here," he said. "There's a harbor below the city. That's where Ombra brought us in his underwater ship. There were sailing ships there."

"Then perhaps we need to borrow one," said George, giving Molly a look.

"Do you think you could be in charge of that, George?"

said Peter. He was reluctant to admit it, but George was quite good at things like getting ships.

"My pleasure," said George.

"Good," said Peter. "So you, Molly, and the boys will get a ship and have it ready to sail. Tink and I will go to the palace and—"

"I'm going with you," said Molly.

No she's not, said Tink.

"No, you're not," said Peter. "Molly, think about it. Tink and I can fly. And we've been inside the dungeon. We know where we're going."

"He's my father," said Molly. She pulled out her locket. "And I have starstuff left. I can fly if I need to." Peter started to object, but she cut him off. "I'm going with you," she said, "like it or not."

Not, said Tink.

"All right," said Peter.

"Thank you," said Molly.

We're doomed, said Tink.

A few minutes later, with the plan settled, they left the market in two groups. George and the other boys headed toward the harbor, with George leading the camel. Molly and Peter, with Tink still tucked away, headed toward Zarboff's palace.

Peter eyed the looming spires, recalling how close Kundalini had come to making a meal of him and his mates.

He glanced at Molly, glad she was with him. But at the moment he had no idea how the two of them, and Tink, could possibly free Leonard Aster from Zarboff's dungeon. He also had grave doubts that George, capable as he was, would be able to procure a ship.

We're doomed, Tink said again.

"What did she say?" asked Molly.

"She says," replied Peter, "that this should be exciting."

CHAPTER 46

TINK'S MESSAGE

LEONARD ASTER SAT SLUMPED against the cell wall, staring at nothing. Next to him, Bakari, equally downhearted, rose to stretch his legs. He glanced out the small barred window, then moved closer for a better look.

"They are working on the rocket," he said.

Leonard rose quickly and stood next to Bakari. The blazing bright afternoon was yielding, slowly, to the softer light of evening. Across the courtyard, the rocket thrust its dark, tapering silhouette into the sky above the palace wall. A tall, thin man—Viktor Glotz, Leonard assumed—was supervising a crew of boys, who appeared to be about Peter's age. The boys were carrying buckets from a wagon to the rocket. Stationed around the rocket were a dozen soldiers armed with rifles; at least fifty more armed men were positioned around the courtyard. Many of the men were shading their eyes with their hands, scanning the sky.

"They're watching for Peter," said Leonard.

Bakari nodded. "Do you think he'll try to return?"

Leonard allowed himself a thin smile. "If I know Peter," he said, "he will indeed try to return." The smile faded. "But I don't see how he can get past all those rifles."

"Perhaps when it gets darker," said Bakari.

"Perhaps," said Leonard. "If it's not too late."

They stood in silence for another minute, watching the rocket preparations. Leonard was about to turn away when he thought he saw movement at the left edge of his vision. He pressed his face against the bars, straining to see in that direction, and saw it again: a darting glimmer against the sky.

"Tink," he whispered.

The tiny shape zigzagged closer as Leonard and Bakari watched anxiously, fearing that she would be spotted. But the soldiers were watching for something far larger. In a moment she had shot through the bars and was hovering in front of the men in their dim cell. She glanced at the corridor, and, seeing no guards within earshot, chimed quietly.

Peter sent me to you.

"Is he all right?" said Leonard.

Yes.

"And Molly?"

She's with Peter, chimed Tink, with a disapproving expression. *They're hiding. They're going to fly over the wall when it gets dark and the men can't see them. They're going to rescue you.*

Leonard shook his head. "No," he said. "Listen, Tinker Bell, this is very important. Tell Peter and Molly that rescuing us will have to wait. The important thing is that they must stop the rocket from going up. Do you understand?"

Tink nodded. *Don't rescue you. Stop the rocket from going up.*

"That's right. Good."

How?

"What?"

How do they stop the rocket?

Leonard rubbed his forehead. "I don't know," he said. "But they must stop it, somehow. If they don't, the world will be . . . there will be no world."

Tink had no response, which was unusual for her.

"Hurry, Tink," said Leonard, glancing out the cell window. "Tell them there isn't much time."

I'll tell them, said Tink. She shot through the bars, a streak of golden light. Bakari and Leonard watched her disappear over the palace wall. The sky was getting darker; soldiers were lighting torches in the courtyard.

"There isn't much time," repeated Leonard.

CHAPTER 47

MOLLY'S DECISION

TINK, ZOOMING THROUGH the darkening evening sky, found Peter and Molly where she'd left them—in a narrow alley between two buildings close to the outer palace wall. Ignoring Molly, Tink landed on Peter's shoulder and chimed into his ear for a full minute, Peter's frown deepening all the while.

"What is it?" asked Molly.

Peter, to her annoyance, held up a hand to quiet her, then said to Tink, "What did he mean by that?"

Tink chimed a few short tones.

Peter shook his head and said, "Strange."

"What?" said Molly, exasperated.

"Tink says your father doesn't want us to rescue him right now," said Peter.

"*What? Why not?*"

"He wants us to stop the rocket from going up."

"What rocket?"

"There's another rocket in the palace courtyard. Your father says if we don't stop it from going up, there will be no more . . ." Peter hesitated.

"No more what?" said Molly.

"No more . . . world," said Peter.

Molly stared at him. "What on earth does *that* mean?"

"I don't know," said Peter. "But he told Tink we haven't much time to stop it . . . the rocket. However it is you stop a rocket."

Molly looked at Tink, then at Peter. "Whatever Tink *thinks* she heard my father say," she said, "I still intend to go to him first."

The soft, golden glow that Tink usually radiated quickly turned to a deep maroon. She fired off a blast of bells.

"Molly," Peter said, "Tink says—"

"I don't care what Tink says," Molly snapped. "I'm going to find my father. I'm going to rescue him, with or without you!" She drew her locket out from under her robe.

Peter grabbed her arm. "Listen, Molly," he said, "we'll rescue your father, I promise. But he told Tink we have to stop the rocket first. Think about it. He wouldn't say that if it wasn't important."

Molly shook Peter's hand off. "You do as you please," she said. "I'm going to find my father *now*." She opened the locket. Instantly the alley filled with a golden glow. She raised the locket and carefully poured a small amount of starstuff onto herself. As the glow traveled the length of her body, she began to rise up into the sky, which was now a deep blue black.

"Molly!" Peter shouted. But before he could say another word, she leveled her body and disappeared over the rooftops. Peter braced to launch himself after her, but then stopped. He turned to Tink.

"Were there people working on the rocket?" he said.

Yes, chimed Tink.

"All right," he said. "We'll go see about the rocket first. Then we'll help Molly rescue her father."

If there's still a world, chimed Tink.

"Right," said Peter softly. "If there's still a world."

CHAPTER 48

THE SHIP WE WANT

GEORGE AND THE OTHER BOYS were hiding amid a cluster of wooden barrels, up a gentle hill from the harbor. As the sun descended, they listened to the bustle of the docks ease into the lazy murmur of evening. As dusk deepened to night, the boys raised their heads and surveyed the scene.

The harbor was shaped like a horseshoe, with five docks sticking out from the rocky shoreline. The docks were crowded with sailboats: some small fishing vessels, and some larger cargo ships. The sails were triangles, with spars connected to masts at odd angles.

"Those are strange-looking boats," said Prentiss.

"Never seen nothing like 'em," agreed Thomas.

George frowned. "You mean," he said, "you've never seen *anything* like them."

"That's what I said," said Thomas.

George sighed. "Those ships are called feluccas," he said.

"Ancient sailing craft. Quite all right for rivers and low seas, but sadly lacking for our needs."

"Yes," said Prentiss. "Sadly lacking, those feluccas." Thomas giggled. George, annoyed, was about to say something when James tugged his robe.

"What about that one?" he said. He was pointing to a tall mast directly below them.

George crept forward between the barrels for a better look. The other boys followed. "Ah," said George. "Now that's more like it. Dutch or French built. Square-rigged. Nearing a hundred feet, I'd say. Excellent, James!"

"But it's not in the water," Tubby Ted pointed out. He was right: the ship sat atop timbers, its stern aimed toward the sea.

"It's being repaired," said George.

"He wants to steal a broken ship," said Tubby Ted. Prentiss and Thomas snickered.

"We're not stealing," said George. "We're *borrowing*. And it's not necessarily broken; it's under repair. Painting, refitting, that sort of thing. It looks to me as though it's ready to be launched. But at the moment it has no crew, so we can easily take control."

"Right," said Prentiss. "Control of a ship that's *not in the water*." Thomas giggled again.

"Laugh if you want," said George. "But that's our ship. That's the only one that can get us home."

"But how do we get it into the water?" asked James.

"That's the problem," agreed George.

"Will there be food on the ship?" said Tubby Ted.

George ignored him, studying the ship. The sky was quite dark now, but there was light to see by, thanks to the fat moon just starting to peek over the horizon. Tubby Ted began to poke around among the barrels, in case one of them contained food. He noticed that one seemed to be leaking liquid from a seam. He sniffed the liquid, then took some on his finger and licked it.

"Umm," he said. "Not bad."

"Ted," said James. "This isn't the time to—"

"What is that?" said George, looking at Ted.

"I dunno," said Ted. "But it's not bad."

George dabbed his finger into the seeping liquid, then tasted it. His gaze went from the row of barrels down the hill to the ship. He smiled. "It's olive oil! Well done, Ted."

"You mean we can eat it?" said Ted.

"No," said George. "But we can definitely use it to our advantage."

CHAPTER 49

THE APPETIZER

SHINING PEARL AND THE PIRATE named Hurky crouched in the thick jungle around the clearing outside the gate to the pirate fort. By moonlight they could see that the gate hung partially open. They had been hiding there for half an hour, not moving a muscle, listening for Scorpion warriors but hearing only jungle sounds.

"They must have left," whispered Shining Pearl, finally.

"Or they're sleeping," said Hurky, his eyes on the fort.

"Either way," whispered Shining Pearl, "I'm going to go in."

Hurky looked at her for a moment. "All right, then," he said. "Let's go."

Keeping to the edge of the clearing, they crept to the gate. Reaching it, they stood still for a minute, listening. Shining Pearl glanced up and saw a bright streak shoot across the sky, then another, then another. She had seen shooting stars before, but never three so close together; she wondered if it was a sign.

Hurky's attention was on the gate. He put his hands on the rough wood and pushed. The gate swung open slowly, making a creak that sounded much too loud to Hurky and Shining Pearl. They waited another minute but heard nothing. They went inside. Shining Pearl jerked to a stop. Just a few feet away, the body of a pirate lay on the ground, an arrow sticking out of his chest, a reminder of the battle that had taken place here when the Scorpions had overrun the fort.

Shining Pearl stared at the body. It looked ghastly pale in the moonlight. Hurky tugged at her arm.

"Nothing to be done about him," he whispered. "The cap'n's cabin is over there." He pointed to a hut across the compound.

They went to the hut, where a piece of canvas served as a door. Shining Pearl pulled it aside and entered. She gagged at the stink of sweat. At first the cabin appeared to be empty, but then she saw something dark on the floor in the corner. She picked it up and examined it by the moonlight. It was a ragged pair of pants, worn, tattered, full of holes. And very smelly.

"That's what you asked after," said Hurky, wrinkling his nose. "The cap'n's pants. He hardly ever took 'em off."

They left the hut, trotted across the compound to the

gate, and slipped out. Hurky pulled the gate shut. Shining Pearl was holding Hook's pants at arm's length; even in the open air, they reeked. She started across the clearing, then stopped, her eyes scanning the dark jungle.

"What's wrong?" whispered Hurky.

"Listen," she answered.

Hurky cocked his head. "I don't hear nothing," he said.

"That's what bothers me," whispered Shining Pearl. "The jungle is too quiet."

"Maybe it's because of us," said Hurky.

"No," said Shining Pearl, pointing across the clearing. "It's because of them."

Hurky looked up and gasped. Four Scorpion warriors, each holding a spear, had stepped out of the jungle and were moving across the clearing, spreading out to prevent their prey from escaping. Shining Pearl and Hurky, with nowhere to go, backed up toward the fort. The Scorpions stopped a few feet away. They were grinning, their teeth bright white in the moonlight.

One of them said something. Neither Shining Pearl nor Hurky understood it. Their backs were now against the gate. The Scorpions laughed at them, enjoying their terror. One of them raised his spear and pointed it at Hurky, then at Shining Pearl, then back at Hurky, then back at Shining Pearl again, as if deciding which one to impale first.

The Scorpions found this game so entertaining that they

didn't notice the movement in the jungle behind them. But Shining Pearl saw it: the treetops shaking as the trunks were shoved aside by something huge and powerful coming through. A moment later Shining Pearl saw the two orbs glowing red in the moonlight—eyes, reptile eyes, impossibly big, impossibly far apart.

Now the taunting Scorpion warrior pulled back his spear for the kill. He had chosen his target: Hurky would die first. Hurky did not see the massive thing in the jungle behind the Scorpions; he had dropped to his knees, his eyes on the gleaming tip of the spear that was about to end his existence. Hurky's lips moved in soundless prayer. The warrior's hand tightened on his spear; his arm tensed for the kill.

And then the jungle night was filled with a blood-chilling roar, and the ground shook as a massive creature longer than a war canoe lunged from the jungle. The Scorpions turned and gaped at the sight of the giant croco-dile known as Mister Grin lumbering toward them, opening jaws huge enough to swallow a standing man in one gulp.

The Scorpion warriors froze for an instant, and that was an instant too long. The huge croc, moving faster than would seem possible for a thing of such monstrous bulk, was across the clearing and upon the warriors, whose spears were no match for Mister Grin's snapping jaws and long, sharp, jagged teeth.

Shining Pearl reached down and grabbed the arm of

Hurky, who was still kneeling and too shocked to react to the carnage in front of him.

"Come!" she said, jerking him to his feet. "Hurry!"

She ran along the fence and into the jungle, Hurky stumbling behind her. They plunged into the undergrowth. Shining Pearl angled to the right, pushing through the thick vegetation until she found the path that led to the place where Smee and the other pirates would be waiting for them. With Hurky right behind, she raced up the path, away from the clearing and the awful screams of the Scorpions.

Gradually the screams grew less frequent. Then they stopped. Shining Pearl was breathing hard, but she dared not slow down. She knew that what had drawn the giant crocodile into the clearing was the pants she held in her hands, which smelled so strongly of the croc's favorite delicacy: Captain Hook. Now that Mister Grin was done with his appetizer, he would be after the next course.

He would be coming after Shining Pearl.

CHAPTER 50

Unanswered Questions

Peter and Tink, keeping to the shadows, flew up the side of the massive palace-compound wall, away from the guard towers. The moon hung low on the horizon, but the heavens above were coming alive. Fiery meteors streaked across the sky every few seconds in a dazzling display.

Peter poked his head over the wall and surveyed the scene. He saw the palace courtyard illuminated by a large ring of torches on poles thrust into the ground; in the center of the torch-lit ring stood the rocket, next to which a scaffold had been erected. Slightly and the other boys were lugging buckets of black powder from a distant wagon to the rocket. There were soldiers everywhere, most of them holding rifles.

As Peter and Tink watched, Slightly and the other boys finished loading the powder. Viktor Glotz shouted an order, and two soldiers appeared carrying a cage containing a monkey.

Franklin! chimed Tink.

"Who's Franklin?" said Peter.

The monkey, said Tink. *I know him.*

"Not well, I hope," Peter said grimly. "It appears he's going to steer the rocket."

He's a nice monkey, said Tink.

They watched as Glotz, aided by Slightly and Tootles, climbed the scaffold and put Franklin into his compartment near the top of the rocket. After they descended, Glotz had soldiers bring the fuse roll.

"He'll be putting the fuse in soon," muttered Peter. "Tink, I've got to get down there."

Tink fluttered into his face. *They'll shoot you.*

Peter nodded, looking at the soldiers. "If I fly in, they will," he said. "I need another way." His eyes scanned the courtyard. The powder wagon was being drawn away. Trudging behind it, surrounded by guards, were Slightly and three other boys. They turned right, heading toward the dungeon. Peter frowned. Then he pushed away from the wall, hovering in the darkness.

What are you doing? chimed Tink.

"Thinking."

About what?

"About Slightly and the other boys. I bet they're going to get the starstuff to load onto the rocket. Glotz and Zarboff don't dare go near it themselves."

So?

"So," said Peter, "they'll be coming back with the trunk."

So?

But Peter was gone, zooming low along the outside of the wall. In an instant Tink was after him, a tiny blur of light, angrily chiming questions that for the moment went unanswered.

CHAPTER 51

Not All Right

MOLLY FLEW OVER THE PALACE-COMPOUND WALL, immediately spotting the rocket, which was surrounded by a ring of torches and the shadowy shapes of soldiers. She flew away from this activity to the far end of the compound, where she dropped to the ground in the deep shadow next to a large building. Entering the compound had been easier than she'd expected. As her eyes adjusted to the darkness, she saw small windows with bars along the bottom of the wall. The building was evidently a prison.

Hardly daring to believe she'd been lucky enough to land next to the dungeon, she ran along the side of the building, looking for a way in. She turned a corner, and in a few feet, came to a large wooden door with iron bands. She took a breath and tried the handle. To her surprise, it turned. She pushed open the heavy door and peered inside; seeing nobody, she stepped into a small space

318

from which low, torch-lit corridors ran off to the left and right.

She jumped when she heard a man's voice coming from the corridor to the right. A moment later, a second voice answered. *Two men*—definitely heading toward her. She hesitated, considering going back outside, but she'd come too far to give up. She hurried down the corridor to the left.

Passing a line of empty cells, she entered a dark stretch of corridor, where the torches were spaced far apart. She smelled a strong, unpleasant aroma, and heard strange sounds coming from very close by.

A hairy hand brushed her neck. She stifled a scream and turned to see, in the dim light, a long, hairy arm reaching through the cell bars. The hand grabbed the air, trying to touch her again.

A monkey! What on earth?

She stepped out of its reach and moved cautiously forward to the next cell. Her heart stopped: a man! He was standing in shadow in the far corner—tall, like her father. Moving closer, she pressed her face to the bars.

"Father?" she whispered.

The figure stepped into the glow of the torchlight. Again Molly fought back a scream. A long black moustache slashed across a familiar hatchet-thin face.

Hook!

The pirate recognized her—she had once been a prisoner

on his ship. He smiled, enjoying her fear, his thin lips pulling back to reveal a jagged row of brown tooth stumps. Molly willed herself on, glancing nervously back at the pirate's cell.

"Molly!"

Relief filled her soul at the sound of her father's voice. His face was pressed against the bars of the cell. She ran to him, and they embraced awkwardly through the bars for several long seconds. Then Leonard, apologizing for his rudeness, formally introduced his daughter to Bakari, who shook hands with her.

"How did you get in here?" Leonard asked.

"The door was unguarded," said Molly.

Leonard nodded. "I assume the soldiers are preoccupied with the rocket preparations." He nodded toward the cell window, which looked out onto the courtyard. "Molly, we've got to stop them."

"I know," said Molly. "Tink gave us your message. She and Peter are going to see about the rocket. But I came to get you out first."

"But how?" said Leonard.

"I've got starstuff in my locket," said Molly. "I'll use it on the lock." She drew the locket out from under her robe and flicked it open, reflexively squinting her eyes to guard against the brilliant light.

But there was no light.

"Oh, no," said Molly. "I must have used it all up. Perhaps

320

I can—" She stopped, seeing her father's expression change suddenly.

"Molly, run!" he shouted. She whirled and found herself face-to-face with a burly soldier who grabbed her arms with a grip that made her cry out in pain. The soldier shouted something in the Rundoon language; moments later three more soldiers came running. They drew swords and gestured at Leonard and Bakari to go to the back of the cell, then opened the door and roughly shoved Molly inside. After making sure the door was securely locked, the soldiers left, laughing loudly.

Molly ran to her father's arms. "Father, I'm so sorry," she said. "I meant to help, and now I've just made everything worse."

"It's all right," said Leonard, gently patting his daughter's back. "We'll be all right."

Still holding Molly, he looked at Bakari. Bakari glanced out the window at the rocket, then back at Leonard. He shook his head, and Leonard understood his expression: things were most definitely not all right.

CHAPTER 52

THE GOLD SUITS

PETER, WITH TINK FLYING ALONGSIDE, landed in front of the big door leading to the dungeon. The door was ajar. Peter poked his head inside and, seeing nobody, stepped into the entry room. He held his breath and stood absolutely still: laughter came toward him from the corridor to his left. He turned toward the corridor to the right, but heard the sound of men's voices coming from that direction. With nowhere else to go, he flew to the ceiling and flattened himself in the darkness next to a wooden beam. Tink tucked herself in beside him. Moments later, four soldiers, still laughing, passed directly beneath them and crossed into the right-hand corridor, their voices slowly fading.

Peter dropped quickly to the floor and trotted down the corridor to the left. He passed the storage room where the gold suits were locked up. He continued on to the monkey cell, then hesitated, weighing the risk of continuing until he reached the cell holding Leonard Aster and Bakari. But then he once again heard men's voices—now coming from behind him—and decided to stay with his plan.

As he'd hoped, the monkey cage had no lock, only a latch. He opened it and, wrinkling his nose at the smell, stepped inside, pulling the door closed but not letting it latch. Immediately, he was surrounded by excited monkeys, hooting and shrieking.

You're scaring them, said Tink, from Peter's shoulder.

"Tell them it's all right," he said. "Tell them to be quiet."

Tink flew down and spoke to the monkeys, making a strange combination of bell and monkey sounds. Whatever she said was effective; all of them quieted. A young monkey approached Peter, sniffed his leg, and made a noise.

She says you smell bad, said Tink.

"Shh," said Peter, listening. The voices were getting closer.

"Listen, Tink," he whispered, wriggling out of his robe. "Tell the monkeys that I'm about to open the door and that they should go outside and distract the soldiers."

Why would they want to do that?

"I don't know," snapped Peter. The approaching voices and footsteps were very close now. "We need a distraction," he whispered. "Make something up."

All right.

As Tink spoke to the monkeys, Peter peered through the

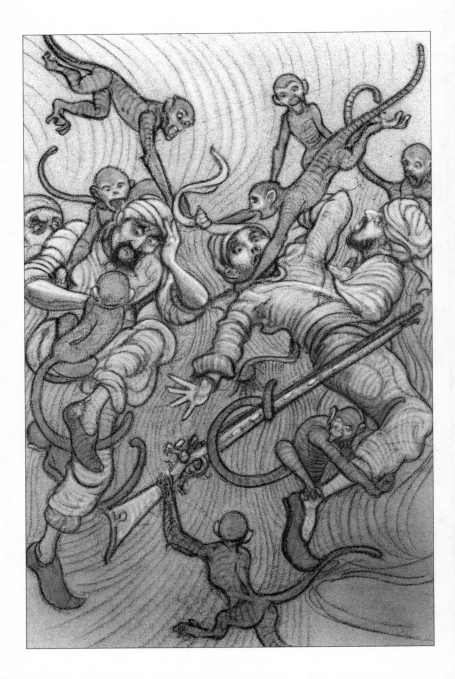

cage bars and saw soldiers approaching. As he'd hoped, they were the ones escorting the four boys—Slightly in the front, followed by Tootles, Curly, and Nibs. They stopped in front of the locked room containing the gold suits. Peter glanced down at Tink hovering among the monkeys and nodded. Then he pulled the cage door open.

Tink emitted a loud chime. Instantly, the monkeys, screeching like banshees, shot into the corridor and leapt onto the soldiers, climbing on their heads, clinging to their faces, yanking off their hats, and pawing through their hair. The soldiers dropped their weapons and frantically tried to free themselves of their furred, frenzied attackers; several stumbled and fell.

Peter held back, waiting. When the corridor was utter chaos, with the monkey-besieged soldiers paying no attention to the four boys, Peter darted out, grabbed the second boy in line—Tootles—and yanked him back into the monkey cage.

"Shh," whispered Peter, cupping Tootles's mouth before the boy could cry out. "Stay in here and keep out of sight until the soldiers are gone. I'm here to help."

To Peter's relief, Tootles nodded.

Peter tucked Tink into his shirt and watched for the right moment, then ducked into the still-chaotic corridor and slipped into line behind Slightly, motioning for the other boys to keep their mouths shut.

A minute or two passed while the soldiers struggled to rid themselves of the annoying monkeys, who finally scampered away down the corridor, screeching and hooting. The disheveled soldiers, clearly upset about the delay, hastily retrieved their hats and weapons. Peter pressed close against Slightly, keeping his face down. The soldiers didn't notice the switch. Barking orders, they opened the door and shoved the boys inside, gesturing impatiently at the gold suits hanging along the far wall.

Peter, following Slightly's lead, began putting on one of the suits. It was heavy, made of a gold-mesh fabric. It felt cool to the touch, and smooth against his skin.

"What did you tell the monkeys?" he whispered to Tink, as he tucked her inside the gold jacket.

I said the soldiers had bananas in their hair.

Peter slipped his feet into a pair of gold boots, then pulled on a gold-mesh head covering. The hood reduced his vision considerably, but now his face was obscured. He fell into line behind Slightly as the boys filed back out into the corridor, four small gold figures on their way to get the starstuff that would end the world.

CHAPTER 53

GREASING THE ROLLERS

As the darkness deepened, George, ignoring the meteor display, studied the ship, making sure the last of the workers had put away their tools and left for the day. The docks were quiet now, the sailors and dock men having found their way into nearby cafés, from which spilled loud laughter and billowing tobacco smoke.

When night had completely fallen, George said, "James, Prentiss, and Thomas, you'll come with me. Ted, you stay here. Wait for my signal."

"What signal? To do what?"

George reached inside his robe and drew out a white handkerchief. He waved it over his head. "When you see this," he said to Ted, "I want you to kick out this barrel." He pointed to a barrel at the bottom of a tall stack.

Ted studied the barrels. "But if I do that," he said, "all these barrels will fall."

"Yes," said George.

"Ah," said Ted, as though he understood, which he did not.

"Once you kick out the barrel," said George, "run for the ship. It will be moving. Jump on quick as you can."

"But—" Ted began.

"Quick as you can," repeated George, cutting him off.

George, with the help of Prentiss, Thomas, and James, then selected two of the barrels of olive oil and carefully rolled them down the hill to the harbor. The dry dock was essentially a large trench dug into the harborside and lined with timbers. At one end of the trench, holding back the water, was a large wooden gate secured at one end by a thick chain. Inside the dry dock, the ship, its stern tilted down toward the water, sat atop a row of big, smooth logs; it was prevented from falling over by wooden braces along both sides. Between these braces netting hung down from the deck, so workmen could climb up and down.

"The way it's supposed to work," said George, "is that when that gate is opened at high tide, the water comes in and lifts the ship until it just barely floats. Then the ship rides on those logs—the rollers—into the sea."

"It must take a lot of men," said Thomas.

"Actually, it's mostly gravity and leverage," said George. "You see those two winches on each side? Those lines pulled the ship up into the dry dock. When they're released, if there's not too much friction, the ship will slide down and into the water."

"But there are only four of us," said Thomas.

"Yes," said George. "One to release each of the winches, one to open the water gate, and one on board to start preparing the sails. The tricky part is the timing. Usually the water gate is opened at low tide. As the tide comes in, the boat is lifted. But we haven't got time to wait for that. That's why we've got this." He pointed to the two barrels of oil.

James nodded. "To help it slide," he said.

"Precisely," said George.

"What about the side braces?" said James.

"Most of them will fall off or break away as she slides in," said George. "We'll have to count on her momentum to keep her upright."

"It might work," said James.

"*What* might work?" asked Thomas, thoroughly confused.

"Never mind that now," said George. "We're about to get very dirty, so I suggest we get out of these robes."

The boys took off the robes. Underneath, George still wore his suit pants and a white shirt. The other boys were in their island rags. James, a good climber, volunteered to board the ship and unfurl the mainsail. George quickly accepted. The boys spat on their hands and shook for good luck, then James was off, sliding down the timbers into the dry dock, then climbing the netting onto the ship's deck. The sky was now bright with meteor flashes, so he was clearly visible as he began ascending the mainmast.

George told Thomas to keep watch. He and Prentiss grabbed one of the oil barrels and, grunting under its weight, worked it down into the bottom of the dry dock. They stopped alongside the rollers; the ship's hull rose over them, blotting out the sky. The air smelled of tar pitch.

Together, the two boys supported the cask above the rollers. Prentiss pulled the bung plug from its side, and oil glugged out, sounding like a big man swallowing. They slid the barrel alongside the ship's hull, allowing the sweet oil to seep down between the rollers. When they'd finished with the left side of the hull, they climbed out of the dry dock, carried the second cask back down, and oiled the other side.

"She'll slip out of here like a bar of soap in the tub," said George. "I hope."

"But, George," said Prentiss. "If Thomas and I work the forward winches and you unchain the sea gate, how will we get aboard the ship once it's moving?"

"The nets," George said. "We'll have to jump for them."

"Jump?" said Prentiss.

"Yes."

They started climbing out of the trench. George looked up at James, who was high up the mainmast working on one of the sails. There were so many meteors in the sky now that at times he was as clearly visible as if it were day-light.

"George!" It was Thomas hissing at them.

"What?" said George, reaching the top of the trench.

"Those men over there!" said Thomas, pointing. "I think they've spotted James!" A group of men had emerged from a hillside café, seemingly to look at the meteors. Several of them were gesturing toward the dry-docked ship and shout-ing. More men were coming out of the café.

"This is it," said George. He pulled the white handker-chief out of his pocket and waved it violently over his head, hoping Ted was watching. The café had emptied now; the men, several dozen of them, were starting down the hill.

"They're coming!" said Thomas, unnecessarily.

"What do we do?" said Prentiss.

"You two release the winches," said George, starting to run to the end of the dry dock. "I'll get the gate."

"But how do we . . ." began Thomas.

"There's no time!" George shouted over his shoulder. "Just release those lines!"

Prentiss and Thomas started running for the winches, not sure what they were going to do but quite sure they had better do it quickly. The mob of angry men came shouting down the hill toward them, the fury on their faces very clear under the meteor-flashing sky.

CHAPTER 54

The Launch

THE STREETS OF MAKNAR, normally empty at night, teemed with the city's inhabitants, who'd left their homes to witness the amazing heavenly display. Children shouted and shrieked with excitement as lines of bright light, dozens at a time, streaked silently but spectacularly across the black sky. The adults remained more subdued, muttering to each other, trying to fathom the meaning of this strange phenomenon. Many of them cast nervous glances toward the dark hulking walls of the palace compound.

The mood inside the walls was no less tense. King Zarboff the Third had emerged from his palace to watch. He was accompanied by his personal guards and the two slave boys known as the twins, who were charged with carrying the heavy basket containing the king's beloved Kundalini. A well-cushioned chair had been set up a safe distance from the rocket so the king could sit and watch the launch in comfort.

Lord Ombra had also arrived, appearing suddenly as though materializing from the night itself. He spoke to nobody, keeping to the shadows outside the circle of torches surrounding the rocket; but the soldiers were quite aware of his presence—and the sudden chill in the air. Even Viktor Glotz noticed it, in spite of his preoccupation with the final preparations for the launch.

All watched as Glotz inserted the fuse into the rocket and laid it out on the ground, cutting it at precisely eight and a half feet. He'd calculated it would burn for ninety seconds before reaching the fuel—plenty of time for him to get a safe distance away. Glotz was not particularly worried about an explosion; this was why he'd decided to launch the rocket from the palace courtyard rather than the desert. Compared to the earlier rockets, this one contained surprisingly little black-powder fuel, given its weight. Most of the lifting force would come from the huge quantity of starstuff; the main function of the fuel was to propel the rocket forward, enabling the monkey to steer it on the correct course.

Glotz glanced at the sky, then checked his pocket watch. The ideal launch time was quickly approaching. He looked around impatiently, and . . .

There!

Soldiers appeared from around the side of the dungeon, escorting the four gold-suited boys who were carrying the trunk of starstuff. They held the trunk by handles at each corner and carried it easily; the starstuff made it essentially weightless.

The gold-lined trunk had been built with great precision; its seams and joints were fitted perfectly, allowing no light to escape. Even so, the air around the trunk hummed and even glowed faintly because of the immense energy it contained. The soldiers kept their distance from it; the gold-suited boys turned their heads away from it as they walked. Ombra drifted back into the deepest shadows as the boys brought the trunk into the torch circle and set it down next to the scaffolding that stood alongside the rocket.

Glotz approached the boys.

"There is an open hatch right above the monkey's chamber," he said, pointing up at the rocket. "You will carry the trunk up there—*carefully*—and set it inside the rocket. Then you will release the trunk lid by pressing the button on the latch. The hinges are on springs, so the lid will open by itself. As soon as it starts opening you must close the hatch. *Quickly*. Then come straight down. Do you understand?"

The boys nodded their gold-hooded heads.

"One more thing you should understand," said Glotz. "I will be watching you closely. If you deviate in any way from my instructions, I will order these soldiers to shoot you off the scaffold. Do you understand?"

The boys nodded again. Glotz looked at his watch and said, "You have ten minutes." The boys, two above the trunk and two below it, took hold of the handles and began ascending the steep ladderway inside the scaffolding.

Peter and Slightly were at the upper end of the trunk. When they were far enough from Glotz, Slightly whispered to Peter through the gold mesh.

"What are you going to do?"

Peter had been thinking about just that. His first idea had been to simply dump the starstuff out of the trunk from the top of the scaffolding, but he'd rejected that idea. For one thing, it would get the other boys, and very likely himself, killed. For another, he feared Glotz would find a way to get the starstuff back into the rocket and proceed with the launch. What he needed, he knew, was a way to get the starstuff away from Glotz, Ombra, and Zarboff, but also to prevent it from being released into the sky. He wasn't yet sure how he would do this. All he said to Slightly was, "I won't do anything until we're back on the ground. Keep the other boys close by, and be ready."

"Ready for what?"

"I'm not sure. But you may have a chance to escape. If you do, run to the harbor. Look for James and the others. They're getting a ship."

"They're getting a *ship?*" said Slightly, his tone suggesting that he found this highly unlikely.

"Well, they're going to try," Peter said.

Slightly nodded. "What about you?" he said.

"I'll be along as soon as I can," said Peter.

They had reached the platform on the top of the scaffolding. They faced a hatch patterned with small air holes. Peter noted it was latched from the outside. Through the holes, he could hear the monkey making soft whimpering noises. Tink, still stuck inside Peter's gold suit, made sympathetic sounds in return.

Above the hatch was an opening just large enough for the trunk, leading into a compartment lined with gold. On the right side of the opening was a small door on hinges. On its left side was a latch attached to a steel cable that snaked down through a hole into the monkey compartment. Peter assumed this was how the monkey, in the chamber below the trunk, would open the door and release the starstuff.

The boys lifted the trunk and slid it through the opening into the gold-lined compartment. When it was inside, Slightly reached for the button on the big gold trunk latch. Peter put a hand on his arm, stopping him.

"I'll do it," Peter said. "You three get back."

Slightly, Curly, and Nibs stepped toward the ladder. Peter reached inside the rocket and pressed the button. With a *snick* the latch flipped open. The lid began to rise. Instantly, the compartment filled with a blinding light and a roaring sound. Peter quickly grabbed the door and closed it; the latch clicked tight. The air around the top of the rocket hummed and glowed.

From below, the boys heard Glotz shouting at them to come down. The four gold-suited figures hastily descended the ladder. As soon as they reached the ground, a group of soldiers dragged the scaffolding away from the rocket. Glotz looked up into the sky, then at his pocket watch. He shouted for everyone to move back, and proceeded to pull a torch from the earth and walk over to the fuse. The sky was alight with meteors now, the courtyard so bright that even through the mesh Peter could clearly see Glotz's face.

All eyes focused on the scientist as he stood over the fuse, checking his watch. King Zarboff rose to his feet to get a better view, though Peter noted that he kept his guards between himself and the rocket. A movement at the outer edge of the crowd of spectators caught Peter's eye. He looked that way and noted, with a small smile, that Slightly and the other boys, including the twins, had slipped away unnoticed, five shadows trotting toward the palace gate.

Peter's eyes returned to the crowd, scanning the spectators until he found Ombra, a dark shape among the shadows on the far side of the torchlight circle. Peter stared at Ombra for a moment, and as he did, the dark hood shape swiveled and seemed to look right at him. Peter felt a chill and quickly looked away, hoping desperately that he had not been too obvious.

His eyes returned to Glotz. The scientist stood holding the torch and looking at his watch for several long minutes.

Then, slowly, his eyes still on his watch, he began to lower the flame to the fuse. The courtyard fell utterly silent as the flickering flame descended until it touched the fuse. Sparks erupted from the ground and began crawling toward the waiting rocket. Glotz watched for a few seconds, then began slowly walking toward the circle of spectators. He stopped near Zarboff and turned back toward the fuse.

Peter was also watching the fuse now, trying to get a sense of when to move. He needed to time it perfectly—too soon and the soldiers would shoot him out of the sky; too late and the rocket would be out of his reach.

The sparks crawled across the dirt and, reaching the rocket, began to climb the fuse. Peter tensed; it would be in a moment, now. A nagging worry made him risk a look across the circle of spectators into the shadows.

Ombra wasn't there.

Peter looked around frantically but didn't see the dark shape. He heard a roar and turned back toward the rocket. The fuse had ignited the fuel; flames and black smoke billowed from the base. The rocket shook and started to lift. Peter, for a fraction of a second, felt something cold and horrible in his legs. With a shout, he crouched and hurled himself upward.

Glotz saw the gold-clad figure flying toward his beloved rocket. He screamed in rage and shouted at the soldiers to shoot. Transfixed by the rocket's roar, they took several seconds to understand what he wanted, and several more to get their rifles into firing position.

Peter flew straight to the top of the rocket. He searched desperately in the billowing smoke for the latch to the door covering the monkey's compartment. He heard a shot; a bullet zipped past. He yanked the gold hood off his head so he could see better. Another shot went past. He found the latch and yanked the door open, hurling himself headfirst in with the monkey as a bullet clanged off the hatch door behind him.

Glotz screamed when he saw Peter duck into the rocket, which was now off the ground, rising slowly on a cushion of fire and smoke. Glotz shouted incoherently, nearly insane with rage and helplessness as he watched his life's work, the crowning achievement of his genius, being threatened by a boy. He ran toward the smoke, his face twisted in fury.

And then, suddenly, he stopped, and the fury on his face turned to hope. For he saw something in the roiling smoke, a dark shape rising, twisting, and contorting itself—now thick, now thin, but always moving upward through the billows, upward to the base of the rocket, and then along its side—a black blot, oozing in through a seam in between two metal plates.

Glotz smiled.

Ombra was aboard the rocket.

CHAPTER 55

The Giant Eye

"Please get up, Mr. Smee," whispered Shining Pearl, glancing nervously back down the jungle hillside. "Hurry!"

Smee lay where he'd fallen, having tripped on a vine for at least the hundredth time. Sweat dripped from his round face; it gleamed in the light of the meteor shower, which filled the normally dark nighttime jungle with an unearthly flashing light.

"I don't think I can keep going," he panted.

"You must!" said Shining Pearl, again looking down the hill. "He's coming!"

Smee turned his head and moaned in fear. The treetops shook as the huge beast shoved his way through the thick jungle growth. Mister Grin had been following Shining Pearl and the seven pirates for hours now, never seeming to tire. At one point he had come so close that Shining Pearl, in desperation, had dropped the lure—Hook's smelly pants—

onto the ground, leaving them behind as the little group continued up the mountainside. This had stopped Mister Grin, but only for as long as it took him to gulp down the garment. Then, with a roar, the monster croc had resumed following Shining Pearl and the pirates, who realized to their horror that the beast thought Hook was still among them.

Now there was no turning back; they had to continue over the mountain to the Mollusk camp and hope that Mister Grin would turn his attention from them to the Scorpions.

Shining Pearl looked up the hillside; the other pirates were almost out of sight.

"Help!" she called. "Mr. Smee has fallen again!"

Two pirates, Hurky and Boggs, turned and came trotting down.

"Cap'n," said Hurky. "You have to get up."

"I can't," said Smee. "I'm too . . . OW!"

"Sorry, sir," said Hurky, as he and Boggs, one grabbing each arm, jerked Smee to his feet, put his arms over their shoulders, and began dragging the little round man up the hill, with Shining Pearl right behind. She stopped for a moment to glance back at the jungle. The shaking trees were only a dozen yards away. She caught a glimpse of a giant eye glowing red in the meteor light. It seemed to be looking right at her.

Shining Pearl turned and started running again.

CHAPTER 56

ᎢHE ᏚECOND ᏞAUNCH

ᏞEANING AGAINST THE STACK of barrels, Tubby Ted sucked olive oil off his fingers, his eyes closed, his lips smacking.

"Mmmm," he said, wishing he had a warm piece of bread.

Then, hearing shouts, he jumped to his feet. A dozen men were running down the hill toward the dry-docked ship. Under a sky alight with streaking meteors, Ted saw the angry looks on their faces. *Very* angry. Some of them were waving knives in the air.

Ted looked down at the ship and saw his mates scattering in opposite directions; George held the white handkerchief in his hand, his arms pumping furiously as he ran.

Ted wondered: *Did I miss something?*

He couldn't exactly describe George's motion as waving the handkerchief over his head, but he decided it was close enough. He turned and, as George had told him to, kicked at the bottom barrel. It was stubborn, but it dislodged from the

stack and rolled down the hill. He jumped back as the entire barrel stack collapsed in an olive-oil avalanche. A half dozen barrels exploded as they struck the ground, sending a wave of slippery oil gushing down the hill, followed by more barrels, rolling and bouncing and spewing their contents as they split open.

Tubby Ted, staying clear of the olive-oil cascade, began lumbering down the hill toward the ship. Ahead, he caught sight of Thomas and Prentiss on either side of the dry dock trench, each struggling frantically with a big winch. As Ted ran toward the ship, the winches—first Thomas's, then Prentiss's—began to turn, paying out the heavy ropes. At once the whole ship began to shudder, groan, and creak. Behind Ted, the sound of the men's shouting grew louder, more frantic. Thomas and Prentiss started clambering down into the trench, running for the ship.

"Wait!" Ted shouted, but neither boy heard. Reaching the ship, they grabbed on to the nets suspended from the decks and began to climb. There was a loud CRACK as one of the big side supports fell away. Then another. The groaning became deeper, turning into a rumbling noise, and now the ship was *moving*, rolling on the huge logs beneath the keel.

"Wait!" Ted yelled again, but nobody heard him over the sound of the sliding ship. He ran alongside the trench and spotted George at the big wooden gate behind the ship. He was struggling with a chain. The ship was moving toward him, rudder first, but George seemed unaware of the fact that he was about to be crushed.

Ted heard screams behind him. He turned and looked up the hill. The mob of angry men, their eyes on the escaping ship, had run right into the olive-oil cascade. They were tumbling and sliding down the hill, knocking each other over, their knives flying everywhere. Ted turned back and began running toward George, screaming unheard warnings about the oncoming ship.

———◆———

George struggled with the chain that held the gate to the piling. It was too heavy, made of massive links that George could barely lift, let alone raise over the top of the piling to release the gate. He glanced behind him and saw with a mixture of elation and alarm that the ship was moving, its stern rising high above him, its huge rudder pointing right at him. To the side, he saw men tumbling down the hillside, shouting in confusion and fury. At least that part of his plan had worked. But what about the chain? If he couldn't release it, the huge links would stop the ship. And if he stayed where he was much longer, the ship would squash him like a bug.

George turned back to study the massive chain. He saw that one of the links was held to the next by an iron bolt. He twisted it with all his strength, and to his relief it began to unscrew. He turned the bolt as fast as he could; it unscrewed and unscrewed, but did not come free. The ship was gaining momentum now; the side struts were splintering and snapping and falling away. The rollers made a deafening grinding sound.

Several of the men had made it down the hillside. One of them saw George at the gate and shouted; he and the others began running toward George. The ship was only a few yards away. George gave the bolt a few more frantic twists. Finally, it came free, clanking on the rocks underfoot. The chain fell away. Water leaked in around the edge of the gate. The ship was rushing toward him, the enormous rudder coming at him like a blade.

The shouting men reached the gate.

George dove. He landed just to the side of the ship's hull. He scrambled to his feet, grabbed hold of a rope dangling from the deck, and started to climb it. One of the men leaned out over the trench, knife in hand, and slashed at George. George, unable to get away, closed his eyes, waiting for the pain of the blade.

Instead, the rope jerked him violently backward as the last supports snapped and the ship suddenly picked up speed. He clung desperately to the rope as the ship smashed into the gate, which splintered into hundreds of pieces. A wall of water roared into the trench, nearly taking George with it; he hung on to the rope, sputtering, and struggled to haul himself onto the deck. Behind him, the man who'd tried to stab him screamed as he fell into the trench, now a deadly boiling cauldron, as the surging seawater tossed huge timbers around.

The ship plunged into the sea stern first and slowed with a shuddering jerk. George, reaching the deck, saw that Prentiss and Thomas had managed to scramble aboard. He looked back to see Tubby Ted standing on the side of the trench where the gate had been, looking uncertain. The ship's bow was just passing him.

"Ted!" screamed George, running toward him on the deck. "Jump!"

For once, Ted—normally not one to act quickly—did as he was told, leaping toward the ship and just catching the last of the nets. As Prentiss helped Ted up onto the deck, George raced to the stern and grabbed the ship's wheel. He looked up the mainmast at James, who was just then releasing the last of the ties. The mainsail fell away, ruffling in the wind. George heaved on the ship's wheel, turning it hard, trying to angle the ship so the sail would fill with wind. But the ship was losing momentum; it didn't answer to the rudder.

"Come on," said George, glancing toward the furious men on the shore, then back up at the sails. "Come *on*."

The sail flapped and snapped, and caught some wind. George held the wheel all the way to starboard. The ship began to turn, but agonizingly slowly.

James shouted something from the mast and pointed toward shore. George looked in that direction and saw a small rowboat in the water with five figures heaving hard on the oars. It was headed straight for the ship. At first George thought it was the men who'd been chasing them, but as the dory drew closer he saw, to his shock, that they were boys— the same slave boys he'd seen in the desert with King Zarboff.

James recognized them as well. "Slightly!" he yelled, quickly climbing down from the mast.

The rowboat reached the ship; the five boys struggled up the netting and onto the deck. Three of them—Slightly, Curly, and Nibs—were wearing golden suits; the other two— the twins—wore their servant garb.

"Where's Peter?" said James.

"He's back at the rocket," said Slightly. "He told us to run here while Zarboff and the rest were distracted by the rocket launch."

"And Molly?" said George.

"Didn't see her," said Slightly. "Peter just said to come here and—"

He was interrupted by a shout from Thomas, who was pointing toward shore. The angry mob, having seen the slave boys row to the ship, had decided to do the same: they had run to a dock where some rowboats were tied, and were in the process of launching three of them.

George looked up at the luffing mainsail, willing it to fill with wind. The ship was moving, but pitifully slowly.

"Untie the nets and ropes!" he shouted. "We want nothing over the sides for them to grab on to!" But he doubted they'd have time to untie a single net; the first rowboat was already launched and making good time. It was rowing straight for the ship; and its occupants did not look at all friendly.

George glanced around in desperation for a weapon, something—*anything*—with which to defend the ship. He saw nothing. Hopelessness filled his heart.

Had he looked toward the city, he would have seen, amid the myriad streaks in the sky, one light of a different color: the fiery tail flame of the rocket, now rising over the palace wall.

CHAPTER 57

THE CREEPING COLD

FRANKLIN THE MONKEY was most unhappy. He hooted and screeched, baring his teeth at the smelly human who had so rudely barged into his little space.

Peter's mood was no better. The monkey's cage inside the roaring rocket was loud and cramped, with barely enough room for the monkey and his control levers. These levers were sticking painfully into Peter's back. At the same time, the monkey was shrieking into his ear, and Tink, still stuck inside his gold suit, was pounding on his chest with her tiny fists and clamoring: *Let me out!*

Peter wriggled sideways and was able to give Tink enough room to escape. She and Franklin exchanged odd noises.

He wants you to get out of his cage, she told Peter.

"I'd love to," he said. "But how?" The only opening was the hatch through which he'd entered; the hatch door hung open and the wind howled as the rocket gained speed and altitude. If Peter went out that way, the rocket would leave him behind.

Tink squirmed past Peter and examined the cage behind him.

Here, she said, chiming loudly to be heard over the howl of the wind and the roar of the rocket. *Open this side.*

Peter craned his neck and saw that the back wall of the cage was held in place by metal pins at the top and bottom. He yanked these out. The cage wall dropped away, clattering as it fell to the base of the rocket. Peter pushed himself out and hovered next to the cage. The starstuff was in the compartment directly above him; he could feel it and see it—the compartment wall glowed brightly, filling the upper part of the rocket with light. Below him was the main section of the rocket, a chimneylike cylinder a bit more than three feet in diameter, filled with smoke from the fuel burning down at the base of the rocket.

Coughing from the smoke, Peter stuck his head back into the cage, which was starkly illuminated by the glow from the starstuff compartment. Franklin, he now saw, was held firmly in place by a leather harness. The monkey had his face pressed against what looked like a telescope eyepiece, and he was manipulating two levers. A third lever, with a red handle, projected into the cage from above; this, Peter assumed, would open the door to the starstuff compartment.

"Ask him what he's doing," Peter said to Tink. She exchanged sounds with Franklin, then told Peter, *He's keeping the light in the circle. If he keeps it in the circle, he gets a banana.*

"Let me see," said Peter, pushing the monkey aside. Franklin screeched in protest.

He thinks you're going to take his banana.

"Tell him he can have his banana," snapped Peter. While Tink calmed Franklin, Peter squinted into the eyepiece and saw a magnified image of the starry desert sky with a small white circle painted in the middle. Evidently, Franklin was supposed to steer the rocket so that a certain star—Peter couldn't tell which one—remained in the circle, thus holding the right course. He glanced out the open hatchway; at the moment, the rocket appeared to be going straight up into the meteor-streaked sky. He would have to change that.

Peter quickly unbuckled Franklin's straps and shoved the still-protesting monkey aside. He looked out the hatchway and pulled on one of the control levers. The rocket veered to the right so sharply that Peter, Franklin, and Tink were almost hurled out. Peter quickly pushed the lever forward, straightening the rocket. He tried the other lever, gently pushing and pulling, getting the feel of it.

What are you doing? chimed Tink.

"I'm steering it," said Peter.

Steering it WHERE?

Peter was pondering the same question. He looked out the open hatchway. Below—quite far below—he saw the city of Maknar and the palace; in the distance to one side was the desert. To the other side lay the harbor and the sea. His eyes rested a moment on the vast expanse of dark water. Then he gently pushed on both levers. The rocket began to turn to a horizontal position.

What are you doing? said Tink.

"I'm going to fly it into the sea," said Peter. "That way they can't get the starstuff back. We'll jump out before it reaches the water."

What about Franklin?

"I'll hold him."

The rocket leveled off. Peter, sticking his head out the hatchway to see, put it into a sweeping turn over the desert, aiming toward the harbor. He brought the rocket lower, lower; he passed over the palace and could see, hurtling past, the ring of torches still burning around the launch site in the courtyard. Ahead, he saw the curve of the harbor, the masts of ships. He squinted against the rushing air as he looked out toward the sea.

He angled the rocket even lower. The roar of the wind filled his ears. Thus he did not hear the urgent warning sound from Tink, nor the shriek from Franklin.

Then he felt the cold creeping into his feet. He turned to see Ombra just outside the cage. He was shrinking from the light of the starstuff in the compartment above but managing to reach a black tentacle out to touch Peter's shadow, cast in that same light. Peter felt his strength being sucked away. He whirled back to the hatchway and, sticking his head out, saw that the rocket was just about to reach the harbor; ahead, almost level with the rocket, was the mainmast of a large sailing ship.

Peter felt the cold rising in his legs. There was no more time. He reached up and yanked on the red lever. He heard the hatch on the starstuff compartment opening, then saw a flash outside, like lightning. He heard a roar of rage and felt the warmth flood back into his legs as the flash drove Ombra back. Before Ombra could touch his shadow again, Peter released the red lever and dove out of the opening.

As he did, he heard a *clang* above him, and he realized to his horror that the starstuff hatch—either because of the motion of the rocket, or Ombra's actions—had swung closed. He whirled back, hoping to reach the lever again, but the rocket was already hurtling past, faster than he could fly. With a desperate lunge he managed to grab on to its side, but the smooth metal gave him no purchase. He slid down to the end of the rocket, finally stopping when he caught hold of one of the four hinged steering plates sticking out of the base.

He clung to the plate, the wind roaring past. He dared not let go of the rocket for two reasons: one was that Tinker

Bell was still inside; the other was that, although he had dumped some of the starstuff over the harbor, he had not dumped it all—he could see that the top of the rocket was still glowing brightly. He didn't know whether there was enough starstuff left to accomplish Glotz's mission, but he did know this: the rocket was no longer descending. He felt a movement in the plate he was clinging to as it was pulled by the cable attached to it. Something—either the monkey, or Ombra himself—was operating the steering levers.

The rocket began to rise.

CHAPTER 58

CHE ROAR in the SKY

FROM THE DECK OF THE *De Vliegen*—the name carved on the prow of the ship he and his mates had just commandeered—George watched helplessly as the three rowboats full of angry men drew closer. The nearest rowboat had almost reached the ship; by the light from the meteor-streaked sky George could clearly see the rage on the men's faces.

Suddenly, the rage turned to fear. The men stopped rowing and pointed at something, shouting. George heard a roar in the sky and turned to see a rocket thundering toward the ship. It was spitting orange flames and billowing black smoke and seemed impossibly close to the water, so close that George was sure it would hit the ship. As it bore down on him, he saw what looked like a door flapping open.

In the next instant, the night turned to brilliant day as the rocket released a glowing mass of yellow-gold light, brighter than anything George or the others had ever seen.

James, Slightly, and the other boys were hurled to the deck, thrown on their bellies against the rough wood as if a giant hand were pressing down on them.

George tried to hold on to the helm, but he was ripped away from it and thrown against the mizzenmast by what felt like a hurricane wind. Yet it wasn't wind at all—not a line fluttered, and the mainsail still hung limply from the yard. And despite its terrifying force, the "wind" also had a strangely pleasant component, imparting a feeling of well-being that George recognized instantly, having felt it before.

"Starstuff!" he shouted to the others. "Stay down! Don't look at it! Keep away from it!"

The glowing sphere sank slowly, like a giant balloon. George prayed it would land in the water, but it descended directly onto the *De Vliegen*. As the starstuff touched the ship, bolts of golden light raced down the masts and spread across the deck like melted wax. It washed over the cowering boys, whose fear turned to joy as they felt their aches and hunger disappear, felt their bodies grow lighter.

Then something rocked the ship, port to starboard, bow to stern. With their eyes pressed shut against the brilliant glare, the boys could not see what was happening, but the ship was now glowing—every sail, every plank, every line, cleat, pulley, and nail, shining with golden light. And then, as swiftly as the light had spread throughout the ship, it began to contract, re-forming itself into a huge glowing orb, which rolled across the deck to the main cargo hold, whose hatch had been left open during the repairs. The sphere stopped on the brink, then plunged into the belly of the ship.

The glare was gone; the boys opened their eyes. The ship looked normal again, save for a column of golden light rising from the hold into the night sky.

George and James were the first back on their feet.

"Is it gone?" said James, blinking.

"I don't think so," said George, pointing toward the light column.

"Maybe we should close the hatch," said James.

"No," said George. "It's too dangerous."

"Not for us," said Slightly, arriving on the quarterdeck. "These suits will protect us." He, Curly, and Nibs went to the hatchway and heaved the doors closed. The intense light now escaped from the cracks of the hatch, reaching into the night sky. Then, as the boys stared in astonishment, the light began to change color, from gold to yellow, from yellow to orange, then to a feverish red, and then . . . nothing.

"Do you think it's passed through the hull?" said James.

"I don't know," said George. "I don't know where it is."

"They're coming!" shouted Thomas.

George spun around. He'd forgotten all about the attackers in the rowboats. They had retreated during the starstuff spectacle, but now that the ship appeared normal again, they were rowing toward it furiously.

"Prepare to be boarded!" George shouted. "Loose the nets, let fly the belaying pins!" He'd dreamed of being a sea captain and issuing these orders.

The other boys stood still, looking confused.

"Untie the nets!" shouted George. "And throw anything at them that isn't tied down!"

The rowboats quickly closed the distance. One bumped up against the hull.

"Hurry with those nets!" George shouted. "James, climb the forward mast and give me more sail!"

James started running toward the mast, and then a wonderful thing happened: his feet left the ground. He was flying, like Peter! With a whoop of elation he swept up the mast and began untying the sails.

The other boys, seeing this, leapt from the deck and found, to their utter joy that they, too, could fly—at least for now. Prentiss, Thomas, and Tubby Ted began swooping around the deck, untying nets as quickly as they could. Slightly, Curly, Nibs, and the twins were scooping up wooden pins, empty barrels, and anything else they could find and dropping them on the first boatload of attackers, now climbing the nets. The missiles hit two of the men on the head, causing them to fall back into their boat, which tipped and capsized, throwing its occupants into the water. Prentiss and Ted joined Slightly and Curly. They flew up and dropped a heavy box of nails into the next rowboat from seventy-five feet in the air. The box went right through the bottom of the rowboat, sinking it immediately as the men dove into the sea. The boys cheered.

But more rowboats were nearing the ship, and still more were coming. George, with James's help on the sails, had the ship moving now, but not fast enough. Two more rowboats banged into the ship. More men jumped onto the nets and started to climb. The boys swooped overhead, raining objects on them. But the men kept coming.

George felt the ship lurch. He looked up, but it wasn't the wind—the sails were no fuller. Another lurch, and then a loud groaning noise rose from the ship's bowels, as though its beams and planks were being torn apart. The masts shook; the sails shivered; the lines danced.

James, standing high on a yardarm on the forward mast, shouted something to George and pointed toward the water.

George, unable to hear over the groaning of the ship, assumed James was pointing out the attackers. "I know!" he shouted. "Just get us more sail!"

But it wasn't that at all. James was gesturing frantically now. George looked, and his mouth fell open.

The *De Vliegen* was rising. George ran to the rail. The ship, its timbers groaning and creaking in protest, was lifting out of the water. The terrified attackers were letting go of the nets and dropping back into the harbor, then swimming frantically away from the dripping hull. The men still in rowboats were staring up at the rising ship in slack-jawed amazement.

George heard a whoop from James; the forward sail was free. He ran back to the wheel and gave it a spin; the ship answered, slowly turning. Its sails filled with wind, and it began to pick up speed. And still it was rising: now fifty feet above the water, now sixty. George put the ship into a long, slow turn to port, coming fully around, and ordered his flying crew to adjust the sails. The flying ship passed over the dry dock, its former attackers staring up at it helplessly.

George spun the wheel, straightening their course. He grinned.

The spires of Zarboff's palace lay directly ahead.

CHAPTER 59

THE STRUGGLE

THE AIR GREW COLDER as the rocket rose, rushing past Peter's bare arms and legs and causing him to shiver as he desperately clung to the metal steering-plate. The rocket flew high over the desert now, Maknar barely visible far below. Above, a thousand meteors slashed the sky.

Soon, he thought.

The fuel couldn't last forever. At some point, the monkey—or whatever was now piloting the rocket—would release the remaining starstuff. If Peter was going to do something, he had to do it now.

He loosened his grip on the metal plate, testing whether he could, for at least a brief burst, fly fast enough to keep up with the speed of the rocket. He wasn't sure. Perhaps if he used his legs to push off from the metal plate . . .

He looked up the side of the rocket. The door to the monkey compartment was perhaps thirty feet away. If he could get just that far, he could grab on to the latch. Thirty feet. He had to try.

Carefully, bracing himself against the rocket's side, he climbed onto the plate. He crouched, tensing his legs, then silently counted: *one . . . two . . .*

THREE!

He pushed off with all his strength. Added to the rocket's forward momentum, the effort sent him skimming upward. He reached out for the latch, but his hand fell a foot short. The rocket slipped past. He grabbed for purchase, his hands sliding along the cold metal, desperately trying to get a grip. His fingers caught a small ridge where two metal plates were joined. Somehow he held on to it, stopping his slide down the rocket. He squinted up through the cold, blasting wind—the latch was five feet above him. He gripped the ridge and with a grunt heaved himself upward. He flung his hands forward and managed to get his right hand on the latch. He clung to it as his legs swung wildly away from the rocket. He got his other hand on the latch and steadied his body. He yanked the latch; the hatch door swung open.

Peter hauled himself up and peered inside. To his relief, he saw that the rocket was being flown by Franklin, his face pressed to the eyepiece, his hairy hands on the control levers. Peter saw no sign of Ombra; apparently the bright glow from the starstuff compartment was keeping him away,

at least for the moment. And there was Tink! She flew to him, chiming something. But Peter had no time to listen. Franklin, intent on earning his banana, was raising an arm toward the red lever that released the starstuff.

"No!" shouted Peter, shoving the screeching monkey away from the controls. He grabbed the levers and, ignoring Franklin's frantic protests, began to turn the rocket.

Urgent chimes from Tink. Peter glanced to his left and saw the blackness seeping into the monkey's cage. A tentacle reached for Peter's shadow. He squirmed to keep it away, at the same time pushing the levers and putting the rocket horizontal. The tentacle touched his shadow. He felt a chill.

"Stop him, Tink!" he shouted, closing his eyes. Even through his eyelids, he could see the flash as Tink filled the rocket with a brilliant light. Peter felt the chill leave him immediately. He opened his eyes; Ombra was gone again, for now. Franklin was gibbering hysterically, temporarily blinded. Tink lay motionless on the bottom of the cage. Peter picked her up and tucked her gently inside his shirt, then returned his attention to the controls. He stuck his head out the open hatchway and, getting his bearings, began steering the rocket back toward Maknar, and the sea beyond.

He glanced back into the cage.

The tentacle was there again. It was slithering forward, reaching for Peter's shadow. He shifted away, but there was little room to maneuver in the cage, especially with Franklin whimpering in the corner. The tentacle kept coming. Again it touched his shadow; again he felt the cold. He looked out the hatchway; the rocket was still over the desert, too far from the sea. The cold was creeping up inside him. He felt Ombra now, as he had felt him at Stonehenge. Peter had won that struggle, but he was losing this one, the darkness flowing into him through the tentacle attached to his shadow, filling him, taking him over.

"No!" he shouted, resisting, willing his arms to push the levers forward, to put the rocket into a steeper dive. He pushed his head out the window and saw that the city and harbor were closer, but still too far. His eyes fell on a dark shape in the desert. He heard Ombra's roar of rage and realized that he was hearing it *inside his own mind*, as Ombra saw—through Peter's eyes—what Peter was looking at.

Now Peter's arms and hands were moving. But Peter was not moving them—Ombra was. He was making Peter pull the control levers back.

"No!" Peter shouted, this time at his own hands. But they continued to betray him. The rocket was turning back toward the sky. Ombra was going to make Peter finish the job.

"N—" he started to repeat, but now Ombra had control over even his mouth, and he heard himself say in a ghastly voice, part his and part Ombra's: "Quiet, foolish boy." Peter watched in helpless horror as his own hands began to steer the rocket upward, and he realized that as soon as it was vertical again Ombra would make him release the starstuff.

And that realization gave him an idea.

He concentrated on it, keeping it in the tiny part of his mind that was still just Peter, and not Ombra/Peter. He could not let Ombra know there was any of him still free. He would hide inside himself, waiting for his one chance to make his plan work, if it could work at all.

The rocket pointed straight up. Peter saw his right hand reach for the red starstuff-release lever.

Get ready . . .

His hand grabbed hold of the lever and pulled. As before, there was a blinding flash. And as before, the light flash forced Ombra away. He detached from Peter's shadow and shrank back into the dark bowels of the rocket. The instant he felt Ombra leave, Peter focused his mind on his right arm and shoved the red lever forward. With a *clang* the starstuff hatch slammed shut. Peter heard Ombra's angry roar and an instant later saw the tentacle coming at him in the cage, reaching for his shadow, touching it.

But this time Peter did not try to shift his shadow away.

This time Peter *separated from his shadow*.

He didn't know how he did it—not exactly—it was more of an intense feeling than a conscious thought. But suddenly he was on one side of the cage with the screeching Franklin, his shadow on the other. Ombra's tentacle still grasped the shadow. But now Peter no longer felt the cold.

He was different in other ways as well—very different—but he had no time to consider the changes. He had something else to think about. He stuck his head out the opening, saw the meteor-filled sky above him, the dark desert below, and . . .

There.

He grabbed the levers, shoving them forward, turning the rocket in a stomach-churning dive. He heard another roar from Ombra, who knew what Peter planned to do. Franklin's screeches grew suddenly louder. Peter glanced over his shoulder and saw that the dark shape, despite the bright starstuff glow, was billowing into the cage. He turned back to the window, forcing himself to concentrate on steering the rocket . . . lower, lower, almost to the desert floor and now leveling off, hurtling along the dune-tops toward the target.

"It's useless, boy." He heard the hideous groaning voice in his ear, over the howl of the wind. Ombra, unable to get inside Peter through his shadow, was now enveloping him like a cloud. "If you stop this rocket, we will build another."

Peter said nothing, concentrating on holding the rocket level as it hurtled forward, closer, closer . . .

"You will not be free of me," said the groaning voice. "No matter what happens, *you will not be free of me.*"

Closer . . . closer . . .

NOW!

Peter grabbed the shrieking Franklin by the arm and, with all his strength, heaved against the rocket hatch. It came open; he and the monkey flew out, followed an instant later by what looked like a puff of black smoke.

The wind caught Peter and hurled him backward, head over heels. He almost slammed into the sand before he got his bearings and righted himself, just in time to turn and see the rocket.

Its fuel finally expended, the rocket coughed out its last tongue of flame as it hurled directly into the huge, gaping, dark mouth of the Jackal.

And then the desert night exploded.

CHAPTER 60

$\mathcal{B}$RIGHTER THAN $\mathcal{D}$AY

$\mathcal{L}$EONARD ASTER WAS SURE the flash meant the end of the world.

He had watched the rocket launch, standing with Molly and Bakari on either side of him, their faces pressed against the bars of the jail-cell window. As the rocket climbed, they heard anxious shouting—Viktor Glotz's voice especially— and saw a hundred palace guards running around in the torchlight. But they couldn't tell what was happening. All they knew was that the rocket had gone up.

Peter had been unable to stop it.

A short while later, they once again heard shouting. They'd looked out to see the rocket cross the sky directly above the palace. For a few minutes, nothing; the three of them had stood by the window watching, listening, waiting. . . .

Then the sky grew brighter than day, illuminated by a

blinding white light that seemed to come from everywhere at once.

This is it, Leonard thought. *This is what Ombra described.*

He held his daughter close and looked over at his friend, awaiting the end of the world.

The brightness dimmed. Night returned, the sky still streaked with meteors. The palace walls still stood. Men were shouting from the courtyard, their voices tinged with panic.

The world had not ended.

But *something* had happened.

Leonard stared out the window, wondering what it was.

CHAPTER 61

THE CELL DOOR

THE BLAST OF BRILLIANT LIGHT sent Peter tumbling through the desert air like seaweed tossed by a giant wave. There was no sound and no sensation of wind; it was as if the light itself swept him along.

The brightness disappeared as suddenly as it had come, leaving Peter lying on his back on the sand, temporarily unable to see. He felt something clinging to his chest, and he realized that he was still holding the whimpering form of Franklin the monkey. He sat up, blinking. "Tink!" he called.

I'm here, came the chimed response, and he felt wings fluttering against his cheek. Tink said something in Monkey to the frightened Franklin, who relaxed his grip. As Peter's eyes readjusted to the night, he stood, slipped out of the golden suit, and checked himself for injury. He was unhurt, but he felt quite strange—*different,* although he didn't know exactly how. He looked up; the moon hung high in a sky still alight with meteor streaks. In the distance he saw the spires of Zarboff's palace rising over Maknar. He turned around and scanned the desert—once, twice, then a third time to be sure.

The Jackal was gone. He studied the spot where it had once stood; there was nothing, not even a hole in the sand. Just desert.

Tink saw this too.

Good riddance, she chimed.

"We've got to get back to the palace," said Peter.

Wait, said Tink.

"Wait for what?" said Peter.

For you, said Tink.

"What do you mean, 'for me'?" Peter said. "I'm right here."

Not all of you, said Tink. She pointed out at the desert. Peter looked, and at first saw nothing. But Tink kept pointing, and then he saw it, sliding swiftly across the white, moonlit desert sand—a shadow.

Peter tensed, as the first thought in his mind was *Ombra*.

No, said Tink. *It's you*.

The shadow slid to his feet and as it touched Peter, he instantly felt right again. He looked down at his attached shadow for a moment. Then he said to Tink, "Let's go."

Don't forget Franklin, said Tink.

Peter sighed and scooped up the monkey, which

shrieked—from delight or fear, Peter couldn't tell which—as Peter launched himself from the sand. With Tink at his side, he swooped across the desert, his moonlit-cast shadow keeping pace on the sand below. Within minutes they reached the palace compound. Peter alit gently on a shadowy section of the massive outer wall. The torch circle was still burning around the rocket-launch site; dozens of figures milled about. Most of them were soldiers, but in the middle of the throng Peter saw Viktor Glotz and King Zarboff engaged in an angry exchange, both of them shouting. Peter looked toward the dungeon but saw nobody near it.

"Come on, Tink," he whispered. Keeping low in the shadows, they flew along the wall to the dungeon, landing by the big wooden door. Peter released Franklin, who, recognizing the building where he and his fellow monkeys lived, scampered inside. Peter and Tink followed more cautiously, alert for guards. Seeing none, Peter ran down the corridor.

"Molly!" he called as he neared her jail cell.

"Peter!" she cried, rushing to the cell door. "You're all right!" She reached through the bars and touched Peter's arm.

"Yes, I'm all right," he said, putting his hand over hers for a moment, then pulling it back, blushing.

"What happened to the rocket?" said Leonard.

"It flew into the Jackal," said Peter.

"Was that what caused the flash of light?" asked Bakari.

"I think so," said Peter. "I'm not sure what happened. But the Jackal isn't there anymore."

Now it was Leonard's hand reaching through the bars, resting on Peter's shoulder. "You stopped Ombra," he said. "It seems grossly inadequate to say this to a person who just saved the world—but thank you, Peter."

Peter blushed.

He had help, noted Tink.

"Thank you, too, Tink," said Leonard.

"We need to get you out of here before the guards return," said Peter. He rattled the door lock, to no avail. "Do you have any starstuff left, Molly?"

"I'm afraid not," she said.

There was shouting from the courtyard.

"I'll go find the guard with the keys," said Peter. "He's got to be around somewhere."

"No," said Leonard, his voice grave. "You could be caught, and then we'd all be stuck here. You must leave immediately and get back to England, so you can tell the rest of the Starcatchers about Glotz's rocket and the Others' plans."

He's right, said Tink.

"I'm sorry, sir," said Peter, "but I won't leave without you." He shot a glance at Molly. "*All* of you."

"I appreciate that," said Leonard, "and I expected you to say it. But this is not a time for heroism. You cannot risk being caught. It is absolutely vital that this information be passed along to the Starcatchers before the Others can mount another threat. This is far more important than our lives, or anyone's. Please, Peter, go."

"He's right, Peter," said Molly. "You must go."

Even she's right, for once, said Tink.

Peter looked from Molly to Leonard, then shook his head. "No," he said. "I'll get you out somehow."

The shouting in the courtyard grew louder. There was a gunshot, then another. Bakari went to the cell window and peered out.

"Peter, *listen,*" said Leonard, his voice desperate. "Even if you do manage to get us out of here, we've no way to get out of Rundoon."

"Yes, you do," said Peter. "George and the others went to the harbor to get a ship."

Leonard shook his head. "I'm sure they'll try," he said. "But I seriously doubt that a group of boys will be able to commandeer a ship."

"You are mistaken, Lord Aster," said Bakari. "It seems that the boys have, indeed, obtained a ship."

"How could you possibly know that?" said Leonard, turning to his friend.

"Because," said Bakari, pointing out the window, "it's just now coming over the palace wall."

CHAPTER 62

UNDER FIRE

THE FLYING SHIP *De Vliegen* approached the palace wall, leaving a trail of chaos on the streets of Maknar, where crowds wailed and scattered in terror at the sight of the massive, dripping, barnacle-encrusted hull passing overhead. George, at the helm, was frantically trying to learn how to pilot the ship. He was getting a feel for the steering, but having little luck controlling the altitude. He saw now, as the *De Vliegen* reached the palace compound, that it was too low. He felt a lurch and heard a grinding sound as the hull scraped the wall, knocking some stones into the courtyard below.

The crash of the stones drew the attention of the men in the courtyard, who shouted and pointed in alarm. Their shouts interrupted the heated argument between Glotz and Zarboff, who looked up at the flying ship, gaping in amazement. Zarboff's surprise turned to wrath when, by the light of moon and meteor, he saw heads poking over the ship's rail, looking down. With a roar of rage, Zarboff recognized his slave boys.

He whirled and, with spittle flying from his mouth, screamed an order to his soldiers. Immediately they raised their rifles and began firing at the ship. As muzzle fires flashed, the slave boys jumped away from the rail.

Bullets thunked into the ship, splintering the woodwork. George spun the wheel hard. The ship began to turn, but it was now below the top of the wall; unless George could gain altitude, they would be trapped inside the courtyard and eventually cut to pieces by the riflemen. Bullets struck the hull and whistled through the rigging, some puncturing the sails. George looked high overhead and had an idea.

"Take in the topsail!" he shouted up to James, who was crouching high up on a yardarm.

"Do *what* to the topsail?" James shouted back.

"Make it smaller!" shouted George.

James flew up to the highest sail and, as bullets zinged past him, began trimming it. Slowly, ever so slowly, George felt the bow of the ship rising. As more bullets zinged past, he yelled commands to Slightly, Prentiss, Thomas, and the other boys, ordering them to pull in this sail, let out that one. The ship was rising more quickly now and moving with greater speed. George got it high enough that he felt reasonably safe from the bullets, though the occasional shot still came close. Using both rudder and sail, he put the ship into

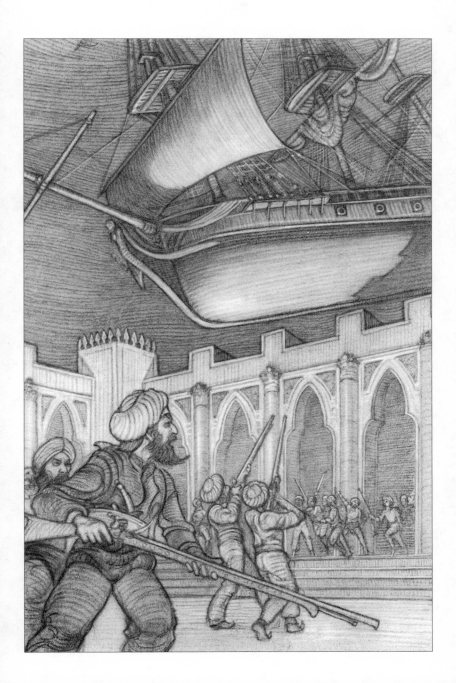

a gentle turn, such that it circled high above the palace. He assessed the damage; there was a good deal of splintered wood and a few tattered sails, but, incredibly, nobody had been hurt.

George wasn't sure what to do. He didn't know how long the ship would keep flying. He also didn't know where Peter was, or even if Peter was still alive. He had no idea how to go about trying to rescue Molly and her father from the hornet's nest of angry, shooting men below. He peered over the side: the soldiers had dragged a catapult onto a rampart and were busy setting a burning cauldron into its sling. They were going to try to burn the ship out of the sky!

We can't stay here, George thought. But Molly was down there somewhere. Lord Aster. Possibly Peter. How could he just fly away and leave them? But what choice did he have?

Waving urgently, Prentiss shouted at him from the bow. "To the right! To the RIGHT!" He and Thomas and Nibs had a large crate of nails, which they were hoisting onto the gunwale.

George looked down: the boys meant to bomb the catapult. He spun the wheel to port and steered directly over the rampart. The boys heaved the heavy box up and over the gunwale and let it drop. It fell directly onto the catapult, smashing it and hurling the cauldron of fire down the wall and into the courtyard, scattering the soldiers. The boys on the bow whooped in triumph.

George, allowing himself a brief smile, steered the ship back over the courtyard, still pondering a rescue attempt.

Maybe . . .

He jumped as a hand tapped his shoulder. He whirled and saw . . .

"Peter!"

They had never been great friends, but in that moment they came very close to hugging each other, each stepping hesitantly forward before stopping and settling for a manly handshake.

"I know I asked for a ship," said Peter. "But *this* . . ." He gestured at the flying vessel, grinning. "Well done, George!"

"Your wish is my command," said George, with a mock bow. His face became serious again as he asked, "What about Molly?"

"She's still in the dungeon, with her father and Bakari. I couldn't get them out. Aster demanded we leave them here, but of course we won't do that."

"I should say not!" said George.

Idiots, observed Tink, sitting on Peter's head.

"What did she say?" asked George.

"She says we need a rescue plan," said Peter, as a volley of gunshots rang out below.

"I agree," said George, ducking away from the gunwale.

"Peter!" The shout came from James, who was high up on the mast and had just spotted his friend. As Peter watched in delight, James flew down to him; the other boys quickly followed, flying to the quarterdeck.

"Peter!" shouted Prentiss. "We can fly!"

"So I see!" said Peter.

"Although I think it's wearing off," said Thomas, who had hit the deck a bit hard.

"No, it's not," said Ted. He jumped upward, then came right back down, landing on his rear. "Yes, it is," he amended.

The boys gathered around Peter and began to pepper him with questions about the rocket, the starstuff, and Ombra. He waved them off.

"There's no time," he said. "We need to get Molly out of the dungeon. The door's locked, and I've no idea who has the keys. Does anybody have any ideas?"

"What about that black powder, for the rocket?" said Prentiss. He pointed down at the powder wagon, still in the courtyard. "Could we use it to blow open the cell door?"

Peter, looking at the soldiers milling in the courtyard, shook his head. "We can't get near it," he said. "They'd cut us down." As he spoke, another volley of shots forced the boys to move away from the gunwale.

"I wish *we* had guns," said Thomas.

James frowned. He poked his head back over the gunwale.

"What about those?" he said.

Cautiously, Peter leaned over the rail and looked where James was pointing. He smiled at James, and James smiled back. Then Peter stood up.

"George," he said, "do you know how to fire a cannon?"

CHAPTER 63

The Golden Moon

Molly's face hurt from pressing against the cell bars as she strained to see what was going on in the confusion of the courtyard. Behind her, also looking out, were her father and Bakari. They didn't see much, other than soldiers shouting and firing their rifles at the sky. Every now and then they caught a glimpse of the flying ship, but usually it was too high overhead, clearly trying to stay out of range of the bullets.

The three prisoners speculated about the ship, concluding that it must have somehow become infused with starstuff. Leonard grew increasingly agitated as the ship sailed back and forth, a fat target for Zarboff's soldiers.

"I wish they'd just leave," he said. "They're going to get themselves killed."

Molly turned to her father. "Would *you* leave?"

384

Leonard smiled ruefully and shook his head. "No," he admitted. "I'd try to rescue you."

Molly nodded and turned back to the courtyard.

"Someone's coming," said Bakari. He looked down the corridor. "It's Peter!"

Molly and Leonard rushed to the cell door as Peter, with Tink on his head, trotted into view. Across the corridor, Hook, who'd been sitting in the shadows of his cell, rose to his feet.

"Peter," said Leonard, "what's happening?"

"No time to explain," said Peter. "You must lie on the floor, as far from the window and outside wall as possible. And by all means, cover your heads."

"But what . . . ?" began Molly.

"Please, just get down!" said Peter.

Before Molly could speak again, he was gone.

⬤━◆━⬤

King Zarboff the Third frowned at the meteor-streaked sky. Several minutes earlier the flying ship had stopped circling the palace and flown off on a straight course; it was no longer visible from inside the courtyard wall. Zarboff went over to Viktor Glotz, who was staring intently at the sky. Minutes ago the two men had been arguing heatedly over the apparent failure of the rocket, but now their anger at each other was replaced by shared concern about the strange ship. They

385

had no doubt that starstuff was involved, but how had the boys gotten hold of it? And where were they now?

A soldier shouted something from one of the ramparts; he was pointing to something in the distance.

"The ship is coming back," said Zarboff. He barked a command in the Rundoon language; the soldiers readied their rifles. Zarboff turned to Glotz, his expression a mixture of anger and puzzlement.

"What do they want?" he said. "Why do they return?"

Glotz had been thinking about that. Now, as Zarboff asked the question, the answer came to him.

"The Starcatchers in the dungeon!" he said. "They're trying to free them!"

"The Starcatchers will die before they escape my kingdom," snarled Zarboff. He barked another order. A half dozen soldiers started running toward the dungeon. As they did, a chorus of shouts arose in the courtyard, and a hundred fingers pointed toward the sky.

The flying ship was swooping down toward them under full sail.

"We're a minute away!" shouted George, peering ahead at the palace courtyard. He saw muzzle flashes; the soldiers were already shooting. "Slightly, are you ready?"

"Almost!" came the reply from below, where Slightly,

Nibs, Curly, and the twins were frantically loading the fourth and last starboard cannon. The boys had been very lucky—the shot, powder, fuses, and matches had all been stored close by the cannons. George, whose family kept an antique cannon at their country estate and fired it on ceremonial occasions, had raced below and hastily demonstrated the loading process on the first cannon; Slightly and the others had done the rest. George prayed they had done it right—cannons, even when properly loaded, had been known to explode.

George looked aloft, where James and Prentiss were working from the topsail yardarm. They had let the topsail out fully; the force of the wind on it was what was pressing the *De Vliegen*'s bow downward, causing the ship to descend. It would be James and Prentiss's job to take the sail in when it was time to make the ship rise and escape. They were vulnerable to rifle fire up there, but there was no other way. Thomas and Tubby Ted stood by George, ready to pull in or let out sail as needed.

George looked forward again. He had judged the angle of descent well; the ship would just clear the compound wall on its dive into the courtyard. The rifle fire was increasing, the bullets again slamming into the ship's hull.

"Take what cover you can!" shouted George. "We're going in!"

They passed over the wall. The rifle fire was constant.

George heard a high-pitched scream and saw Thomas crumple to the deck, holding his leg. He felt a thud in his left arm, as though somebody had punched him; he looked down and saw blood. A second later, he felt the searing pain. Using his right hand, he spun the ship's wheel to the right, then left again, angling the ship so that it would run parallel to the massive dungeon building, which would be off the starboard side. The ship was still descending; its keel was now no more than twenty feet above the courtyard itself. Soldiers ran behind, firing upward at the ship.

The dungeon was just ahead; George saw the row of barred cell windows along the bottom of the wall. Peter had told him Molly was in the fourth cell from the near end. He hoped the cannons were aimed low enough. His arm was throbbing intensely now.

"James!" he shouted, "a bit less topsail!" He needed to stop the ship's descent before it hit the ground. As James and Prentiss worked above, George returned his attention to the dungeon, now almost alongside.

"Slightly!" he shouted. "Ready on the forward cannon!"

"Ready!" came the shout back, over the sound of the rifle fire.

George watched the wall, trying to judge when the cannon would be lined up with the fourth cell window. A few more feet . . .

"Fire one!" he shouted.

Molly, lying on the cell floor, heard the cannon's boom. It was louder and deeper than the *crack-crack-crack* of the rifles. Then she heard a resounding crash as the cannonball struck the dungeon wall near the cell. A cloud of dust filled the corridor. She struggled to her feet. Her father was already at the cell window.

"They're firing the cannons at the dungeon!" he shouted. "They're trying to—"

He was interrupted by the shout of "Fire two!" and another huge boom as a second cannonball slammed into the dungeon wall directly outside their cell, hurling all three occupants to the ground in a hail of flying stone. Coughing and choking in the thick dust, their ears ringing, the three struggled back to their feet. Blood poured from Leonard's chin, where he'd been cut by a shard of masonry, but they were otherwise unhurt. Their relief lasted only a few seconds, however; there were shouts coming their way and now soldiers in the corridor. One of them produced a ring of keys and began to open the cell door. Behind him, the others drew their swords, and the looks on their faces told Molly the frightening truth: *they mean to kill us*.

"Ready on three!" shouted George. The first shot had gone

too early, striking the cell next to Molly's. But the second had been right on target, blasting big chunks of stone out of the wall. A third ball in the same spot should poke a hole through it.

"Fire three!" he shouted.

———◆———

The third cannonball blasted through the dungeon wall just as the soldiers entered the cell. Molly, Leonard, and Bakari, having heard George give the order to fire, dropped to the floor, but the soldiers ran head-on into a hail of stone fragments that knocked them over backward, some of them screaming in pain. The ball shot across the corridor and knocked the door to Hook's cell off its hinges, very nearly decapitating the crouching Hook himself.

Molly, disoriented by the dust and the noise, felt her father's hands pulling her to her feet. Over the ringing in her ears she dimly heard a familiar voice shouting her name . . .

Peter!

He was extending his hand through the jagged hole in the wall left by the cannonball.

"This way!" he shouted. "Hurry!"

Leonard pushed Molly through the hole, then Bakari; then he climbed through himself. The three of them, turned ghost white by the dust, stood with Peter by the dungeon wall. The action in the courtyard had moved on, following the flying ship, which was traveling away from the dungeon. Its stern loomed against the meteor sky as rifle-wielding soldiers ran after it. Molly could make out George at the helm, shouting to the other boys, who were working on sails and ropes as bullets whistled around them. For the moment, nobody seemed to notice Peter and the three escaped prisoners in the shadow of the dungeon.

"Now what?" Leonard asked Peter.

"George is going to turn the ship and bring it back this way," said Peter. "They'll lower a rope. I might be able to fly Molly up to it, but I doubt that I can lift you or Bakari."

You can't lift her either, observed Tink, who was perched in Peter's hair. *She's a cow.*

"Tink!" reprimanded Peter, glancing at Leonard. But Leonard's attention was focused on the ship. "Let's hope George gets back here before anybody notices us," he said.

He had barely gotten those words out when they heard angry shouts behind them. They turned to see a soldier, his sword drawn, coming through the hole in the wall. And there were others right behind him.

—◆—

"Loosen that rope, Ted," shouted George. "No, not that one. *That* one. James! After we tack, give us more topsail so we can get down and pick them up. Ready about!"

George spun the wheel hard to the left, using only his

391

right arm. His left arm was useless and throbbing with pain. The ship began to turn; below, the soldiers scurried to get better shooting positions. Fortunately, they were miserable marksmen; they also appeared to be running low on ammunition. The shots were coming less frequently. As the ship came around, George peered ahead and found the dungeon wall, the place where Peter was to wait with Molly, her father, and Bakari. His heart jumped when he caught sight of the four figures near the dark wall. Then he saw other figures with them—soldiers.

This isn't good, he thought.

"More topsail, James!" he called. "Let's take her down!"

<hr />

"Stay behind me, Molly!" said Leonard, putting himself between his daughter and the tips of the soldiers' swords.

Seven soldiers had come through the wall, four of them bleeding from the cannonball blast, all of them very angry. They were advancing in a semicircle toward Molly, Peter, Leonard, and Bakari.

"Peter," said Molly, "get out of here while you can."

Listen to her, said Tink.

Instead of answering, Peter took a step directly toward the nearest soldier. The man thrust his blade forward, but struck only the air. Peter had launched himself straight up and was now coming back down, hitting the top of the

392

soldier's head with both feet. The man cried out in pain and crumpled to the ground, dropping his sword; in a flash, Leonard stooped and picked it up. As he did, Peter swooped sideways, delivering a hard kick to another soldier's right wrist. His sword tumbled loose, and Bakari was on it like a cat.

Now the fight was on. Peter no longer had the element of surprise; the soldiers knew he could fly. But he could still serve as an annoyance, swooping at them from above as they slashed at him with their swords. Meanwhile, Leonard and Bakari, both strong swordsmen, were able—barely—to keep the soldiers at bay, the two of them standing with their backs to the dungeon wall, protecting themselves and Molly from the five remaining blades arrayed against them.

As he swooped and darted, Peter kept glancing at the *De Vliegen*. It had turned around and was heading back toward the dungeon. Unfortunately, the ship was bringing with it a horde of angry soldiers following behind, still getting off the occasional shot. Somehow Molly, Leonard, and Bakari would have to break through the ranks of their attackers and get aboard—*before* the rest of the soldiers spotted them.

The big ship was close now, its bow filling the sky.

"Get ready!" Peter shouted. But as he did, he saw that, skilled as they were, Leonard and Bakari, two blades against five, could not force their way through the wall of flashing steel.

"Ted!" shouted George. "Throw the rope over!"

Tubby Ted—getting it right the first time, for once—picked up the heavy coil of rope on the forward port-side deck and heaved it over the rail. One end was tied to a winch on the ship, the other would fall to the ground to be grabbed by whoever was down there. George, unable to see the end of the rope from where he stood at the wheel, watched the rail intently, not knowing whether the rope would be bringing friends aboard, or killers.

Peter saw the rope drop down over the side of the ship; Leonard saw it, too.

"Take Molly, Peter!" he shouted between blade thrusts.

"No, Father!" said Molly.

"YES!" thundered Leonard, in a voice that even Molly dared not defy. He glanced at Peter, then Bakari, and said, "On the count of three."

Bakari nodded. Peter arced into the air.

"One," said Leonard. "Two . . . THREE!"

Leonard and Bakari lunged at the soldiers, thrusting furiously, momentarily driving them back. At the same time, Peter dove, leveled off, and scooped Molly into his arms, praying he had enough momentum to reach the deck. He lifted her off the ground and veered toward the ship, rising, rising . . .

. . . and then stalling and starting to descend.

"Let me go!" shouted Molly.

Yes! Let her go! concurred Tink.

"Hang on!" shouted Peter, and he swerved desperately sideways.

UNNH! Molly and Peter grunted together as they slammed into the side of the ship. They started to slide down the wood. Peter reached his left arm out and managed to grab the dangling rope.

"Here!" he gasped, yanking it toward Molly. She gripped it and hung on, letting go of Peter. He looked up and saw Tubby Ted leaning over the rail, his arms outstretched. As Molly began struggling her way up the rope toward Ted, Peter turned and darted back down toward Leonard and Bakari.

They were losing the fight. Their backs were against the dungeon wall; the soldiers were closing in on them. To make matters worse, more soldiers were running toward them. Soon they would be impossibly outnumbered. And the flying ship, their only hope for escape, was getting away, the rope end dragging on the ground.

Peter swooped down at the swordsmen, shouting and punching as he dodged their blades. Tink did her part as well, darting into their faces, delivering surprisingly painful kicks with her tiny feet. But it was not enough. More soldiers were arriving, and the ship was leaving. For a fraction of an instant, amid the furious clash of blades, Peter's eyes met Leonard's, and Peter saw only despair; Leonard knew the fight was lost.

"OUT OF MY WAY, YOU SCURVY DOGS!"

The roar came from the right, a booming voice that Peter knew well but had never before been grateful to hear: Hook. He had just emerged through the cannonball hole in the dungeon wall and, with snakelike quickness, snatched a sword from the hand of a soldier with his right hand while clubbing him to the ground with the stump of his hookless left arm. Bellowing fearsomely and wielding the sword with a pirate's ruthless efficiency, he began hacking his way through the soldiers, who were thrown into confusion by this blindside attack. Hook quickly joined forces with Leonard and Bakari, the three of them forming a deadly triangle of steel, their combined skills overmatching any soldiers able to get close. In a few furious seconds, they had fought their way free of the wall and were moving faster and faster toward the receding ship, its rescue rope still dangling tantalizingly.

Peter darted ahead, his intent being to tell George to slow the ship, if possible, to allow the men to reach it. But he was stopped by Tink's sharp chime in his ear.

There's a boy back there.

Peter turned, his eyes scanning the mob of shouting soldiers running this way and that. He spotted the small figure crouching near the hole in the dungeon wall: Tootles. Peter had completely forgotten about the slave boy whose gold suit he'd borrowed. He swooped into a turn and headed back, praying that Tootles weighed less than Molly. A good deal less.

━◆━

"James!" shouted George. "Take in the topsail!"

As James and the others got to work aloft, George, for the dozenth time in the last minute, peered nervously ahead. The ship was nearing the massive wall and was far too low to clear it. Unless they gained altitude soon, they'd smash bow-on into the stone. But so far, only Molly had made it up the rope; Leonard and Bakari were still trapped in their fight with the soldiers. If they didn't reach the ship soon . . .

George glanced back, and his heart leapt. Bakari was running toward the ship, with Leonard right behind, followed by a mob of soldiers. George glanced ahead again. The wall was very close; the ship was still too low.

"Hurry, James!" he shouted, praying that the ship would rise very soon—and that Leonard and Bakari would reach the rope before it did.

━◆━

Bakari had almost reached the rope. Its end was off the ground now; the ship was rising. Bakari glanced back. Leonard was right behind him, followed by Hook, the two of them slashing their swords back at the pursuing soldiers.

"Go on!" shouted Leonard. "I'm right behind you!"

Bakari let go of his sword, grabbed the rope, and—despite arms aching from the furious swordfight—began to climb, hand over hand. The dangling rope end was now more than six feet off the ground and rising. Hook and Leonard reached it at the same time, and, flinging their swords back at the soldiers, jumped together and caught the rope. Leonard began to climb. Hook, with but one hand, could only cling desperately to the rising rope end, wriggling to evade the swords of soldiers slashing at him from below.

Leonard, gasping from the arm-wearying rope climb, reached the ship's rail and was helped over by a smiling Bakari and a tearful Molly. Leonard looked around, assessing the scene aboard the ship. George, at the helm, was shouting frantically at some boys aloft in the sails. Just ahead loomed the compound wall. To Leonard it looked too close, too high.

Something thumped on the deck next to him. He turned and smiled at the sight of Peter, who was carrying a very scared-looking young man on his back.

"HELP!"

The shout came from below. Peter and Leonard leaned over the rail and saw Hook, still dangling from the end of the rope above the thrusting blades of the soldiers. The pirate looked up; his glittering black eyes met Leonard's, then Peter's. There was a plea in those eyes but no groveling; Hook did not beg.

Peter and Leonard looked at each other, both thinking the same thing: it would be easy to simply untie the rope and be done with the man who had tried, more than once, to kill them.

Then Leonard said, "He saved my life, Peter. And Bakari's."

Peter nodded. Together, he and Leonard began hauling on the rope, pulling the pirate onto the ship.

———————

"James!" shouted George. "Hurry!"

James was working furiously on the topsail, but the *De Vliegen* was still too low. The bow was only feet from the wall. They weren't going to make it.

"Hang on!" shouted George, a second before the ship's keel struck the top of the wall. The sudden stop sent every-one sprawling to the deck, save George, who clung to the wheel. There was a horrible grinding sound from below, wood scraping over stone, and then a crash as a chunk of wall broke off and fell to the ground. The ship began to turn to the right, pivoting slowly clockwise on its keel. It finally ground to a stop, its starboard side now facing the courtyard. George spun the wheel, but nothing happened. They were stuck.

A roar went up from the courtyard as the soldiers realized that their prey had not escaped after all. Zarboff was screaming orders at his men. In moments, soldiers appeared with a ladder, then another. They rushed these toward the wall where the ship sat, immobile.

"James!" George shouted. "Take in more sail! Take in all you can! The rest of you lighten the ship! Throw everything overboard!"

James worked the sails as Peter, Leonard, Molly, Bakari, and the others—even Hook—scurried around the deck, grabbing barrels and boxes and heaving them over the side. The *De Vliegen* shifted but did not rise. The soldiers had leaned the ladders against the wall on either end of the ship and were starting to climb. Zarboff stood in the middle of the courtyard, still screaming orders. More barrels went over the side; the ship shifted again. It *wanted* to rise—George could feel it. He needed just a little more lift . . .

"Slightly!" he shouted. "The fourth cannon—is it loaded?"

Slightly, lifting a barrel, answered, "Yes!"

"Fire it now!" shouted George. "Hurry!"

Slightly hurled the barrel over the side and raced down

the companionway. The soldiers were on the wall now, coming toward the ship from both ends. Seconds passed . . .

"Hurry!" shouted George again. *What was Slightly doing down there?*

———◆———

Slightly was aiming. He'd lit the cannon's fuse, and now, in the few seconds left, he was heaving his body against the heavy barrel, shifting it until he hoped it was pointed where he wanted.

The sparking, smoking fuse fire disappeared into the touch hole. Slightly closed his eyes and clapped his hands over his ears.

———◆———

BOOM!

The cannon thundered just as the first of Zarboff's soldiers reached the ship. George felt a lurch and then let out a whoop. *The ship was rising.* The cannon shot had jolted it free. George spun the wheel to port and got the bow turning; wind filled the sails, and the ship began to gain speed, rising and moving away from the palace. The courtyard was in an uproar now, Zarboff's thwarted soldiers shrieking in fury, while the few riflemen with ammunition remaining fired ineffectively at the receding ship.

Such was the clamor in the courtyard that, for a few

moments, nobody noticed where the cannonball had gone.

———◆◆◆———

It had gone where Slightly aimed it—right at King Zarboff the Third. But the ball had not hit him; the portly king had seen the flash and somehow sensed the ball sizzling at him through the night air. In the instant it took to fly from the ship to him, Zarboff managed to lunge to his left just enough so that the ball barely brushed him as it whistled past. That was lucky for Zarboff.

Not so lucky for him was the fact that his momentum sent him stumbling sideways, right into the heavy basket that had been sitting in the courtyard for hours now, unnoticed. Zarboff fell, and, grabbing the basket for support, pulled it over with him. As he did, its lid came unfastened and its occupant spilled out onto the portly king as he lay on the ground. Kundalini's tongue darted out, tasting Zarboff's scent. It was familiar, but familiarity did not translate as affection for a snake. Food was food.

Zarboff struggled to get free, but struggling was useless against Kundalini. The giant snake was perfectly designed for just this situation; each move made by his prey only gave Kundalini another opportunity to tighten his muscled coils. Zarboff emitted a few panicked cries, but they were

402

lost amid the courtyard din. And then he could no longer breathe; he could only struggle in silent horror as his beloved pet began the slow, relentless process of feeding on him.

The last thing Zarboff saw, before he received the gift of unconsciousness, was the silhouette of a ship sailing past the fat, golden moon.

CHAPTER 64

THE ONLY HOPE

TORCHES FLICKERED DIMLY against the cave walls, the flames barely visible through the thick dust swirling in the air. The cave echoed with the sound of rock hitting rock, underscored by the groans and coughs of Mollusks toiling under the glare of their whip-wielding Scorpion guards.

Fighting Prawn, not daring to stop working, sneaked a glance around him. He saw his people: men, women, and—most heartbreakingly—children, with sweat pouring from their bodies; rock dust turning their hair white, their fingers bloody and broken from the endless smashing of lava.

The Scorpions were literally working them to death. If a Mollusk passed out from hunger and exhaustion, the Scorpions whipped him until he resumed working. Those who did not awaken were dragged away, unconscious, and never seen again. Fighting Prawn didn't want to think about what happened to them.

Fighting Prawn knew his people were beyond despair. They no longer looked to him, as they once had, for hope; they knew he had no hope to give them. He wanted more than anything for this ordeal to be over. He wanted to simply lie down on the hard cave floor and let the end come. But he would not do that. He was the Mollusk chief and would not leave his people, even though in his heart he knew he had failed them.

Fighting Prawn felt a nudge from the man working next to him, Leaping Toad. He was holding something in his hand so that only Fighting Prawn could see it. It was a piece of rough lava, with a different type of rock nestled inside, glittering in the torchlight.

It was a rough diamond the size of a knuckle. Diamonds appeared from time to time among the volcanic rock that formed the island; the Mollusks had traditionally called these "hard rocks," and viewed them as amusing trinkets. But Fighting Prawn knew, from his experience as a slave aboard British ships, the great value placed on hard rock by the outside world.

The diamonds were what the Scorpions were after; Fighting Prawn was convinced of that. Somehow they had known of the hard rock on Mollusk Island. Twice in recent days, Mollusk workers had uncovered glittering stones, and both times the Scorpion guards had become very excited, only to be disappointed when they realized that the stones were ordinary minerals. But the rock in Leaping Toad's hand was no ordinary mineral. Fighting Prawn knew it was a diamond, and a big one.

A Scorpion guard, seeing that Fighting Prawn and Leaping Toad had stopped pounding, shouted and came striding toward them. Fighting Prawn, with the slightest shake of his head, indicated to Leaping Toad that the guard was not to see the discovery. Leaping Toad dropped the rock and put his knee over it.

The guard looked briefly at the rocks in front of the two men, then shouted something at them and, raising his whip, gave them each a lash to put them back to work. Fighting Prawn resumed pounding rocks, his mind racing. If the Scorpions saw the diamond, he knew, they would work the Mollusks even harder—if that was possible—in their frenzy to find more. He had to pass the word to the others—any hard rock they found was to be kept from the Scorpions' sight. Maybe if no diamonds were found, they would give up.

Maybe.

It was the only chance Fighting Prawn saw, in the dim, despair-filled cave, to save his people.

CHAPTER 65

THE SECRET WEAPON

IN THE LIGHT OF THE MORNING SUN, Peter leaned over the rail of the *De Vliegen*, looking at the water far below. With no landmarks in sight—only the vast, uninterrupted blue of the sea stretching out below them in every direction—he couldn't judge how far the ship had flown during the night. But he knew it had to be a great distance because the ship was flying very, very fast.

They were headed for Mollusk Island. It had been Leonard's intention to sail the flying ship straight back to London so he could confer with the rest of the Starcatchers about the alarming events in Rundoon. But Peter had begged Leonard to go to the island first, to see what could be done to help the Mollusks. Leonard had reluctantly agreed, deciding that when the ship reached the island, he would use the porpoises to send a brief report on the Rundoon situation back to London.

Peter was sure they were close to Mollusk Island, with the ship traveling at such amazing speed.

That was Hook's doing. Leonard and George, recognizing the pirate's vastly superior seamanship, had reluctantly given him command. Hook had taken the helm, and after experimenting with the flying ship's rudder and sails, issued a crisp series of commands, adding, then adjusting, sail after sail, each time gaining speed and altitude. Now the ship was flying every scrap of canvas it had, soaring thousands of feet above the waves, pressed forward by winds far stronger than those at the surface of the sea, winds that made the taut rigging whistle. The air here was crisp and cold; the sun's rays were welcome.

Peter turned away from the water and looked at his shadow stretching across the deck. It was twice his own length. He stared at it for several seconds.

You're afraid he'll come back.

Peter jumped, the sudden movement nearly throwing Tink off his head.

"I didn't know you were awake," he said.

Awake and cold, she said, snuggling down into his hair. *Why are you afraid of him? He's gone.*

"He was gone once before," Peter said, still looking at his shadow. "And he came back."

But he's not here now.

"I know. But he could be at any time. I feel a bit silly,

but I keep looking at my shadow, wondering if he'll come back."

"Who will come back?" said Molly, her voice startling Peter. He hadn't seen her approaching, clutching a gray blanket around her shoulders to keep warm.

"Um, nobody," said Peter. "Tink and I were just talking."

"I see," said Molly.

No, you don't, said Tink.

"What did she say?" asked Molly.

"She said, ah, we must be getting close to Mollusk Island," said Peter.

"That's what I came to tell you," said Molly. "We may be there quite soon. George found a sextant and took some sights. The only question is whether we have the correct time. George found a clock belowdecks. It's the strangest thing—the clock *glows*, and it ticks quite loudly. Father thinks it must have come into contact with the starstuff. But it seems to be working, and if the time it gave is correct, we're getting quite close to the island." Molly pointed to a speck of white on the horizon. "George thinks that cloud might be over where the island is."

Peter nodded. "Good," he said. He stared at the cloud, thinking of the gentle Mollusks and the vicious Scorpions.

"You're worried for your friends," said Molly, seeing his expression.

"I just hope we're in time," said Peter. He started to say

410

more, but his chest was too tight. He looked away, hoping Molly wouldn't see his eyes glistening.

Molly reached out her hand, and—ignoring Tink's glare—touched Peter's arm. "We'll do what we can," she said. "All of us. We owe you that, for what you did back there."

He had help, noted Tink.

"What's important is that you're safe," said Peter, reddening. "We're all safe."

"You saved more than just us, Peter." She paused. "Will you stay on the island?"

Of course he will, said Tink.

"I'll stay on the island if there's anything left," said Peter. "It's home for me, Molly."

"And your friends? George says they should be in school."

Peter stiffened. "Well, if that's what *George* says . . ."

"I didn't mean it like that, Peter."

Yes, she did, observed Tink.

Peter was about to speak when he saw George clomping toward them, his hair blowing and his smiling face ruddy with the cold. His injured arm had been expertly bandaged by Bakari, who had also tended to Thomas's leg wound; fortunately, neither boy had been seriously hurt.

"Well, well!" George called out. "Smashing bit of wind Hook has managed to find up here, what? With no resistance

411

from the water, we're making three or four times the speed we could make on the sea, and perhaps more! If I'm not mistaken, Peter, that means we should reach your island quite soon. What do you think of that?"

I think most of the wind is coming from him, chimed Tink.

"What'd she say?" asked George.

"She said the sooner the better," said Leonard, just joining them. He and Peter exchanged a look; Peter grinned.

"So, Peter," said Leonard. "I assume George told you that we believe we're nearing Mollusk Island."

"Yes, sir," said Peter. "I suppose the question is, what do we do when we get there?"

"That's what I wanted to talk to you about," said Leonard. "I need you to draw a detailed map of the island, so we can plan our attack."

"I can do that," said Peter, "but there are hundreds of Scorpions, and they're brutal fighters. All we've got is . . ." Peter looked around and shrugged.

"We have a ship, Peter," said Leonard. "A *flying* ship. And we have the element of surprise. And we have . . . a pirate." They turned and looked at Hook, still at the wheel. Hook, seeing everyone staring at him, glared back.

"You *trust* him?" said Peter.

"I trust him to do what's in his interest," said Leonard. "Right now it's in his interest to take us where we want to go so that we don't toss him over the side, which I

412

have assured him we will happily do at the first sign of treachery."

Peter smiled and was rewarded with a personalized glare from Hook.

Leonard added, "And let's not forget Tinker Bell."

Tink chimed with delight. *You can see who got the brains in the family.*

"After all," said Leonard, "she's our secret weapon."

CHAPTER 66

A Miserable Night

Shining Pearl crept to the mouth of the cave. It was little more than a hole in the mountainside, the cave itself barely big enough to hold Shining Pearl and the pirates.

They had found it just in time. With Mister Grin close on their heels, they'd crossed the mountain ridge and started down the other side, tripping and falling in the darkness. It had soon become obvious that they could not outrun the relentless beast. They stumbled upon the cave with seconds to spare, crowding inside just as Mister Grin reached them. They huddled together in terror against the back wall as the hungry crocodile thrust his monstrous jaws into the narrow opening, his dagger teeth snapping at them from only a few feet away. But the entrance was too small by just inches. Finally, Mister Grin had backed out, roaring in frustration.

But he did not go away. All night long he stayed close to the cave, pacing in front of the opening, sometimes stopping to try yet again to force his way in. It made for a tense and miserable night; Shining Pearl and the pirates crowded together in the cramped darkness with no room to stretch out.

Now, as the sun rose over the island, Shining Pearl realized that Mister Grin had stopped patrolling past the cave. Cautiously, she poked her head outside to get a look. Her heart leapt. The cave was directly above the Mollusk compound. In the clearing far below, she could see the high pole wall that surrounded it and smoke rising from cooking fires. She saw figures moving about, though from this distance she could not tell which were Mollusks and which were Scorpions.

She hunched over and warily took a step outside. Coming upright, she looked right and left; she didn't see Mister Grin. Another step, then another . . .

There!

The giant croc lay motionless—*asleep?*—some fifteen yards away. Shining Pearl watched him carefully for a full minute. She waved her arms in his direction. He did not react.

She returned to the cave, where the pirates waited anxiously.

"Well?" whispered Smee. "Is he still there?"

"To the right, about fifteen yards," whispered Shining Pearl. "But I think he's asleep. We might be able to get away if we're quiet."

"What if he wakes up?" said Smee, with more than a hint of fear in his scratchy voice.

"That's why I said we need to be quiet," said Shining Pearl. "That is, until it's time to wake him up."

Smee's eyes nearly popped out of his head. "Why would we do *that?*" he said.

"To get him to follow us, of course," said Shining Pearl.

"But I don't *want* him to follow me," said Smee. "He keeps trying to *eat* us."

The pirate named Hurky cleared his throat. "Cap'n," he said. "That's the plan, remember?"

"Plan?" said Smee. "What plan?"

"The little girl's plan," said Hurky, "which we agreed on, is the croc follows us, and we lead him to them savages, and he eats them or runs 'em off."

"Ah," said Smee, looking doubtful. "*That* plan." He glanced nervously toward the cave entrance. "Maybe we need another plan."

"With all due respect, Cap'n," said Hurky, "we been through this already. Them savages outnumber us a hundred to one, and they're all over this island. Either we get rid of them, or they hunt us down like rats. That croc is our only hope."

His face pale, Smee stood looking at the cave opening. Shining Pearl put her hand on his arm; he jumped.

"You can stay here, Mr. Smee," she said. "You'll be safe in

the cave." She turned to the rest of the pirates. "You can all stay, if you want. I'll lead Mister Grin down the mountain. This was my idea, and I know it probably won't work." She paused a moment to steady her quavering voice. "But I have to do something to save my family, and this is the only thing I can think of."

A few seconds passed uncomfortably. Then Hurky said, "I'll go with you, little one."

"Me too," said the pirate known as Boggs. "I ain't staying in a cave while a girl does my fighting for me."

That was all it took for the other pirates to declare—quietly—their intention to go with Shining Pearl. That left only Smee, who looked at the men, then at Shining Pearl, then said, more to himself than anyone else, "I'm acting captain. I'll lead my men."

Shining Pearl nodded, too moved to speak. She went to the cave entrance again and looked out. Mister Grin had not moved. She beckoned to the pirates; one by one, they crept from the cave and—casting wary glances toward the sleeping beast—began to make their way down the mountainside. When they had what Shining Pearl judged to be an adequate head start, she turned, looking up to where Mister Grin's massive form lay, still motionless. She took a deep breath and emitted an ear-piercing whoop.

Instantly, the enormous head rose. With alarming quickness, the croc slithered over to the cave on thick, powerful legs. He poked his snout inside, and a moment later withdrew it with a roar of rage. The giant head swiveled left and right, seeking the scent of its prey. Then, with another roar, the beast began lumbering down the mountainside right toward Shining Pearl and the pirates, who were already running toward the Mollusk Village as fast as their legs would carry them.

As the trees crashed and snapped behind her, Shining Pearl could only hope they were fast enough.

CHAPTER 67

BAD NEWS

HOOK AND LEONARD STOOD on the quarterdeck, eyeing the sails and discussing strategy. They were getting along surprisingly well for two men who, had they met under any other circumstances, would likely be trying to kill each other. Leonard was in command—there was no doubt of that. But Hook was proving to be such a master of the flying ship that Leonard could not help but feel, if not admiration, a certain respect.

Hook, for his part, felt a grudging respect for Aster, but that had not prevented him from thinking of how he might get rid of him and have the ship to himself. Hook's dark eyes glittered as he pondered the possibilities.

With a ship like this, a man could pirate as no man has ever pirated before. A man could . . .

". . . tuck in behind that cloud bank there," Leonard was saying.

"What's that?" said Hook, coming out of his daydream.

"I said we can tuck in behind that cloud bank over there," said Leonard, pointing to a low line of clouds to the right of Mollusk Island. "That way we can approach the island without being seen by the Scorpions."

Hook studied the cloud bank, then nodded in agreement. He shouted some orders to the crew—actually, to George, who translated the nautical terms for the other boys—then turned the wheel to set the new course. This drew the attention of Peter, who flew up to the quarterdeck, alighting next to Leonard. Hook glared at him, but Peter ignored the pirate; the two had not spoken to each other once on the ship.

"What are we doing?" Peter asked Leonard. "Why have we turned away from the island?"

"We don't want them to see us," said Leonard. "At least not before we know what we're going to do."

"What do you mean?" said Peter. "We're going to rescue the Mollusks, aren't we?"

Hook snorted, which irritated Peter greatly. Leonard put his hand on Peter's shoulder.

"Yes, we're going to rescue them," he said. "But if we simply fly in there, they'll see us coming. We want to see *them* first—where they are, what defenses they have. Then we can make a decision as to how to proceed."

"But we *will* attack them," said Peter.

"Yes, of course," said Leonard. He hesitated, then added, "But we might want to send Ammm to get reinforcements first."

"You mean reinforcements on ships?" said Peter.

"Possibly," said Leonard.

"But that could take days!" said Peter. "Or weeks!"

"Yes," said Leonard. "But if we charge in there vastly outnumbered, we could all be killed, flying ship or no. And what good would that do the Mollusks?"

Peter thought about that, then said, "So what are we going to do?"

"We're going to send in our secret weapon," said Leonard, pointing to Tink, who'd been listening from her perch in Peter's hair. "She'll have a look and let us know what she sees."

A wise plan, chimed Tink.

"I'm going with her," said Peter.

"No," said Leonard, his voice suddenly stern. "They're likely to see you, and then we've given ourselves away."

"But I'll be careful!"

Like the last time? When they shot you with the poison arrow?

"She's right," said Leonard, suppressing a smile. "We'll send Tink alone. I promise, there will be plenty for you to do once we're ready to attack."

Peter pouted, but that was the extent of his objection.

He couldn't argue with Leonard's caution; he'd seen how easily the Scorpions had defeated the Mollusks.

A half hour passed, and Hook had the *De Vliegen*—flying much lower now—tacking smoothly back and forth behind the cloud bank, which nicely shielded the ship from the island.

"We'll stay here," Leonard said to Tink. "Come back as soon as you can."

I will, said Tink, and she was gone, a golden streak disappearing among the clouds.

Leonard told George and the boys to help him load the ship's cannons. They went below, leaving the deck empty, save for Hook at the wheel; Molly, sitting forward with a blanket wrapped around her; and Peter, staring over the rail at the spot where he had last seen Tink. There was no sound other than the whistle of the wind and the extraordinarily loud ticking of the starstuff-touched clock, in the captain's cabin below.

After a few minutes Molly rose and went to where Peter was standing, staring at the clouds.

"She'll be all right," she said.

Peter looked at her. "Tink? Right, I'm sure she'll be fine. It's . . ." He stopped.

"It's what?"

"What if the Mollusks are . . . What if they've been . . ."

Molly put her hand on his arm. "We'll just have to hope for the best," she said.

Peter turned to her, suddenly angry. "What good does *that* do, hoping for the best? What help is *that?*"

Molly reddened and removed her hand.

"I'm sorry," she said. "I was just trying to . . ."

Now it was Peter's turn to redden. "Molly, *I'm* sorry," he said. "It's just that I feel as though the Mollusks are all I have right now, and if they're gone . . ."

"You have me," said Molly. "And Father. And James and the others. You have all of us."

Peter looked down. A tear fell, then another, both whipped away by the wind before they reached the deck.

"I have you now," he said, his voice breaking, "but you're growing older, all of you. And I'm not. I never will. I won't have you later. That doesn't trouble me so much on the island. I feel at home there. But if I lose that . . ."

"Peter," said Molly, putting her hand on his shoulder, "no matter . . ."

Before she could finish, the ship lurched to port. Hook spun the wheel to correct it. Seconds later, Leonard was on deck.

"What was that?" he shouted to Hook.

"I don't know," said Hook. "It felt like we hit something, but there ain't nothing up here to hit."

"Peter!" called Leonard. "Have a look, will you?"

Peter, quickly wiping his eyes, vaulted over the rail and swooped alongside the ship. He saw it right away—a bulge in the keel just forward of amidships. A few of the planks were being spread apart; light gleamed through the cracks.

"What do you see?" called Leonard, leaning over the rail.

"There's a sort of bump on the bottom of the ship," Peter called back. "I think it's the starstuff, pressing against the wood." As he spoke, the timbers groaned, and the bulge bulged a bit more. Peter flew back up to the deck and landed next to Leonard.

"I think it's getting worse," he said.

Leonard and Hook exchanged worried glances, both thinking the same thing: if the starstuff escaped through the hull, the ship would no longer fly. With a hole in the hull, it wouldn't even float. They'd have to get to land before that happened. But the only land around was currently occupied by the Scorpions.

"Mr. Hook," said Leonard. "Perhaps we should . . ."

"Tink!" shouted Peter, spotting a sparkling speck zipping toward the ship through the clouds.

Seconds later she was perched on the ship's rail, her tiny, delicate face deadly serious, chiming so fast that Leonard had to ask her to slow down as the bad news tumbled out. . . .

Bad men everywhere with whips and sticks . . . making Mollusks work in the mountain . . . Mollusks hurt, sick, hungry, the children . . . very, very bad . . .

"What did she say?" asked Molly. "What is it?"

Peter, ignoring her, spoke to Leonard. "We can't wait any

longer," he said. As he spoke, the ship's timbers groaned again.

"I agree," said Leonard. He look over the rail, rubbing his chin. "Mr. Hook," he said. "This cloud bank goes all the way to the water, does it not?"

"Aye," answered Hook. "We calls it the White Beard, when the clouds meet the sea."

"Well, can you set us down on this side of the White Beard?"

"Into the *water?*" said Peter and Molly at the same time.

If Hook was surprised, he didn't show it. He looked at the sails, gauged the wind.

"I can bring her down," he said. "But it might be a bit rough on her."

"Do it," said Aster. He turned and spoke quietly to Tinker Bell for a few seconds; she nodded and disappeared over the side. Meanwhile, Hook was shouting orders, which George quickly translated. The boys jumped to the sails. Almost immediately, the *De Vliegen* began to descend.

Peter, frowning, said to Leonard, "I don't understand. Why are you putting the ship in the water?"

"Yes, Father," said Molly. "Aren't we giving up our advantage?"

"We're giving up one advantage to gain a greater one," said Leonard. "Molly, do you remember the last time we approached this island?"

"I most certainly do! We were lucky to escape with our lives—especially you, Father—when those red-painted warriors attacked us in canoes."

"Precisely. And what do you think they'll do if they see this ship sailing in?"

"I suppose they'll attack again. . . . Wait, Father, is that what you *want*?"

"Precisely," said Leonard.

"But—"

Molly was interrupted by Hook, bellowing a string of commands, rapid-fire. The sails fluttered and flapped loudly. The ship, its bow tilted down, was descending to the sea with frightening speed.

"Hold on tight to something!" roared Hook. As the ship neared the wave-tops he gave the wheel a violent spin, pointing the ship upwind. At the same time, he ordered George and the boys to take in the topsails and let out the main. For a moment, the ship listed hard to starboard; then the wind caught, and it leveled off just as it touched down on the sea. There was a splash and a violent lurch as the ship slowed to a near stop, forcing all aboard to hang on as hard as they could to keep from falling. Timbers creaked in protest as the ship sank down, then bobbed back up, sending large, foam-frothed waves outward from both sides. A few more bobs and the ship settled, now sailing like a regular ship.

"Brilliant!" shouted George.

"Well done, Mr. Hook," said Leonard.

Hook waved his stump dismissively, as if he'd sailed a hundred flying ships into the sea. But the glint in his eyes betrayed him; he was quite impressed with himself.

"I still don't understand," said Molly. "Are we going to just sail in there and be attacked?"

"That is the plan, yes," said Leonard, glancing over the rail. "But we won't be sailing in alone."

Molly started to ask him what he meant, but before she could, she heard a voice from the sea call her name . . . in Porpoise. She turned and saw a smiling silver snout poking out of the waves.

"Ammm!" she shouted.

Her old friend was surrounded by at least two dozen more porpoises. Tinker Bell, having guided them to the ship, hovered proudly above. Leonard leaned over the rail and conversed with Ammm for several minutes in fluent Porpoise. When he was done, he turned to the quarterdeck and called, "Mr. Hook!"

"Yes, Cap'n?" replied Hook, with a hint of sarcasm.

"Make your course for Mollusk Island," said Leonard. "And let's have plenty of sail. We wouldn't want them to miss us."

CHAPTER 68

THE ALARM

THE SCORPION LOOKOUT BLINKED: A piece of the cloud bank had broken free and was moving toward him. As he stared, the moving cloud took shape, fog spilling off . . . its sails.

A ship!

Instantly the lookout raised the conch shell hanging from his side. He pressed it to his lips and trumpeted the alarm; the sound echoed down toward the compound from the lookout's mountainside post. He took a big breath and sounded it a second time.

From down the mountainside, he heard another lookout repeat the alarm. Then he heard shouts, and within a minute dozens of red-painted Scorpion warriors hurried out of the jungle and onto the beach, sprinting toward their war canoes.

The Scorpions had a simple strategy for dealing with

sailing ships: strike immediately, and in overwhelming numbers. Some of the ships would shoot cannons—the Scorpions called them fire-throwers—but there were never enough cannons to stop all the war canoes. And once the Scorpions, with their deadly poison arrows, got close to the ship, the battle was over quickly.

The first canoes were already in the water, moving swiftly toward the ship; many more were right behind. The lookout smiled. He expected to enjoy the show.

———◆———

Fighting Prawn heard the moaning of a conch shell reverberate down the lava-tube tunnel. He lifted his head to listen; it was not a Mollusk signal.

The sound was repeated, closer this time. The Scorpion guards were agitated, some of them shouting, seemingly unsure about what to do.

The guards fell silent as a large man strode into the cavern chamber. At first Fighting Prawn saw only a silhouette against the dim tunnel light, but as the man passed a torch, Fighting Prawn recognized the bone necklace, the red-painted face, the gleaming black eyes of the Scorpion leader.

The leader surveyed the chamber, his eyes lingering an extra second or two on Fighting Prawn. What he saw, Fighting Prawn knew, was a bunch of exhausted, hunger-weakened slaves, their chief a beaten man, pounding rocks with bleeding hands. Fighting Prawn could feel the contempt in the Scorpion leader's eyes.

The Scorpion leader said something to his men, speaking in harsh syllables. When he finished, five guards ran from the chamber. The Scorpion leader looked around again; then, after barking another command to the remaining guards, turned and strode back up the tunnel.

Fighting Prawn glanced left, then right. Five guards had gone; that meant that only five remained. The guards were strong men, armed with knives and whips. But now it was just the five of them, guarding about fifty Mollusk men and a few pirates—the only slaves still able to work. Many of his men, Fighting Prawn knew, were barely able to move. He prayed that at least some of them could still summon the strength, and the will, to fight. Because this was their only chance.

He gripped a rock and started to rise.

There were more than thirty canoes in the water now, with still more being launched: the Scorpions slicing skillfully through the waves, paddles flashing in the sunlight. Most of the canoes carried ten warriors, ready to put down their paddles and pick up their bows and arrows when they came within range.

The canoes were aimed, like waterborne arrows, straight

at the ship. As the canoes drew closer, the ship began a slow turn to port, presenting its starboard side to the canoes. The Scorpions saw four cannons sticking out of the gun ports, a sight that caused them to whoop and shriek with delight. Four cannons, they knew, would have no chance of stopping the attack.

The forward canoes were almost within range. Some of the warriors set down their paddles and readied their bows. The war whoops were constant now; the ship was a fat, slow, inviting target. It would be an easy kill.

CHAPTER 69

REVOLT

𝒯HE CLOSEST GUARD was looking away when Fighting Prawn reached him; he went down without a sound. Fighting Prawn, the rock still in his hand, took three quick steps toward the next guard, who turned just in time to emit a shout before he, too, went down.

The element of surprise was gone now. Fighting Prawn shouted for his men to rise and take the remaining guards. Pride swelled his heart as three men, then four, then more, struggled to their feet, despite their desperate weakness. Two of the pirates were up as well. The three remaining Scorpion guards, clearly stunned by the revolt, at first tried to run toward the tunnel; but, finding their path blocked, had backed against the cavern wall, lashing out with whips and knives while shouting for help. But no help came, and the Scorpions were soon brought down by a hail of rocks hurled by the slaves they had once tormented.

When it was over, Fighting Prawn put his hands on his knees, gasping for air. The fight, short as it was, had left him, in his weakened state, barely able to stand. He looked around; the others looked no better. Fighting Prawn gave them a few more moments to recover, then ordered his men to strip the fallen Scorpions of their knives and whips. When they were ready, he turned and started out of the tunnel, followed by every Mollusk and pirate who could still walk. None of them knew what awaited them outside the cave, but all of them knew there was no turning back.

CHAPTER 70

*F*IGHT OR *F*LIGHT

*T*HE CANOES WERE NOW CLOSE enough that Molly, from the deck of the ship, could make out the red-painted faces of the howling Scorpion warriors. Some of the closer ones raised their bows and shot; the poisoned arrows arced through the air. Most splashed into the sea, but several thunked into the hull.

"Father," said Molly, "they're getting awfully close."

Leonard, his eyes on the canoes, nodded. "Steady . . . steady . . ." he said to Hook, whose dark eyes danced between the Scorpions and the sails. The *De Vliegen* continued on a steady course that kept her broadside to the oncoming Scorpions—an easy target.

Leonard turned to Peter—actually, to Tink, on Peter's shoulder.

"Now," he said.

In a flash, she was over the side.

435

More arrows thunked into the hull. One, then another, hissed across the deck.

"Take cover!" shouted Leonard. Molly ducked below the rail, peeking over the top. Peter and the other boys, having climbed to various posts in the rigging, hid behind masts and spars. Leonard and Hook crouched by the wheel. All eyes were on the onrushing canoes. The closest Scorpions were crouching in the front of their war boats, ready to make the leap toward the ship, now only yards away. The warriors rose to their feet, howling.

In an instant, their howls turned to cries of fear as the forward canoes rose straight out of the water, lifted by the blunt snouts and powerful tails of Ammm and the other porpoises, shooting upward from the depths in perfect unison. Four canoes were hoisted high and flipped over, sending the Scorpions and their weapons flying into the sea.

With a flash of tails, the porpoises disappeared, diving deep. The next wave of Scorpions, fearful of capsizing, stopped paddling and grabbed bows and spears, warily watching the water around them. Suddenly they heard hoots and whistles coming from behind. They turned and saw . . .

Women?

A dozen mermaids had surfaced among the canoes; they waved and beckoned to the Scorpion warriors, who stared at them, openmouthed, not knowing what to make of these strange creatures. As it happened, they had no time to decide, as seconds later they, too, were hurled upward and out of their canoes as the precision porpoise team struck again.

Now the water foamed with chaos. Scorpions splashed in the water as they tried to pull themselves into the remaining upright canoes. These, in turn, were capsized by the porpoises and the mermaids. The would-be attackers—now set upon from every side—struggled to keep from drowning. They paid no attention to the *De Vliegen*.

"Mr. Hook," said Leonard, surveying the scene, "I believe the time has arrived."

Hook spun the wheel, shouting out orders. George interpreted and repeated them. As the ship began its turn, the boys quickly changed both the arrangement and the angles of the sails. The effect was exactly as Hook had planned. Slowly, the bow began to rise. Water slapped against the hull; timbers groaned; masts and yardarms shook; lines sang. A shudder passed from bow to stern. For a moment it sounded as if the ship was going to break apart.

Instead, it flew.

The bow lifted free of the surface, followed by the rest of the hull, water cascading from it like a rainstorm. The deck tilted steeply. The boys hanging on to the rigging let out a cheer.

"Well done, Mr. Hook," said Leonard. Hook's lips twisted into what could possibly be described as a smile.

"Slightly!" called Leonard. "Take your crew and man the starboard cannons."

"Yes sir," answered Slightly, climbing quickly down the rigging. Reaching the deck, he paused and said, "Which one is starboard again?"

"That side." Leonard smiled, pointing to the right.

The *De Vliegen* soared over the capsized canoes. The Scorpions, already spooked by the porpoise-and-mermaid attack, pointed and shouted in fear as the dripping hull passed overhead. When the flying ship had passed over the Scorpions, Hook put it into a starboard turn; the ship was now between the island and the dozens of swamped canoes. One by one, the porpoises and mermaids surfaced beneath the ship, forming a line in the water.

The Scorpions struggled to get their canoes righted; they bailed them out with their bare hands. They had recovered some of their paddles, but most of their bows, arrows, and spears were lost. They now faced a choice: they could try to get back to the island, which meant fighting their way past the demonic sea creatures that had capsized their canoes and the flying ship—*a flying ship!*—only to face the wrath of their chief, a man who was not merciful to those who had failed him. Or they could do something unthinkable for a Scorpion warrior—retreat.

BOOM!

The fire-thrower blazed from the ship's side; a cannonball hurtled across the water, barely missing a just-righted canoe. It skipped twice across the water before sinking.

BOOM!

A second ball—this one blasted an overturned canoe to smithereens as the warriors who had been in it swam for their lives.

The mermaids, hooting and whistling, began swimming toward the Scorpions. The porpoises, squeaking and clicking and dancing high on their tails, did the same.

The Scorpions were panicked. How could they fight this enemy?

BOOM!

Another ball whistled past.

The line of mermaids and porpoises drew closer. One of the canoes in their path began to turn away, its occupants using hands and paddles to escape the oncoming creatures. Another canoe turned with them, then another, then another . . .

———◆———

Panic swept through the Scorpions as the unthinkable became thinkable. They all turned away, every canoe, the entire attack force, paddling out to sea as fast as they could, away from these magical foes, away from their wrathful chief, away forever from this cursed island.

A cheer went up on board the *De Vliegen*.

"Cease firing!" Leonard shouted to Slightly and the gun crew below. A moment later Peter landed on the deck next to him, soon joined by Molly.

"That was brilliant, Father," she said.

"The credit goes to Mr. Hook and the crew," said Leonard.

I beg your pardon? chimed Tink, alighting on Peter's shoulder.

"Not to mention Admiral Tinker Bell and her naval forces," said Leonard.

Tink glowed brighter with the compliment.

Peter watched the Scorpions paddle toward the horizon. "Is that all of them, do you think?" he asked.

"Not likely," said Leonard, his voice suddenly grim. "They wouldn't have left the Mollusks unguarded. There will be more of them on the island, and they will be well-armed. We'll have to face them without the element of surprise, and—unless we can get them into the water—without the help of Ammm or the mermaids. We've improved our odds considerably, but I fear we may still be in for a battle."

Just then the *De Vliegen* lurched again, this time more violently than the first time. Leonard looked at Hook, who shrugged, having no idea of the cause. Peter quickly vaulted over the side. He returned less than a minute later with a worried look on his face.

"The bulge is worse," he said. "There's a good-sized crack in the hull now."

Leonard and Hook exchanged glances.

"It didn't do her no good, coming down in the water," said Hook. "No telling how long she'll hold together."

"No," agreed Leonard. "If we're going to attack, we must do it now." Leonard looked his crew over. *Children* . . . But what choice was there?

"Mr. Hook, make your course for the Mollusk camp."

CHAPTER 71

THE MONSTROUS MAW

THE SCORPION CHIEF, surrounded by four of his senior warriors, had watched the water battle with disbelief from a rock outcropping just above the compound. He had watched his warriors paddle their canoes toward the ship; had watched as they were attacked and overturned by sea creatures, both natural and unnatural. He had watched—though at first he doubted his eyes—the ship rise from the sea as though its sails were wings, then fly over his men, and finally turn and fire on them.

And he had watched in disbelief, then fury, as his men—*Scorpion warriors*—had fled to the sea. He watched them for a full minute, then spat on the ground. *Cowards.* He knew every man in those canoes. When the time came, he would find them and kill them all.

But first he had to deal with the flying ship. It was turning now, clearly coming to the island. The chief glared at it.

If the men on that ship expected to frighten the Scorpions on the island into fleeing, they were greatly mistaken.

He would see to that.

⸺·⸺

Shining Pearl emerged from the thick jungle onto the path. The pirates stumbled out behind her one by one, the last being Smee.

Shining Pearl held her finger to her lips for quiet, and they all listened for a moment. They heard the now-familiar crashing sounds of Mister Grin following them, but the sounds were coming from farther away than they had been. Shining Pearl allowed herself a small smile. She had deliberately led the pirates through a part of the jungle where the trees grew very close together. It had been hard going for the pirates, squeezing between the trunks; but it had been harder still for the monster croc. They had gained both distance and precious time.

"Where does this path lead?" said Boggs.

"To the village," said Shining Pearl, pointing. "It's not far now."

Boggs started to speak again, but he was interrupted by the sound echoing from the direction of the village.

"What was *that*?" said Smee.

"That's a cannon," said Hurky.

"And what is *that*?" said Boggs, pointing skyward.

443

"That," said Hurky, not quite believing his own words, "is a flying ship."

———•———

"Fire two!" shouted Leonard.

BOOM!

The second ball whistled through the air. This one, better aimed than the first, smashed a hole through the high tree-trunk wall surrounding the Mollusk compound.

"Fine shot, Mr. Slightly!" shouted Leonard.

"They don't seem pleased about it," observed Hook, gazing down at the Scorpion warriors. They were swarming beneath the *De Vliegen*, shouting and shooting arrows up at it. But the ship, thanks to Hook's deft airmanship, was just out of reach of all but the strongest archers. The few arrows that reached the ship had lost most of their velocity and bounced harmlessly off the hull.

"No," said Leonard. "They're not pleased. But they don't seem frightened, either. I had hoped we might scare them into fleeing. But clearly they intend to defend the compound."

Most of the Scorpion warriors were gathered in front of the main gate. Inside the compound itself were the sleeping hut and cooking fires, which were tended by Mollusk women and children, now slaves to the Scorpions. Peter, standing next to Leonard and Molly on the *De Vliegen*, felt his heart ache when he saw the condition of his Mollusk friends—gaunt, exhausted, barely able to lift their heads, even to see the flying ship.

"They look awful!" said Molly. "Father, what can we do?"

"I don't know," Leonard admitted. "We can irritate them with the cannon, but we can't defeat them from up here. And we don't want to risk harming the captive Mollusks."

The ship lurched. Leonard exchanged glances with Hook, then said, "For that matter, I don't know how much longer we can stay up here. What we need is . . ."

He was interrupted by a shout from James, high up the mainmast.

"People coming!" he called.

"Where?" shouted Peter.

"There!"

Peter looked where James was pointing, and in a moment he saw them—a line of tiny figures on one of the paths leading down the mountainside toward the compound. At this distance, he couldn't make out who they were.

"Do we have a spyglass?" asked Leonard.

"There's one below," said Molly. She ran down and quickly returned with the glass, which she handed to Leonard. He put it to his eye.

"Well, now," he said.

"What is it?" said Peter.

"Take a look," said Leonard, handing over the glass.

Peter put it to his eye and looked at the mountain. It took him a few moments, but he found the path, and then the men, and then . . .

"Fighting Prawn!" he exclaimed. The Mollusk chief looked gaunt and filthy, but he was trotting down the path with dogged determination, followed by what looked like at least fifty men, including . . . Were those *pirates*?

"What's happening?" asked Molly.

"It looks as though Fighting Prawn intends to attack the compound," said Leonard, frowning.

"That's good, then, isn't it?"

"I wish it were," said Leonard. "But he's still outnumbered. The Scorpions will cut him and his men to pieces. Unless . . ." He looked at Peter. "Is there a rear gate to the compound?"

"Yes," said Peter, pointing. "It's back behind those huts. But it's always barred shut." He looked at Leonard. "But if it was open . . ."

"Exactly," said Leonard. "We can use the cannon to distract the men in the front, but the rear gate is likely to have guards. If you go in alone . . ."

Excuse me? chimed Tink

"I won't be alone," said Peter.

"But what about the arrows?" said Molly, looking down at the Scorpion archers.

Does she ever stop nagging?

"What did she say?" asked Molly.

"She said we'll be careful," said Peter. He took two quick steps and launched himself off the deck, with Tink right behind.

Leonard and Molly watched them go, two figures arcing high across the sky to stay out of range of the Scorpion archers.

"Yes," Leonard said softly. "You be careful."

———◆———

Fighting Prawn, staggering down the mountain as fast as his hunger-weakened legs would carry him, kept his eyes on the path, occasionally glancing up at the miraculous sight of the flying ship. He didn't know how it came to be there, although he suspected his flying friend Peter was involved. What he did know was that the ship was firing on the Scorpions, and therefore was, at least for now, his ally.

He reached the base of the mountain. Ahead, on the other side of a clearing, lay the village. *His village.* He turned and looked at the ragged band of Mollusk warriors and pirates—a few armed with whips and knives but most holding only rocks. Not much of an attacking force, but it would have to do.

He raised his head and, with all the strength he could muster, shouted the Mollusk war cry. His men answered in parched, hoarse voices. Fighting Prawn turned and began trotting across the clearing toward the compound, and the battle that would decide the fate of his people.

———◆———

Peter and Tink flew high in the brilliant blue sky, their plan being to come down with the sun behind them, thus blinding any Scorpion looking up in their direction. At the moment, though, the Scorpions were occupied with the *De Vliegen*, which was firing on the front of the compound, providing the distraction that Leonard had promised.

He heard faint shouts, and looked down to his right; Fighting Prawn was leading his men across the clearing. If Peter was to get the rear gate open, he would have to move quickly. He glanced up to check the sun's angle, then, with Tink alongside, went into a steep, fast dive. He hoped to reach the gate and have it open before the Scorpions saw him.

It nearly worked. As Leonard had expected, Scorpion sentries—two of them—had been posted at the rear gate. Both sentries, however, had been distracted by the cannon attack, and had wandered toward the center of the compound to get a better view of the action. Peter dropped gently to the ground behind them and ran to the gate. It was a single door, barred shut by a log set into forked tree trunks on either side. Peter went to the left side and strained to lift it, but it barely budged. He glanced behind him; the sentries were still looking away. He put his shoulder under the log and strained upward with all his strength. Slowly he inched it out of the fork.

Look out! chimed Tink.

THUNK!

The arrow slammed into the log two inches from Peter's head. Trapped under the log, Peter gave it a desperate heave. He got it clear of the fork and let it fall, diving to the side as a second arrow pierced the gate where he'd been standing. Facedown on the ground, he turned sideways to see one of the Scorpion sentries aiming another arrow at him. He started to push himself up, but as he did, the Scorpion released the arrow. Peter was sure it would hit him—yet somehow it didn't. It skimmed just past his face, making the strangest sound, and as it slammed into the gate next to him, Peter saw that it had been deflected by Tink, who had somehow grasped it in mid-flight. She was still clinging to the shaft with her tiny hands, a dazed look on her delicate face.

"Thanks!" said Peter, springing to his feet.

I am NOT doing that again, she replied.

There was no more time for conversation; the sentries, having abandoned their efforts to shoot the elusive boy, were sprinting toward him. Peter waited until they were close, then flung himself upward, leaving them grasping air and grunting with surprise and a hint of fear—*A flying ship, and now a flying boy.*

Peter hovered just above their heads, shouting at them, hoping to distract them from the log now resting in only one fork. The Scorpions leapt up and down, trying to reach the infuriating boy's dangling feet. Realizing that was hopeless, they reached for their bows again. As they fitted arrows to strings, Peter shot over the compound wall.

⸻

Fighting Prawn's lungs burned, and he was having trouble moving his legs. Twice he had stumbled and fallen, as had many of the men behind him. Each time he willed himself to get back on his feet and move forward. Assuming that the rear gate was locked, he had decided to divide his force in half and send them around both sides of the compound to attack the Scorpions in the front. He was about to issue the order when he saw a familiar figure fly over the compound wall.

"Peter!" he shouted.

"Push the gate!" answered Peter. "Hurry!"

Fighting Prawn, understanding immediately, altered course and ran toward the gate, yelling at his men to follow. Peter ducked his head back over the wall and saw that the Scorpion sentries, having realized what was happening, had dropped their bows and were wrestling with the log. They were too late. With a roar, Fighting Prawn and his men slammed into the gate, knocking the two Scorpions to the ground. Neither would ever get up again. In moments, the Mollusks and pirates were inside. Peter dropped to the ground next to Fighting Prawn, and they embraced briefly. Peter was shocked by the Mollusk chief's filthy, weakened condition.

"Where are the rest of them?" asked Fighting Prawn.

"In front," said Peter. "The ship is distracting them so you can attack from the back."

"Good," said Fighting Prawn. He called his men together and quickly gave orders in the grunt-and-click language of the Mollusks. In a moment, with Fighting Prawn leading the way, they were running toward the main gate, using the sleeping huts to screen their approach. Peter watched them, wondering if this small band of exhausted men, brave as they were, stood any chance against the strong, well-armed Scorpions. He rose into the air, preparing to fly back to the ship and report to Leonard.

Look, chimed Tink, pointing.

Peter turned and looked. Another group was descending the mountainside. This was a smaller group—eight figures. Peter squinted, trying to make them out.

It's Shining Pearl, said Tink, who literally had the eyesight of a bird. *And some smelly-looking pirates.*

Peter hesitated, then decided he had better warn Shining Pearl that she was heading into a dangerous situation.

"Come on," he said, zooming across the clearing. In less

451

than a minute, he and Tink reached Shining Pearl, who beamed when she recognized her two friends. Peter noticed that Shining Pearl—could it be possible?—seemed to be *leading* the small band of pirates, which included Hook's short, round first mate. They appeared to be quite tired but also in a great hurry to get down the hill.

"Who's that?" said Shining Pearl, pointing at the ship as Peter landed next to her.

"It's the Starcatchers," said Peter. "Molly's father is in command, although Hook is actually sailing the ship." Peter noticed that the pirates perked up when he said that. One of them mumbled, "Alive?"

Peter also noticed that nobody stopped running.

"Listen," he said, trotting next to Shining Pearl. "You shouldn't go to the village now. Your father . . ."

"My father is down there?"

"Yes," said Peter. "But there's going to be a fight."

"Then that's where we need to be," said Shining Pearl.

"But . . ."

"Peter," said Shining Pearl, "we couldn't stop even if we wanted to."

"Why not?" said Peter.

"Mister Grin," said Shining Pearl, "is right behind us."

There he is, chimed Tink, who was hovering above the group, looking up the mountain.

Peter rose and looked back. About one hundred yards up

the path he saw trees being shoved aside, and then the monster croc himself. Peter dropped back to the ground and resumed trotting next to Shining Pearl.

"Why is he following you?" he asked.

"He thinks Hook is with us," said Shining Pearl. "He . . ." She stopped speaking, her eyes widening. "That's it!"

"What is?" said Peter.

Shining Pearl explained her plan, finishing just as they reached the clearing. Peter took off and flew as fast as he could toward the ship. He glanced back; Mister Grin, having reached the wide part of the mountain path, was gaining on Shining Pearl and the pirates. He'd have to make this quick.

<hr />

From the quarterdeck of the *De Vliegen*, Leonard saw that the battle was not going well for the Mollusks. Their unexpected attack from inside the compound had surprised the Scorpions, who had been focusing their attention on the flying ship; for a chaotic minute or two, it looked as though the Mollusks might have a chance. But the Scorpion chief had rallied and reorganized his men, and the tide had turned again. The weak, outnumbered Mollusk warriors were fighting valiantly—desperately—but they were being driven back, deeper and deeper into the compound, joined by the Mollusk women and children who were fighting now alongside their husbands and fathers. It was only a matter of time,

Leonard saw, before the Mollusks would be backed against the rear wall and destroyed—if they even got that far.

"Father!" said Molly. "Peter's come back."

Leonard turned to see Peter land on the deck. Leonard started to speak, but Peter cut him off.

"I need Hook's shirt," he said, panting.

"What?" said Leonard.

"Are you *mad*, boy?" sneered Hook.

Peter ignored him. In urgent tones, he explained the situation to Leonard, who turned to Hook and said, "Give him your shirt."

"I won't," said Hook.

Leonard took a step toward him and said, "Then I'll take it from you."

Hook glared at Leonard, then Peter, then back at Peter.

"I won't forget this, boy," he said. He removed his shirt and tossed it on the deck. Peter snatched it up and was over the side in an instant, streaking over the compound, hoping he was in time.

<hr />

It was hopeless, Fighting Prawn knew. The fight was lost. Soon they would reach the back wall; they would make their stand there. What choice did they have? And then it would be over.

Hopeless.

Shining Pearl and the pirates ran across the clearing as fast as their tired legs would carry them. It was not fast enough. Mister Grin, roaring at the sight of his prey, had also reached the clearing and was gaining with every step. Ahead lay the wall to her village. The rear gate, she noted, was open. The opening was too narrow for the giant croc. If they could just get through it . . .

She glanced back. Mister Grin was getting close to Smee, the last in line as usual.

"Hurry, Mr. Smee!" she called. But the look on his face told her he could go no faster. She looked up at the sky.

Where was Peter?

Shining Pearl reached the gate and ran through the opening—right into the battle between the Mollusks and the Scorpions. She saw in an instant that the Mollusks had been driven back to the rear wall by the Scorpions, who were now closing in for the kill. Shining Pearl saw her father in front of his men, preparing to fight the Scorpion chief, who was advancing toward Fighting Prawn with a spear in his hand and a scowl on his red-painted face.

Behind her, Smee, the last of her pirate band, was coming through the gate with Mister Grin just a few yards behind.

Again Shining Pearl looked toward the sky.

Where was . . . ? THERE!

Peter, a blur of darkness against the bright blue sky, swooped low over the compound.

"There, Peter!" shouted Shining Pearl, pointing toward the Scorpion chief. "That one!"

Peter saw her and swerved toward the chief.

"Get out of the way!" shouted Shining Pearl, shoving Smee and the other pirates away from the gate opening. She was repeating the warning in the grunts and clicks of the Mollusk language when Peter reached the Scorpion chief and dropped Hook's shirt on his head, covering his face. With a howl of rage, the chief yanked the shirt off his head and hurled it to the ground. He whirled around, determined to hurl his spear at the flying boy. But the fury on his face turned to surprise and then fear as the rear gate and the walls on either side of it came crashing down, logs flying everywhere, and Mister Grin roared into the compound. The Mollusks and pirates dove to the side as the massive scaly body hurtled into their midst, seeking the source of the scent he craved. Fighting Prawn was knocked sideways by the mighty croc just as it reached the Scorpion chief, who drew his spear back in a desperate effort to defend himself.

He had no time to bring it forward. The monstrous maw opened wide, then snapped shut. The Scorpion chief was gone.

For a few moments, time seemed to stop in the compound.

Scorpions, Mollusks, and pirates alike stared at the beast, which was, for the moment, cheerfully chewing the chief.

Only Peter kept moving. He swooped down next to Mister Grin and snatched up Hook's shirt, still on the ground where the chief had thrown it. Then he swept low just above the heads of the Scorpion warriors, with the shirt dangling down, brushing their heads. At first, still stunned by the loss of their leader, they didn't understand what was happening. But soon enough it became clear. With a roar, Mister Grin, his hunger far from sated, lunged forward again, seeking new morsels.

The Scorpions were brave fighters, but they had seen enough this day—a flying ship, a flying boy, and—worst of all—this hideous creature that, having eaten their chief, now hungered for them. They were brave but not suicidal. They turned, and with Mister Grin on their heels, ran out of the compound and down to their canoes, desperate to escape this infernal island and to seek the safety of the sea.

The Mollusks watched them go—too stunned and weak to rejoice in their victory. Shining Pearl found her father, who knelt and hugged her. She hugged him back with all her strength, her tears bathing his whip-scarred skin.

CHAPTER 72

Hook's Dream

Leonard Aster, leaning over the rail of the flying ship, allowed himself to relax for the first time since sunrise. The Mollusks had won. The last of the Scorpions had crowded into the remaining canoes and were now paddling furiously out to sea, still pursued by the gigantic crocodile, which was thrusting itself easily forward with lazy sweeps of its powerful tail.

Leonard turned to Hook, who was also watching the crocodile, but not smiling.

"Mr. Hook, set her down," said Leonard. "There, in the lagoon."

"It'll be hard on her hull," Hook warned.

"Perhaps," said Leonard. "But she might not stay up much longer even if we wanted her to." The *De Vliegen* had taken to lurching every few minutes. "And," Leonard continued, "those people down there need help." He turned his gaze to the Mollusk compound, where families were joyfully reuniting after their forced separation by the Scorpions. Many of the Mollusk warriors had been injured in the battle; all of the tribe showed ill effects from hunger and mistreatment.

Hook gave Leonard an odd look, then spun the ship's huge wheel and shouted some orders, which were repeated by George. The other boys complied; the ship turned slowly toward the turquoise lagoon and began to lose altitude. The fluttering sails and the loud ticking of the clock belowdecks were the only sounds. Leonard looked back out to sea. The canoes continued toward the horizon, though the crocodile had apparently given up. Leonard scanned the water looking for the beast, but saw no sign of it.

Hook and his young crew did a better job of bringing the ship down this time. It cut a gentler angle through the sky, descending low over the compound, getting a weak but heartfelt cheer from the Mollusks. Leonard, Bakari, and Molly waved from the rail; George, James, Slightly, and the other boys did the same from the rigging. The ship sank lower and lower, its hull just brushing the tops of the palm trees. The sparkling lagoon was up ahead.

"As close to shore as possible, Mr. Hook," Leonard called. "I'm afraid we'll have to swim in."

"That you will," said Hook, in a tone that sounded odd to Leonard. He looked back at the pirate, who seemed occupied with turning the wheel and watching the sails. The ship's keel was now only ten feet off the water. Leonard and Bakari tied several thick ropes to the rail and heaved them over the stern, preparing to slide down them into the lagoon.

"Look, Father!" Molly shouted, pointing. The mermaids, along with Ammm and the other porpoises, were now alongside the descending ship. The porpoises rose to their tails and, racing backward, clapped their fins together as though applauding. Leonard, Bakari, and the children cheered and applauded back.

"Splendid, Mr. Hook!" called Leonard. "Right here will do!"

"Aye, aye," said Hook. "Right here it is, *Captain.*" He said this in a tone so unmistakably hostile that Leonard, Molly, and Bakari all turned to look. As they did, Hook suddenly gave the wheel a furious yank, spinning it so fast that the spokes blurred. He then lunged to his left and pulled two pins from the port rail, releasing a total of four lines. Instantly two sails went slack. Hook then dove back to the wheel and wrapped his good arm around the steering post— an act that at first made no sense to Leonard.

Then, too late, he understood what Hook was up to: suddenly, violently, the *De Vliegen* tilted hard to starboard, as though hit by a hurricane wind. The boys aloft were hurled into the lagoon, followed quickly by everyone on the starboard rail—everyone, that is, except Leonard, who had managed to grab the rail with one arm. He hung on—barely—his feet dangling.

"Hook!" he yelled. "What in heaven's name are you doing?"

"I'm throwing the rats off my ship," Hook answered. "D'you hear, Aster? MY SHIP!" With that, Hook yanked the wheel again, and the ship shuddered, loosening Leonard's grip; he, too, plummeted to the lagoon. Leonard plunged below the surface, then felt himself quickly being gripped by both arms and lifted up, propelled by the powerful tails of two laughing mermaids, who began towing him swiftly toward the beach. He looked around and saw that the other mermaids and the porpoises were rescuing Bakari, Molly, and the boys.

Meanwhile, Hook had gotten the *De Vliegen* upright again, but it had lost altitude; the stern was almost brushing the lagoon's surface. Hook tied off the wheel and, working furiously with his one hand, started raising the sails he'd dropped. He looked around, quickly considering his options. The wind direction prevented him from steering the ship out to sea. Nor could he turn directly toward the island with its steep and tall central mountain peak. The best he could do without a crew was to maintain his current course. He was headed toward the side of the lagoon, just beyond which was a small mountain with a waterfall cascading down. He would have to gain enough altitude to clear that mountain. Then he and his flying ship would be free.

Hook darted around the deck, adjusting sails. When he'd done what he could, he raced back to the wheel, getting the course precisely right. Then he waited, expecting to feel the ship climb again.

The bow did, in fact, lift, and for a moment so did Hook's heart. But then he felt it—something was wrong. The bow was well clear of the water, but the stern was not rising. The deck tilted steeply as the bow pointed still higher. Hook frowned. It was as if something was holding the stern down. He glanced ahead again; he needed to go higher, and *quickly*. He checked the sails again: there was nothing more to be done there. He decided he had to lighten the load at the stern. There were two large cannons in the captain's quarters—stern chasers. If he could jettison those . . .

Hook tied the wheel once more and hurried down the companionway, his mind's eye picturing the mountain getting ever closer. He darted into the captain's cabin, which echoed with the loud ticking of the starstuff-infused clock, a massive pewter thing that sat, glowing, on a table in the corner. Hook kicked open the stern portholes, which allowed the cannons to be rolled into firing position. The lagoon's soft, blue water played out behind the ship. Hook unfastened one of the cannons and grunted as he shoved it out of its stern hole. It splashed into the lagoon and was gone.

The stern barely rose an inch. Hook frowned. This was not right. He poked his head out the cannon window to see what could be the matter. . . .

His heart stopped when he saw what was holding down the stern.

The crocodile.

The beast had its massive jaws clamped onto one of the thick ropes that Aster had tossed overboard. Its enormous body was being dragged along behind the ship like a giant sea anchor. Hook stared into the croc's huge eyes—glowing red even in the daylight—and he felt a chill, for there was no doubt that Mister Grin was looking, hungrily, *at him.*

Hook looked frantically around for a blade—a knife or sword—to cut the rope. He saw none. He'd have to untie it. He raced up the companion way to the rail where the fat rope was tied. He struggled with the knot one-handed for a few seconds, then shouted an angry oath; the massive weight of the croc had pulled the knot too tight for mere human hands to undo. He looked around; the mountain loomed ahead. Hook's mind raced. He had to make the croc open its jaws and keep them open long enough for Hook to pull the rope free. . . .

A desperate plan came to him. He ran back down to the captain's quarters, untied the sash at his waist, and let his pants drop to the floor, leaving him in a pair of threadbare knickers. Using his teeth and his good hand, he tied the pants to his handless forearm. He looked frantically around the cabin for something sizable that he could throw . . . the clock! He snatched it up—it was warm to the touch—and ran to the gun hole. He leaned out the window, waved his stump with the pants tied to it, and shouted, "HERE I AM, BEAST! COME HAVE A BITE!"

Mister Grin's mighty tail swished, and the croc shot forward. The rope slackened, and the ship's stern started to rise, but the crafty croc quickly stopped that, working his way up the rope, releasing it and grabbing it with lightning-quick snaps of his teeth, getting closer and closer to Hook and his dangling pants. Closer and closer . . .

Steady now . . . Hook tried to calm himself as the hungry beast reached the stern. Hook leaned farther out, dangling the pants as close to the nose of the beast as he could. The pants leg brushed the crocodile's nose.

With a horrifying roar, Mister Grin lunged upward, his jaws opening to reveal rows of spiked teeth and a long, pink tongue the length of a tuna, with the rope lying across it. He was ready. Just as the jaws began to snap shut, Hook tossed the clock into the croc's massive mouth, and at the same time let the knotted pant leg slip off his stump. He then grabbed the rope and quickly pulled it toward him; Mister Grin was trying to chomp down, but the clock, wedged in his teeth, prevented him from fully closing his mouth.

In a moment Hook had freed the rope—and with it, the

De Vliegen. Instantly, the ship began to rise. Seeing his prey escaping, Mister Grin made a last lunging snap upward; he got close enough that Hook could see the clock tumble to the back of the beast's mouth and disappear down its throat, along with the ripped remains of his pants. And then the croc fell back while the stern lifted out of the water into the air.

She was flying!

With the roar of the frustrated croc in his ears, Hook turned and, wearing nothing but a pair of knickers, hurried topside. He cursed when he reached the deck: the ship had reached the edge of the lagoon, and it was clearly not going to gain enough altitude to clear the mountain. Hook untied the wheel and frantically spun it. Slowly, the bow responded.

The ship continued its gentle climb, but now the sky ahead was blotted out by the green mountainside. It was so close that Hook could smell the dank soil of the jungle. He kept the wheel turned fully left, the bow moving faster now, the sails fluttering. The ship shuddered, nearly knocking Hook off balance as the hull brushed the tops of some palm trees. The ship was now traveling parallel to the mountainside, still gaining altitude but losing speed as it turned into the wind. A monkey jumped up onto the ship's rail and screeched at Hook. He cursed at it, but halfheartedly; his attention was focused on a massive rock outcropping protruding from the hillside ahead. Hook could do nothing but watch as the black lava drew closer. . . .

A sudden gust wafted up the mountain and caught the ship from the jungle side. The ship leaned heavily to port, its hull lifting and turning. For a moment Hook thought the ship would miss the rock entirely. He willed the ship to go higher, watching the bow rise inch by inch . . .

But it was not enough. With a violent lurch and a loud grinding noise, the keel struck the jagged rock. As Hook clung to the wheel, the *De Vliegen* bounced forward once, twice, three times, the masts shaking and groaning with each bump. And then . . .

It floated free!

Hook looked around; the outcropping was behind him. He now was heading over a lush valley laced with waterfalls and streams, at the head of which was a large spring—the source of all the fresh water on the island. From here Hook had an easy path out to sea. He turned the wheel and the ship responded nicely. He had made it! He, Captain Hook, the most feared pirate ever to roam the seas, was now in command of the air as well! He'd rename the ship, of course, with something that was more . . . *piratical*. And he'd get a crew of real cutthroats, not like the pathetic lot he'd had on this island. And then he'd . . .

Hook's dream was cut short by a tremor passing up his legs. He frowned; the ship was high above the trees—it couldn't have hit anything. He felt another tremor, this one more powerful. And then the entire ship was shaking, masts waving like palm trunks in a storm.

What the . . . ?

He ran to look over the starboard rail and immediately staggered back, temporarily blinded. Where the valley had been, there was now only a light brighter than the sun, streaming from the ship's hull.

"*NO!*" wailed Hook, as he felt the ship stop rising. He staggered to the wheel, holding it for support, and said "No," again, softly this time, as the starstuff drained from the hull, cascading into the valley below, sinking into the springwater, then disappearing. And then the ship—his wonderful flying ship—began to descend toward the sea, never to soar again.

On the beach, Leonard, Bakari, and the children shielded their eyes as the brilliant light poured from the *De Vliegen.* Suddenly, the sky flashed with colors, and for a few moments a brilliant rainbow arced from the ship down toward the other side of the mountain. It was an enormous amount of starstuff, Leonard knew; what he didn't know was what effect it might have on the island.

The rainbow flashed and was gone. Leonard scanned the skies and found the ship, sinking fast—almost falling— toward the sea. Hook was still on board, Leonard assumed.

Apparently Mister Grin assumed the same thing; Leonard could see the giant croc swimming out of the lagoon in the direction of the descending ship. What would happen to the treacherous pirate, Leonard did not know; nor, at the moment, did he care. He had bigger concerns, such as the welfare of the Mollusks, the recovery of the starstuff, and the need to return to England and report to the rest of the Starcatchers. And, of course, Molly.

He turned and saw her; she was cheering, along with the other children, as Hook's ship disappeared behind the mountain. Just then, Peter, having flown from the village, landed among the others. Molly hurried over to hug him, causing Peter to blush, and George to frown, and Tinker Bell to emit a rude sound.

Watching Peter and Molly embrace, Leonard was struck by two things: the first was how happy they made each other; the second was how much older Molly now looked than Peter. As if thinking the same thing, Peter, his face beet red, pushed himself away from her and walked over to join the other boys. Disappointment flashed across Molly's face, and she started to follow him, but then she stopped, remaining where she was, next to George.

CHAPTER 73

THE PROMISE

*I*T WAS TEN DAYS BEFORE the ship from England arrived at Mollusk Island. It was escorted past the reefs by Ammm and his cohorts, who had gone to England to inform the Starcatchers there that Leonard, Molly, and the others needed a way home.

Leonard had spent most of the ten days searching for the starstuff, but he found none; evidently it had seeped deep into the island.

For the Mollusks, the ten days had been a time of healing from the wounds, physical and mental, inflicted by the Scorpions. The physical healing happened surprisingly quickly, and the Mollusks began to suspect, correctly, that the reason was the starstuff-infused water. It tasted subtly different—a bit sweeter and *lighter* somehow; it sparkled more in the sunlight; and at night the waterfall cascading down the hill above the lagoon seemed to glow.

In time, the Mollusks—and the other inhabitants of the island—would discover that, as long as they drank the island's water, they would not age, not so much as a day. But for now, all the Mollusks knew was that the more they drank from the spring and bathed in it, the better they felt. Soon there was laughter in the village again—although the Mollusks found themselves, from time to time, casting anxious glances toward the sea. It would be a while before they stopped doing that.

For the pirates—the ones who'd been enslaved by the Scorpions, as well as Smee and his band of six—it was a confusing time. The Mollusks, their former enemies, were now treating them as friends, offering them shelter and all the food they could eat. At first the pirates had enjoyed this hospitality, but after a few days, they became restive.

On the fourth morning after the Scorpions left, Boggs and Hurky had hiked across the mountain to see what had happened to their fort. They returned that night with the news that the fort was still in decent shape—*and Hook was living in it.* Somehow he'd managed to bring the *De Vliegen* down in the lagoon by the fort. Because of the large hole in the hull, the ship had settled to the bottom, but in water only a few feet deep. Hook had fled the ship to avoid Mister Grin, who was still lurking about. Hook had holed up inside the fort wearing only his underwear and living on rainwater and coconuts.

"Just coconuts?" Smee had asked, when Boggs and Hurky finished their report. "Raw?"

"That's all he can prepare," said Boggs.

"Cap'n don't like his coconuts raw," Smee said softly, looking at the ground. The other men nodded.

The pirates mulled over the situation. Yes, Hook was a scoundrel who had abused them relentlessly. Yes, the Mollusks had treated them well. Yet the inescapable fact remained: they were *pirates*, not villagers. Hook was their captain. And he had a ship. Granted, it was sitting on the lagoon bottom. But it was a ship.

The next evening, when darkness fell, the pirates quietly crept out of the village to return to piracy. They told only one Mollusk: Shining Pearl. She saw them off, giving a hug to each of the seven men she'd led across the mountain. The last to leave was Smee. They embraced for a full minute, the little round man snuffling into Shining Pearl's shoulder.

When they pulled apart, Smee said, "Will you come visit us at the fort?"

"I don't think Captain Hook would like that," said Shining Pearl. "Once you're back with him, I think we'll officially be enemies again."

"I suppose you're right," said Smee. "But even if we're official enemies, you know I'd never hurt you, don't you? Truth is, I never hurt nobody. I'm not really much of a pirate."

"Yes, you are!" said Shining Pearl. "Why, you were the captain of the pirates! And you did a fine job."

"Really?" said Smee, his face brightening. "You really think so?"

"Of course I do," said Shining Pearl. "Now, hurry, before you're left behind." Then she kissed him on the cheek, and he turned to waddle after the men he had once commanded as Acting Captain Smee.

The orphan boys who'd been Zarboff's slaves—Slightly, Curly, Tootles, Nibs, and the twins—took to Mollusk Island as though they'd been born there. They loved the lagoons, the beaches, the jungle, the mountains, the caves. They were enchanted by the Mollusks and amazed by the mermaids. Above all, they reveled in the freedom. After years spent in the harsh confines of St. Norbert's, then under Zarboff's brutal thumb, the boys were finally free to do as they pleased. They moved into the underground lair with Peter and the other boys, and spent their days exuberantly exploring the island—hiking, climbing, fishing, and swimming, from sunrise to sunset and beyond.

They were not happy when the ship arrived from England. They went to the beach, along with Peter, James, and the other boys, and stared glumly at the longboats rowing to shore. A moment later, Leonard joined them, with Molly, George, and Bakari. Fighting Prawn emerged from the jungle and walked down to the group. The Mollusk chief thanked the Asters, Bakari, and George for their help, and told them they were always welcome back on the island. Leonard, in turn, thanked Fighting Prawn for his hospitality. When he was done, he turned to Slightly's group.

"Are you ready, boys?" Leonard asked.

"No, sir," said Slightly.

"What?" said Leonard.

"We're staying here, sir," said Slightly. "We talked about it, me and Tootles and them. We don't want to go back to England."

"But we agreed you would return," said Leonard. "I'll look after you. You won't be returned to St. Norbert's. You'll be placed in a good school. You have my word."

"We believe you, sir," said Slightly. "But we like it here better than any school. We don't want to go, sir."

Leonard stared for a moment at Slightly, and the other former slaves gathered behind him, barefoot and sun-browned.

"Are you certain?" he said.

The boys nodded.

"All right," said Leonard. "I won't force you. You've been forced enough. But if you change your mind—if you decide to return to England—you tell Peter, and he'll get word to me through Ammm. Promise me that."

"I promise, sir," said Slightly. "And thank you."

Leonard nodded, then turning to Molly, George, and Bakari, said, "I suppose it's just us, then."

James cleared his throat.

"Sir," he said, "we want to go."

"What?" said Leonard.

"*What?*" said Peter.

James looked at Peter, then at the sand, and then, in words so soft that Peter could barely hear them, he said, "I'm sorry."

"But *why?*" said Peter. "You love it here, don't you? He looked from James to Prentiss, Thomas, and Tubby Ted. "Don't you?"

"Yes," said Ted. "We love it *now*. But . . ."

"But what?" said Peter.

"But we're not going to be boys forever," said James, looking at Peter, tears streaming down his cheeks. "Don't you see? We're going to be men."

"Why can't you be men here?" said Peter. "The Mollusks are here! The pirates are here! They're men!"

"We're not Mollusks," said Prentiss. "Or pirates."

"And there's no books here," said Thomas. "Sometimes I wish I could read a book."

"And no pudding," said Ted.

Peter stared at his four friends. James took a step forward. "Peter," he said, "come with us."

Now it was Peter who looked at the sand.

"I can't," he said. He heard a sob and looked up; Molly had pressed her face into her hands. "I can't," he repeated.

477

"I'm not like you. I'll never be like you." He glanced down at his shadow. "I'm not sure if I'm really still me."

The longboats had reached the shore. The sailors were pulling them up onto the sand.

"Well, then," said Leonard. "It appears we'll have boys with us on the journey home after all—just not the ones we expected." He turned to James, Thomas, Prentiss, and Tubby Ted. "Is there anything you boys want to take with you?"

The boys shook their heads; they had no possessions, other than the rags they were wearing.

"I have something for them," said Fighting Prawn. He untied a small brown leather bag from his loincloth and handed it to Leonard, who looked inside, then at Fighting Prawn.

"Are these *diamonds?*" he said.

The Mollusk chief nodded. Leonard looked into the bag again.

"But they're enormous!" said Leonard. "They're worth a fortune!"

"In your world, yes," said Fighting Prawn. "Here they are trinkets—troublesome ones, at that. Use them for the benefit of these brave boys."

Leonard nodded and told James and the others to thank Fighting Prawn. This they dutifully did, though none of them understood that he had just transformed all four of them into very wealthy young men.

When they were done, Leonard walked over to Peter,

and, putting his hand on the boy's shoulder, said, "Will you come to visit us in London?"

That horrible place? said Tink, from atop Peter's hair.

"It's not so bad," said Leonard, smiling. "What about it, Peter? Will you visit?"

Peter glanced at Molly. "Maybe," he said. "Someday."

"I hope so," said Leonard. He put his hand out, and Peter took it. "Peter," said Leonard, "I—we—have no proper way to thank you. I've given up trying. But if you ever need anything, *anything* . . ."

Peter nodded, and the handshake turned into an awkward hug. Then Leonard pulled away, red-faced, and in a businesslike voice, said, "All right, then. We'll want to catch the tide." He started toward the boats. Bakari was next, giving Peter a brief, heartfelt hug before turning to go. Then George stepped up to Peter. They shook hands, the handshake of two people who respected each other far more than they liked each other.

"Perhaps I'll see you again, Peter," said George.

"Perhaps you will," said Peter, and George was gone.

Peter turned then to his mates, four boys becoming young men, four boys with whom he'd set out to sea . . . how long ago? It felt like a hundred years. Peter went down the line, hugging Prentiss, then Thomas, then Tubby Ted. After he hugged Ted he stepped back and said, "You know, Ted, you're not really tubby anymore."

"I'm not?" said Ted. He looked down at himself.

"Not really," said Peter. "You're big, is what you are. And strong. And a good fighter."

"I am?" said Ted.

"You are," said Peter. "And I think we should call you just plain Ted from now on."

"Plain Ted," said Ted. "I'd like that." He paused. "But when I get back to England, I still want pudding."

The last in line was James. Peter hugged him, and that was the hug that broke the dam, the two friends sobbing into each other's shoulders for a good minute before they could separate, their teardrops spattering the sand.

"Come see us, then?" said James, his voice a croak.

Peter answered only with a shrug. James turned and, with the others, trudged toward the boat.

And then there was only Molly. He stepped toward her, and she toward him. Her face was red and wet with tears. She thought she looked awful; Peter thought she had never been more beautiful. She held out her hands, and he took them in his.

Wake me up when this is over, said Tink, lying down in Peter's hair.

"I don't want to know what she said," said Molly.

"No," said Peter, managing a tiny smile. "You don't."

"Will you really visit some day?" said Molly.

"Do you really want me to?" said Peter.